Between The Lies

Louise Tickle

Hardback published October 2023
Paperback published May 2024
ISBN 978-1-7391349-9-0

Text © Louise Tickle
Typography © Bath Publishing

This novel is a work of fiction, and the names, characters and incidents portrayed in it are the work of the author's imagination.

Published by Cinto Press (an imprint of Bath Publishing Limited).

27 Charmouth Road
Bath
BA1 3LJ
Tel: 01225 577810
email: info@bathpublishing.co.uk
www.bathpublishing.co.uk

Bath Publishing is a company registered in England: 5209173
Registered Office: As above

For Sylvia, my extraordinary, complicated
and brilliant mother.

I wish your world had been different.

I try every day to make it so.

Prologue

The electric glare of a too-bright bulb bleaches the room. The backs of Cherry's legs sweat into the armchair he'd sat her in before getting started.

Her socks are damp and itchy and her red blonde hair is wet with tears. Her yellow party dress is soaked and reeks of pee from her accident earlier. The puddle, she observes, has spread across the carpet. Her mum is lying in it. Slumped on the floor, Marianne moans.

Cherry looks out from deep inside the armchair. Her eyes are doing something strange because everything in the room looks further away than usual.

She decides to count up what she can see.

Numbers one and two: clumps of her mother's hair, the blood drying now. One long red tress lies across Cherry's lap. The other is by the door. They had been hard to pull out and the noise had woken her brother which is why her mum and dad went upstairs. Her dad is still putting him back to bed. Number three: sunflowers and hot pink cosmos in a vase on the window sill. Four: a slick of blood across the floor, bright against the carpet.

1

He'd got out a small grey knife with a triangle blade when he unpacked his bag. He'd told her mum not to make a single sound but she'd made such a scary scream that he'd had to come over to Cherry, two slashes on her cheek and he'd held her chin and done it fast. It bled so she tried to mop it with her skirt but it hurt so she stopped.

Her mum hadn't come to help. She'd wanted to. Cherry had seen her try. But then she couldn't anyway because he'd sat on her and she'd sunk in like a popped balloon. He'd used the grey knife again and her mum had breathed and breathed and managed not to make a sound, and then he'd held her hair scrunched in his hands and wrenched her head back and forward and blood flew everywhere, all over the living room and the telly, which was still on, and all over Cherry too. Then the hair came out, handfuls, and her mother did scream and Bill woke up crying and they'd both gone off upstairs to calm him down.

How many minutes later Cherry didn't know but Marianne had stumbled downstairs on her own.

Now, Marianne crawls. Grips her daughter's hand, raises her head, looks up through shallow breaths. Her mother hardly had a face now, Cherry observes, just grazed and broken skin and snot and hair cut off uneven which he'd done first, earlier, when he was shouting and angry. Before he calmed down and started properly.

Too hard to look. So I won't but I want my mum and I want to go back to the party and my cake in the shape of a nine with silver balls all over. When it was fun.

'Get out,' Cherry just hears her mum say, a sticky cough at the end. 'Tell him you need to go to bed. Open the window. Climb out.

'Then run.

'Run.'

Dare to breathe? Dare to move? Unpeel my legs from the chair. Don't look. But I'm holding her hand. I'm holding her hand and she's holding my hand and to get to the door I have to let go.

Our fingers press.

My hand hot in hers.

How do I let go when I can't let go?

All I can feel is my hand inside her hand, holding me. I hold her hand back, hard. My fingers are strong. I stare at the door while I count. One, two, three, four, and five is my thumb which I squeeze to keep us together.

I am still, still, still.

Then I feel air on my hand.

Oh.

She's let go.

To the door.

Yes I'll be careful.

Up. To Bill's room, head round the door. He's kneeling next to Bill.

'Daddy,' Cherry says firmly. 'I need to brush my teeth. Then I need to go to bed.'

Chapter One

May 2018

Hauling herself out of bed, Cherry Magraw saw through her window the first shreds of morning light. Her body ached for sleep. There was no traffic yet. A cat had walked past, and a fox, just after she'd woken the first time. She had watched the fox for a few minutes as it nuzzled at the recycling crates, wiped its nose along the wheelie bins, then disappeared in a flicker.

She padded on cold floorboards to the table. Her laptop screen glowed, open where she'd left it – Cherry looked at the clock – just over an hour ago. She read back what she'd written and cringed. Even those few lines were crass. What was she telling him that he didn't already know?

She felt chilled. Her feet and fingers were icy from the forty-five minutes she'd spent at the table, no socks or jumper, just in her t-shirt, trying and trying again to compose the email. This was way past the beginning of the end. The end had started ten months ago when Garth's wife had come home to him and the twins.

Cherry had told him they could no longer carry on. He'd agreed. They would each survive, they knew. She had survived, Cherry thought, but the daily effort was too much now that she could no longer sleep either.

She'd thrown herself into reporting on the violence that seethes behind closed doors, making herself the go-to journalist for editors who knew that misery and violence always sells. She'd been to

Bristol's courts so often the security guards barely glanced in her bag, waving her through as they did the lawyers and social workers who frequented the courts every day.

Her editors were pleased. At least, they kept commissioning her, which was the only feedback a freelance journalist could rely on.

Cherry had just published a feature about a young woman's sudden death which police had not recognised as murder and refused to investigate. As the weeks in which she had researched the story went on and each new police failing came to light, Cherry found her nights broken and her mind buzzing with frustration at the chances squandered to investigate a death she was sure was a crime.

She sighed and closed her laptop. Her article had forced the police to reopen the case. It was what the family had hoped for, and the best reporting could achieve. She should be feeling vindicated, professionally thrilled. Instead, her personal life was a shitshow and she was feeling bleaker than she could remember.

Grabbing a blanket off a squashy blue velvet sofa that dominated the room, Cherry wrapped it tightly round herself, tumbled into the softness of cushions and groaned. She had to find a way to tell Garth that she was going to up sticks and leave the country. She would pick up the itinerant life she'd once led reporting from the knife-edge tension of post-conflict states, in the swirling international community of here-today, gone-tomorrow aid workers, ex-military personnel raking in fortunes as private security, UN consultants of variable quality and freelance stringers like herself. The years she had spent travelling across these fragile new nations had introduced her to women and girls who had been raped as part of the wars they had somehow survived; it had fired Cherry's reporting and brought her to the attention of national news editors. It was also what had brought her back to Bristol two years ago, burnt out and knowing that, at least for a time, she needed to call a halt to stories of lives broken and sometimes obliterated by sexual violence. It hadn't worked, in the end – Cherry had been inexorably drawn back into these stories, and in the excitement of meeting Garth, she had been able to cope. But now, bereft and alone, it was too hard.

She had to take action, had to move, had to do something. Somehow, somewhere, she needed to create a new start. So, the email to Garth was one she would have to send, and soon. But it needed more focus and equanimity than she could muster right now.

Cherry stretched her legs out against the sofa, digging her toes into its softness, trying to find some pleasure in the sensation. Eyes stinging, she drew her eyelids down and tried to conjure a place of calm. But she couldn't. She couldn't find peace.

No. Goddammit. If she couldn't sleep, she might as well get up, get out, and try to engage with the world beyond her laptop.

Cherry slung on her clothes, grabbed her backpack and walked down the two flights of stairs to the front door. She wheeled her bike quietly along the communal hallway of the terraced house which had been split into two flats, emerging into a faint dawn. Wishing she was at her family home on the Pembrokeshire coast, she hankered for the sea, but the Bristol Channel was as good as she was going to get now that her ancient car had finally succumbed to a total lack of upkeep. Why was she always so bloody skint?

As she clipped into her pedals Cherry thought wistfully of the lane from her family's farmhouse, Waun Olau, that would take her in less than half a mile to the cliffs of Ramsey Head and the churning, choppy waves below. The Severn estuary into which Bristol's River Avon debouched could be beautiful too, but it could never hold the drama of the jagged coastline which had anchored her childhood.

Picking up speed in an attempt to warm up, she headed west for the estuary. Depending on the tides she would soon be looking out over mudflats or, given the pink-tinged sunlight now breaking through from the east, a shining sheet of water stretching from England to Wales.

Cherry pumped her legs, grateful to be absorbed by the physical sensations of breathing and speed. On her bike she didn't have to think. If she cycled fast enough her whole attention was required. Cycling hard and fast, and rock-climbing, either outdoors or at the wall, had recently become her only relief from the visual flashes of crime scene photographs and grisly details of abuse disclosed in interviews that increasingly punctured her nights. Why now, after years of doing these stories, she had wondered – before shutting down the thought.

Swooping down the Portway, traffic was already building under the Clifton Suspension Bridge. Cherry headed on towards the mouth of the river. Not wanting to engage with the industrial hardness of the port, she cycled across the Avonmouth Bridge alongside the rushing M5 motorway. Pale light was just striking the shallow intertidal waters that were, she saw, at their lowest ebb, hundreds of metres out to the west, by the Royal Portbury Docks. Massive red crane arms hovered waiting to swing containers from ship to land and back again.

As Cherry left the port behind, she glimpsed a footpath sign across the road from a line of pebble-dashed council houses perched on a high bank. Their windows looked out across the Severn estuary to the Brecon Beacon mountain range beyond, as yet invisible in the low light.

She'd stop here. Explore the estuary. Maybe a tramp along the mudflats would help her hold off sliding back into the misery of knowing she could not see Garth again, and had not managed to make a life for herself in Bristol without him.

Dumping her bike behind a clump of brambles, Cherry clambered along the shore and crouched low in the shingle, staring out. Waders, their spindly legs seemingly hinged backwards, picked delicately for invertebrates in the sticky grey mud. Exhaustion suddenly dragged at her again. The broken nights sapped her but the constant anxiety she now felt as a result, she knew, of her reporting, had made her brittle.

Her stomach clenched. She had to eat, and with the realisation of her need for breakfast, Cherry knew that her attempt at escaping the realities of the day was over. She didn't have the energy or the willpower for a walk. There'd be no adventure, no matter how small, today. Stomach gnawing, she pedalled lethargically back towards Avonmouth, wobbly on her bike.

Since she'd zoomed past, the port had rumbled into life and the bright yellow lights of a greasy spoon seemed to sizzle as she approached. A workers' café, two shipping containers on a platform with steps up. She pushed through the plastic door into a welcome fug of warm, oily air.

'Bacon bap with fried egg, one coffee,' called the waitress to the man cooking but barely seen, out the back. She looked up at Cherry. 'Yes love?'

'Cappuccino,' said Cherry. 'And one of those baps please. With an egg.' Her Welsh lilt contrasted with the waitress's raucous tone.

The waitress nodded in the direction of the menu above the counter. 'No cappuccino. Black or white.'

Cherry spotted a glass jug on a hotplate and resigned herself to instant dressed up as filter. 'Black then.' She turned to face the café as the waitress turned to chivvy the chef.

A table of four lads in overalls, all in their early twenties, were applying themselves enthusiastically to plates filled to the edge. A man in a sweat-stained tracksuit scrolled through his phone as he forked pale scrambled egg into his mouth. A woman at a corner table, who had sat as far away as she could from the other customers, was weeping.

Cherry saw this with the internal jerk that accompanies witnessing a socially awkward situation play out.

The woman didn't fit the surroundings. A little older than herself, Cherry thought, mid-30s. Dark, shoulder length hair that was slightly dishevelled. An expensive pink wool coat that was both feminine and deliberate – not a colour you'd wear without meaning to. A light grey roll-neck jumper, slate grey suede boots. More at home in a chichi deli selling sourdough in Bristol's Montpelier or Clifton neighbourhoods than here in a dockers caff.

The woman's shoulders shook.

Cherry paused, then decided. She turned back to the counter. 'Another coffee please.' The waitress sloshed the dark, burned liquid into thick, white mugs.

Carrying both coffees, Cherry walked to the woman's table and stopped a pace away. Not too close. Lean out, not in.

'Coffee?'

The woman half-looked up, then scrubbed a hand over damp cheeks and dug in her coat pocket for tissues that emerged in a clump. A child's sock fell on the floor together with a marble that rolled across the worn vinyl.

'Oh for Christ's sake.' The woman bent to pick them up but Cherry was there before her. She put the marble and the sock on the table.

'Thanks,' the woman said, stuffing them roughly back in her pocket. Her voice was clipped. A hint of aggression, Cherry thought. Or maybe embarrassment.

The woman's chest heaved. 'I'm always losing something.' She looked down, couldn't seem to raise her eyes from the smeared formica table. 'I can't even keep the bloody socks in pairs.'

'Hey,' said Cherry quietly, sitting down diagonally across the table. She nudged the mug across the table. 'It's hot. Might help.'

She watched the woman reach out and clasp the mug tightly as if trying to extract every scrap of heat and channel it up through her arms into her body.

Cherry watched as she tried to gather herself.

'Early to be out,' the woman managed through clenched teeth.

'Slept badly,' Cherry said. 'Some nights I wonder if I'll ever sleep again.'

The woman's eyes widened. Then she laughed. It came out as a hoarse bark. 'You and me both.' She picked up the mug more steadily this time, managed a sip. 'It's not very good.' A whisper of a smile.

Cherry grinned back. 'No. They need a decent coffee machine. Don't expect they'll get one.' She took a slug from her own mug. The woman was breathing more calmly now, she noticed, each sip seeming to revive her a little.

Cherry thought back to the sock. 'Girl or boy?'

The woman looked startled, then understood. She reached for her pocket, felt inside as if to reassure herself the sock was safely there.

'Girl,' she said. 'Lola. Seventeen months.' The woman looked up. Cherry saw her register the two faint scars across her cheek. There was always a moment. And she hadn't bothered to hide them this morning. 'And a boy. He's five.'

Then the woman ducked her head, but it wasn't with embarrassment at the scars. She was entirely bound up with her own story, and Cherry saw her mouth twist as she tried to regain control. A sigh shuddered out of her.

'They're with their dad,' she said. She waved a hand towards the grey rows of pebble-dashed council houses on the hill. 'Well, they're at his mum's. I'm picking them up in a minute. Though actually I've been here all night.' She took a gulp of coffee and closed her eyes.

'Here?' asked Cherry bemusedly.

The woman grimaced. 'No, my car.'

Cherry considered this. What would compel you to stay out all night in your car, here by the docks?

She felt a spurt of curiosity shoot through her. Deliberately, she retreated, leaning back in her chair. She had always been able to make herself small. Unthreatening.

The woman drew her pink coat around her, its collar high, her dark hair trapped inside, billowing over the lapels' edge. She shook her head, drew in a breath and glanced out of the window. The metallic sounds of a port coming to life jangled into the café. The woman turned back to Cherry, exhaustion paling her face.

'It's the kids' first night on their own with him. I don't think they're safe.' She paused. 'I mean with him. Not safe with him. I mean, I'm not safe with him. Why would they be?'

Cherry's attention tightened.

'People think I'm ridiculous. I know they do.' She sounded distant. 'But I know him. He holds them too hard when he picks them up. He does it to show me. To show me he can hurt me even if he's not got me. He's...' The woman spat the words out, 'angry with me. For reporting him to the police. For making him leave. So I stay close, in case...' She stopped again. 'In case.'

'Bacon bap with fried egg.' The waitress clanked over with Cherry's order and placed the plate on the table with a clatter.

'I don't know why I'm telling you,' said the woman abruptly, looking down.

Cherry smiled. 'It's fine.' She thought about whether to tell the woman what she did for a living. People reacted in a variety of ways to the word 'journalist'. 'It's sort of my job.'

The woman glanced up. 'Oh?' Uninterested.

Cherry pointed at the floury bap in front of her. 'Half?'

The woman hesitated.

'Go on,' Cherry said. 'Might be better than the coffee.' She cut the bap in two and pushed one half over the table on a serviette.

'I'm Cherry,' she said.

The woman glanced up. 'Right.' She sipped her coffee, then shook her head, impatient with herself. 'Kathie. Sorry. I'm in a bit of state.'

The door was pushed open again and cold air rushed in around their ankles. A man encased in yellow oilskins ambled heavily to the counter.

Lean out, not in. Never crowd someone. 'You're all right,' Cherry said. Shift her away from the distress. 'I've never been to these docks. Everything's huge. Impressive.'

Kathie glanced around. 'Not so much in here.'

Cherry laughed. 'True. Though the bacon baps aren't bad.'

Reminded, Kathie looked down. 'Oh yes.' She took a bite, chewed, swallowed. 'It's good. Thank you. And sorry.'

As the café filled up and the chatter around them got louder, Kathie lost some of her stiffness. Yes, she worked. She was a translator. But she'd been off sick a lot since going back after Lola. Then, as if pulled back inexorably to the catastrophe unfolding in her life, she abandoned the standard social chitchat.

'I know everyone wants Ed to be able to see the kids on their own. 'Unsupervised contact' the lawyers call it.'

Cherry had nodded. She had spoken to a couple of mothers going through the family court process through her contacts at domestic abuse charities. And, she recalled, one father standing tensely outside the Bristol Family Justice Centre, who had been shaking and tearful. She'd followed him inside, slipped in at the back as his hearing started. His ex, he told the judge, had picked up their six-year-old daughter from school the Friday before and disappeared with her, on the weekend the little girl was meant to stay with him. His voice had trembled at every word.

'I got an injunction after Ed... after last time.' Kathie stopped abruptly. Embarrassed, Cherry thought. She didn't want to say what he'd done.

'Anyway, I agreed in court that he could have them once a fortnight, just for the meantime. And one overnight, teatime to breakfast. But only at his mum's. I could see it would go badly with the judge if I said no.' Kathie stopped, tears suddenly threatening.

'I only went to the police at the very end.' She blinked. 'Stupid, stupid me. And now I've got to prove he's a risk or he'll get to have them on his own whenever he wants.'

Cherry felt a surge of interest. Family court cases were held in private – effectively in secret. Journalists were allowed to watch, but unlike in criminal trials where the press had the right to publish a blow-by-blow account of everything and anything that went on in court, the media was strictly banned from reporting a single word that was uttered in front of a family court judge.

Twice, she had applied for permission to report on the details of family law cases where a council had taken children into care; both times the judge had refused.

'Is anyone helping you?' Cherry asked.

Kathie laughed. 'Do you have any idea what lawyers cost? I had one for that hearing but I'm on my own now.' She blew her nose and looked at the clock. 'I need to head.' She looked at Cherry. 'You've been kind. In return, here's some advice. Don't ever end up in a family court against your ex. Because it's fucking brutal in there.' She picked up her bag, then swayed, eyes closed, lips pressed together.

'Are you all right?'

'Mmm. Low blood pressure. Takes a minute sometimes.' Kathie leaned against the table.

Cherry got up. 'How about I walk with you? Just to the car.'

How could she approach this, without it seeming just too weird? Cherry wondered. How could she ask to report on this woman's court case without frightening her off? And what on earth was she thinking?

She was meant to be getting out of Bristol. She was done with the city, she had acknowledged she could not cope being so close to Garth and yet so far from all she'd hoped for with him, and she knew the grimness of the stories she was investigating had, once again, become too much to bear.

But. She had never followed a domestic abuse case through the family court. And from the insights she had gleaned through reporting on domestic assault and rape in the criminal courts, she knew the powers wielded in family courts when children were removed from victims who could not prevent their abusers' violence, could change people's lives forever.

Awkwardly, as they reached Kathie's car, a smeared and dusty Ford Focus estate, Cherry rifled through her wallet and handed over her card.

'This is going to sound odd, but I'd really like to talk to you again. Professionally, that is.'

Kathie looked up from opening the door in distracted bafflement.

'Only if you want,' Cherry hurried on. 'You see, I'm a journalist.' She let it sink in. 'I write about situations like the one you're in. About safety. About risk.'

'Right.'

'I think your story's important.' Cherry thought fast. How to convince her it mattered. 'I'd want to describe how you're fighting for your kids. That you think they're in danger. That the judge might not believe you. And what happens if they don't.'

Kathie was staring at her.

'Sorry, I know you need to go.' Cherry stepped back, turned her bike towards the road. 'Will you think about it? If you want to find out more, give me a ring.'

Chapter Two

With her phone alarm set for 3.30 that afternoon when she was due to call her editor, Patrick Daunt, Cherry collapsed into bed as soon as she got back to her flat.

To set against the unpredictability of work, increasingly poor rates and chasing unpaid invoices, one of the best things about being free-lance was the ability to manage her own time. And if you'd had a terrible night – or several weeks of terrible nights – then not having to drag yourself into an office and pretend everything was all right was a blessed relief.

Despite being bone weary, she struggled to sleep. She found herself interrogating again and again the scene she'd just observed. Was the interaction at the handover of the children as bad as it had seemed? Or had it merely been an ill-judged moment of poor parenting provoked by the almost inevitable micro-aggressions that erupt when a relationship breaks down?

· · · · ·

Cherry had watched Kathie steer the Ford Focus towards the council estate above Avonmouth port. After seeing her turn left up the hill and disappear from sight, she'd decided to follow.

Pulling up the incline on her bike, she hadn't known quite where to go but it was a small estate with a one-way system, so she'd been filtered into a loop before glimpsing, in an offshoot from the main thoroughfare, Kathie's car parked in a cul-de-sac in front of a semi-detached council house. A small boy with a shock of dark hair was trying to lift a hessian shopping bag stuffed with books and toys into the open boot.

Kathie emerged from the white plastic front door carrying more bags. A few steps behind her, a man in his mid-thirties holding a toddler emerged.

To her surprise he seemed familiar. Lean, about five foot ten, with tousled dark hair like his son's but longer and somehow wilder.

Kathie turned to the man and held out her hands for the little girl. Lola, Cherry remembered.

The man didn't hand her over, but hoisted her higher with one arm and walked over to the car leaving Kathie on the pavement. Kathie followed, her stride quick and jerky. She held out her arms again, remonstrating.

But the man turned the toddler so the little girl was facing him, and threw her up into the air, catching her, over and over again.

Kathie stood stiff and silent.

Why isn't he handing her over? Cherry wondered. She glanced the man up and down again, memory tugging at her.

Then he threw the girl into the air again, stretching high, and his extended stance, muscles stretched, head tilted, meant that with a jolt of memory, she placed him.

Ed, Kathie had called him. He was a regular at the climbing wall at the converted church in St Werburgh's where Cherry climbed every so often. He wasn't a casual enthusiast but one of the best climbers she'd seen there. As the cogs turned, Cherry realised she'd met him briefly, through a climbing instructor, around a year ago. He wouldn't remember her. But she remembered him; he'd just finished a fiendishly difficult pitch with moves requiring strength and immense control. Watching someone unleash just enough force to vanquish a testing, risky climbing problem was, well, Cherry grimaced – it was hot. She'd noticed him at the wall since, now and again. Not that strange a coincidence really. Bristol wasn't a big enough city to be completely anonymous.

There was a cry. Ed had hoisted Lola back up onto his arm again, and with the other hand drew Kathie to him so her head was held against his chest. It could have been an embrace but the movement seemed crushing. She could see Kathie struggling to free herself. Her hands grasped for Lola. The toddler's laugh was changing to a rising shriek of alarm.

'Jesus Christ, Ed just *give* her to me,' Cherry heard. 'Get the fuck off me. Give her to me *now*.'

Cherry watched as the man dipped his lips to Kathie's neck and kissed it lightly. His hold only broke when Kathie sank downwards, using her weight to escape him.

The little boy, alarmed, had looked up on hearing his mother's raised voice, and was now gazing up at his parents, bewildered. Kathie grabbed for his hand, opened the passenger doors and bundled both children inside.

Glancing over to Ed as this unfolded, Cherry was astonished to see him cross his arms and observe the panicked scene with an amused smile.

She'd seen that smile before, a more vigorous, triumphant version of it, as the man had punched fists with his belay partner at the climbing wall. She was too far away to hear every detail of what had just happened. But it seemed to Cherry that Ed had held Kathie too hard for his embrace to be an affectionate goodbye, even if such a sentiment were likely to be welcomed under the circumstances. And the kiss... the kiss had felt startlingly misplaced. Cherry frowned as an echo of unease assailed her. And yet, what, really, could be said to have happened that might worry someone?

The car engine roared into life and Kathie drove past Cherry in gear crunching fury. When she looked back, Ed had gone.

· · · · ·

Cherry's phone rang. She scrabbled to find it, glanced at the unfamiliar number and considered not answering. But it might be someone calling her about work. She couldn't afford to miss a potential commission.

'Yes. Cherry Magraw.'

'Hello.' The voice stumbled slightly. 'It's Kathie. You know, from this morning.' The voice tightened. 'That... utter... shit... has just had me served with a court application for shared care of Brandon and Lola.'

Cherry's eyes snapped open. 'Ah. Right.'

'He's sent me papers saying there's a hearing next week. I've looked you up, read some of your articles. I'd like...' Cherry heard Kathie take a breath, 'well, I'd like you to write about it. So people know how arseholes like him manipulate the courts to get what they want...' Faint sobs came down the line.

Cherry pulled herself up to a sitting position in bed and let Kathie cry for a minute before speaking. Should she tell her she'd followed her after saying goodbye, seen the row, recognised Ed?

'Let's meet up,' she said, carefully. 'There are some really tricky factors in writing about a case that's going through the family court. We'll need to talk it through.'

Chapter Three

That familiar first buzzing of journalistic interest Cherry had felt on meeting Kathie now flared into an excitement that she couldn't ignore. In the ten minutes before her scheduled call with her editor, Cherry frantically typed her thoughts into a pitch ready to discuss with Patrick Daunt.

She'd need a commission of several thousand words to make the job financially viable. So many people had acrimonious splits and came to blows about who got the children – surely it was vital that readers understood the stress and fear involved in going to court, the difficulty of representing yourself if you couldn't afford a lawyer, and risk that it would all, from the point of view of one person or another, go horribly wrong? The fear Kathie clearly felt was an added factor: was Kathie a victim of domestic abuse, and would the court believe her?

But... the time it would take... Family court hearings were almost unique in dispensing justice out of public view. To have any chance of getting permission to report on the details of what happened in the hearings, she'd need to ask for special permission from a judge, with no guarantee of a 'yes'.

Cherry started totting up the likely hours, and sighed. Even with a longform commission, even with Patrick paying her as much as he could screw out of his ever-tightening budget, she could easily end up working at a hopeless loss. But this sort of story, one that might matter, that might make a difference – and especially one that nobody else had managed to get access to – was why she did the job.

Cherry called up her contacts and dialled Patrick.

In the few seconds before he picked up, she imagined him in the London office, one of the brightest of the bright young things employed at the paper. She'd met him twice. Three years older than her and a Middle East specialist, he'd come back to the paper's HQ from a Jerusalem posting after recognising – unusually for a foreign correspondent – that he was suffering from post-traumatic stress. The first time they'd met, he'd clocked her scars, then seen her notice with an apologetic wince. The second time, it was as if they didn't exist – which was unusual, as facial disfigurements tended to fascinate people to the point that their gaze was inexorably pulled back, almost without their being able to control it.

'How on earth are you going to convey the facts, let alone that this woman is scared to death for her kids if you can't write about those pivotal, dramatic moments in the courtroom?' Patrick demanded.

Cherry doodled on her notepad, digging her pen almost through the paper. The truth was, she didn't entirely know the answer.

'I can't guarantee I'll be able to report anything,' she finally said. 'But it's a chance that rarely comes along. I want to try.'

There was silence on the line. Patrick was pondering.

Cherry took a breath then blurted out 'Patrick, can't you just trust me? This story has conflict, children pulled from one parent to another, and potentially domestic abuse. Thousands of people are in this situation every year. My instincts are good, you've often said so.' She exhaled deliberately to relax.

'All right.' Patrick was laughing. 'But look, this might be too difficult to get past our lawyers. I'm just not sure. I know you'd do a great job. And sure, the risk to children is really significant but we'd absolutely have to have the court stuff. That interaction with each other, and the judge is pretty much the point. I just don't know if you'd put weeks of work in and then not be allowed to write a word. No...' he cut across her protests. 'We're pushing at the edges of what we can do on this. We won't go anywhere near contempt of court, not a hope, not when it's kids involved. We'd be crucified.'

Cherry stared at her feet, trying to work out what to say to convince him. She'd have to take on some of the risk.

'Why don't I feel out the lay of the land,' she suggested cannily. 'Go to the next court hearing. Meet the judge. If you think it's an important issue in principle, why don't I see if I can get *both* Kathie and Ed to agree that I can report? If they say yes, then it'll be harder for a judge to say no.'

There was a vanishingly slim chance, she thought, of Ed agreeing, but it had to be worth a shot.

Patrick's voice sharpened. 'Hmm. That's not a bad idea. This isn't a commission yet though,' he warned. '*If* we do it, we'd need to reflect both sides. And Cherry, keep in mind that right now, this stuff about the violence and the threat to the kids is only what she says. It's an allegation. We're not her mouthpiece. We need his side too, right?'

More than two hours later, as Cherry was engrossed in trying to fathom out yet again the intricate law on reporting family court hearings, she idly picked up her phone and saw it light up with an incoming text. She'd muted calls after the conversation with Patrick: sometimes she cursed the outside world for having such easy access.

Steffan. Her brother. Well, cousin really. But she considered him her brother.

'Ding dong – not sorted your doorbell yet?' it read. 'I'm outside.' There was a string of unread messages above that one.

As Cherry dashed to the window and heaved the sash open, a pale freckled face peered up at her, eyes crinkling.

'Finally. I was thinking I'd have to take shelter in the crack den next door.'

'Steff? What are you doing here?'

'I've been *trying* to let you know.' The gangly figure sighed flamboyantly. 'Gonna let me in? It's taken ages to get here in the old banger.' A beaten-up Land Rover, the farm workhorse, was parked behind him. His soft accent echoed Cherry's. It sounded out of place in this street of hard brick and litter.

She buzzed him in and heard the familiar bound of lanky legs springing up the stairs. They hugged, then Cherry, who only came up to the young man's shoulders, leaned back.

In the time Steffan had taken to reach her apartment, her surprise had taken on an edge of unease. It wasn't unusual for him to come and stay with her in Bristol when he needed an escape from what could easily end up, for a 19-year-old buzzing with energy, as the dull grind of life on the farm, but despite being nearly 10 years younger than her and a bit scruffy and unkempt, her cousin, adoptive brother, whatever – she never knew quite what to call him – tended to be reasonably considerate. He would usually announce his arrival before turning up on her doorstep.

Well, not entirely unannounced, Cherry had to acknowledge, as Steffan dangled his phone with its text trail in front of her. It seemed he'd alerted her three hours ago that he was about to set off from their family home just west of St Davids. But he hadn't said why.

'Mum sent me.' His usual light-hearted demeanour turned suddenly serious. 'She wants you to come home. Er, tonight.'

'*What?*' This was so out of character for her aunt Margaret that Cherry could only gape.

'I know.' Steff looked uneasy. 'She wouldn't say what it's about.'

'What's happened?' Cherry demanded.

'Who knows? It was lunchtime. I'd come in starving and she was stood at the kitchen table looking so awful I had to make her sit down.'

'What did she say?' Cherry's alarm was growing. 'Is she ill?'

'No. She said to tell you it's not that. But she wouldn't say much. It was weird. She practically shoved me in the car, told me to come and get you.' Steff scrubbed at his hair, a darker shade of auburn than Cherry's, and sank into the blue velvet sofa. 'I'm knackered. The lifeboat got a call out at four this morning.' He stretched out, long legs dangling over one armrest. 'We only got in at ten. Then I had to help mum get the flower orders sorted. I've hardly eaten. Can I have a sandwich? God, this sofa's comfy.'

Scouring the fridge to see what she had in – a thin end of Cheddar, a packet of ham and a wrinkled tomato seemed about the sum of it – she busied herself with the breadknife.

'Steff, go back. Think.' She looked at the sandwich, then glanced over at the recumbent figure taking up the entirety of her sofa. 'Crusts on or crusts off?'

'Oi!' Steffan's head shot up. 'Cheeky.' He collapsed back into the sofa, grinning. 'On. Don't want to waste any.'

Cherry handed over the sandwich and perched herself on the other armrest, the only sliver of sofa that remained uninhabited. 'Come on. Something must have happened.' Irritation swelled. 'I can't just be summoned home without any reason at literally no notice. It's mad.'

Steffan chewed energetically.

'Dunno. We had a quick chat about the rescue when I got back. Mum did the picking as usual. I helped her finish the bouquets in the barn. Then she went into the house to sort out lunch.' He looked over to the kitchen. 'This sandwich is obviously a gourmet treat but it's not going to be enough by a long shot. Toast?'

Cherry punched him. 'Get on with it.'

He bolted the rest of the sandwich. 'Okay. So, the post van came and I loaded it up, then went in thinking I'd have a kip. That's when I found her standing at the kitchen table.' He paused, his brow furrowed. 'She was shaking.'

Cherry frowned, baffled. 'Shaking? What about Tom? Was he there?'

Steffan shook his head. 'Dad's been at the livestock sale in Haverfordwest. He's not back till tonight.'

'And that was it? Just 'go and get Cherry'?' She rolled her eyes. 'Steff, I can't just up sticks. I'm busy! I'm working!' She reached for her phone. 'Look, I'll call her now. Find out what this is all about. I mean, what happens that you can't say on the phone these days?'

'Don't.' Steffan sat up. 'She's... I think she's really upset.'

'I'm upset! I'm being hauled three hours down the motorway and I don't know why!'

Her cousin shook his head. 'I said you'd go mad. She just said you could work at the farmhouse if you brought your laptop.' He looked at her pleadingly. 'Look. I'm sorry, but I think you have to come. I've never seen Mum like that. She looked...' he struggled for the right word, '... haunted.'

Chapter Four

A s the last shards of sunset disappeared, Cherry swung off the Haverfordwest roundabout and hit the final stretch towards St Davids.

Until this moment, when the familiarity of the Pembrokeshire landscape wrapped itself around her, she'd felt Margaret's unexplained demand to come home as an intrusion. But driving westwards to meet the vast sweep of beach at Newgale, Cherry caught sight of swathes of glowing gorse and breathed in deeply. This coastline, which she'd explored in its every bay and inlet, cave and cliff edge, was always home.

Approaching the fishing village of Solva, Cherry shook Steffan awake. 'Nearly there. And don't you dare disappear upstairs when we get in.' A muffled protest emerged from deep within his hoodie. Cherry poked him. 'Nope, you're staying. Whatever this is about, I'm going to need you.'

Cherry's home since she was nine years old was the most westerly farm in Pembrokeshire. Even in the late evening light, its whitewashed buildings glowed against the scrubby rise of the Carn Llidi outcrop to the north. Massy stone walls, their edges rounded by centuries of weather, hid cobwebbed rooms with enticing alcoves and cool flagged floors. Ancient wood-wormed beams delineated and enclosed the interior spaces that had become her place of safety.

The instant she'd arrived at the farmhouse, Waun Olau, on that long-ago evening, Cherry remembered, the building had enveloped her, a small, unspeaking girl in a torn green cardigan held tight over grazed and stinging arms.

Wide, long-lashed eyes – lashes so sweeping her mother had sometimes scarcely been unable to wrench her gaze away – observed details of the cobbled farmyard from the social worker's car. A mounting block, a rusty disused pump, a plastic jerrycan, lidless, on its side. Her gaze took in a pair of dented metal gates propped against a barn, and a woman walking fast out of a wide front door towards the car who opened the passenger door and scooped her up.

The touch of not-as-familiar-as-her-mother's skin was what struck Cherry first, then being grasped tight and high and carried in her aunt Margaret's arms into the darkness of the farmhouse interior. Soon, there was warmth, the glow of lamplight, and without being undressed from her yellow party dress, Cherry was placed deep inside a worn sofa and wrapped in blankets.

Her mother's sister barely left her side for weeks. To Cherry, used to being considerably alone, the constant company of her aunt was a strangeness that became just another distinct element of this peculiar time when all she could do was watch and make lists and count her observations when she could not name them. And all this with no desire – and no prompt, and no need – to speak.

Her cheek had needed to be dressed each day. Her aunt did this, gentle in almost precisely the way Cherry's mother had been gentle. In fact, Margaret was so shocked at the cutting of her niece's face she could hardly bring herself to touch it. The horror of what Cherry's father had done never left her even as her niece's face healed, and over decades, the scars somewhat – but never completely – faded. Though it was never mentioned, as she grew up Cherry sensed that for Margaret, her scars were a daily reminder of her grief.

From the second Cherry had arrived, she'd felt the harshness of farmers' lives over generations as a reality that her entire being grasped as part of a natural order. There was life here, and there was death, and animals were slaughtered sometimes in the farmyard and dark beads of blood oozed from the hens' wrung necks before they were plucked and eaten, and dead children and babies too from years before were buried in the churchyard along the way, quite a lot of them once you started to look, and her mother and brother had been killed and now she was here because she hadn't.

* * * * *

The front door of Waun Olau opened at the exact moment Cherry and Steffan pulled into the yard. Margaret had been waiting, Cherry realised, and listening, probably for the past hour in expectation of the sound of the Land Rover's rattle. Her aunt was the personification of calm. She never panicked, and she rarely inflicted her worries on the rest of the family. What was going on? Light blazed from the porch as the woman who had taken her in, and within the year formally adopted her, emerged from the house and stood waiting on the cobbles.

The Land Rover doors banged shut. Cherry slung her bag over her shoulder and made for the house while Steff decanted her bike from the boot. Something was very wrong. She had never seen Margaret like this, uncertain and – Cherry hugged her – so tense that she was physically stiff.

'I'm sorry my lovely.' Her aunt dropped her hands to Cherry's and grasped them. She tried to laugh. 'I know this is odd.' The laugh failed. Though it wasn't yet cold, Margaret wrapped her arms tightly around herself. 'Let's get you into the house. No,' she said, seeing her niece's face. 'Not here. Inside.'

The slate-flagged hallway and the kitchen's familiar, well-worn chaos greeted Cherry. Her eyes fell on an arrangement of white ranunculus and pink tinged apple blossom that overflowed from a jug on the table; leftovers from the bouquet orders earlier in the day she guessed.

The kettle shrieked on the range where it had been left to boil. Cherry rubbed her temples, her eyes stinging with tiredness. 'Mags, I think I'm going to need a proper drink.'

'So you are, and here it is.' A giant figure in an ancient, holed sweater emerged from the door of the old dairy, a bottle of amber liquid and four mugs in his hands which he dumped on the table. 'My lovely girl.'

Her uncle Tom pulled Cherry into the broad sweep of his arms. Crushed against the rasping wool, Cherry clung to him, grateful for the normality of his welcome.

'Right then.' He sloshed liquid into each mug. 'My latest recipe. Tell me what you think. And remember – what happens on the farm stays on the farm.' He winked.

Cherry managed a grin. Her uncle's illegal distilling hobby had been a secret between the two of them for years until one afternoon, seven-year-old Steffan had wandered into the furthest away barn and found the copper still. The alcohol slid down her throat.

'Marks out of ten?' Expectant, Tom held out the bottle for another slug.

'Bit raw yet. Perhaps... six?'

'Harsh. But maybe fair.' He held the bottle up to the light. 'We'll keep trying.' He knocked his mug back, swallowing the contents in a single gulp. 'Right, best we don't string it out... this girl's shattered.' Tom looked at his wife. Margaret was sitting ramrod straight at the table, her hands clenched. At his words she flinched slightly, then took out an envelope from a manila folder.

'This came for you. Via the newspaper. They sent it here.'

The letter had been forwarded to Cherry's family home by the features desk administrator at one of the national newspapers. The envelope had been opened. Astounded – her family was punctilious about privacy – Cherry looked up, her eyes wide.

'I'm sorry.' Margaret's head dipped.

Cherry fingered the sliced edges of the envelope, then drew out the letter. It was just a single sheet.

My dear daughter, Cherry, it said. Unable for a split second to compute the words, Cherry read on. *It has been twenty years since we last saw each other so this letter will be a shock.*

Tom sat down heavily at the table and watched her, troubled. Margaret's eyes were pinned to her niece.

Cherry's focus lengthened past the sheet of paper and fixed on the tabletop, scattered with buttery crumbs. Adrenalin surged through her and she waited for the rest of her body to react. A split second later she felt her heart begin to pound.

Careful now.

To help herself survive the next few moments she found herself analysing the letter as an artefact. Blue biro on cheap foolscap. They allowed him first class stamps in jail, it seemed. The paper was con-certina-folded twice. The handwriting, neat and even, formed part of the shock, Cherry noticed. His hand had rested on this piece of paper, formed the words, addressed the envelope.

Ever since I knew you had become a journalist I've followed your career, her father had written. *I've tried to read everything you've published. Your recent articles about women's murders are what prompted this letter. This is to ask, will you come and meet me? There are things I need to tell you. Things you need to know.*

Cherry's vision blurred. Her legs no longer felt solid beneath her. Unaware of Steffan's exclamation or her aunt and uncle starting up, Cherry sank onto the floor. She pushed her hands into the cold, smooth slabs. These were the last moments, her heartbeats spelled out, of the time before. She knew this feeling, from the other last moments. Because there was a line. On one side was your life so far. Then there was the rest of time, after.

Her aunt Margaret was by her side, crouched. Cherry felt her aunt's arms wrap tightly around her, like a vice, holding her together, holding her in. Her ribs compressed with the pressure of the embrace.

Steffan half pulled, half carried Cherry to the armchair by the range. Silent, all three of her relatives stood around her, on guard, a frieze of anxiety and fury.

'I didn't want to tell you,' said Margaret. 'But Tom,' she flung a fierce look at her husband, 'said that we must.'

Into the silent kitchen a black cat skidded fast as if fleeing an at-tacker outside, then leapt elegantly onto Cherry's lap.

'Why was it opened?' Cherry asked into the silence.

'Cherry, when we saw the postmark, your aunt had to know what he was saying.' Her uncle Tom looked wretched and suddenly old, his fingers pushing anxiously through thick, greying hair. 'She was upset. Worried. Yes, yes, I know,' he responded to Cherry's pale, set face. 'It is your letter. Darling girl, we understand that. And he is your father.'

Sharply, Margaret turned away.

Tom shook his head, positioned between the two women, fearful of what would come next.

Margaret's hands gripped each other, her arms braced. 'You don't have to do what he wants. You don't have to go.'

'But I do.' The words came so instinctively Cherry was amazed. 'I want to know what happened that night. And that is much more important than *whatever* it costs.'

Margaret flushed. She slammed the table with both hands: the kitchen echoed to the sound. Astounded, Steffan started towards his mother as he watched a wine glass tip and smash against the floor. Cherry recoiled. In their entire childhoods Margaret had never done such a thing.

'That monster,' Margaret choked out, 'cannot have you.'

She knelt in front of Cherry in the armchair and holding her chin, gently cupped her niece's cheek.

'My gorgeous girl. Remember? He did this,' she ran her finger over the two ridges, 'and now he clicks his fingers and you run?' She drew air into her lungs in ragged breaths, now gripping Cherry hard.

'You don't know him. You have no idea. He will lie. He will lie and lie again. And you'll believe him.' Her laugh came out as a thin, bitter sound.

'We all believed him. Do you understand? You've done so well. You think you're strong enough. You think you'll resist. But he destroys people. He'll destroy you. And he'll enjoy it.'

Upstairs in her room, wrapped tightly in her duvet, Cherry tried to forget the memory of Margaret's distress. Tom had intervened, pulling his wife away and wrapping her in his arms as she wept, fists clenched in front of her, before her aunt had flung herself out of the room, muttering that she had to finish some chores.

Her uncle had collected the broken glass into sheets of newspaper. Cherry swept the floor. Scooping the cat up, finding comfort in the softness of fur against her face, Cherry then allowed Steffan to push her gently upstairs to her room. Filling the window's deep reveal was a vase spilling over with headily scented blooms. No remnants these, but the best of the day's pick.

With the cat draped across her chest, Cherry closed her eyes. She rehearsed, again and again, the sensation of reading her father's words. Then, for the first time in weeks, she slept peacefully until early light filtered through the cotton curtains, and she awoke, feeling energised – and renewed.

Chapter Five

A pair of choughs tumbled through the thin morning sunshine. Scimitar beaks gleamed scarlet as the birds wheeled high above the cliff then dropped, losing air fast, down past the glowing gorse, down through the shadowed grass, down the reddish scree of the rock face. Quick-turning, feather fingered wings beating, they rose again, past two figures, a man and a woman, climbing.

The muscles in Cherry's right hip cramped as her toes reached for a thin edge of rock. She gasped as the muscle seized. Suddenly her leg collapsed, falling slackly away from the cliff.

'Shit,' she gasped, fingertips digging deeply into knotted muscle. 'My sodding hip. Again.'

Braced against a grassy indent twenty metres below her, holding the belay, Steff grinned.

'I could've led,' he called. 'It *is* my new route.'

'Never.' He felt the rope jerk crossly and muffled a snort. Cherry was the better climber but she was out of practice. Steff squinted up, seeing his cousin flex her leg as best she could while barely attached to the rock face.

Cherry had shaken Steff awake just before six. They'd collected their climbing gear and crept out of the farmhouse. Without needing to say it, both wanted to put off dealing with the fallout of the night before when Margaret, furious and crushed, had pushed her way out of Tom's encircling arms and banged the back door behind her.

Both had instinctively craved the simplicity of climbing, and the concentration that would take them away from the upset at home. Neither mentioned the letter. But deep inside, Cherry hugged her father's words. He had followed her career. He had read her articles. He wanted her to visit. Their warmth bathed her.

Twice more Cherry attempted the reach and fell, caught by Steffan on the rope. She clamped down on the incipient panic she couldn't afford at this point. She knew she had been hanging too long and was tiring. But the thick slabs of rock they'd clambered out on when the tide was at its lowest were now being slapped by the incoming waves.

'There's two holds you can't see that will get you out, but...' Steff hesitated. Climbing blind, being held on the rope, was the opposite of ideal. He would have to take all her weight while she scrabbled for traction on holds she couldn't see.

'Yep. Up.'

Steff began to shake his head, and then realised. She had to ascend, else they would need to embark on an awkward down-climb that held its own risks, but worse, with the tide now sweeping in fast, they'd have to wade, possibly even swim through fast-moving water to reach their get-out point. That was riskier still.

If anyone had been watching the two figures on the cliff from an opposite headland, they would have noticed nothing out of the ordinary as the man called instructions, guiding the woman's hands and feet into small indentations in the rock face.

The blind move was done fast. The woman rose smoothly again, reaching the cliff top in under two minutes, hauling out to be joined by the man shortly after. As so often in climbing, just a few brief seconds held safety from disaster.

At the top Cherry and Steff lay flat out on the thrift-speckled grass. Close by, half a dozen choughs dug busily for insects. Above the narrow finger of land that poked out into the sea, the morning air had started to warm. The slick of fear each had felt began to seep away as their bodies relaxed in the sun.

Cherry sighed. Over the years she'd saved Steff's bacon a few times on difficult climbs he'd wrestled with, and now he'd saved her back. But she knew he'd be kicking himself, angry at his mistake this morning.

Cherry had taught Steffan to climb when she was fifteen and he was five. For a long time she was by far the stronger, and had an intuitive sense how to scale these cliffs.

As he'd moved into his teens, she'd shown him how to stretch the edges of risk and how to think through the implications of each decision that might, if poorly judged, lead to a fall or worse. Today she'd let him make the decisions, and he'd forgotten about the incoming tide. Cherry rolled over onto her stomach and prodded her cousin.

'S'alright you know.'

Steff groaned.

'Come on.' Cherry tickled him. 'We didn't lose a grand's worth of kit to the bottom of St Bride's Bay. Plus we didn't drown. *Or* fall off.'

'Might've been worth it not to have to go back home this morning,' Steff muttered.

'Oi!' Cherry propped herself up on her elbows and frowned.

'Sorry, sorry.' Steff looked strained. 'But I don't get it, just like Mam doesn't. Why do you want to see him?'

'I don't *want* to.' Cherry pulled at the springy tussocks of grass. She struggled for words, her thoughts unformed and hard to express.

'He's never been in touch,' Steff said accusingly. 'In all these years.'

But now he wants to see me, she thought, feeling again the shock of pleasure that had shot through her last night when she read those words.

'He said he was interested in my work.' It sounded lame even to her.

'How can you think he cares?' Steff's words cut through her little flush of happiness. 'Cherry, be serious. What he did... I know I wasn't even born. But it's shaped my life, all our lives. He doesn't care about you. No.' He saw her expression shift. 'He doesn't. We do. We're your family. It's us who love you.'

A few feet away, the small gathering of choughs dashed upwards. Whirling chaotically the birds flung themselves about, no longer concentrated on feeding but a panic of wings and hoarse cawing.

Cherry and Steffan rolled over onto their backs and scanned the sky, knowing what they'd see.

It hurtled into view. Still hundreds of feet above, the bird seemed small by comparison with its hoped-for prey. Its body solid and compact, its scything wings sliced the air, refining its trajectory of attack. No surplus effort was expended as it plummeted towards the clifftop. An explosion of black feathers against blue sky showed the successful culmination of the hunt.

Talons grasping its bloodied meal close, the hunter flew swiftly away. A peregrine falcon – the efficient, shadowed shape of death.

They didn't talk as they cycled home in between high hedgerows tangled with bluebells and red campion. The morning light had solidified and turned the fields luminous, the greenest green ever. Margaret would be waiting with eggs and bacon and she would, Cherry guessed, have marshalled her emotions well enough to smile and dish up the breakfast with at least an appearance of normality. But she was, Cherry knew, deeply hurt and racked with worry.

As their bikes clattered into the yard and the door was opened by her aunt, Cherry's mind telescoped back in time.

Margaret seemed hardly any different to how she'd appeared twenty years before. Her body had never developed the thickened heft typical of farmers: her toughness was of the wiry variety and all about endurance. There had always been a poise to Margaret, which this morning expressed itself as a deep, exhausted stillness.

Cherry's guilt bloomed as she made her way over and hugged her aunt. Margaret's arms went round her in response but the embrace felt briefer, lighter, somehow, than she was used to.

'Breakfast is ready, so come on in now.'

Cherry found she couldn't meet Margaret's eye. She had to be out of here soon, yet didn't want her leaving to be rushed which would hurt Margaret even more. For the very first time, she felt ill at ease in the house that had been her home for so long.

On the big kitchen table, set out as she'd known there would be, were eggs and toast and fried bread. A pat of butter on the blue dish, the knife dug in.

Steffan followed her in, peeling off clothes and dumping kit in a trail behind him. He took the chair next to Cherry, side by side, just as they'd sat as children. They both sliced bread, spread butter and jam and ate. Before the silence completely overwhelmed her, Cherry took a breath. She'd have to try again. Try to convince Margaret that this was not rejection, but survival. A way to understand the horror of that night. Why it happened. A chance to share her knowledge that she caused her brother's death with the only other person who had been there.

'It's nine years I don't have, Mags,' she said. 'That I don't really remember. I want them back.'

Her aunt, interrupted in her careful placing of boiled eggs into egg cups, paused.

'Only he knows about it. He's the only one who can tell me.'

Steffan stopped crunching.

'*You're* my family.' She saw Margaret's body shrink. What to say to get through this, Cherry thought; to make something better that can never be better. She spread her fingers, pressing each one down, fingertip by fingertip, on the scrubbed tabletop, gripping it hard. 'It's about knowing everything there is.'

Margaret flinched.

Cherry took a breath.

'I want to know what went on before. Between them.'

Margaret's face bleached. 'He won't tell you that.'

Cherry started towards her aunt, but Margaret held up a hand.

'You're expecting the truth, *now*? From him?'

Cherry heard her anguish.

'He will tell you exactly what he wants to tell you.' Margaret could barely look at her niece. 'He will find a way to justify himself. That's why he got in touch, no matter what he says.'

Cherry shook her head.

'I know he'll have his reasons for writing,' she said. 'But if he wants me to go, he has to give me something back. And I want to find out how he could have ever...'

Margaret turned away. 'There's no possible way for him to justify what he did.' Her aunt was trembling so hard her teeth were chattering. 'What you really want to know,' Margaret stumbled over the words, 'is why we didn't save her. Why we didn't bring her back. Help her leave. Make her safe.' She stopped, folding into herself, spent.

'And Bill.' There was nothing left in Margaret now, her voice a sobbing whisper. 'You want to know why we didn't save Bill.'

• • • • •

Hawthorn blossom poured creamily through the hedges but went unseen as Cherry stared blankly out of the car window. Steff drove the Land Rover fast along winding lanes away from St Davids, towards Haverfordwest so she could catch the next train home. The blur of wildflowers rampant in the hedgerows tore across Cherry's gaze as the car bowled along.

No one had been able to stop her father's sporadic outbursts of violence. Margaret and Tom had known and had worried for them all but had not ultimately insisted that at least the children should stay at the farmhouse when her mother returned to him that final, fatal time. Cherry had long sensed that Margaret and Marianne had been estranged at the end, and her aunt had just confirmed it.

'How do you welcome a man into your home when he's chipping away at someone you love till she can hardly say a word or think a thought of her own?' As she poured from a large teapot, Margaret's voice was so quiet Cherry had to strain to hear.

'She tried to leave him. You'd come for a weekend and often stayed longer. Then she turned up that last summer and said she wasn't going back.' Margaret's face flushed. Tom took her hand.

'We couldn't believe she'd done it,' he said gruffly. 'We got you signed up for school. Your mother got a job in the pub.'

'We'd started to convert the barn,' Margaret said. 'For a place for you...' At this, her face collapsed and tears took over entirely.

'But then he came – to see you and Bill, he said.' Tom's voice was grim. 'Stayed a few days. Told your mum he wanted a 'fresh start'. Here on the farm. Said he'd help out.' Tom looked at Cherry, shamefaced. 'I said no.'

'You said no?' Cherry could hardly push out the words.

Margaret closed her eyes. 'Your father would have poisoned our life here.' Her voice shook. 'His moods. His rages. He wasn't welcome. We couldn't pretend.'

'There was some pull he had on your mum,' said Tom. 'After he'd been, she lost faith in herself. Packed you all up and went back to Bristol.'

Cherry felt ice-cold. 'You didn't stop her? When you knew what he was like?'

'We'd worked so hard to get you all set up here – we'd done so much to make it work. I was angry,' said Margaret, her voice not far off a whisper. 'We didn't know it would cost her life.'

Or Bill's, were the unspoken words that clanged loud and clear across the scrubbed kitchen table. And so Cherry came to understand that Margaret and Tom, who had brought her up as their own daughter and swaddled her with love since that dazed October afternoon, felt it was their fault that her mother had been killed, and Bill along with her.

But Cherry knew different. She knew it was nobody's fault but hers that her brother was dead.

Chapter Six

Newport had not been Cherry's intended destination but feeling steadily more bereft as the train pushed through South Wales towards Bristol, it had suddenly made perfect sense to get off as her carriage pulled in beneath the sleek new silver concourse.

Cherry was already kicking herself as she stepped off the train. She hadn't called Garth. He wasn't expecting her. It was going to be awkward. Worse than awkward. But this time, she knew she wasn't going to resist the urge. She ignored the small, tight knot of dread forming at her centre. He might be surprised, but he wouldn't refuse to see her. He couldn't.

Twenty minutes later she cycled into the truck depot. A dozen or so yellow and green liveried articulated lorries were parked in neat diagonals, each emblazoned with the words *Garth Morgan – Getting Your Goods There Safely*. A couple of drivers were checking their vehicles over. It was the end of the day. Nobody gave more than a brief nod to Cherry as she reached the hangar-like office building, leaned her bike against some railings and slipped inside.

Everyone who worked in the office had gone home. Cherry walked quickly to the staircase that ascended through the middle of the building. A large glass fronted office set apart from the cluster of desks in front beamed out light. Inside it she could see Garth on the phone, wandering slowly around the table in the centre as he dealt with whatever problem his client was throwing at him. She watched, transfixed to see once again how he moved, the dip of his head, his hands – she could not take her eyes off his hands.

Quietly, Cherry walked over to stand beside the wall of glass.

Garth's head turned at the movement, and a startled mixture of surprise, pleasure and – she'd known it would be there – dismay flashed across his face.

She raised her hand. Garth didn't stop talking, and he didn't stop looking. Cherry waited. Then the call was done. A silence stretched. Then, as if it was a normal thing, as if she were still an everyday visitor, Garth opened the door, leaned against the glass and rubbed his eyes.

'Hello you.' Guarded. But his Valleys accent rolled warmly over Cherry, the familiarity of his greeting a sound she settled into.

Cherry crinkled her eyes. A small smile. But she couldn't go further. She couldn't go to him, couldn't cross the last few yards between where she stood and where he stood. He would have to come to her.

What seemed like miles was only a few steps, if you wanted to take them. His arms wrapped around her, his hand cradled her head and his whole body pressed into hers. Surrounded entirely, relief flooded through Cherry in an echo of the heady sensation she'd felt that morning as she completed the blind move and hauled herself up and over the cliff edge. They stood silently, not rushing. Her mouth muffled against his chest; she could feel laughter about to explode out of her at the sheer wonder of being with him again. It had been too long.

'Sorry,' she whispered into Garth's shoulder. He gripped her harder, then unclenched his body from hers to look down at her face. The sloughing off of the ache of months happened in seconds.

'It's been too hard,' he said.

Fat tears spilled down Cherry's face. Yes. It had been hard, she thought bitterly, remembering her determined edict the autumn before, a bid to do the right thing, cutting off contact to save them both more pain. He'd agreed. There was no option, after all. Once his wife came back.

Garth studied her again, frowning.

'Something's happened.' He pushed her hair back from her face. She felt him decide. 'I'll call home. We've got the rest of the evening. And I'll take you back.'

Garth's arm around her shoulder, they walked back into his office.

Their exact, perfect physical fit still shocked Cherry, and she gloried in it afresh at every time of meeting. Still holding her close, Garth rang his wife, made sure the au pair was at home to help out, said goodnight to the girls and made his excuses.

Cherry's head dipped as she heard him lie. There was no triumph in her, only a hot wash of pleasure that for the next few hours at least, they would be together.

* * * * *

They sped along the M4 over the second Severn bridge, Cherry's bike in the back of Garth's car. She loved this bridge, the pale green of its suspension cables whipping past as they drove across the estuary. They only ever talked in glancing terms about his home life, but she knew his twins would be five now. Aline, his wife, was presumably stable now on her medication. Stable enough to stay. Stable enough that he trusted her with the girls.

It was nearly two years since they'd met, thanks to a story she had been working on about refugees trying to cross the Channel. The weeks she'd spent living and volunteering in the makeshift Calais camp called the Jungle had convinced her that the plight of children, somehow surviving on their own, after travelling by themselves across Africa, the Middle East and even Asia, was a story that had to be told.

She'd followed a group of teenagers as they jumped the lorries, night after night, in a desperate bid for a life beyond the wretched existence they endured in the camp.

One night, five had made it, climbing into one of Garth's trucks. Propelled by adrenalin, Cherry had climbed on with them, noting their exhilaration in the huge, silent grins they darted at each other as the vehicle pulled away and onto the ferry. She'd had hours to do interviews, and because they knew and trusted her by now, they talked to her, the ones who had some English. Four of the stowaways jumped off when the driver took a break on a motorway, but Cherry and the youngest child, Zahra, a whip thin, iron-willed twelve-year-old from

Mali, had been sleeping when the others dropped silently off the back of the truck. The driver, unaware, had headed on down the M4 and back into Wales. Cherry and Zahra had woken only when he pulled into Garth's yard, parked up, and discovered them with a horrified yell.

Garth had run out, blazing. He'd torn strips off her in full view of everyone who'd gathered at the rear of the truck. Reckless, dangerous, irresponsible, he'd said furiously. There hadn't been much of a lilt in his voice on that occasion.

'Say what you like to me after you've called the police and got this child somewhere safe to sleep for the night,' she'd spat back. 'She's on her own. She has been for months. She needs looking after.'

Garth hadn't reported Cherry to the police when they came. When he'd seen Zahra emerge from her hiding place in the back of the lorry, grubby and thin, he'd been visibly shaken. When the girl stepped carefully off the ramp, her tiny, delicate body seemed on the point of collapse. Only her unflinching gaze and her fierce hug for Cherry when they'd had to say goodbye spoke of the determination to survive that had got her this far.

Garth had watched as Cherry held Zahra tight, reassured her that she'd be safe and made sure the girl had her phone number. His anger somewhat dissipated, he'd brought her a coffee and a platter of leftover catering sandwiches once the police had gone. He'd asked her how she had come to do such a reckless thing – didn't she mind it was illegal?

And so it had started.

'Now,' said Garth as they pulled off the bridge, his voice amused, but with a twinge of tension underlying the warmth. 'Going to tell me what brought you today?'

Cherry knew the question had been coming. It was hard, though, to navigate her way to the answer.

'When we... well, when we stopped being together, I had to find something different,' she began. 'I needed to be swallowed up by something else. Something that mattered.' She stopped. The pause lengthened as the car sped on. Garth glanced over at her, concern flickering. Cherry regrouped, tried to arrange her thoughts. What to tell him? What could possibly explain why she'd turned up out of the blue?

'I started finding out about babies being taken into care, and then adopted. I spent weeks hanging round the courts. Going into hearings, watching really young women – they looked like children, often – losing their kids. Parents who are splitting up battling to see their kids or fighting to stop the other one getting custody.'

An image suddenly assailed her. A few weeks ago, on the first floor of Bristol's lofty central family court, Cherry had noticed a woman in her early forties wearing an elegant silk scarf and heeled leather boots, talking to a younger woman Cherry knew to be a worker at Bristol's biggest women's refuge. Leaning against the ushers' desk, she had been perusing the court lists, trying to find a divorce case where at least one of the parties didn't have a lawyer.

Fergus, the head usher, pointed at the woman she'd noticed.

'Don't know where he is but she's on her own and they're due in shortly.' He raised his shoulders in a half-shrug. 'Honest to god, if I had a hearing listed for 10am I'd be here by 9.30 on the dot but some people, they fetch up at the last minute, rush through the doors, no solicitor let alone barrister, and not a bloody clue. It's a car crash.'

He'd sighed at the hopelessness of the litigating public.

'Then they don't like what the judge tells 'em and it all kicks off. Had people screaming at each other down the stairs. Echoes all the way up here it does. You can hear every word.'

'So, does he have a lawyer?' Cherry asked.

Fergus shook his head.

'Nope, neither of 'em.' He looked down his lists again, ticking off each case with a well-sucked pencil. 'I'd say they're your best bet for this morning. Though there's lots coming in on their own now. All in a state. Every hearing takes hours. Ties up the courts. Puts our judges on a very sticky wicket if you ask me, trying to make it fair for everyone. It can be like hand-to-hand combat in there. 'Course, it's the kiddies that suffer. I've seen some terrible things,' he'd concluded. 'Take my word for it. Never get divorced. And if you do, stay out of court. People fetch up here and they turn into animals.'

Cherry had made an approach to the woman, nodding hello to Janine, the refuge worker she'd spoken to a couple of times. Closer up, the woman's eyes were red-rimmed, wide, exhausted.

'You want to come into court and watch?' the woman asked.

Cherry nodded.

The woman looked sceptical. 'Because?' A look of comprehension came over her face. 'You know Janine at the refuge, so you think I've been abused?'

'Well. Not exactly. Because you don't have a lawyer and I want to find out how things go for you in court.'

'Christ, you people are vultures,' the woman had hissed, her lip curling. 'Get away from me. Absolutely not.'

Garth listened intently.

'That's not what brought you to the yard though,' he observed. 'Not by a long shot.' He swung the car off onto the approach road into the city.

Cherry realised that she still didn't know how to start. She'd begun too far back.

'It's not just that case,' she said. 'It's all of them. The ones where women are killed. And there's this woman I met yesterday. Same thing. She's frightened for her kids. I might be able to write about her. I hope I can. I have to tell this story. But it's so hard to get anyone to agree. And if they don't it's not likely the judge will either.'

Garth thrummed his hand against the steering wheel.

'I'm not following why this is a problem. Yes, it's upsetting, but this stuff is what you do.'

Cherry dug herself deeper into her seat. To explain about her father's letter she'd have to talk about her mother and Bill. And think about them. And speak the words that would make real the prospect of seeing her father again. And she would have to think again about Bill's death.

Garth knew what had happened. The bones of it. She'd explained the scars when he'd noted them with his fingers, not on their first night together, but the second. She mostly didn't give the real version when people asked. But when Garth had run his fingers over her cheek, she'd sat up in bed, wrapped the duvet tightly around her, and recounted the bare facts.

He had heard her out without comment or exclamation of sympathy or horror.

Most of it, she told him, she didn't remember in detail. But at that point, she hadn't been getting the flashbacks that had begun to assail her in the months since they'd split up, traumatic in the details they etched into her mind as they wrenched her from sleep. At first, the flashbacks had only been fleeting. But not any more.

'It's since starting to do these stories. I worry about the women. I'm scared for their kids. And it's all got mixed up. I'm not sleeping, and when I do, it's barely.' She pushed her hands between her thighs, hunched. 'I've started to see the room where we were. Me, what I was wearing.' She stopped. 'I see movement, and the light in the room, and colours.' Her mind's eye was suddenly flooded with the brilliance of smeared blood.

Her throat closed painfully.

'I don't see my mum. Not so far anyway. But I hear her voice.' Cherry fought for control. 'I hear her talking to me.'

They'd arrived at her flat. Garth parked, the smartness of his car incongruous against the shabby terraces and equally shabby cars in front of them. He reached over to touch Cherry's cheek, ran his fingers over the raised lines of her scars, so neatly parallel.

'Come on Cherry. Everything. Might as well.' He smiled slightly. 'We're here now. We've got time.'

Cherry closed her eyes.

'He wrote to me.' It came out quietly. 'My dad. From prison. I found out yesterday. He wants to see me.'

Garth inhaled, held the breath then turned, his arms open. He folded her into him. Cherry felt the cabling of his sweater against her face and burrowed into it, smelling him, nuzzling at the warmth. So very near to safety that she could almost fool herself. *This* was why she had gone to the yard. The comfort, the pull, of a sense of safety. She let herself luxuriate in the feeling, knowing it wasn't real, trying to forget.

'I told my family I'd go,' she said, tears suddenly wet on her cheeks again.

Garth leaned back and sighed.

'What is it that you want?' he asked. 'You must have decided to go because you want something from him. Not just because he's clicked his fingers.'

The silence stretched as Cherry struggled. There were so many layers of wanting.

'Nobody has ever told me exactly what happened that night,' she managed. 'Or what happened before. What led up to it? Why didn't anyone think we were in danger? I need to know about every second of that night. And,' her voice was steely now, 'I need to know precisely what happened to Bill.' Her fingers traced her scars. 'And to me. And why.'

Garth held her away from him, bracing her shoulders.

'Will knowing make any of it better?' he asked gently. 'The nights? The nightmares? And will he tell you – really?'

Cherry sat up straighter.

'Finding out what people don't want me to know is my job,' she said. A flash of energy ran through her. 'It never comes for free, but he wants something too. That's why he got in touch.'

Garth looked at her, eyebrows raised.

'So, a challenge,' he said. 'And whatever he asks for, are you willing to pay?'

Chapter Seven

Garth hadn't stayed. She'd known he wouldn't – couldn't, and shouldn't – but Cherry felt an aching tug of abandonment as he stepped out of their embrace at her front door and she heard his car door slam. Quickly, she turned away, keys already in her hand, and let herself in.

Bizarrely, she slept well – this was the second morning in a row she had woken feeling rested, she thought wryly.

Today she would embark on discovering more about her father in the same way as she would find out the background to any story: she would do her research.

She spent two hours searching for national coverage of her father's trial, but there was barely anything online from twenty years ago. Frustrated, Cherry ran downstairs, swung onto her bike, and headed into the city centre, making for Bristol's Central Library.

'Newspapers on microfilm?' A boyish-looking librarian, dressed in scruffy drainpipes and a pea green sweater sounded amused. 'How far back?'

'From the eighth of October 1998 to the end of 1999, please.' She didn't know exactly when the trial had been held, but it would surely have been within a year.

'Hmm. Well, you might find some national papers have their stuff from that period online, but yep, regional ones definitely won't have.' He tapped into his computer. 'We've got the Western Daily Press in hard copy up to mid-2006. There's a room where they're stored for viewing.'

Swivelling smartly, he propelled his office chair across the reception area towards another computer and tapped into a different keyboard.

'But if you want the local Bristol papers, the ones that had morning and evening editions then, yes, for that period we've archived them on microfilm. I'll have to order them. Don't worry,' he said, as Cherry looked alarmed. 'They're on site so you'll have them within half an hour or so. Have you viewed microfilm before?'

Cherry shook her head.

The librarian – his name badge said 'Eric Wilder' she now noticed – grinned as he sprang from his chair.

'It's all a bit analogue, knobs and dials and so on, but come on, I'll show you how to use it.'

The librarian scudded down the long corridors so fast Cherry had to put on a burst of speed to keep up. She expected to be shown into a dusty room with buzzing strip lighting, but was instead ushered into a grand octagonal chamber with a central atrium that allowed daylight to stream in.

It was empty but for four enormous wooden desks facing each other. With their tilted tops, they looked as if they'd come direct from a Victorian draughtsman's office. Affixed to the side of each with a metal clamp was a substantial brass desk light. Lining all eight walls of the room was a continuous run of polished wooden shelving interspersed with cupboards.

'Beautiful, isn't it?' Eric Wilder waved an arm expansively. 'The Western Daily Press editions you're after are all stored in here. I'll pull them out. Then I'll chase up that microfilm.'

Cherry watched him heft open a worn, leather-bound ledger at the back of the room then glance around the shelving.

'October 1998 to end 1999,' he murmured. Keys in hand, the librarian moved to the opposite side of the octagon and unlocked two of the cupboards built into the shelving, opening their doors and fixing them to small hooks that held them back securely.

Peering inside, Cherry could see hundreds of newspapers hanging neatly on rails like ironed shirts in a wardrobe.

'All yours,' he said. There was a hint of an enquiry in the librarian's expression that Cherry chose to ignore.

'Great,' she said. 'Thanks.' He was endearingly enthusiastic but right now she wanted to be alone. She was itching to begin. 'I'll get on, then.'

The paper's lunchtime edition on the eighth of October had only mentioned that a serious domestic incident had taken place at a property in the Easton area of the city, with the added titbit that an unnamed schoolgirl who had lived at the property was missing. That was a pooled report taken from the Press Association, she noted. By the evening edition it was clear that a staff reporter had been tipped off by police and had legged it to the house in time to find the forensics teams still at work.

Police have not confirmed the names of those found dead but at around 1.15pm, two body bags were brought out, one adult-sized, the other child-sized, the reporter had written, sticking, exactly as he should, to the facts while making the pathos of the situation heartbreakingly clear to his readers. *A 32-year-old man has been arrested and is helping police with their enquiries.*

The report continued: *A nine-year-old girl living at the property who was thought to be missing has been discovered at her school. According to the girl's headteacher she is safe and being cared for by family.*

Cherry took a careful breath and quietly exhaled, counting to five, as the unknown reporter's words tugged at her memories of the day. By the time that edition had hit the streets, she'd already been taken to have her face sutured and was staring blankly from the window of the social worker's car, heading west towards her aunt and uncle's farm.

By the next morning, her mother and brother were front page news, and her father had been charged with two counts of murder. As she lifted a copy of the Western Daily Press dated the ninth of October 1998, Cherry was jolted by a picture of her mother she'd never seen before. Her hair, so wild and curly, had its coppery colour transformed to sober monochrome in the black and white newsprint rendition of Marianne in the garden holding Bill, who was grinning.

Turning to page three, a photograph of Cherry in her school uniform was printed as an inset to a larger picture of the forensic team in front of the house. Seeing it, Cherry's heart thudded. Her face hadn't been pixelated. A sign of the times. A child who had survived a murder scene today would never have their face emblazoned all over the media. But a more uneasy feeling crept in as Cherry read the article and the reports that followed over the next few days; it was clear that journalists wanted to know how she had escaped. They had staked out her school as well as, predictably, interviewing neighbours and friends who had been at her birthday party that afternoon.

Not much was said by any of them – nobody knew what had happened that night after all – but the reporters' fascination was evident. How had she got out? Or, alternatively, some speculated... why had she been spared?

Cherry's mind started to spin. But no. She couldn't afford to lose focus. She leaned backwards in her chair and stared upwards at the ornate ceiling of the library, fixing her gaze on the plasterwork, following its curlicues, disciplining her thoughts. She had to focus on the words written by reporters closest to the case at the time. If she was going to meet her father in prison, she had to know as much as possible about the facts. She needed to be armed.

Her father had pleaded guilty to her mother's murder at Bristol Magistrates' Court the morning after being charged, but had entered no plea to the charge of murdering her brother. The trial was set for the following July.

The flurry of articles in the Western Daily Press had died down a week after her mother and brother were found dead. But as she read the first few days' coverage, Cherry's exhortations to herself to hold hard to her present purpose were becoming more difficult to sustain: reading the words that told her what was happening to her father, she was swept back to what had suddenly become her parallel life, alongside but apart from his, forever separated from the fate of her mother and brother.

She had barely understood at the time how much her future would change, much less that she and her father would not see each other again.

That first morning of her new life, Cherry had lain in her aunt and uncle's bed, surrounded by hot water bottles, her cheek aching beneath the wadding bandaged to her face.

As the smell of bacon rose through the house, her aunt Margaret had come in, engulfing the nine-year-old Cherry in her firm, comforting arms.

Her aunt had dressed her, she remembered, carefully, so carefully, in borrowed clothes.

She'd eaten a jam sandwich in the kitchen but had not said a word. Misery hung in the air. The welcoming farmhouse she'd always known had changed into a place of silence broken by abrupt comments from her aunt and uncle, trying and failing to ease the atmosphere.

Then Tom had taken her hand and told her he was taking her to see something. A surprise.

She hadn't answered, but had allowed her coat to be put on and her aunt's woolly hat to be gently pushed down onto her head. Then she and her uncle had walked hand in hand down the farm track to the road and turned right towards the lifeboat station, and Ramsey Island. It was only a short walk.

Another man met them by the old concrete jetty, stilts rising to the lifeboat station high above. She'd been there before, climbed up the gridded metal steps and into the cavernous home of the giant boat that was held taut on a winch rope at the top of the steep slipway by a single hook. It hung there, poised above the sea on a ramp that was thickly greased all year round. You couldn't get the thick oiliness of that grease off your clothes, but Cherry had liked the feel of it when she'd touched it.

That day though they hadn't ventured up the metal steps. Instead, beneath the stilts, a small grey rib was waiting in the shallows. Cherry was lifted into the boat by Tom who wrapped her in an engulfing yellow oilskin. With the other man at the helm and Cherry leaning against her uncle, the rib purred away from the jetty and across to the island. Ramsey. Her first trip there.

From inside her cocoon, Cherry heard Tom tell the man to go carefully.

'Slow is fine for today,' he'd said. 'Keep her steady.'

She'd gazed over the front towards the island as it loomed closer, its cliffs topped by green pasture and a scatter of sheep.

The man pointed at a narrow inlet.

'There were two white coats here yesterday.'

Cherry had no idea what he meant.

Tom glanced at her. 'Watch the beach now,' he said.

As the boat had slid quietly along the south side of the inlet, Cherry could only see a narrow strip of pebbles. Tom pointed and she followed his finger till her eyes alighted on a small pale blob.

Her blankness as she looked at the blob flipped to comprehension in the moment between one heartbeat and the next. Once she'd seen the barely perceptible rise and fall as the seal pup breathed, it was impossible to remember how a second before she hadn't understood this was a living creature.

The man driving the boat cut the engine.

'Born last night I reckon,' he'd said. 'Look, fur's still yellowish.'

Cherry's eyes now scanned the beach and found two more seal pups lying flopped on the pebbles. They were at least twice the size of the first tiny creature and their fur had turned pure white. They lay beside large grey boulders that she realised, as they raised their heads to peer at the boat, were their mothers.

'We'll just watch a few minutes, not disturb them,' Tom said.

Cherry gazed intently, not speaking. The man who'd brought them chatted quietly to her uncle.

As Cherry watched the first pup she'd spied, the tiny creature raised its nose and peered upwards and around, dark button eyes searching helplessly. It opened its mouth and called, a piteous sound.

Ten metres from the boat, a gleaming charcoal grey shape parted the water's surface. Cherry heard a snort and a shiver of whiskers as the pup's mother swam strongly to the shore. She moved surprisingly quickly up the beach, flippers levering her heavy body over the stones. Then, a couple of metres away from the pup still, she eased over onto her side exposing her nipples.

In minute increments it inched towards its mother. Those two metres seemed like miles and it appeared to Cherry at first that the pup would never manage. So young it had barely any muscle tone, the newborn kept sinking back exhausted. Cherry could not tear her eyes away.

A few minutes of sustained effort later however, and it was suckling. As she saw its body relax in the bliss of filling its belly with fat-rich milk, Cherry released her clenched fists and flicked a glance at her uncle. He was smiling.

'They always get there in the end.'

She'd nodded.

'Better go now,' he'd said. 'Don't want to scare the mums away. But we can come back.'

Again, she'd nodded. She wanted to see the seal pups again. But she couldn't tell her uncle. She still had no words.

'Microfilm at your service.' The door in one of the octagon's panelled sides had opened so softly Cherry hadn't heard it and was startled to hear the librarian's voice. She looked up to see Eric Wilder wheeling a trolley towards her. It held two dozen or so cardboard containers and a machine that he explained was the microfilm viewer.

'If I show you how to set up the first one you'll soon work out the knack. What dates do you want first?' he asked.

'October the eighth 1998.'

'Here you go.' Deft fingers fitted the selected film into the machine linked up to the viewer. Squinting as he turned the dial to shift the microfilm along, Eric Wilder checked the dates.

'Bingo.' He looked up and grinned at Cherry. 'Reminds me of those Fisher Price binoculars with slides you wound round on a wheel. Anyway,' he gave the viewing screen a wistful stroke, 'over to you. Give us a shout when you're done. I can keep the microfilm out of the archive for a week if you want to come back and view it without having to wait.'

As he turned away, his gaze fell on the newspapers Cherry had spread out across the desk.

BRISTOL MAN CHARGED WITH MURDERING WIFE AND TODDLER the headline blared. Beneath it, the standfirst read, 'Ralph Lester, 32, held on remand. 9-year-old daughter found safe at school'.

Cherry saw him absorb the headline, and saw his eyebrow twitch. None of your business, she thought.

The librarian gave Cherry a professional smile.

'Right, well, I'll leave you to it,' he said, making swiftly for the door. 'Come and get me if you need any help.'

The city's main newspaper, the Bristol Post, had dedicated its crime reporter Ben Temple to the case. He had followed the story assiduously from the day her mother and brother's bodies were found and appeared to have attended every day of the trial. His report on the day the two police officers who'd found Bill's body were cross-examined had merited a front-page splash.

POLICE OFFICER FIRST ON SCENE: TODDLER FOUND 'LYING IN A POOL OF BLOOD' was the headline. Across pages two and three, Temple reported their graphic descriptions of the scene. Cherry read every word.

Scrolling through each day's reporting to get an idea of how the murder trial had progressed, Cherry saw that Ben Temple's articles were a mixture of straight news enlivened by the occasional lurid flourish. He had clearly heard about her cheek being slashed during the trial and so had interviewed a plastic surgeon to find out about her chances of healing without major scars. Reporting on the day Margaret gave evidence, when her aunt had told the jury of her mother's attempts to protect herself, the headline blared, JUDGE PUT TRAGIC MUM IN HARM'S WAY.

Cherry's brow wrinkled as she read on.

Temple had quoted Margaret as telling the jury, *My sister asked a judge to ban him from the house, but he didn't think she was in any real danger.*

This was the first Cherry had heard of her mother making any trip to court, but despite the headline, the article said no more on the subject, the reporter having chosen to focus on her aunt's harsh words about her father's destructive rages.

On the second day, she saw that the pathologist who had done the post-mortem examinations of Marianne and Bill had given evidence. She steeled herself to read on.

The newspaper had printed outline drawings of a woman and child's body in order to illustrate in detail the injuries the pathologist described.

Cherry scanned the description of her mother's injuries. *Broken cheekbone, contusions to the forehead, skull fracture, bruising across the face, hair missing from three areas of the scalp, two broken ribs, left lung punctured, stab wound to neck severing carotid artery.*

Each injury had an arrow showing where it had been inflicted. The pathologist had explained that all Marianne's injuries had been survivable except for the neck wound, which, Ben Temple recounted, had caused her to bleed out in minutes.

Next, the pathologist had detailed her brother's injuries. She started to read, but while Cherry had been able to absorb how her mother had been killed, she found after reading the first sentence she could not bear the dispassionate description of how her brother's life had ended. Instead, she looked at the outline drawing of a child's body, noting the cross hatching, line-shading and labelled arrows. Blinking, she raised her eyes from the viewer. She had been the last person to see Bill. To hold him tight. She knew what had happened.

She took a breath. How much more could she cope with today?

There was no case for the defence. Her father had pleaded guilty to the murder of her mother. He had entered no plea to the charge of murdering her brother, effectively refusing to engage with that accusation. Cherry felt baffled but read on. Despite being repeatedly given the chance to do so by the judge, her father had offered no explanation to the court as to how Bill had died.

She forced herself to keep reading. *The defendant did however take the opportunity to make a statement,* Temple had reported. *In a one-line sentence read out in court he said he had not killed his son.*

Cherry suddenly realised she was stiff. She'd been hunched for too long over the viewer and her notebook was full. As she moved, motes of dust swirled in a shard of sunlight. She gazed into the dancing dust particles. Her father had said nothing at all about her dropping Bill as she made her escape. He could have told the court about her part in Bill's death. But he had stayed silent. Rigid on her chair as her mind raced, Cherry knew why. Her father had refused to tell the court that Cherry's actions had resulted in her brother's death. It was the only thing left he could do to help her. To protect his daughter. To keep her safe.

Weariness dragged at her now. She had to keep going. She scrolled quickly to the date of the verdict: 29 July 1999. She would have been on school holidays then, her cheek healed, still not speaking. Still walking the lanes and clifftops hand in hand with Tom in search of choughs, ravens, and sometimes spying gannets at a distance, diving. Saying nothing.

SLAUGHTER OF THE INNOCENTS: BRISTOL DAD GUILTY OF DOUBLE KILLING, the Bristol Post had printed in enormous type.

With a photogenic young mother now found to have been murdered along with her sweet-faced toddler son, the paper had gone to town. The entirety of the front page was taken up with a picture of her mother and Bill. The ink dots blurred as she stared into the viewfinder. Her mother and brother, just an image printed quickly one afternoon on cheap paper that would be thrown away by the next morning. As she twisted the dial of the microfilm machine to take her to the next pages, Cherry saw with a jolt that the reporter Ben Temple had managed to persuade Margaret to give him an interview.

She'd never been told about this.

A picture of her aunt some twenty years younger accompanied the article. Margaret had always been fiercely protective of the family's privacy and so while Cherry was astonished she'd been willing to speak, she also felt professional admiration that Ben Temple had managed to persuade her.

His interview with Margaret had merited a double page spread.

BLOOD ON HIS HANDS – WHY DID FAMILY JUDGE IGNORE THE RISK? the headline demanded.

Two weeks before the murders, Marianne went to court, Temple had written. *Her sister Margaret told me she was frightened. She wanted an order to stop her husband from going to the family home. Her fears were ignored.*

'She begged me to give evidence,' Margaret said, her fists clenched, knuckles white. 'Her barrister said it might help.'

Margaret travelled to Bristol, but in the end she wasn't called to the witness stand. 'The judge had said her husband needed to be able to get into his workshop in the garage to keep his business going, to support the kids. So it was easy for him to get into the house. Women like my sister need to be believed when they say they're scared. That judge has blood on his hands.' Speaking through sobs, Margaret clearly has regrets: 'I should have made her stay here with me. I'll always regret I didn't fight harder to keep her here.'

Cherry winced. She had done these kinds of interviews. They were often intrusive. But news reporters couldn't shy away from asking questions. And sometimes traumatised relatives wanted to talk.

It had only been a few months before that Marianne had turned up at the farm unannounced. 'I thought then she'd made the break. We got the kids registered at the local school and nursery. But he'd phone up and she'd talk to him. I'd be begging her not to, but she said he was the children's father and he wanted to know how they were. And somehow he wheedled himself back in.

'I don't know why Marianne believed him. We didn't believe him for a second,' Margaret said, bitterly. 'We could hardly bring ourselves to speak to him.'

Ralph told Marianne he loved her and couldn't live without her and the children. And one fateful day, Marianne decided to go back.

'I was so furious,' said Margaret. 'I told her if she went back, she shouldn't come crying to me next time it all went wrong.'

Margaret struggled to speak as she told the Bristol Post: 'I'd tried for years. I was so frustrated. It felt like she'd just flung everything we'd done back in our faces. So this is my fault too. I said not to come back. And she didn't really talk to me afterwards, not about what was really going on, until that phone call about the court case.' Even when I knew the judge had let her down, I didn't change my mind. I didn't tell her, 'come home with me'. I didn't insist.'

Cherry rubbed at her eyes, trying to clear her head. She had to get a grip on this new reality. Her aunt had known her mother was so scared she'd gone to court to get an injunction. Scared enough to swallow her pride and beg Margaret to come and give evidence. But then her aunt hadn't been called into court. Why not? And why hadn't she insisted on them all returning to Warn Olau when the family court judge failed to protect them?

Pushing her chair back abruptly, she switched off the microfilm viewer, swept up her notebook and rucksack and almost ran from the room.

What had Ben Temple not written in his article, she wondered, as she swung down the corridors in search of the exit. Space in a paper wasn't infinite. So much had to be left out. Exactly how had her father persuaded her mother to return? Just telling a woman you love her when you've abused her isn't enough, surely? What had he promised?

Chapter Eight

Scooting down the corridor to the main desk, Cherry barely flung a goodbye at the young librarian, who looked up over the reception desk with a grin that faded slightly as he saw her back disappearing fast towards the exit door.

'Want that microfilm kept out?' Eric Wilder called after her.

Uncertain how to respond, she stopped in her tracks and half turned.

'I don't know. Er, maybe.'

He raised a quizzical eyebrow. 'I need to know whether to pack them up and take them back to the archive. Or not. I'll need a scan of your library card to keep them out if you want to come back. If you've got one. Or we can sign you up?'

'Oh, yes, sorry.' Her mind wasn't on it. Cherry turned back to the desk, forced a smile. 'I think I've still got one.' She rifled through her wallet and handed over her card. 'Please keep them out. I'll come back.' As soon as she had the card back, she stuffed her wallet in her backpack and headed for the heavy glass doors. She emerged squinting into the brightness of the afternoon.

Arriving back at her flat slick with sweat, she stripped off her cycling gear, pulled on a clean t-shirt and leggings and opened her laptop. She would write a list.

One column she headed 'Personal', the other 'Kathie'. Cherry looked at the headings, reconsidering. This couldn't just be Kathie's story, so she struck out that title and replaced it with 'Family court/ DV?/kids'.

Under the Personal column, she wrote;

Ben Temple – contact re trial evidence.
Maggie – ask why press interview.
Get my social services/adoption info.

After a few seconds' thought, she began a new line and typed 'Reply'. And then she paused. She couldn't write the word 'daddy' though it hung in her mind. Instead, she typed the letter D.

* * * * *

An hour later, Cherry looked up from her laptop. It had turned out after a quick search online that there was an established process for adoptees to see not only their social services case files, but also associated court orders relating to their adoption. But Cherry also saw that she might be prevented from seeing certain information. The Bristol City Council website made it clear that anything disclosed in her social services file was at the discretion of a case manager; information could be redacted.

When it came to information about her adoption, the website told her, the decision was taken by the local senior family judge, who could opt to let her see it, or withhold her file.

Cherry felt indignation surge hotly through her. How dare anyone redact information relating to her life, preventing her from knowing everything other people knew? The emotion was familiar; she typically felt it when a council or government official tried to obstruct her from finding out information that might be embarrassing or damaging. In those cases, she knew, her reflexive fury was based on principle; because information was power, restricting access to it was a deliberate decision, and sometimes a policy choice, intended to disempower. In this instance, though, it was personal.

Rapidly, she scanned her passport and emailed it along with her application. She would fight that battle if she came to it. Now, she had other work to do.

She drained a pint glass of cold water and set out to locate Ben Temple. It wasn't hard – few people have no online footprint, and it turned out that Temple had abandoned journalism for a new life running a sailing school. Cherry paused as she saw that his training centre was based in the Pembrokeshire fishing village of Dale, on the Marloes peninsula which scooped and enclosed the southern edge of St Bride's Bay. That wasn't far from St Davids. On narrow country lanes, maybe a forty-minute drive.

Had she ever come across him? It would hardly be surprising: the population of Pembrokeshire was tiny and anyone who ran a business along the coastal strip was likely to come into contact with others doing the same. But she felt no spark of recognition at his name.

The photograph of Ben Temple on his website looked typical of someone who lived their life in the outdoors; crinkled eyes with creases spidering towards sun-lightened hair, roughened skin and an expression that spoke of someone at ease with their life. Late forties, early fifties? She tried and struggled to imagine him in his twenties, in a rumpled suit that might, at a stretch, have come from Marks and Sparks but which probably came from one of the cheaper high street shops, dashing to the scene of a murder after the call came through to the newsdesk.

He'd have seen her aunt give evidence, approached her in the corridors in a break, built a relationship of enough trust that Margaret had been willing to talk to him about her family...

Where had Temple done the interview? In the courtroom café, a hotel lobby, or, Cherry suddenly wondered, at the farmhouse? She hadn't considered this before. She thought back to the picture she'd seen emblazoned across two pages of the Bristol Post earlier that day.

The interview must, she now realised, have been done at Waun Olau, for her aunt had been holding the picture of Cherry with her mother and Bill which had been a permanent feature on the living room dresser.

So. Temple had come to her home. Where, as a bereaved small child, she had been living, knowing little of the trial, only watching, still unspeaking, as her aunt disappeared and then appeared again.

A fuzzy memory came to her of Margaret driving off early each day that summer having set out Cherry's breakfast on the kitchen table, then her coming back late, tucking Cherry into bed and lying with her during long nights when she still couldn't sleep. When she woke up, her aunt would be gone again.

What had Ben Temple wanted from that interview with Margaret? What would she want to find out from a relative, if she was covering a murder of a mother and toddler, where an older child had escaped?

Oh.

Her heart thumped hard in her chest.

Of course.

Margaret had been just a way in.

He had wanted to know about Cherry. He had wanted to see the girl who'd fled the scene of the crime, find out how she had escaped, her state when she'd been found, what she had seen. He'd have wanted to know how come she had been spared.

Had he seen her?

Talked to her?

Cherry felt revolted at the thought.

The point, her purpose, in contacting Ben Temple was to find out more about her father's defence, to ask him about the information, interviews, tip offs, rumours, gossip and undoubtedly some facts that he would have collected and *not* reported on after the guilty verdict came in – either because there wasn't space, or because the information was tangential to the main thrust of the murder trial. Police officers sometimes told journalists key pieces of information that were then ruled inadmissible in court.

She wanted to know everything he'd heard, everything he'd suspected, everything he knew but hadn't been able to prove.

And she wanted to know what had happened when he travelled to Waun Olau to interview her aunt. What had Margaret said that he hadn't put in his piece?

Would he tell her? Would he even agree to meet her?

Cherry shook herself. Of course he would. A former journalist wouldn't be able to resist finding out what had happened to the nine-year-old girl who was the only survivor of a double murder. She began typing. She wouldn't mention that she had read his interview with her aunt. Not yet.

Dear Mr Temple, she wrote.
My name is Cherry Magraw. In 1999 you reported on my father's trial for the murder of my mother Marianne Lester and my brother Bill. I would be glad of the chance to ask you some questions. Would you be willing to meet me?
With best wishes
Cherry

She pressed Send.

Methodically, Cherry now considered the outstanding items on her list. She took her father's letter from the top of her bag, placed it on the table. She couldn't respond to it yet. She didn't know enough. Yet.

The words he had written gnawed at the edges of her mind. She had no bulwark against the warm shame of knowing how much it mattered to her that he had read her work. Searched out her name. Seen what she had achieved.

She couldn't dispose of the letter, that she already knew. But she didn't want to be confronted by it, either.

Cherry padded to her bookcase. From the bottom shelf, she took out her world atlas, the largest, heaviest hardback she could find and sandwiched the envelope in the middle. Then she shoved the atlas back on the shelf.

Out of sight. Not out of mind.

He had never, she was realising, truly been out of her mind.

Her phone pinged.

Steff.

'Mum's in an even worse state. Not seen her like this. Worried. Dad too. Call me,' the text message said.

Christ. This was all getting too much. She was busy. Cherry muted her phone and typing rapidly, emailed Kathie with a request for a time to conduct an interview.

Then she texted Eliza Wynne, a barrister she'd met through her reporting on the family courts. A year or so before, over an unpleasant coffee from a court vending machine, the lawyer had given Cherry a tutorial on how to find her way around the impenetrable daily 'cause' lists pinned up on notice boards in court lobbies around the country to inform the public of what cases were being heard. Cherry had taken her for a more palatable coffee to say thank you.

Six months on there had been a quick drink after Cherry had observed a hearing in one of Eliza's cases; just before midnight, after an unexpectedly entertaining evening with a bunch of Eliza's lawyer colleagues and clerks, they had been decanted unceremoniously onto the cobbles from one of Bristol's riverboat bars. Cherry had been amused at how Eliza's shiny glamour drew eyes and attention that the lawyer could not fail to notice, but – clearly a matter of long practice – simply ignored.

The night in the bar had warmed a professional acquaintance into something that was perhaps poised on the edge of friendship. But right now this was business. She wanted advice on how to ask for reporting restrictions on Kathie's case to be relaxed.

Could they meet tomorrow, she tapped onto her screen. In town? Her treat.

Now she looked again at the text from Steff.

Contacting Margaret was on her list. But dealing with her aunt's distress now would, she realised, overwhelm her. She didn't have the emotional resources that conversation would demand.

Eyes squeezed shut, Cherry pressed the power button on her phone.

Off. She was turning off.

Chapter Nine

'It's all a mess, obviously.'

It was two days later when Cherry pushed past the scatter of small shoes that littered the hallway of Kathie's large Victorian house in the Montpelier area of Bristol.

'The place is always a tip, sorry, after getting Brandon to school, but thanks for coming. We're along here.'

Kathie's back disappeared into the kitchen. Lola's dark eyes, peeping up from over her mother's shoulder, pinned themselves to Cherry as she followed on behind.

On entering the home of someone she was about to interview, Cherry always swept her eyes swiftly around every corner. Absorbing as much as she could from the few seconds it took to walk through to the kitchen, she saw the hall was substantial and elegant. Light streamed through brilliant gold and red glass set into the front door. Victorian encaustic tiles in blue, mustard and turquoise screamed high-end restoration job, in a house which in this part of Bristol certainly hadn't been cheap, whatever state they'd bought it in. A long row of Shaker coat pegs stretched along the pale painted wall, the chaos of family life hung along them.

Though the children had, as Kathie had said, created a tip, it was a tip that would easily be swept away leaving the bones of a kitchen that was utterly plain and quietly expensive. Kathie's translation work wouldn't have bought them this house, or this kitchen, no matter what dilapidated state it had been in originally.

'All this,' Cherry indicated around her. 'Did you do it?'

Kathie, tidying the breakfast detritus, looked distracted.

'Oh, yes. Well, Ed did. It's not my taste.' She cast her eye around the kitchen, her mouth pursing. 'A bit magazine smart for me.'

It sounded churlish, Cherry thought, as she sat down at the dining table and got out her audio recorder. Kathie had a home many people would envy.

'So, thank you for agreeing to do this.'

Kathie nodded. 'Mmm.' She kept on tidying, her face turned away.

She was uncertain, Cherry thought, now that the reality of a journalist in her house had actually materialised. When Kathie had called her, she'd been desperate for Cherry to write about the battle she faced.

'Maybe we could start with the court hearing tomorrow.' She paused. Too fast. Cherry retrenched.

'How are you feeling?'

Putting down her cloth, Kathie stalked away from the central kitchen area, disengaging Lola from her shoulder. Bending, she placed her daughter in a playpen. As she straightened stiffly, Cherry saw her hands clench. She stayed standing, unmoving, staring through the French doors into the garden beyond. It wasn't that she was being unfriendly, Cherry realised. Kathie was in such a state of tension that she was finding it hard to keep herself together.

'I'm going to have to turn up at this hearing on my own.' Kathie's voice was without energy, without emotion. She sounded empty.

'I got scared and thought I'd see what it would cost to get a lawyer. But when I rang a couple they couldn't tell me. Not if he keeps fighting, anyway. It could end up being tens of thousands. I just don't have it.'

Kathie's shoulders heaved and she sobbed so hard she shook.

Cherry made coffee and persuaded Kathie to drink it, then tried again.

'Can I see the papers?'

She shouldn't ask for these, she knew, and Kathie shouldn't show her. They were part of private court proceedings. But no one would ever know.

A shrug from Kathie directed Cherry to a manila envelope at the far end of the table. The documents she pulled out were photocopies of Ed's official application form for a child arrangements order. He was asking for the children one night a week, every other weekend and half of the holidays. It wasn't the 50:50 split she'd assumed from what Kathie had said in her phone call. But it sounded like the kind of arrangement a judge would consider normal and unremarkable.

'The point is he'd have them on his own,' said Kathie. 'Look.' She pointed.

Kathie saw that Ed had specified that the address at which Brandon and Lola would normally be staying was a flat in Clifton.

'Not his mother's, which is how we do it now. Her being there means I know at least that there are other eyes on them. This is a flat that he's...' Kathie raised her eyebrows cynically, 'borrowed from a friend who's working abroad. Of course he's not paying any rent. Landed on his feet. As usual.' The bitterness in her voice was tangible.

Kathie was not just frightened for her kids' safety, Cherry realised. She was eaten up by a sense of unfairness.

Presumably, however, Ed was still paying towards the mortgage on the house Kathie and the children were living in. She couldn't be bringing in much now, on sick pay. She'd ask, later.

'How will you argue against what he's asking for?'

A harsh laugh was followed by a hiccup as Kathie tried to catch her breath.

'That's the problem, isn't it? I don't have *evidence*. Not apart from that last thing that happened. All I can do is tell the judge why I'm scared. And it sounds ludicrous if you've not seen it. If you've not lived it. And then *he'll* find a way of making it all sound perfectly ordinary. At best, I'll come out like an overwrought, over-anxious mother. At worst, I'll sound like...' And here Kathie sank her head onto her arms and cried again.

At best, Cherry thought, you'll sound like a fantasist. At worst, like a spiteful liar out to deprive a man of his children on the basis of allegations you can't prove.

'There was this thing when he bit me. That was the only time I went to the police.'

Kathie reached into her bag that was hanging off the back of her chair and brought out a file. Among the paperwork was a plastic envelope holding three photographs.

'They took some pictures at the station but I don't have those. I took my own.'

The pictures had been taken at an awkward angle. The first, dated 15 February 2018 showed a nearly complete double arc of teeth marks, and skin on what looked like someone's upper underarm that had been partly broken.

Kathie hugged herself. 'He'd pushed my hands up over my head.'

He would have had to, Cherry saw, to reach the soft flesh of Kathie's underarm.

According to the date stamp, the second photograph had been taken two days later. Streaks of deep puce reached up into Kathie's armpit as the bruising took hold.

The final picture was date-marked four days later, when an infection had set in and the entire upper arm was swollen.

Cherry frowned. 'When did you report this?'

'When it got infected. My GP said she'd support me.'

Silently, Cherry took out her phone and snapped each picture. These injuries were doubtless what had secured Kathie both the non-molestation order stating that Ed must not come within 100 metres of her, and the occupation order – far more difficult to secure – which stated that she could live in the family home, but he could not.

'What did he say to the police?'

'Oh, it was a mistake, apparently. He said it happened when we were in bed. He said we liked that sort of thing – that I liked it like that.'

Cherry's eyes narrowed.

Kathie laughed, for the first time in a way that made Cherry warm to her. Kathie was genuinely, if cynically amused.

'And here's the awkward thing. Because I do sometimes. But not to the point of having my husband bite me though my skin. And anyway, we weren't in bed. We hadn't had sex since Lola was born.'

Cherry tried to imagine what the police reaction would have been. A liking for rough play during sex was hardly unusual but it wouldn't make it any easier to get an assault charge to stick.

'What did the police say?'

Kathie's eyes blazed.

'I told them I wasn't big into biting and that if I was it wouldn't be when I was trying to get the kids' packed lunches sorted for the next day and was dead on my feet because it was nearly 12 at night.'

Cherry laughed. 'Fair enough.' But Kathie's eyes were now glittering with tears again, her face turning blotchy.

'I found out later it could have been a charge of grievous bodily harm because he'd broken my skin. I'd have gone through with it. But the police officer said that given our...' she stopped and shuddered slightly, 'sexual history, and lack of any previous police callouts and me not contacting any domestic abuse charities, it would be hard to prove even actual body harm. I begged them, but it was no go.'

Cherry thought about this. She knew that crimes of intimate violence were often downgraded from the most serious charge possible to a more minor offence in order to secure a guilty plea or, if the charge was defended, a conviction. Juries, which the police and Criminal Prosecution Service knew all too well, weren't keen to convict a man of a serious assault carrying a prison term when there was any other interpretation of events.

'His lawyer did a good job for him, I'll say that. He accepted a caution in the end.'

'Okay.' Cherry took a breath. 'What happened next?'

'Nothing. I mean, I'd already been to the family court to get the injunction against him coming near me. And to keep him out of the house. That wasn't a problem.' Kathie suddenly stood up and strode over to where Lola was now sleeping. She made to scoop up her daughter, then stopped. She knelt at the playpen, gazing through the mesh.

'Do you understand?' Kathie's voice was harsh. 'It wasn't enough for a criminal trial, but a family judge said it was serious enough that he wasn't allowed to live here any more. And now as well as fighting me for the kids, he's fighting me on that too. He doesn't see why he shouldn't be able to come here, where we live. Where I should feel safe.'

Given the photos and the police caution that Ed had accepted, Cherry wasn't surprised that Kathie had got her non-molestation order and a ban on Ed living in their home. But, privately, police officers had told her that even if a family judge put this sort of injunction in place, it could be impossible for them to persuade the Criminal Prosecution Service to pursue a criminal charge. It was something victims often found hard to comprehend.

'Did he ever apologise?'

'Christ no.' Kathie sounded weary. 'I'm so bloody stupid. I didn't grasp the simple fact that he won't change, not ever.' She rubbed the back of her hand over damp cheeks. 'And you know what? There are times I still, *still*, want what we had. But it feels so long ago. And was it even real?'

The loss of trust in one's own judgement was the most debilitating part of any relationship breakdown, Cherry thought. How could you have been so dazzled, when in fact the object of your desires turned out to be – she ticked off instances of delusion from her own past – self-obsessed, sketchy on matters of honesty, egotistical, casually sexist, insecure, unreliable or just plain weak?

'The hearing tomorrow. What's that about?'

Kathie reached for the documents in her court bundle and began flicking through.

'I don't really know.' She stared blankly at the paperwork, then gave a short laugh. 'I guess he'll say I exaggerate everything. I really have no idea how it works.'

Cherry flicked forward in the court bundle and scanned Kathie's statement.

When I was driving to the playground, my husband criticised me in the car when I didn't parallel park close to the kerb the first time, Kathie had written about one incident. *He shouted inside the car which frightened me and the children. As I was trying to park for a second time, he grabbed the wheel to try to 'help'. His criticisms of my driving carried on for the next half hour. The children could see I was being undermined by their father. When we left, he would not let me drive my own car out of the parking space and pushed me away from the driver's door, grabbing the keys off me. He was also rough when he belted Brandon into his car seat. I was worried for Lola so I put her into her car seat myself. This was typical of how a family outing would descend into an opportunity for him to slate me in public. The morning was spoiled, and as usual, I had to pick up the pieces afterwards for Brandon and Lola.*

Cherry could perfectly imagine the scene, but she could also see how Kathie's account sounded, well, verging on petty. A marital argument in front of the kids. She didn't think it would elicit the level of sympathy which would be essential if Kathie was to persuade a judge that her fears for her children were a mother's natural reaction to a genuine threat posed by Ed. She looked at the woman in front of her who was watching keenly for her reaction.

'Is there any chance at all you might be able to pay for even a couple of hours with a lawyer?' Cherry ventured.

'No. Ed is paying some money towards the children but I don't have any savings.' Kathie frowned. 'I know this house probably makes you think there's loads of cash sloshing around, but when I kicked Ed out, he took his salary with him. All this,' Kathie swept her arm to indicate the expensive kitchen, the understated, elegant decor, 'was paid for by him.'

She looked quizzical at Cherry's surprise.

'You don't know what he does, do you?' Kathie sighed. 'He's a professor in the IT department at Bristol uni. The youngest they'd ever appointed. He created bespoke software for one of the big banks while he was still a student. Still does, when someone comes to him with a big enough cheque. That's where the money comes from. So there's no mortgage on this place.'

She stroked the burnished wooden top of the kitchen table with her thumb, then using her fingernail, scraped it hard.

'Don't get me wrong, he's always been generous. I can't fault him on that. Well, until we split up.' Panic suddenly flitted across her face. 'Why are you suggesting a lawyer? Is what I've put down in my statement terrible?' She banged her fist on the table. 'Of course it is. I spent hours on it. Hours. Christ, am I so useless I can't even write a decent account of what he's put us through?'

Cherry reached out her hand.

'No, that's not what I meant.' Internally, she sighed. 'I just think that when so much is at stake, if humanly possible it would be helpful to get some expert advice. Just in terms of how to put things across. It's hard to be objective when you're hurt.' She saw Kathie's shoulders shudder.

'And scared.'

'The whole lawyer thing. It's not just the money.' Kathie turned her face to Cherry, distrust clear in her narrowed eyes.

'The one I went to see, she didn't rate my chances. She was pretty hard-nosed. She said I didn't have enough to argue against him having the kids unsupervised. She wasn't going to fight for me, I could tell. So shelling out thousands of pounds I don't have for the pleasure of having someone rip my statement to shreds – what would be the point?'

Chapter Ten

How much should she believe of what Kathie had told her? Cherry remained unsure. She still needed to do an interview with Ed to find out his version of events, and he wasn't even aware yet that a journalist was sniffing around his court case. Cherry knew to be alert against being swayed by the account of anyone with skin in the game. From hard-earned experience, she also knew that the deeper she dug into Kathie's story without hearing Ed's, the harder keeping hold of her objectivity would be.

Pushing her bike against the wind through Bristol as the streets filled up at lunchtime, Cherry made for her favourite bolthole, a tiny café next to the old criminal courts. Two earnest young men with a passion for coffee had gone into business a few months before, offering discerning customers a choice of single origin coffee beans and an education in where they came from. *Artisan Roasted* said their sign, and while Cherry didn't pretend to be able to tell one coffee variety from another, she did take pleasure in the vivid blue cups in which her cappuccino was served.

Glimpsing a young woman with gleamingly upswept near-black hair through the café's glass frontage, Cherry waved. Seeing her, Eliza Wynne slid a file of paperwork back into her briefcase as Cherry bundled herself and her bulging backpack through the door.

From Merthyr Tydfil, a town she loved but told Cherry she'd fled without a second glance once she'd secured her place at law school, Eliza was the same age as Cherry, also single, and had a filthy sense of humour that belied her polished appearance.

Eliza represented parents who stood to lose their children to foster care and adoption, and was a committed and persuasive advocate on their behalf; Cherry had seen her in court. She could also be scathing about some of her middle-class clients as they bickered endlessly, unnecessarily – and expensively – about money and access to children. Eliza's stories about their outrageous and occasionally ludicrous behaviour seemed even more preposterous when regaled in her lilting Valleys accent.

Not yet ground down by decades of acrimonious litigation, Eliza seemed untouched by the grimness of family breakdown.

'What I keep in mind when I get fed up with people's *total* idiocy,' she'd declared to Cherry on the riverboat bar of their most recent encounter, 'is that it's my job and my privilege to stop some arsehole robbing my client blind in between getting sucked off by his shiny new girlfriend.'

Eliza stood back, looking hard at Cherry.

'Where has the rest of you gone?' she exclaimed. 'I know it's been a couple of months, but Christ, let me order you some cake.'

She waved at the bespectacled young man behind the counter for a menu. 'What do you have in the pudding department?' she demanded, scanning the counter. 'No cakes? Call yourself a café? Ah well, two large chocolate chip cookies it is then and two of whatever kind of coffee it is you're planning on teaching us about today.'

Her dazzling smile took any sting from her words and the proprietor grinned back before trotting off to play with his coffee machine.

Cherry blinked in admiration, feeling suddenly scruffy and unkempt next to the elegant barrister. She sank down into one of the battered iron-framed school chairs set around a scrubbed wooden table and tried to neaten her hair which was still squashed and damp with sweat from her helmet.

'So,' Eliza squinted at Cherry. 'Apart from having to feed you up, what can I do for you today? And remember, my hourly rate is ruinous which means you'll be buying the next round of drinks.'

'Given what these coffees cost I might prefer an invoice.' Cherry dug into her bag for her notebook and pen. 'Can I pick your brains for some insider knowledge about how judges think?'

'You can. Off the record,' Eliza grinned. 'Don't get me in trouble with their lord and ladyships.'

'Yep, got it.' Cherry chewed her lip, wondering how much detail she needed to go into. 'I'm doing this story about a woman who believes her ex could be dangerous if he's left alone with kids. Problem is, she's got a hearing tomorrow, and she doesn't think she's going to be able to convince the judge.'

Eliza listened, doodling on a yellow legal pad. 'Who's her lawyer?'

Cherry shook her head. 'No lawyer. And the judge, well, she got the non-mol extended, but she thinks the judge feels she's exaggerating, to keep her ex away from the kids.'

'Hmm.' Eliza sounded quizzical. 'Yep, well, that does happen.'

Cherry sighed. 'The photos of an injury to her arm look pretty bad. What she says he does when nobody's there to see could easily make you feel like you and your kids were at risk. But how she can prove it is beyond me. To other people I can see how it just sounds like she's lost the plot.'

'What's the ex like?'

'I've not met him. Well, not as part of this case.'

Eliza arched a pair of sharply delineated eyebrows.

Cherry shrugged. 'I've seen him at the climbing wall. I don't know him. It's a coincidence.'

Eliza took a bite from the enormous chocolate-flecked disc that had just been placed in front of her and chewed thoughtfully.

'Relationship breakdowns where children are involved can tip people into a state of blind panic,' she said. 'I've seen it lead women *and* men into exaggerating their ex's failings, and that's the best case scenario. Worst case, you're into character assassination. It gets ugly. People are desperate, and, well, maybe a quarter of the bad stuff they're saying is true but by the time they get to court they've convinced themselves their ex is a monster.' She looked pointedly at Cherry. 'Are you going to eat your cookie? Because you need to.'

Their coffees arrived, borne by the café owner. As he placed the cups reverently on the table he began to explain precisely which mountainside the beans had been grown on. Cherry restrained a snort as Eliza tilted her head and put a hand on his forearm.

'We'll take a rain check,' she said. 'I'll admit I'm a philistine, but I don't need to know the life cycle of the plant my drink is made from.' She crinkled her eyes at him. 'Though I think it's amazing that you do.'

She turned back to Cherry rolling her eyes comically as he wandered away, ever so slightly bewitched. She really did have the knack, thought Cherry with a flash of envy.

Eliza settled herself back in her seat. 'There's a lot at stake when it's one person's word against another. And judges won't stop a dad seeing their kids simply on mum's say-so.'

Cherry twiddled her spoon in her cup. 'Mmm. I've seen her statement for the hearing tomorrow.'

Eliza's eyebrows shot upwards.

Cherry laughed. 'I know, I shouldn't have. But you know journalists are shown loads of stuff they shouldn't be. Anyway. I read it and I don't think she's painted much of a picture of what she's scared of.'

Eliza shook her head, frustration mingling with resigned exasperation. 'Sometimes, when it's all perfectly true – actually, *because* it's all true – you can get a victim in court who's so petrified she can hardly speak because her abuser is right there, a few seats along from her. And if he's representing himself, then he's the one asking the questions when she takes the stand.'

The barrister laughed at Cherry's look of horror.

'Not seen that yet? Well, who else is going to do the cross-examination? There have been protests that it's still allowed, but if you don't have a lawyer in a family court, that's what happens, unless the judge doesn't allow it. Some still do.'

Eliza brushed biscuit crumbs smartly off her pale silk blouse. 'Right, I have to shoot. So briefly, this is the situation. *If* she's telling the truth, but has no criminal convictions to rely on *and* she's unlucky enough to get some fuckwit of a judge who doesn't get it that a man can be abusive to his partner without beating her black and blue, then it just looks like she's being spiteful. Trying to blacken his name to stop him seeing his kids. And then she's properly stuffed, because she's seen as the aggressor, not him.'

Cherry was scribbling all this into her notebook.

Eliza's tone changed as she had another thought. 'Actually, it can almost be worse if the victim isn't scared anymore.'

Cherry looked up inquiringly.

'I've had cases where she's taken a year or so to get herself together, during which he's carried on trying to control her through the kids. It's subtle stuff, but nasty. She decides to go to court and fight because she knows none of them will ever be free of him otherwise. By now, she's feeling strong, she's determined, she's eloquent and she doesn't back down – and my heart sinks because sometimes, you can see a judge thinking, 'Look at this woman! She can stand up for herself – how can she claim this very reasonable sounding man who she agrees never once hit her somehow managed to control her for years, and still is?' '

Cherry winced. 'It sounds like you're damned either way.'

The barrister drained her coffee and spoke with a degree of suppressed fury.

'If you want to argue you've been coerced and abused and you're asking a judge to curtail your children's relationship with their daddy who loves them, you'd better have plenty of evidence – and god help you if you don't also pitch your performance in the witness box exactly right.' Eliza rose to leave, her expression suddenly stony. 'Not too downtrodden. Not too uppity. We're still in search of the perfect victim. And no, you're not quoting me, this is all just for info.'

'Or there'll be a writ in the post, yes, I know.'

'On top of my invoice.'

'Christ. Well. How about I pay you in dinner?' Cherry hadn't planned this. Not at all. 'At mine, tomorrow. I'll cook,' she rushed on.

Eliza cocked her head. 'A home-cooked dinner.' Her voice turned dreamy. 'There's an offer a woman who lives on ready meals can't refuse.' She nodded. 'So, yes. But maybe we'll only talk shop *half* the time?'

Having paid a bill that made her decide that the chocolate chip cookie would have to do for lunch, Cherry made her way swiftly on foot towards the river, across the bridge and towards Bristol's central court building. If she wanted to find out more about her adoption, and more particularly, what social services knew about her family life before the night of the murders, she would have to convince judge Judith Vail, the newly appointed senior family judge for the area, to release her adoption file. Her appointment was for half past four.

The court building was virtually empty. Nodding at the security staff, Cherry made for the first floor where she found head usher Fergus tidying the reception desk and getting the cause lists ready for the next morning.

'Miss Magraw, back again – to meet our head judge. And on your own account this time I gather...' he said with a hint of a question.

Cherry kept her tone light. 'Fergus, remember it's Ms for us modern girls.'

Fergus, no fool, pushed no further.

'Yes, well, I'll let her know you're here.' He picked up the phone and dialled. 'Ma'am, are you free? It's *Ms*,' he twinkled, 'Cherry Magraw to see you.'

Cherry rolled her eyes. Fergus slapped his own hand, grinned in apology and nodded her through.

• • • • •

'Let's sit here, shall we?' Her Honour Judge Judith Vail QC indicated a table at the front of the courtroom and pulled out two chairs, which she placed side by side. 'No need to be too formal about the way we do this, though because it's an official application, we have to keep the mics on for the record. Hopefully though, it will just feel like a chat.'

'Right, yes. Thank you.' Cherry sat.

The judge, Cherry noticed, was speaking fast.

'Elsa, might you start the tape?' The clerk clicked on the audio record facility, then diplomatically removed herself to the side of the courtroom and out of Cherry's view.

'Excellent, let's start, so – oh!' Having sat down, Vail rose suddenly and darted towards the raised platform at the front of the court to fetch a jug of water, nearly bumping into the clerk who had risen to help.

'Ma'am, I can do that...' the clerk said.

'So sorry Elsa, yes, thank you.' Vail returned to the table where Cherry was seated. 'I thought you might need some water. And goodness, I'm very sorry, we never shook hands.' The judge reached out her right hand, smiling in a way that Cherry assumed was meant to be reassuring.

As she felt the judge's small, dry palm in hers, she observed that Vail appeared rumpled and careworn in the way that all lawyers and judges tended to look at the fag end of a working day. But, Cherry also noticed, she seemed somewhat on edge.

'So, may I ask, why do you want to see your file?'

The judge had asked in a kindly tone, but Cherry's stomach tightened at the prospect she might not give the right answer.

Why did she have to go through this? It was her life. Not this woman's life, who had it in her gift to withhold the information Cherry had never been told.

'I have to know what happened. To everyone.' Cherry stopped. The floor was falling and she gripped her seat. Her mind flickered back to saying the same words to her aunt at the farmhouse. Flickered again with the cinema image of her birthday party. How she'd loved it. At the end when her friends had gone and they were surveying the mess in the scraggy back garden, her father threw her in the air and caught her and hugged her hard and flipped her upside down and laughed and laughed, and she'd laughed back.

'Me too,' Bill begged. 'Upside-down boy me too.'

'Not your birthday, mister,' her dad had said flatly, and walked back inside.

That had been mean. Her brother's disappointed face zoomed in for a second, and she remembered – did she really remember? – how she'd grabbed for his hand and they'd run off down the garden, her tickling Bill, making him scamper and chuckle so he'd forget their father's slight.

Cherry wrenched her mind back to the present, but a faint wash of nausea pressed her down in her chair. She stared at the judge. How could it be that this momentous decision, one more among so many, was yet again to be someone else's?

'I have to be sure you're able to cope with the information you would discover in the file,' said Vail. 'That's why I need to ask why you want it. What you'll do with what you find out.'

'It's more about how I'll cope if I don't find out.' Cherry tried not to sound sullen but knew she was failing.

Vail's gaze hadn't left Cherry's face, her pale forehead creased. She wanted more, Cherry could feel it. These people. They wanted to wring the juice out of you. Then taste it. Then decide. Jesus.

She breathed in hard.

'I've built up a life. I've got my family. My job. But there's some of me missing. All the years at the start. I need to know why things turned out how they did.' Cherry had to clamp her teeth together as she finished, horrified that she'd started to tremble. With rage or nerves, she couldn't tell.

Vail took a breath.

'Elsa.' The judge's voice was crisp. Across the room, the clerk looked up from scrolling through her phone. 'Stop the tape, please.'

'Oh. Right.' The clerk hesitated, puzzled at this break with strict court protocol. Vail nodded at a sheaf of papers on a desk. 'And I've just seen this file from the last case. They can't hang around here unsecured. Return them to the court office please, then you can go for the day.'

Bundling the papers together, the clerk clicked off the recording machine with a shrug and exited the courtroom.

'May I call you Cherry?'

Surprised, Cherry looked up, then nodded.

Vail gave a brief smile. 'You won't understand why this is yet, but meeting you is a strange experience for me.' She saw Cherry wrap her arms around herself, uncomprehending.

'I'll release your file. It is, as you say, information that belongs to you,' said the judge. 'But I need to run through some aspects of what you'll read when you go through it.'

Vail rested her chin in her hands and looked up at Cherry. 'I knew your mother.'

There was a beat as she watched Cherry register her words.

'I represented her when she tried to leave your father – when she tried her hardest to make sure he couldn't come anywhere near you.'

She saw Cherry's eyes widen.

'It was my job to secure for your mother the best protection the courts could offer her,' Vail said. 'I'm extremely sorry that I failed.'

For a long moment Cherry stared at the judge. She could see the small broken veins spidering across her cheeks, and a film of sweat on her brow.

'You were my mother's lawyer?' she said slowly.

Rubbing her temples, Judith Vail looked down, then did her best to meet Cherry's eyes. 'I'll try to explain.' She sighed. 'Twenty odd years ago women weren't always taken seriously when they said they were being assaulted in their home,' she said quietly. 'But with the photos and the police testimony, plus your mum giving evidence, I was appalled that the judge let your father come and go from your house as he pleased.'

'Did my mum,' Cherry stopped, her throat seizing up, 'not do very well?'

Vail looked at her, uncertain.

'I mean, when she was saying what my dad was like. In her evidence,' Cherry choked out. 'Did she not do a good job?'

Swiftly, Vail reached out her hand and grasped Cherry's.

'Your mother,' she said, 'did brilliantly. She was scared but she fought. She tried her best to keep him away. Away from her but also away from you two.'

'Then why didn't the judge believe her?' Cherry whispered.

'I'm so sorry. Sometimes... judges have their own biases. Sometimes they don't feel that evidence is strong enough. Sometimes, they get it wrong.'

Inside Cherry, a dense ball of fury, latent for decades, ignited.

'I see,' she said. Her fists clenched. She could not speak her rage; she feared speaking at all in case it erupted and obliterated the room and everything in it.

'Some water?'

Cherry shook her head, unable to raise her eyes, tears filling them.

'Well, you'll want to start reading your files, I expect,' said Vail, her tone brisk. 'They're all here.' Her heels clicked on the wooden steps up to the judge's bench. Handing the files to Cherry, she turned to leave. 'You're fine to stay until six o'clock. Please return everything to the court office downstairs when you're done. You can't take them with you but you're welcome to view them at any time.' A brief, formal nod. 'Good luck, Cherry.'

Vail had taken only a couple of steps when she hesitated.

'Perhaps,' she said, 'you might like to meet again.' She stumbled slightly over the words. 'I mean for a coffee. Or... lunch? In case you have any questions. About your mother. About the day we went to court.'

Cherry glanced up from the files. The invitation seemed odd. But perhaps no stranger than learning that this judge had been her mother's lawyer. She paused, unsure how to respond. But... why not try to find out more? And so she nodded.

'Fine,' said the judge, suddenly businesslike again. 'Then let's say, Friday?'

Cherry nodded again, her eyes flickering to the files.

'1pm then. Excellent.' With that, Vail turned and walked away, her head and shoulders held stiffly straight.

Cherry did not acknowledge her exit. Deliberately compressing her anger, she was already opening the first of three faded green box files and only distantly registered the soft click of the courtroom door.

She knew she should try to be methodical. From the first file she lifted out assorted bundles of papers and began to sift, glancing quickly at each page. She was taken aback at the sight of a signature – her mother's – at the bottom of a police witness statement. She didn't recall ever seeing Marianne's writing before.

The file mostly dealt with events leading up to the murders. Her mother's first contact with the council had been in the first week of June 1998, four months before the day of Cherry's birthday party. She'd asked to be rehoused. The paperwork stated: *Refused - family already housed, privately owned.*

She moved quickly to the start of the second file, where the first page was the hospital record of treatment for the slashes to her cheek. 'Taken to Frenchay hospital for specialist surgery,' someone, presumably a social worker, had written.

A consultant plastic surgeon had apparently put three sutures in the top cut, five in the longer wound beneath. Her medical notes included a record of what she'd been wearing when she'd arrived at the hospital. Vest and pants, a lilac party dress, a green cardigan. No shoes. No socks.

Cherry frowned. Her dress had been yellow. All the way through the assault, every image of herself on the leatherette chair in the living room was imprinted with the yellowness of her dress, a light, happy yellow that had set off her hair. Well, someone must have got that wrong as they were logging her clothing.

Wanting to see ahead in time now, Cherry flicked quickly through the files' remaining contents.

While he was on remand and awaiting trial, her father had made a formal application to the court for Cherry to visit, she read in the social worker's rounded, blue biro'd handwriting. Decision: rejected. After the conviction, he'd tried again with the same result. An appeal against that decision failed. By this point, at the back end of 2000 – Cherry noted the dates of each request and subsequent ruling – over two years had passed since the murders, and she had turned eleven.

She had known none of this.

Cherry was suddenly struck with an awareness of the stress it must all have caused Margaret and Tom, who were then, she calculated, still only in their early thirties, trying to look after their traumatised and silent niece at the same time as having just become parents to Steffan, who had arrived unexpectedly in the wake of the disaster.

This was the point, Cherry saw, when her aunt and uncle had applied to adopt her.

Unsurprisingly, given the determination with which he had tried to see his daughter, her father had contested it. The rest of the second file and much of the third was taken up with paperwork from the family court hearings which had needed to be convened, where Margaret and Tom had argued that her father was unreasonably withholding consent to her adoption. Next, she saw the social services copy of her change of name documentation; Margaret and Tom had ensured she would no longer be known as Lester, but instead, by her mother's maiden name, Magraw. She remembered the conversation about it in the farmhouse kitchen; she'd practised signing her new surname with a flourish, over and over again, as children do. She didn't recall feeling any emotion attached to the name change.

Further on was a photocopied legal bundle containing a copy of the non-molestation order her mother had secured, with Vail's name on it as her barrister. No order preventing him from coming to the house though – her father had been free to use his garage workshop. There was also a welfare statement by her school, a six-page statement by her aunt and uncle, and a carbon copy of a long statement by her father, signed by him at the bottom.

It was closely written on lined paper. She hadn't known about this. Cherry glanced at the clock. She couldn't read it now, though every part of her was screaming to. There was no time.

Quickly, she got out her phone – no judge was present, clearly, but she knew very well that photography in courtrooms was against the law – and snapped photos of her father's statement.

There was so much more. She had to work fast.

She'd worked halfway through the second file when there was a knock at the door. She only just managed to put her phone down as Fergus stuck his head round.

'Just checking the rooms Miss – er, Ms,' he said affably, mostly succeeding at keeping a lid on his curiosity as to Cherry's business in the court. 'It's nearly six. Can you be out in five? We need to clear the building for the night.'

'You couldn't give me ten?' she asked. 'I'm nearly done. And then I'll be quick down the stairs and out, promise.'

'Fair enough, but don't get me hauled out of bed when the police ring to say there's an intruder locked in the courts.' The usher's head disappeared round the door and it was silent once more in the courtroom.

Cherry pulled out her phone again, this time feeling no compunction. Continuing her work, she systematically photographed every page.

Having deposited the paperwork with the single clerk left in the court office, Cherry walked to the exit and pushed against the revolving doors. As she left the building, an email pinged in. Bristol Library. Would she be needing access to the microfilm in the next twenty-four hours? Please could she let them know, as otherwise the material would need to be returned to the archive. It had been sent by Eric Wilder.

Cherry sighed. So much research to do, so little time to do it. She needed an assistant. In her dreams.

'Very sorry. I'll come in tomorrow,' she typed back. 'I hope that will be all right.' She pressed Send, pushed off on her bike, and instantly forgot the appointment she'd just made.

Chapter Eleven

At her flat, Cherry sent the pictures of each document she'd photographed from her phone to her printer, then watched as dozens of pages spooled out, then – as far as she could work it out – organised the papers on the floor in date order.

Three slices of toast fuelled the next few hours of reading until, around midnight, her brain still fizzing with questions, she forced herself to go to bed.

Sleep came far more quickly than Cherry had imagined possible. When her phone alarm went off at eight, the sound wrenched her from an unfamiliar peaceful slumber. She felt rested. Energised. And curiously, she realised, at peace.

Scrunching her eyes against the morning light, Cherry fought her body's desire to slump back into her cocoon and dismiss the rest of the day. She couldn't. She was meeting Kathie at court this morning. And whatever state Kathie was in, to have any chance of reporting events as they unfolded Cherry had to be there.

But Cherry's whole being longed to return to the state of relaxation her alarm had just interrupted. It had been so rare in recent weeks for her to wake feeling anything other than sad and fraught. The temptation to flee back to the sanctuary of peaceful sleep was too much to resist. She would give herself just a few more minutes. Then get up. Cherry allowed herself to sink back into softness.

But as the alarm buzzed once again Cherry's waking mind veered automatically to Garth. As it always did. She was right back there again, stuck again in the familiar, deeply etched tracks of grief and loss. She could not divert her thoughts, and felt the comfort of her restorative sleep ebb away like a fast-dropping tide. Was Garth getting the girls dressed for school? Finding their toothbrushes? Or was he being trodden on by small determined legs as the girls clambered into bed with him – and Aline?

As always, this image floored her, but no matter how hard she tried to divert, avoid or replace it with other thoughts, physical activity, work or social life, Cherry could not rid herself of it. Each time it flooded her mind she felt sick. Now, she hugged herself, swamped in a bleakness that overwhelmed her every time she failed to quash the various imagined scenarios that ran through her head of Garth living again with his wife.

The next inevitable thought arrived, right on cue. He'd taken Aline back, but did they sleep together? Did he make love to the wife he'd told her he would never return to? She'd never asked. But suddenly, this morning, she couldn't push the question away. She had to know.

She picked up her phone.

Reckless. Stupid. She shouldn't be calling when she was feeling needy. She shouldn't be calling him at all. Exerting the immense self-discipline required to resist asking this question was the only way she had been able to retain a sliver of self-respect. It was how she'd survived. And never being the one who got in touch. Never emailing. It had been her rule since she'd told him it was over. And here she was breaking it. Yet again.

She called Garth's number.

There could be no satisfaction, Cherry knew as she waited, hearing each ring with the hopeless knowledge of her own idiocy.

'Cherry?' The familiar warmth of Garth's voice slid over her. 'Hang on. Sorry. I'll just be a sec.'

As Cherry heard him issue instructions on a route and the answering murmurs from a driver, she realised with relief that he was already at the yard. Of course, it was she who had woken late.

Garth came back on. 'Right. What's up?'

Cherry stared at her feet, poking out from the duvet. 'I needed to ask you something.'

'Ah.'

She battled with herself. A giddy momentum carried her forward.

'Look. I know this is awful of me. I shouldn't ask. But I want to know.'

Cherry gripped the phone and banged her fist against her head, furious with herself.

'Do you?'

'Do I... oh.'

There was a pause.

This was masochism but she had always wanted to know the truth of any situation. Only then she'd always told herself, could she deal with it. The silence lengthened. She couldn't speak.

'Sweetheart.' Garth's voice in her ear, weary and sad.

Her world tumbled.

No point in asking why. No point berating him. No point in demanding that he didn't. But how was she going to manage her day after this? And, yes, goddammit, why? How *could* he?

'Garth, I don't know what to do.' She drew a breath, ragged with tears, barely able to control her speech. 'I can't bear,' she stumbled, the words forming so thickly she had to push them out, 'I can't bear we never had a chance to find out... if we could work.' She tried to breathe. 'But I thought we could.' She squeezed her eyes shut as hot tears rushed down her cheeks. 'I thought we would.'

Across her mind flashed a picture of two small, dark-haired girls shrieking in the sea. Drying off their small sandy bodies pushing still damp legs into shorts, wet feet catching on stretchy fabric. Garth's daughters. She'd come to love them.

'I miss us.' She tried to breathe, but the next words came out as a wail. 'And I miss the girls.'

'Cherry.' Garth's voice sounded deadly serious now. 'I'm sorry. I could not be more sorry for all of this.'

She heard someone ask him a question. It sounded urgent.

'You need to go,' she said.

'I do, but...'

Cherry heard him turn away again to deal with the matter at hand.

'I'm back,' he said. But she could hear the distraction in his voice.

'So.' His voice was strained. 'Cherry. I don't know what I think about this, yet. I need some time and I don't have any right now.'

She'd put herself in the position now of having to wait. She wasn't in control any more. And she hated it. Stupid, stupid her.

'Cherry, are you going to be all right?' His words came out in a rush. 'I don't want you to feel like this. It's a mess. It's my fault. I should never have let it happen.'

• • • • •

Hollowed out, Cherry stood up and walked to her bookshelf. Bending over, she pulled out the world atlas into which she had placed her father's letter. Large and unwieldy, the book was hard to handle. She shook it impatiently and after a few seconds the envelope fell to the floor.

At the kitchen table, she pulled out her laptop. What to say? She didn't want to see him. She needed to see him. But she couldn't let him know that. What was the meeting for, she asked herself. What do I want from this man?

She was a writer but she couldn't find the words. The more she wrote, the more he would understand of her, and the more power he would have. And Cherry, who was unafraid of words and used them daily with such facility, now felt frightened of their ability to reveal her deepest self to a man who must, she knew, be a monster.

'I want to know what happened that night,' she typed.

But no. He would surely know that – else why on earth would she be going?

Delete.

An editor's voice echoed from the past. 'Stick to the facts,' he'd always said. Use the fewest words required to tell the reader what they need to know.

With a thankful sigh, Cherry reapplied herself. No explanation. No elaboration.

This is Cherry, she typed. *I've read your letter. Yes, I'll visit.*

She left it at that.

She wrote out her father's name, Ralph Lester. The surname that had been hers, once. Copying the prison address from her father's letter onto an envelope, she printed out her note and put it inside. Taking no particular care, she placed a stamp in the corner.

It was done.

Next, Cherry washed her hands for a long time before drying them and reaching for her first aid kit from the shelf under the sink. It was extensively supplied with field dressings, cannulas, blood giving bags, needles of various sizes, sterile sutures, medical blood coagulant for traumatic injuries and a tourniquet, as well as the more standard plasters, antiseptic wipes and bandages: she'd carefully chosen each item when she was working in the field. All out of date now. It also contained a Stanley knife and cigarette lighter.

She knew she should use razor blades which caused less damage, but the point was that it should hurt.

She stroked her right thigh up and down, considering the skin, pressing to find the fleshiest part. A quick rub with an antiseptic wipe, then she took the Stanley knife, held its blade in a lighter flame for thirty seconds and drew it horizontally across her thigh, ten inches below her knicker-line. The cut was made between old scars. Instantly the blood welled up and she grabbed the folded tea towel, pressing down hard to staunch the flow.

The pain as the blade sliced through flesh was a vast, familiar relief. The deep throb as her hand pushed down against the wound provided comfort in a different, though equally familiar way. As her heart beat faster with the adrenaline rush, Cherry remained sitting, concentrating on the physical sensations of release.

After five minutes, she lifted the tea towel to inspect the bleeding. Still oozing, she reapplied pressure as she glanced at the clock on the wall. Not long till she had to leave.

From the first aid kit, she soaked a gauze pad in antiseptic fluid and cleaned the cut. Blood began oozing again but she had no more time.

She selected a packet of butterfly stitches which she used to join the edges, then taped two non-adhesive pads firmly over the wound. Then she called a cab, got dressed and headed out to court.

Chapter Twelve

As the taxi drew up Cherry knew she only had ten minutes till the hearing. Damn. Not good. She'd planned to introduce herself to Ed in good time, use her best emollient manner to explain what she was hoping to achieve, giving him every chance to ask her as many questions as he wanted. No time for that now.

After clearing security she dashed up the stairs. and as she reached the waiting area, cast around for Kathie. She could feel her leg throbbing.

No Fergus on reception this morning. Instead, Cherry found herself asking his rake-thin deputy whose name she kept forgetting – Jonathan? Joshua? She peered at his name badge – Jasper – to inform the judge that she would be sitting in on Kathie's case and intended to make an application to report.

Jasper drew his pencil down the morning's list.

'Sams v Sams – think that'll be District Judge Hobson.... Oh, no. What's happened there then?' He leant over and typed into his computer monitor, scrolling down the screen. 'Right. Looks like it's been bumped to Her Honour Judge Fosse.' Jasper smirked. 'She'll be pleased. Had the day marked off to write a long judgment, or so she told me earlier.'

He picked up the phone and dialled.

'Good morning ma'am. Just calling to let you know that I have the journalist Ms Magraw with me.' He paused. 'Yes, a reporter. She's asking to come into court.'

Cherry bridled. She wasn't asking the judge if she could sit in. She was entitled to attend.

Jasper listened for a few moments, his eyebrows raking upwards, then smiled thinly at Cherry, almost in sympathy.

'Her Honour says she will need to see your official press accreditation before you can be admitted. And she will hear any objections to your attendance before the case begins.'

As Jasper photocopied her National Union of Journalists press card and scurried off to deliver it to the judge, Cherry glimpsed Kathie standing by one of the floor-to-ceiling windows, talking tensely to an Asian woman who wore a deep pink and gold embroidered headscarf.

'Hi Kathie, how are you doing?' Cherry said, approaching the pair carefully, almost tentatively.

Kathie barely looked up, distracted by a bundle of papers she was flicking through.

'Yeah. Okay. Well, not really,' she managed. 'Thanks for coming.' She looked up properly and Cherry saw her eyes slide away, tears forming. 'Sorry, I'm not great.' Kathie chewed at her lip. 'I need to find somewhere to sit. Somewhere he can't see me.' She inclined her head across the room. Cherry's eyes followed.

Ed Sams was sitting on his own at the opposite side of the waiting area. She felt the same sense of shock as she had when she saw him before, when she'd realised she knew him from the climbing wall. She'd need to go over to introduce herself in a minute, let him know she would be sitting in. She turned to the woman accompanying Kathie.

'Hi. Are you Rachida? Kathie mentioned you.'

The woman nodded. 'From The Haven. I'm hoping the judge will let me come in.'

Cherry nodded as they shook hands. 'Has Kathie told you she wants me to cover the case?'

Rachida smiled uncertainly. 'She has.' Her tone was not warm. She was worried for Kathie, Cherry sensed.

'Let's see how it goes. Unless there's a serious objection that can't be overcome, journalists have the right to be in court. I just need to speak to...' she indicated Ed.

This was going to be delicate. And – she glanced at the clock, which showed four minutes to 10 – she had almost no time left.

Ed looked up as Cherry approached.

'Mr Sams. Hello.' She paused to give him time to absorb her presence in front of him. 'May I sit down?'

Cherry clearly wasn't a member of court staff. Ed looked puzzled but nodded.

'I'm a reporter.'

She let him grasp what she'd said.

'Journalists are allowed to sit in on family cases, but I wanted to introduce myself to you first, just so you knew who the person was at the back of the court.'

Ed's look of polite enquiry had shifted to concern. 'You're going to write something?'

Cherry knew that as the realisation sank in properly, bewilderment would likely turn to suspicion.

'I can't report your name,' she said quickly. 'I'm interested in how people use the courts to help sort out situations where relationships have broken down. But nobody can be identified. Especially children. Or,' she tried to lighten the mood, 'I end up in jail.'

There was a pause. He didn't smile. 'I guess – well, if the press has the right to be there, there's not much I can do.'

Inside, Cherry wobbled, feeling torn. Should she say? He didn't have a lawyer to advise him, she thought. Damn it. She had to be fair.

'You can say to the judge that you don't want me there,' she said, her reluctance to explain this fact masked by a scrupulously polite tone.

Ed looked at her, puzzled. 'I thought you said journalists were allowed?'

'Yes, but you can object. You'd have to say why. Then the judge decides if your reasons are valid, or strong enough to make it necessary to exclude me.'

She was saved from further explanation by the announcement system. 'Court 3, Case BS18P00126' the call went out.

Ed rose immediately. With a brief nod to Cherry, he gathered up a folder and walked swiftly towards the courtroom door. Trailing behind, Cherry watched to see if he would acknowledge Kathie.

As he passed, Kathie looked away, but just a couple of metres ahead, and before reaching the courtroom doors, Ed stopped suddenly and turned around. His bright blue eyes fixed on Cherry.

'Why *this* case?' Ed asked. His tone held a definite edge.

She'd anticipated the question. She couldn't honestly say her interest in this case was random. But if he knew Kathie had asked her to write about it... in a very real sense, Kathie was a source, and she had to be protected.

'I'm writing an article about family breakdown,' she said blandly. 'I was looking for cases where there was a dispute about children.' She hadn't said anything untrue.

Ed gave a brief nod then turned and walked into court.

A hushed silence hung oppressively over the courtroom until a door at the far end behind the judge's raised platform was pushed open and the court clerk, a cheerful young woman with a bouncy ponytail bustled in holding a stack of files which she plonked noisily on the desk at the front.

'Morning all,' she exclaimed. She peered at the room. 'This everyone?' She flicked a curious glance at Cherry. 'Righto. Well, Her Honour won't be long.'

Over the ensuing thirty seconds the silence grew thicker.

To the left of a large, scarlet leather chair in the centre of the raised dais, another door, almost hidden in wooden panelling, opened into the court. Carrying a laptop, Circuit Judge Ruth Fosse walked in.

In her early fifties, Cherry assessed, she was short and round, with a sharply cut silver bob.

Fosse perched herself, seemingly precariously, on the judicial chair, before looking up over narrow, violet-framed spectacles.

'Good morning,' said the judge. Her voice was tiny and precise. 'I'm aware I'm not the judge you met last time you were in court. Judge Hobson, who I think you were expecting, chose yesterday to, shall we say, pass this hearing up to me.' She half closed her eyes and almost imperceptibly sighed.

'First of all, however, I gather that this courtroom has garnered the interest of the press. The national press, no less.' Her gaze switched from the middle distance to land on Cherry at the back.

'Ms Magraw is, as I understand it, a freelance journalist.' Fosse lingered on the word 'freelance' in a way that might imply, Cherry thought, a lower status than if she had been a regular employee of a media organisation. Maybe it was just her own insecurity. She met the judge's gaze, which was now focused tightly on her, unblinking.

'Ms Magraw, I gather from a fellow judge that you have attended some family cases as well as criminal cases here in Bristol. As yet I have not had the pleasure of making your acquaintance. Perhaps you might like to stand up and introduce yourself.'

It wasn't a request and Cherry felt herself flush. No judge had ever got her up on her feet. But they were all different, weren't they? Judges could run their courts in their own idiosyncratic way, and often did if the lawyers she'd chatted to were to be believed.

As Cherry rose, her thigh throbbed below the bandage. She saw Fosse register her wince. She shifted her stance to take the weight off her right leg. Keep this brief, and keep it general, she thought.

'Your Honour. Thank you. My name is Cherry Magraw. I come to court regularly to report on cases the public don't have time to attend.'

Fosse's eyes did not leave her. 'I understand you have a particular interest in the subject of domestic abuse?'

It felt odd to be interrogated by a judge as to her journalistic interests, but it was not, Cherry supposed, an entirely outlandish question. 'Yes. Yes, I do.'

'Domestic abuse is a terrible misuse of power within a relationship,' said Fosse. Had her diction not been so precise, Cherry thought, the judge's voice was so low it would have been almost inaudible. 'But I hope the following goes without saying; no party to any case should believe that having a journalist in court can bring any pressure to bear on a judge.'

Astonished, Cherry gaped. Was this a reprimand? Or maybe Judge Fosse was simply trying to be clear – with a sledgehammer – about the independence of the judicial role.

She now addressed Kathie and Ed directly.

'Mr and Mrs Sams, particularly as you are litigants in person with no legal representative to aid you, I must make sure that you know the media has the right to attend family court, unless there are any objections which I think sufficiently important in terms of impairing the safe hearing of this case as to require the journalist to leave.'

From their opposite sides of the courtroom, Kathie and Ed looked confused at this tortured phrasing.

'What I am saying,' said Fosse, a sliver of impatience now just discernible, 'is that if you do not wish Ms Magraw to be here, you can say so, but you must tell me why.'

Rachida turned to look at Cherry, raising her eyebrows quizzically. Was the judge inviting objections? At the same moment, Kathie half-stood.

'I'm fine with it.'

Fosse looked at her intently. There was a pause. Kathie was left on her feet until Fosse nodded at her to sit. She slid back into her seat, her head down, her hands resting flat on the file of paperwork in front of her.

Fosse's gaze switched to Ed. 'Mr Sams?'

Unhurriedly, Ed stood. 'Your Honour.' He glanced round at Cherry. 'I've not had long to think about it. What I'm concerned about is the children.'

From the corner of her eye, Cherry saw Kathie's head jerk up. Ed making that point made him look good, while Kathie, Fosse might think, hadn't bothered to think about the kids.

'Obviously I don't want our family's names in the press,' said Ed. 'As long as anything that identifies us is kept out of it, I'm happy with that.' He sat.

'Well then,' said Fosse. 'The media is welcome to remain. And I will consider whether to allow reporting of what goes on in this room when the entire matter is resolved, but that will not, I imagine, be today.

'In the meantime,' – her voice turned suddenly steely – 'I must remind you, Ms Magraw, of the tight restrictions on what you may and may not publish about what happens in this court. Above all, children,

and therefore their parents, may not be identified. It is important before we proceed that we are clear.'

Good god, thought Cherry, feeling indignation swell. No judge
had ever responded to her presence in court quite so combatively.
This opening salvo from Fosse did not bode well for her application
later on to relax reporting restrictions. But she couldn't help that.
Right now, it was just about staying in court. She got to her feet for
the second time, noticing as she rose that blood had soaked through
the dressing and now showed as a dark horizontal streak on her trouser leg. She saw the judge's eyes flicker as, from her vantage point on
high, she took in the fact that she was bleeding.

Fosse's eyes narrowed. 'Are you quite well, Ms Magraw?'

Everyone's heads turned to the back of the court. Reflexively,
Cherry clamped her hands over her thighs.

'Yes, thank you judge.' She was desperate to sit down, desperate
not to be the centre of attention but she also knew she was blushing
to her roots. The widening horizontal line of blood was too precisely
drawn to be anything other than self-inflicted.

Fosse leaned back in her chair, her eyes pinioning Cherry. 'I see.'
Cherry knew that somehow, this judge had precisely understood the
situation.

'Well, Ms Magraw, regarding the restrictions on reporting, are we
clear?'

'Yes,' Cherry said, her tone sharper than she had intended. 'Crystal.'

Fosse's lips thinned. Cherry could have kicked herself. This wasn't
about her ego and it certainly wasn't about antagonising the judge.
But Fosse was suddenly brisk.

'Excellent.' The judge adjusted her glasses and turned her attention to the file on the desk. 'Then shall we get on?'

Chapter Thirteen

The judge perused the ring-binder in front of her. A few seconds later, she looked up to address Kathie.

'Mrs Sams, you are applying for an order that means your two children, Brandon aged five, and Lola, aged 17 months, will live with you, and have only *supervised* contact with their father, supervised that is by you or another family member, for one day every other weekend and one evening after school every week. Have I understood correctly?'

Kathie got to her feet.

'Yes. I mean, yes, Your Honour. I... I don't think he should be able to have them on his own because...'

The judge broke in. 'We will come to that. For now, I am simply trying to establish what it is you want. Have I got it right?'

'Oh. Yes.' Kathie seemed to deflate. 'Yes. That's correct.'

'Mrs Sams, thank you. You may sit down.'

At that, Fosse turned a page and looked at Ed. Squinting over her glasses, she read from the court papers.

'Mr Sams, you have issued a counter application asking the court to allow you to spend unsupervised time with your children... yes, I think I see... from Friday evening to Monday morning every other week. One overnight during the week. And half the holidays. Do I have it right?'

Ed stood.

'Yes Your Honour, that's correct.' He sat down, looking unfazed.

Fosse turned the pages of her folder.

'Mrs Sams, I also see that you are, as a result of allegations of domestic abuse contained in your documents, asking me to make findings of fact that your husband has been coercively controlling and violent towards you. You say here that you lived with him under... let me see, 'the sustained threat of violence,' and that on occasion he has been physically aggressive towards you. I do not think you say he actually assaulted you apart from on one occasion towards the end of your relationship, which has been the subject of a police investigation. You also say that he threatened to physically hurt the children to control you and get his own way. Is that right? No no...' Fosse said as she saw Kathie start to get up. 'There is no need to keep standing up and sitting down.'

Kathie sank back in her seat.

'Yes,' she said, her voice barely carrying to Cherry at the back of the court.

'Mr Sams, you are contesting these allegations?'

Ed did not attempt to rise but sat up straight. 'I am.'

Cherry watched him glance across the courtroom at Kathie, then hesitate.

'May I say something?'

Fosse peered down at him, and considered. She nodded. 'Briefly.'

Ed leaned forward.

'We've had rows, like any couple. Some big ones. But these are exaggerations. They've been taken out of context.'

'Well,' said Fosse sharply. 'We will see. I need to explain to both of you however that making such complaints in court – and indeed contesting the injunction which currently prevents you from living at your home address, Mr Sams – will lead to me making a legal finding of fact that domestic abuse has occurred, or that it has not. One of you, inevitably, will be unhappy with my decision.' Fosse paused to look beadily through her glasses at Kathie and Ed in turn.

'My findings will in turn inform my decision on where, how often and under what conditions each of you see your children, and also with whom they will live.' Fosse paused again, Cherry thought, for dramatic effect, before employing the inflection of a world-weary teacher of recalcitrant pupils as she finished with what sounded less like advice than a warning.

'I would encourage you, if at all possible, to find a way to negotiate between yourselves the time your children spend with each parent without the input of the court. You should think of their welfare first, rather than your own feelings. Deferring your responsibilities as parents to a judge will rarely result in a better solution than one you can come up with yourselves.'

As Fosse paused, Cherry saw Kathie speak urgently under her breath to Rachida. She looked panicked.

Kathie had not grasped, Cherry thought, that there could be any question about which parent Lola and Brandon actually lived with.

Fosse continued, attempting to sound more kindly now, Cherry thought.

'Neither of you have lawyers to advise you, so I should make it clear that there is no compulsion on you, Mrs Sams, to seek findings of fact on these matters. Any domestic abuse is serious, but even if I were to make findings, it would not necessarily lead me to restrict their father's contact.' The judge took a small sip of water from the glass in front of her.

'Now, would you like a moment to consider outside the courtroom whether you both wish to go ahead?'

Kathie stood. When she spoke, her tone was uncomprehending.

'Yes. I mean, yes, obviously. Because he's not safe to be with them. The court needs to protect them. That's what I've come for.'

Cherry typed fast into her laptop as Kathie spoke, clenching and unclenching her fists. Kathie's voice filled with anxiety, rising to a thin, wavering sound.

'The children have to live with me, they can't live anywhere else. I mean, you can't seriously...' She gulped. 'I'm still breastfeeding Lola...' She ground to a halt.

Rachida reached up to take hold of her hand, trying unsuccessfully to pull her to her seat.

'Mrs Sams, I do know this situation is difficult,' said Fosse, her tone losing a touch of its studied patience. 'The welfare of your children is the paramount concern of this court. But if you wish to press on with your allegations, I will need to hear the evidence, see it tested, and discover where it leads us. I can only decide that an episode of abuse has occurred when you have proved to my satisfaction that it did.'

Watching Ed now, Cherry saw that he looked surprisingly at ease. He stood, upright and seemingly relaxed, not looking at Kathie. He nodded to the judge.

'I agree that yes, we do need to sort this out properly,' was all he said, before sitting.

Cherry marvelled at his self-possession.

'I see,' said Fosse, picking up pace. 'Let us get on then. As happens increasingly frequently, neither of you has legal representation. This means when each of you give evidence, the other party will have the right to cross-examine. It has recently been pointed out that when one party is complaining of domestic violence, it is invidious to expect that person to be cross-examined by their alleged perpetrator. Some claim,' her gaze took in Cherry at the back of the court 'that this is a way for abusers to continue their controlling and abusive behaviour. Which would of course be appalling.'

Cherry kept her head down. It was the first time she had heard a judge explicitly set out the difficulties that the disappearance of legal aid had caused for warring ex-partners.

'I will not,' Fosse continued sternly, 'permit any intimidatory or threatening questioning in my court. And to protect the complainant, all questions by Mr Sams will be asked through me rather than directly to Mrs Sams. I hope that is understood. This will inevitably lengthen proceedings, but it is, regrettably, the best I can do.'

Clutching her jacket to her leg in an attempt to cover up the bloodstain, Cherry hurried after Ed as he took the stairs at speed and exited the building. It wasn't so much that he seemed chipper, as that he came across as completely at ease she thought, running after him to catch up by the metered parking further down Redcliff Street. She thrust her card at him.

'I'm sorry, so sorry to bother you. I'd like to get in touch,' Cherry panted, noting that Ed drove a new and expensive looking

Volkswagen. 'Would that be all right?'

Ed frowned. 'I guess... well, I suppose so.' He didn't look thrilled but Cherry opened her notebook anyway. She had barely finished scribbling his number down before Ed had got into his car and pulled off.

Kathie and Rachida emerged onto the plaza as Cherry arrived en route back to the court building.

'I need a few minutes on my own,' Kathie said abruptly. She turned towards the riverbank. 'I'll be fine. I just want some space. Meet you at the café in ten.'

There was an awkward silence as Cherry and Rachida walked together to the café, an awkwardness which extended through the buying of drinks and to them taking a seat at a table by the window.

Rachida spoke first.

'The judge doesn't like you being there.'

Was she suggesting Cherry should not have come? She didn't know, but in truth could only nod.

'Yup. I've not had that sort of reaction before.'

'Maybe not. But it was no surprise to me.' Rachida leaned across the table, her delicate features focused intensely on Cherry.

'That judge is one of two in Bristol whose names we dread seeing on the list when our clients go to court. So I'm worried. I know Kathie wants you there. But it could backfire on her.'

Cherry sighed. Battling the court staff had been bad enough a year ago when she'd started trying to report family cases. But having to persuade a women's charity of the value of a journalist observing a hearing felt beyond a joke.

The truth, Cherry knew, was that everyone was scared. Because the decisions in every family court case came down to a single judge. Not alienating that one, all-powerful being was critical. And when it came to a woman's safety, or a danger to children, there was too much at stake to take even a sliver of risk.

'I'm not here for Kathie,' Cherry said. 'Even though I asked her if I could report on this case, I'm not 'for' her or 'against' Ed. The point is to report on the process. I'll have to interview Ed too. And maybe, you, if you'd agree?'

Rachida had been listening carefully, but at this she shrank back.

'I don't think that will be possible,' she said stiffly. 'My concern is Kathie and her children. And the work I do with her is confidential.'

Oh shit, thought Cherry. Too soon. Time to change the subject. 'I wonder where...'

She peered around the plaza. There was no sign of Kathie.

'I'll order a coffee now for when she...'

As Cherry got up, she misjudged the distance and banged the front of her thighs hard against the tabletop. Pain shot through her and she had to bite back on a cry as she fell back into her seat.

'You're hurt,' Rachida said quietly.

'Mmm.' Cherry was still having to control herself as pain throbbed fiercely across the top of her right thigh. She faked a smile. 'Just tender.' She wanted more than anything to press her hand hard down on the top of her flesh and flatten the pain.

'You're bleeding.' Rachida sounded faintly baffled. You don't bleed through your trousers from a bang against a table, her tone said.

Cherry looked down. The line of blood that had earlier marked her trousers was turning into a thick stripe.

As both women stared at the stain, Kathie walked in.

'Hi. Sorry, I needed some time...' She stopped, as Cherry wriggled as nimbly as she could from between the table and chair.

'Kathie. Hi. I'm just...' Cherry tried to pull her bag towards the front of her body.

'You're going?' Kathie sounded surprised, hurt edging her voice.

'No, no. Um... nipping to the loo. Back in a sec.' Cherry flushed as she looked over at Rachida. 'I'll be fine. Honestly. Back in a minute.'

'Right,' said Rachida. She proffered a packet of tissues. 'Take these.'

'Thanks.' Cherry grabbed them, wanting nothing more than to disappear from view. She caught Rachida's worried look as she turned to head for the loos.

In a tiny cubicle that wasn't too clean, Cherry swiftly pushed her trousers down. The dressing was soaked. Peeling it off she saw that the paper stitches had burst. When she flexed her leg, blood welled up through the gash, which wasn't quite gaping but was definitely not going to heal on its own.

With no first aid kit, what on earth was she going to do until she got to A&E? The wound needed stitching, but she'd have to navigate saying goodbye to Kathie and Rachida, and didn't want to have to explain an even more bloodied scene on emerging from the loo.

Quickly, she took her shoes and socks off, then stuffed the tissues into one of the socks. With the scissors from her keyring penknife, she snipped the knot off the drawstring at the bottom of her coat and pulled it through. Wadding the socks together and pushing them down hard against her sliced flesh, she wrapped the drawstring round the makeshift dressing, tied it off tightly and pulled her trousers up. It wouldn't stop the bleeding entirely but it would slow the gush. And if she zipped her coat, at least her alarmingly bloodstained trousers wouldn't show.

Her leg was hurting badly now. She opened the door and leaned against the cubicle, wanting nothing more than to be safely home and in bed. But no, she'd now have to spend hours in A&E. And no doubt face the disapproval of medical staff, as had happened before. Softly, she groaned.

The door to the Ladies opened. Rachida stood in the doorway.

'You need attention for that leg.'

There was a silence as both women looked at each other. Cherry felt embarrassment so deep that she couldn't speak.

'Please. Don't worry. I'll come with you.' Rachida picked up Cherry's bag from the floor.

'No,' she said as Cherry tried to protest. 'Kathie's gone and I've called a taxi.' She nodded at Cherry. 'Let's sort this. Come on. Let's go.'

Chapter Fourteen

In the taxi, Cherry stared out of the window, berating herself. What a stupid time to succumb to the urge to cut herself, just as she was going on a job. Jesus, what had she been thinking? And inexpressibly idiotic to have created the compulsion in the first place by calling Garth when she knew beyond doubt that she shouldn't. Now, it was clear that Rachida had grasped exactly what she'd done. She looked weak. Unprofessional. Out of control. How had she got herself into such a mess?

Cutting herself was too private for anyone to know about. Lovers had seen her scars but rarely commented, whether out of delicacy or uncertainty over how to approach the subject; she'd never discovered or bothered to ask.

'This isn't new to me. And I don't judge.' Rachida's words interrupted Cherry's silent self-flagellation.

Cherry had to work hard to mask her reluctance to meet Rachida's steady gaze.

'Right. Er. Thanks.' She felt like a child. She gave a brief, embarrassed laugh. 'This isn't how I thought today would go.' She blew a deep breath out, which to her horror, ended in a sob.

Rachida did not look away. 'Not far now,' she said.

Cherry could see they were only a minute or so away from the entrance to A&E at Bristol Royal Infirmary. She felt her chest constrict with unwept tears and had to press her arms hard around herself to prevent herself from shaking.

'I'll come in,' said Rachida. 'In case you need anything.'

Cherry nodded, unable to speak. She had no energy left even to think, let alone explain herself to a receptionist. And from experience, she feared the judgement that had shamed her in the past when she'd had to make the same trip. Medical staff had occasionally been impatient, even cruel, in their response to what they saw as self-indulgent, wilful time-wasting. Once Cherry had been denied anaesthetic before being stitched.

'My sister is expecting us,' said Rachida, seeming to read her mind.

'Your sister?'

'Yes,' said Rachida matter-of-factly. 'She's a nurse here. I've texted her. Luckily for us they're not busy right now, so she'll see you as soon as we arrive.'

Now Cherry did weep, silently, tears sliding silently down her face.

'Cherry, please don't worry,' the other woman said quietly. 'This is not a problem for me. I see it all the time.'

'I just want to go to sleep.' The words came out of Cherry's mouth sounding abrupt and rude.

Rachida didn't seem to notice the mulish tone. For the first time since they'd got into the taxi, the refuge worker smiled. 'You'll find a way through this. Let's get you fixed up.'

They'd arrived. Immediately Rachida was paying the taxi, then coming round to Cherry's side of the car, opening her door, helping her out. She grabbed a wheelchair from the hospital entrance and looked determinedly at Cherry until she dropped into the seat.

Her leg throbbed and her trouser leg was damp again with renewed bleeding. She'd really done it this time.

A small, slim woman, her dark hair shot through with grey, had appeared at the entrance. Rachida waved at her.

'Jasna. Thanks so much.' She nodded at Cherry. 'Here we are. Ready?'

· · · · ·

In the taxi home that Rachida had decanted her into at the hospital exit, Cherry fell asleep. She was roused by the driver calling to her from the open passenger door.

Opening her eyes into soft early evening sunlight, Cherry saw the anxious face of a middle-aged man in a tight blue t-shirt looming towards her. His skin was darkest black, and his belly swelled over his waistband. He was smiling worriedly as he stepped back from the car door now she'd woken up. He was trying, Cherry realised, to maintain enough of a distance that she felt safe.

'Are you awake, er, hello? Miss?' She saw him notice her blood-soaked trouser leg and his eyes widen.

'Yes. Sorry. So sorry for falling asleep. And,' she checked around her, 'please don't worry. I've not bled on the seats. The hospital fixed me up.'

'Good news! Thank god for the NHS... they keep fixing all of us up!' he said, grinning.

Cherry smiled back weakly, not knowing how she summoned the energy, then grimaced as she edged along the seat towards the door. Her leg felt incredibly tender and not entirely under her control.

The driver hesitated, watching her awkward shuffle.

'Do you need assistance?' He held out his arm.

Feeling like she needed help at this point just to keep breathing, Cherry nodded. The day had already shown her just how useless she was. Why not accept her own total inability to manage anything, even exiting a cab, and then maybe, at some point she still couldn't see, this shitty day would finally end.

'You know what? That would be great.'

The driver reached in and offered Cherry his bent elbow. 'I have to help my mother-in-law in and out of cars all the time. She has a bad hip,' he winked, 'that she makes sure she tells us all about. So I am very practised.'

Cherry swayed as she dug around for her wallet.

'No, no. No charge.'

She looked up, frowning.

'No, no, that's not okay. I need to pay you.'

The driver handed her a card. 'Clive's Friendly Taxis' it read.

'You are hurt. I was finishing for the day anyway, and my home is not far.' He gave her a kind look. 'Take care. If you need a taxi again, please call.'

Slumped at her kitchen table, Cherry took two paracetamol and two ibuprofen as well as the first dose of antibiotics the hospital pharmacy had sent her home with. As she gulped them down, her front doorbell jangled.

Who the hell could be here now? Her eyes wanted to close, her leg throbbed and she couldn't even self-medicate with a decent glass of wine because of the antibiotics. Cherry closed her eyes.

The doorbell pealed again just as her phone buzzed. As Cherry glanced at the screen her heart sank.

Eliza.

God. How could she have forgotten she'd invited her for dinner? She didn't know if she could muster the energy to utter a greeting, let alone socialise for the evening.

She pushed out one breath fast and hard, then took another deep breath in and plastered a smile on her face before walking carefully down the hallway and pressing the door entry buzzer.

Dark hair upswept as usual, the paleness of her face shining in the light of the bulb above the door to the flat, Eliza stood on the threshold with a bulging plastic bag, smiling widely.

'I called and texted to let you know I was veggie,' the barrister declared cheerfully. 'But no reply. Which I thought was odd. So I thought I'd bring some veggie options to pad out dinner just in case.'

Stepping into the flat and out of her spikily expensive shoes, she wiggled her toes in relief.

'There's rice, poppadoms, one fish, which isn't strictly veggie, one that is strictly veggie and a naan because no matter what you've made, naan will go with it. Plus,' she brandished two bottles of Tiger, 'two beers.'

Her wide smile elicited a feeble return version from Cherry, who trailed behind her into the kitchen.

Eliza's eyes narrowed suddenly as she turned to see Cherry's face.

'But you, my love, look terrible. Worse than last time, if possible. Drained, in fact.'

As she spoke she noticed Cherry's trousers.

'Oh my good god.'

Cherry leaned against the kitchen table. Shit. She'd not even had time to change her clothes. And another wave of tiredness was sweeping over her. She might as well be honest.

'I'd... forgotten you were coming. Sorry.'

She couldn't get through this evening by covering up, it would take all the energy she had just to cope with having Eliza in her space without trying to make up some bullshit story that the barrister would see through straight away.

'I've not cooked. Sorry.'

Eliza fixed her with a beady eye.

'Right. Well, I'm here now and – assuming the source of the blood-bath has been taken care of? – it looks like you need to eat. Then you can tell me all the grisly details.'

She whisked efficiently around the kitchen, finding plates, cutlery, glasses.

'Someone you've written about take umbrage? Or is it a bust-up with that lorry-driving arsehole?'

'No! Definitely not. That is – I've not seen him.'

Eliza's gaze swept over Cherry, her eyes lingering on the thick band of blood on her trousers.

'You take those off and get some joggers on. Now, let me see.' She dumped rice onto each plate. 'This mysterious man you've never really told me about... married? Tick. Kids? Tick. Wife who's in some way 'difficult', am I right? I am? You surprise me. Not. And now,' she flourished a poppadom at Cherry, 'I'll bet you anything he tells you it's all 'just so much more complex than that.'' She cocked her head. 'Am I right? Again? Yes, I thought so.'

Tiredly, Cherry nodded.

'You got it. I'm a living, breathing cliché.'

Eliza tutted.

'My lovely, I'm not judging. If I did I wouldn't have a client left.'

Her gaze swept around the space.

'Nice flat by the way. I might just have to kidnap that sofa.'

She refocused on Cherry.

'Every married fucker with kids is special when you're in love, am I right? But,' she twinkled, 'don't mind me. I only see this every day in court, but obviously in your case it's far more likely that he'll leave his ever-so-annoying wife than that he'll...'

'She has a mental health diagnosis and doesn't always take her medication,' interrupted Cherry, forlornly.

'Of course. Better and better.' Eliza crunched her poppadom ferociously. 'He's not going to leave her. Also, trust me, you don't *want* him to leave her. That would be the mark of a proper shit. Now, eat.'

Cherry instead took a deep draught of the beer. Sod the antibiotics, she thought.

Eliza tipped her chair backwards and held up her fingers, ticking off each point.

'Let's keep going, shall we? So, lorry man is struggling to cope and none of it is his fault. But he's taken her back because of the kids, and oh my god, they love having mummy home again, and so even though it's very difficult he's trying his damnedest to make it work.' She raised a perfectly sculpted eyebrow. 'How am I doing?'

Cherry could hardly speak.

'I love his girls,' she said quietly. A sob rose up in her. 'I miss them.'

Eliza brought her chair back to the floor with a thud.

'Yes. You will, because you love him and you love them and you thought there might be a way.'

Her tone wasn't unkind but it was dispassionate.

'But you're wasting time and I see so much of that. Too much time wasted on these men, who – oh, they're not bad people – well, they don't mean to be – but they behave selfishly. Or maybe,' she chewed vigorously on a torn-off piece of naan, 'they're just not realistic about the options and dream there might be an alternative because oh yes, he loves you too, but in truth he's not brave enough or brutal enough to take a decision. And yes, it hurts beyond anything. But,' she lifted a heaped forkful of curry to her mouth and wolfed it down, 'you still need to keep body and soul together. And when you've finished eating,' she glanced at Cherry's trousers, 'you need a hot water bottle and your bed. And then *you* need to decide. You can't leave it to him.'

They ate for a minute in silence.

How much do I want to tell her, wondered Cherry, about my life? Friends are people you tell about the things that matter. Eliza had warmth and humour and she was tough too, as well as staggeringly capable and bright. And beautiful, added Cherry to herself. Don't forget beautiful. Nobody else would.

Unconsciously, she brought her hand to her cheek, feeling the fine ridges of scar tissue under her fingertips. They were faint, but she hadn't covered them with makeup. Would she ever tell Eliza how they'd come about?

She knew she couldn't face any more talk about the catastrophe that was her love life, so directed her thoughts towards the morning's hearing, and how badly Kathie had come across.

'There was a hearing this morning in that case I mentioned. It was a bit of a car crash. Well,' Cherry corrected herself, 'it was the start of what felt like it could end up as a car crash.'

'Mmm.' Eliza ate as if she was famished. 'Who's the judge?'

'Her Honour Judge Ruth Fosse.'

'Ah.' Eliza's eyebrows had jumped. She looked intently at Cherry. 'Tell me.'

'I couldn't put my finger on it but she didn't seem to like what she was hearing. But then, Kathie – that's the mother – seemed not quite... in control. She was very emotional. It didn't compare well with her ex. He was completely calm.'

"Has she managed to get herself a lawyer yet?'

'Nope.'

Eliza sighed. 'Doesn't surprise me then. Litigants in person haven't a clue how to put their case across. Understandably.'

Cherry gulped some food down. She was starting to feel better.

'This judge. Ruth Fosse. What do you think of her?'

'Clever, but not as clever as she thinks,' said Eliza, her mouth quirking. 'Not been promoted as high as she believes she should have been.' Her amused tone was mixed with what Cherry read as distaste. 'I don't relish being in front of her.' She smiled sourly. 'She doesn't like me being in front of her either.'

Cherry's curiosity was piqued. 'Why not?'

'Oh, I showed her up on a point of law. Last year sometime.' Peals of laughter suddenly erupted and Eliza finished on a snort. 'Oh god it was awful. I shouldn't laugh – but it was beautiful.'

'Was there any comeback?'

'Oh no. She thanked me at the end, in that ultra-polite-but-actual-ly-rude way we lawyers specialise in. But my card was marked. Thing is,' Eliza licked her fork, 'I'm a better lawyer than her.' She grinned, Cheshire cat-like. 'And a better advocate than I gather she was from people who knew her as a barrister.'

'I'm guessing you're smarter than most people.' It wasn't so much a compliment as a statement of fact, Cherry thought. Eliza was formidable.

'My lovely, I am, but the only thing to do is shoulder the burden.' Eliza was suddenly serious again. 'So, your woman. What's next?'

'A fact-finding hearing in two weeks. To decide on whether her allegations of domestic abuse are true.'

Eliza frowned. 'She can get a free half hour with any solicitor's firm. Then it would cost oh, I dunno, a few hundred quid for someone to guide her through the points she needs to make in her schedule of allegations, and how to put her case in court. It'll be the best money she ever spends.'

'She's like a rabbit in the headlights. I just don't think she's up to doing it on her own.'

'Huh.' Eliza wiped her fingers. 'Imagine you were standing up in court in front of someone who terrified you. Someone you might still have feelings for. The father of your kids, who you know loves them to bits, and they love him, and you've not got any bruises to show but it's all about ways of behaving that scare you and that you can't really prove. Your arguments are going to sound pretty weak.'

'But the thing is, I've seen him,' said Cherry quietly. 'Doing something. The sort of thing she's talking about.'

Eliza looked at her inquiringly.

'I saw him the day I met her. I followed her. It was nothing obvious. But he was holding onto the baby in a way that...' She broke off, remembering the moment she'd seen Kathie arrive to pick up the children. Ed's hands gripping onto Lola. Kathie reaching for her daughter. In vain.

'He wouldn't hand the baby over for, well, for too long. He was holding on to her. Of course parents hold onto their babies. But he was using her, holding her away from her mother.' Cherry shook her head frustratedly. 'It sounds like nothing when I say it. But it looked wrong.'

'And it's all stuff like that?'

'I think so.'

Eliza looked thoughtful. 'Well, unless she has some good ammunition he may have a perfectly good case.' She pointed at the plates. 'Finished?'

Efficiently, the lawyer began clearing takeaway detritus from the table. Cherry made to get up.

'No, you, stay right there.'

Rinsing the plates, Eliza mulled out loud.

'Rare – very – for a judge to stop a man from seeing his kids at all. Pretty rare to get an order saying only supervised contact.'

Unexpectedly, Cherry found herself relaxing as Eliza padded back and forth putting cutlery and plates away, thinking aloud.

'From your point of view, for your story, it's better she doesn't have a lawyer, am I right?'

Cherry was startled. She hadn't thought of that. But Eliza wasn't wrong. The risk of injustice – and its potential for drama – was far greater if neither Kathie nor Ed had a lawyer on their side.

'You're right,' she said, reluctantly. 'The more unfair and awful it feels to each of them, the better the story.'

Eliza whirled around.

'It's not just about it *feeling* awful for Kathie or her ex.' Her face was suddenly bleak. 'It's that if they can't advocate effectively on their own behalf, the court won't hear everything it needs to make a decision that's safe for those children. It's not just about it being unfair. It's about it being dangerous.'

Cherry saw her guest grip the back of the kitchen chair.

'Sometimes children do get hurt. And sometimes, they get killed. So courts have to get it right.'

Eliza stopped, took a breath then swigged at her beer and smiled. 'I'll stop lecturing you now.'

Cherry had no idea what to do. If she didn't tell Eliza her history now, the moment might never come, but she was so tired that the prospect of the emotional toll it would take felt daunting.

Maybe she could do it fast, she thought. Maybe she could set a boundary first. This far and no further. Eliza would surely respect that.

She sighed, then made up her mind.

'Eliza, when you get home would you do something? It sounds odd, I know. Would you google my first name together with the names William and Marianne Lester?'

She heard her brother and mother's names leave her mouth with the same slight surprise as she always felt on the rare occasions that she spoke them. They were always with her. They would always be with her. She would never lose the sensation of Bill's small hand in hers though she struggled to remember his face. She would never lose the feeling of air on her hand when her mother released it. So she could run. Escape. Live.

She watched as the barrister's face posed a question. Was she asking too much, too soon, of this friendship, Cherry wondered. But she found that she trusted Eliza. And nobody could truly know her without knowing this.

'I can't explain now,' Cherry said. 'Today has been... a lot. But I will tell you, I promise. If you don't mind doing that online search first.'

As Cherry closed the door she gave a groan of relief. Awkwardly, she sat on the edge of the sofa, the throb from her wound insistent again. 10 o'clock. Three hours since she'd taken the painkillers.

Probably too soon for any more.

With both hands she lifted her bandaged leg onto the sofa and felt the velvet envelop her. She lay down, pulled a blanket around her, burrowed her head into a cushion and curled her body around another.

She stared ahead. How long would it take Eliza to work it out?

Cherry curled herself more tightly. Had it been too soon to tell her? Possibly too soon – they'd met each other, what, four or five times socially. But... sometimes... you felt that someone could cope with the knowledge. Though she had known one or two to flee from it.

Her eyes closed. She felt Bill's hand in hers. So small and warm, his fingers wrapped around hers. Her father's handwriting on the application forms in the bundles flashed across her mind. He'd wanted to see her. He'd followed her work. Her whole body seemed to clench in pleasure at the thought.

No. Why did it matter to her what he thought? And yet, the delight that he knew of her, had followed her, read her work, had cared enough to...

No. No. Redirect.

What is it like to live in jail for so many years? What is it like to kill your wife? Are you a different person before you do it from the person you are afterwards? Or... were you always that person? What is it like to have altered the trajectory of so many people's lives? To have changed a family's history? To take away your children's future?

Cherry felt the softness of velvet against her cheek.

Why did you cut me?

Her eyes tightened against the throb in her leg. She slept.

Chapter Fifteen

An hour into attempting to decipher printouts of much-photocopied handwritten notes from her adoption file, Cherry's email notified her that a message from the Bristol Central Library had arrived. *Subject: Archive* it said.

Cherry groaned. She'd completely forgotten she'd said she would go in.

Another email from the librarian, Eric Wilder. But it wasn't another reminder, or even a message telling her that the material she'd requested had been put back.

Dear Ms Magraw, Eric Wilder had typed. *I hope you will forgive me, but in collecting up your materials for re-archiving, I came across some items you might want to see in the hard copy editions of the Western Daily Press. I've marked them for your attention if I'm not in when you next come to the library.*

Unsettled, Cherry sat back in her chair, trying to work out what had just happened. It seemed the librarian had snooped on her research. On her life story. She shook her head, bewildered. Why would he do that? People came into the library every day requesting research materials; did he read through everyone's stuff when they'd gone?

At this, Cherry's train of thought suddenly halted. The microfilm. On realising her aunt had given Ben Temple an interview, she had left the microfilm in the viewer in her rush to leave, the article in plain sight. It would be natural, really, for a librarian to take a glance at the antiquated screen to remark to themselves with amusement, probably, just how far technology had moved on.

So. He would have seen the feature. Even though she, her mother and Bill had been known by the name Lester in the newspapers, he would have seen Cherry's first name from her library records. There wouldn't be two Cherrys asking for those archived articles; it was hardly the work of an expert sleuth to put two and two together.

But *what* had Eric Wilder found in that stack of newspapers?

She had nothing else pressing to do, she decided. Plus she was weary of the morning's trawl of court documents. Leaving paperwork strewn across the kitchen table, Cherry pulled on her jacket, locked the flat and got on her bike.

Eric Wilder clocked her the moment she entered the library's central lobby, raising a hand in acknowledgement as she crossed the floor. Uncertain how to react, Cherry nodded in reply. On her ride into the city, she'd wondered what she would say to this person she didn't know at all, but who now knew at least some of the most traumatic details of her life.

She placed her hands squarely on the desk, tilting her chin.

'You looked at my stuff.' It came out more harshly than she'd intended and she saw his smile fade.

'I did.' He took a breath. 'The microfilm jagged as I tried to get it out of the machine. I had to fiddle about a bit. So I ended up looking at the screen as I was trying to extricate it, and saw what you'd been reading.'

'Right.' Cherry's throat felt thick. Tears suddenly pricked her eyes and she was looking down at the floor, following the parquet's zigzag pattern up and down, up and down. 'And you knew my name so you saw it was about me.' Suddenly her eyes filled.

'I'm sorry.' Eric Wilder's voice was low. 'Your name is unusual so I remembered it. I didn't mean to intrude.'

Shaking her head, Cherry scrabbled around in her pocket and retrieved a scrap of tissue into which she blew her nose.

'Oh god.' As Cherry looked up, she was met by the librarian's face creased into a worried frown. 'I really am sorry,' he said. 'Can I get you a coffee? It's shit coffee, but it's arguably better than no coffee.' He pointed down the long room to a vending machine.

Cherry sniffed. Why was he offering her coffee? Why was he being nice – or was he just feeling guilty?

'The machine does chocolate too.' He was still smiling, though his expression was anxious.

Cherry blinked, then internally rolled her eyes. It was a cup of vending machine coffee. No big deal. Why did she always have to complicate things?

'Okay. Coffee it is. Though if it's properly awful I'll be having a KitKat as well.'

They walked in silence to the end of the room where, as always, the pictures on the coffee machine promised the earth and charged more. It whistled and steamed its way to an approximation of two cappuccinos.

Cherry took hers from Eric Wilder and sipped.

'That is filthy.'

'Yup.' The librarian smiled. Then, tentatively, 'Call me Eric?'

Cherry rubbed at her face. 'Fine. I suppose. I'm Cherry.' She rolled her eyes. 'But you knew that.'

His chuckle reverberated through the room causing readers to look up with narrowed eyes. 'I'm not assuming that means I'm forgiven. I'll get that KitKat, then we can go and I'll show you what I found.'

This time the octagonal reading room was completely empty.

Eric swiftly moved to a cupboard in one of the walls, unlocked it and heaved out a pile of editions of the Western Daily Press. Not the paper Ben Temple had worked for, then, Cherry thought.

Dumping the newspapers onto a table, he picked up the two copies at the top. They were dated January 2002 and November 2003, Cherry saw. Eric flicked the 2002 edition open.

Taking up three columns, half the width of page three, was an article headlined *Double-Killer Begs Judge To See Daughter He Spared*.

Cherry froze. Her father's face was juxtaposed against a pixelated picture of her as a child. A cut-out of the photograph her aunt had provided, she realised. But a few years on from the murder, it seemed that papers had developed qualms about identifying her.

'It looks like your father wrote to the newsdesk, telling them he'd asked for you to visit him in prison,' Eric said. 'Then, when your family refused, see...' he picked up the second newspaper, and pointed to the front page headline, 'it seems as though he asked a judge to order you to go.'

Now Cherry read the headline. *Judge Tells Bristol Killer 'You'll Never See Daughter Again'*.

Forcing down instinctive revulsion that a judge could have made her visit the father she was terrified of, Cherry felt bewildered at what she was reading.

'These kinds of court cases are heard in private,' she said, her brow crinkled. 'Journalists couldn't even get into family courts in 2003... oh...' She suddenly understood. 'My dad told them. He went to the press. And once a case is over, papers can publish whatever the judge ordered. With names.'

Then fury rose up in her, fury so fierce she felt she might burst. It was fury at her father for daring to try to make the child whose family he'd destroyed visit him in prison. And sick rage at a system that could countenance allowing a murderer to try to see the child whose mother he had killed.

The force of emotion was so strong that Cherry felt herself sway on her feet.

Eric looked at her with concern. 'You... don't look great,' he said. 'Maybe... sit down?'

'Thank you,' Cherry managed to say. 'Yes. I...'

And now she cried, her sobs soaking her sleeves as she buried her face in her arms.

When she dragged herself upright in her chair, Eric was still there.

'That was a shock,' he said, his eyes crinkling with concern.

Cherry nodded, wondering how she had found herself in this situation, crying her heart out in front of a man she had met precisely twice.

'You need something stronger than shit coffee,' Eric said. 'Cake is good for shock. Let's go and eat cake.'

Chapter Sixteen

The hour she'd spent in a café with Eric eating cake danced delightfully in and out of Cherry's mind over the three days since her trip to the library. He had listened. Really listened, she thought, with attention and yet without intrusive questions, to her story.

As a journalist she was always the listener, the questioner. She had felt reluctant, creaky, somehow embarrassed at first, to be the one doing the talking. To have someone's attention fixed on her. It was tables turned, she acknowledged wryly, thinking back to how interviewees often started, haltingly, to explain the most painful and traumatic moments in their lives, before their stories, almost always, began to flow.

As they left the café, Eric had asked for her number. He had texted later on that day to see if she was all right. She wasn't, and said so, and he had called her shortly after.

An actual phone call, these days... she smiled. They'd chatted. He'd told her he wasn't a full-time librarian, but a PhD student researching into lichens. She'd laughed fit to burst. Mock offended, he'd insisted that lichens were way more fun than the domestic homicides she wrote about. In among her feelings of grief for Garth and rage, sorrow and confusion about her father, it felt sweet.

In the following days, Cherry continued to work on researching Kathie's court case. Ed had responded immediately to her text asking for an interview. He would meet her in a pub not far from the climbing wall in the St Werburghs area of the city.

'Happy to discuss in principle whether I am prepared to speak to you once I know more about your angle,' Ed's message said. 'I'll be finished at uni by 4. There by half past.'

While elated at the prospect that she might, if she was lucky, secure Ed's agreement to set out his side of the story, Cherry had hoped he might suggest she meet him at home. It was always better to see people in their own space – they were often more relaxed – but her briefly proffered suggestion that she would be happy to come to his flat in Clifton had been brushed off. And of course he set the terms. Interviewees usually did, though they didn't always know it. Typically, you needed them far more than they needed you. And Cherry needed Ed. She wasn't sure quite whether he grasped that fact, and she hoped he wouldn't for as long as possible.

Glancing around as she walked into the bar, Cherry recoiled slightly. As so often with pubs in the daytime, the room felt charmless. A florid carpet was just unpleasant and the whiff of bar towels scrumpled up in their own dampness lingered in the air.

She'd arrived ten minutes early but Ed was already holding a half-drained orange juice.

The ring finger of his right hand was bent, she saw, as he put his hand out to shake hers. Each finger pad was calloused. Also on his right hand, she observed, the webbing between forefinger and thumb was bisected by a thick, shiny scar. Not recent. It reminded her of her own.

'Tore it on a climb.' His voice held a tinge of amusement. 'Almost off, in fact. In Ecuador. We had a long walk out. All a bit remote, so it wasn't stitched for days.' He saw her eyes flick to his ring finger. 'Busted that too, on a route. Rushed a move. My own fault.'

Cherry flushed. She had been staring at his hand.

'God, I'm sorry.' She looked up into blue eyes that were gazing back steadily at her. She saw Ed notice her own scars for the first time now that they were standing up close.

'Really sorry,' she said again. 'I should know better.'

He shook his head, then re-offered his hand. 'It's fine. And sorry for dragging you out here. Appreciate that it's not a particularly...' he indicated the bar with a quizzical sweep of his eyes, 'salubrious venue. But I didn't want to do this at the university. Or at home.'

The very first moments one-to-one with an interviewee were always a sensory assault. Ed was a presence in the room. It was this, more than any aspect of his appearance, that Cherry had felt when they were in court, but now sensed even more strongly.

He had that rare thing, a charisma brought of quiet self-assurance. Her job was to put him at ease – but Ed was already at ease. She put her hand in her rucksack to find her purse.

'What can I get you?'

'Another orange juice is fine,' said Ed. 'I'm heading to the wall after. That's why I suggested meeting here.'

Cherry nodded. Alcohol and height didn't mix: nobody serious would drink before a climbing session.

As Cherry got out her voice recorder and notebook, she considered again whether to tell him she already knew he was a climber, had seen him at the wall – and that she climbed, too. It seemed as good a way as any to build rapport.

The decision was taken out of her hands.

'It's strange to see you here, like this,' Ed said.

Cherry's eyes widened. 'I'm sorry?'

'At court... I thought I knew you from somewhere, but I was a bit distracted. Anyway, I thought I'd better tell you I've seen you at the climbing wall. Seems weird not to say.'

Wrongfooted, Cherry felt her colour rise.

'Oh. I – well, er, you're much better than I am, I didn't think you'd have noticed me,' she stuttered. Christ. What was she saying? That had come out wrong. 'I mean, I've watched you but there wouldn't be any reason for you to...' Cherry tailed off. She was making it worse. Ed, however, grinned.

'You're all right. I've seen you be creative on the tricky bits. Technique-wise you're just a bit rusty.'

'I don't get chance to climb as often as I used to,' Cherry rushed out. 'Mostly I've climbed with my brother, but he's not here and I don't have anyone else in Bristol...'

Ed didn't seem to think the situation was awkward. He just sat back, took a slug of juice and planted his hands on the table.

'So, how do we do this?' he asked. 'Tell me how it works.'

The dynamics in interviews shifted from moment to moment: this was Ed being generous, Cherry realised, not pressing his advantage gained by her inept start. She nodded briefly, still recovering as she marshalled her thoughts.

She had to be truthful but she didn't have to give him a lengthy exposition on everything her article would explore. She simply had to tell him clearly what she was trying to achieve.

'First of all,' Cherry began, formally, 'given what you're going through I need to say first up how grateful I am for your time. And acknowledge that it can't be easy turning up at court to find a journalist hanging around.'

Ed shook his head. 'It did feel awkward, and I was surprised. But I did some research. I know you have the right to be there.'

Cherry nodded. 'Yes. But still. I'm grateful you didn't object.' She looked directly at him. 'I'm researching a feature on how courts deal with domestic abuse. Allegations of, sorry. And how judges make decisions about whether it's happened, and how that affects what happens to the children.'

Cherry paused as she studied the man in front of her who was calmly listening.

'I don't want it to be just one person's version of events.'

Ed nodded slowly, his eyes suddenly flicking up at her.

'Let's cut to the chase shall we? How did you know about this case? And how do I know you're not going to make me look like a woman-hating shyster?'

His tone was perfectly pleasant but the bluntness of his words carried a sting, one that cut to the heart of whether he would continue to sit here and agree to talk to her.

She took a breath.

'I met Kathie by chance, in a café,' she said. 'She was upset. She talked to me a bit about what was going on.'

Ed's mouth twisted. 'Right.' He sat back in his chair, his brow furrowed. 'Well. That feels pretty shit. And you've got her version first, of course.'

Cherry looked directly at him. 'Yes. But it's my job to look at all sides of a story.'

Ed shook his head. 'Hmm. That's hard though, isn't it?'

It was, Cherry thought.

'It's what we're trained to do,' she said. 'It's what makes it journalism.'

'So, Kathie asked you to come to court, didn't she?' Ed's tone was sharper now.

Careful, Cherry thought.

'It didn't happen like that,' she said. 'I asked if I could come.' She would never tell him that after she'd taken her card, Kathie had phoned and begged her to cover the case.

Ed's body relaxed. Until that moment, Cherry hadn't realised he was at all tense.

'Riiiiight. I thought she'd seen your articles and got in touch to... well, to, I don't know, drum up sympathy from the judge.' He lifted his glass and half-drained it. 'I'm guessing I don't get to see what you write in advance, or get to agree or disagree with what's in the article.'

Cherry nodded. 'Nope. Nor does Kathie.'

'How do I know where you're coming from?' Ed asked. 'Or that you'll give me a fair hearing? I'm fighting for my kids. You do get that, don't you?' His voice was suddenly gruff.

'She's saying I've done awful things. That I'm a risk to the kids. Which is not true. How do I know you'll put my side of what's gone on, as well as hers?'

'It's my job to be fair and balanced,' Cherry said simply. 'If I'm not sure of a fact I'll always check it with you. I won't ever discuss what you tell me with Kathie. And I won't take sides.'

It was always precariously poised, this moment when someone decided whether or not they would talk to you, and in how much depth.

'Any parent would get it that you want to be a dad to Brandon and Lola. That's why they'll want to know how things play out in court, and understand how the judge comes to whatever decision you end up with.' She looked at Ed steadily. 'They'll also want to know how you behave towards each other in court. Whether you want to destroy each other and are doing this for selfish reasons, or whether you're in court because you really do want the best for the kids.'

Cherry closed her notebook. She felt so far behind the blocks that this interview wasn't likely to start in the next twenty-four hours, let alone the next few minutes. Fine. If he wanted time, she had time.

'If you tell me how this whole experience feels as you go through it, I will be duty bound to report that. I'll *want* to report it. And remember, you'd be anonymous.'

Ed leaned back and sighed quietly, then shook his head.

'How did I get here?' he murmured to himself.

Then he looked directly at Cherry. 'Do you believe what she says about me?'

She'd anticipated the question but hadn't known if he would ask it this early. But, she thought, he was a climber. An accomplished and gutsy scaler of heights that would scare the living daylights out of most people. And like anyone who took big risks, he anticipated problems, analysed the danger, then planned, planned, planned.

'I don't know what's happened,' Cherry said quietly. 'I can't. I know what Kathie says. And if you talk to me I'll know your version. But,' she took a breath, 'this article isn't about who I believe. *No,*' she cut through his short, barked laugh, 'it's not.' She had to take a risk of her own now because Ed was the opposite of stupid.

'In some ways it's not even about you and Kathie.' She had his attention now. He wasn't smiling any more.

'It's what happens in court that I'm interested in,' she said.

'How it affects a man who has to stand up in front of a judge and argue for his right to see his kids. How it affects a woman who says she's terrified of her ex. What you both think about whether the court hearings play out fairly and whether the judge makes a reasonable hash of the decision. And then... the effect on you if it all goes wrong. If you can't see the children on your own. And if the judgment goes your way and Kathie is frightened for the children as they grow up, how will she cope with that?'

Ed massaged his crooked finger. He wasn't looking at her. But his stillness told her he was listening.

'I know this is as serious as it gets, for both of you,' Cherry said. 'But I don't spend time thinking about who I believe, because it's not relevant to my reporting. In terms of my article,' she finished starkly, 'who did what is beside the point.'

Ed cracked his fingers and sucked in a breath.

'Right,' he said. 'Let's do it.'

Cherry swallowed a gasp.

Ed gave her a cautious smile. 'I'll trust you. But you have to trust me too.'

Cherry felt a tremor of faint unease.

'This is the deal,' he continued. 'I'll talk to you. People need to understand just how bloody punishing this whole court thing is. To know your entire future and your kids' futures are in someone else's hands. You lose control of your life. It's the opposite of everything I've worked for.' He leaned forward, his eyes narrowed.

'So here's the quid pro quo. I'm going to teach you how to do that bugger of a route you watched me on the other night.'

Astonished, Cherry's mind raced. Then she realised. Just as he would be in her hands in the article, she would be in his on a belay at the end of a very long rope.

Ed smiled suddenly, his whole demeanour transformed.

'That's my offer. You'll have to trust me and I'll have to trust you.'

It was clever, she had to admit. He'd found a way to make their positions equivalent. This was never the usual dynamic when writing about a subject – once the interview was done typically the journalist held all the power. To find the tables turned so adroitly felt uncomfortable. She had to stop herself voicing an instant refusal.

But his proposition was a nightmare. There were so many reasons not to agree, not least that climbing together would look to Kathie as if Cherry was indeed taking sides.

There was a particular closeness in the relationship of two climbers on either end of a rope. If she was going to learn how to navigate a route that was far more demanding than anything she'd managed before, she would have to trust him, not to put too fine a point on it, with her life.

'You do get why this is impossible?'

Ed's lips twitched. 'You see the symmetry, surely?'

Yes, thought Cherry. I could destroy your life in print or you could destroy mine with a mistake on the belay. A vision of her body smashing from height into the floor flashed across her mind. The crunching thud, the panicked shouts, the feet rushing towards her, the shattered bones, the pulped flesh.

Christ, Cherry told herself angrily, don't be so dramatic. What was wrong with her?

What she wanted to say was screamingly obvious; that the relationship would look – and could become – too close for her to be seen as an objective commentator. What she did say sounded idiotic.

'It's probably not allowed in our editorial guidelines.'

Ed spluttered with laughter, then knocked back the rest of his juice. He set the empty glass on the table and looked at her directly.

'Guidelines,' he said, drawing the word out with a sliver of sarcasm. 'Right. We're not talking about tabloid phone tapping here, or breaking the Official Secrets Act. Listen. This is my life and my kids' lives. I'm guessing you've been to the house, talked to Kathie, met Brandon and Lola, spoken to the woman from the domestic violence charity who's busying herself with Kathie's case – am I right?'

Warily, Cherry nodded.

'If you want me to trust you, then I need the same back,' said Ed. 'I hold your risk. You hold mine. And anyway,' he smiled disarmingly, 'you want to smash that overhang, right? I saw you looking at it. You're aching to give it a go. You're good enough. I can get you up it. So – you get your interview *and* you get a new route. I'd say it's win-win, no?'

He was grinning at her mischievously. 'We could make a start right now. No time like the present.'

Incredulous at the 'choice' she'd been shunted into making, and despite her misgivings, Cherry saw his point. She was going to accept Ed's proposal because she couldn't see that she had much of an option. She had to give it to him, he was good. And in person, one-to-one, he was persuasive, plausible... and attractive. Just as Kathie had said. Remember that, Cherry warned herself. And remember what she'd seen at his mother's house after her first encounter with Kathie at the docks.

That hadn't looked attractive. Not at all.

* * * * *

A waft of old sweat mixed with worn rubber and damp air hit her as they entered the old church building. All climbing walls smelled the same.

Ed was a good teacher. It hadn't been easy, and she hadn't mastered the whole route, but after demonstrating the sequence himself, Ed had talked her up and through two painfully difficult moves and she'd managed, just, to navigate the overhang after many attempts.

He was patient too, she thought. When they stopped for a drink, he'd taken her methodically through the technical moves required, making her practise on the ground until she felt secure that her body as well as her mind understood what had to be done.

Eight metres up, gazing down over the overhang she'd just messily scrambled her way over, Cherry indicated that she was going to belay down. Landing lightly, flushed with exertion, she began to unbuckle her harness. She felt exhilarated from the climb in a way she hadn't experienced for a long time.

'Enough? Really?' Though his climbing buddy Brian had arrived half an hour before and was now bouldering alone, waiting for them to finish, Ed seemed happy to carry on. 'You've done great but I reckon you could crack the whole route tonight if you pushed on through.'

'Nope.' Cherry could feel a pull in a tendon in her groin, and the pads of her fingers were scraped and burning. 'It's been enough.'

As she pulled on her fleece and caught her breath, Cherry began to be aware once again of the niggling unease she'd first sensed in the pub, when Ed had set out his 'deal'.

Now that she wasn't mentally focused on the demands of the climb, she felt uncomfortable again. The set up had thrown her off-kilter from the start, and it seemed even more wrong now she and her interviewee – never forget he's been accused of a serious assault, she reminded herself – were sharing a moment of climbing triumph.

'I need to head home. And,' she looked at him pointedly, 'we need to set up a time to do our interview.'

Ed nodded, his head bent over the ropes as he unclipped his gear.

'Sure.' Ed was in profile, so she only glimpsed the edge of his smile. 'That was the deal.'

'So, when?'

He looked up, his expression unfathomable.

'You put some decent effort into that route. It's nearly the week-end and I've got the kids again, but how about you give me a ring?' He moved off towards the bouldering wall. 'We can sort something out for early next week.'

Chapter Seventeen

It was Friday. 4pm. Cherry's phone alarm went off. She typed frantically at the email she was writing, pressed Send, then snapped her laptop shut. She'd be late for this meeting with Her Honour Judge Judith Vail QC, which the judge had postponed from the morning to virtually the last gasp of the working week.

Cherry felt muzzy and sweaty. She'd not eaten since breakfast, and she needed food. Eliza had been right, she thought, as she passed her reflection in the flat's bay window and noticed that she just... seemed to take up less space.

Cherry couldn't help feeling that this rendezvous was somehow more for Vail's benefit than her own, but if she could extract any more information about what the judge knew of her mother's last weeks of life, then it would be worth it.

Vail had suggested the café. It was across the river, inside the covered market. Not quite close enough to the courts for lawyers to frequent it, Cherry surmised.

The judge had been rushing, Cherry could see from the moisture beading on her upper lip.

She stood, offering her hand. 'Hi.'

The older woman smiled briefly as she shook hands, then took off a rumpled jacket and dropped it on the back of a chair.

'I'm so sorry. It's never not busy – and getting busier.' She gave Cherry a careful smile. 'Sometimes I wonder if we'll end up sitting through the night.' Formally, as if retrieving control of the meeting, she then said, 'Thank you for coming. I'm sure you thought it was an odd thing for me to suggest.'

'Well, yes.'

Vail glanced around for a waitress but when she didn't see one, sighed impatiently and brought her attention back to Cherry.

'How much of your file did you manage to read?' the judge asked. 'I know it's not been logged out again since that day.'

'I've read every word,' Cherry said simply. 'In fact, I'd say I've studied it in detail and at length.'

Vail's eyebrows shot up. 'How did you...?'

Cherry flicked her eyes to her phone which was lying on the table.

'Ah.' Taking photographs in a court was against the law. A serious contempt. Taken aback, the judge frowned, began to speak, then quickly regrouped. 'Best perhaps that we move on.'

Belying her words, the pause that ensued stretched uncomfortably. Cherry realised that the judge was struggling.

How could she exploit this situation? She would have to deal with it as she would approach an interview. Help someone say what they wanted to but felt too upset, worried, frightened or ashamed to come out with.

'I think you want to tell me something about representing my mother,' she said. Her tone was gentle, interested.

Vail sighed deeply. There was a long pause. Cherry did not fill it.

'Yes. I suppose I do.'

Cherry waited, unspeaking.

'I didn't...' Vail paused again. 'I didn't do the best job I could have done for her.' She came to an abrupt halt as the waitress arrived.

'We'll have two teas,' said Cherry briefly. She had to keep Vail in the moment. No accusation. Careful of the words she picked. Never ask 'why'. It was too close to blame.

'Can you explain a bit more?'

Briefly, Vail closed her eyes.

'It meant that although I talked to your mother's sister – I think she was called Margaret?' – Cherry nodded – 'on the phone, for about an hour, and though she gave me detailed examples of what she'd seen of your mum's life with your dad, I decided...' Vail's voice stumbled slightly and she had to take a breath before carrying on, 'even though

138

she came to court that day, I decided not to call her as a witness.' Vail pressed her lips together and fell silent.

Cherry felt her fingers clench. *Why not?* But she mustn't scorch this woman with recriminations if she was to find out all there was to know.

Vail's throat was now covered in blotches that were seeping down towards her chest.

'When we arrived, your mother was frightened. But somehow, she rallied when we got into the courtroom. She was determined to get across what you'd all been put through. But I could tell, to that particular judge, she sounded too 'together'. Too, well, feisty.'

That trumped up shit of a judge, Vail thought, *who'd bollocked me the week before for taking up too much of his precious time. A small-town solicitor promoted beyond his ability and puffed up with an overblown sense of importance.*

Vail's voice hardened.

'It's apparently too difficult for some people to imagine that a woman's been hit when she's not covered in bruises because it's a few weeks since it happened. And that's made an even more impossible concept when she's found the strength to speak out so she's not sounding like a victim. Or whatever our idea of one is.'

Then getting arsey with me in front of everyone for wanting to call more witnesses. 'Miss Vail, given the pressures we are all obviously under and the fact that other people too have a call on the court's time,' *he'd said,* 'when am I supposed to hear your witnesses if you want me to take your contested hearing today?'

The colour had risen to Vail's face and the warmth of the day seemed to be bothering her. Rapidly, Cherry rose and went to the counter.

'Water please, with ice.'

Vail was fanning herself with a file she'd taken out of her handbag when Cherry returned and placed the glass on the table. She looked as though she would rather be anywhere else.

'So why didn't you ask my aunt to give evidence?' she asked.

A frown shadowed Vail's face. 'All judges are different. With your mother we were in front of one who had slated me just the month before for wasting court time in a domestic abuse case.'

She drew a breath, her eyes distant, remembering.

'He mocked me for over-egging the abuse, then told me to stop dragging it all out with more witnesses who, according to him, were just repeating the identical bad character evidence. It meant I was worried, in your mother's case, of repeating what he clearly saw as my mistake.'

So, yes, I didn't argue the toss, and dropped a witness. I decided to lose the sister because I couldn't drop the police officer.

Vail paused.

'That particular judge seemed to have it in for me. He had, I suppose, shaken my confidence to the point that when I saw our case listed in front of him I found that I was dreading it. And then that morning, he called me and all the other barristers into his chambers and told me off in front of everyone for having wasted his time before. He told me to get on with it without too many – what he called – 'unnecessary' witnesses.'

Cherry kept absolutely still, listening intently so she would have total recall of the judge's words.

'So... I thought I'd rely on the police officer's evidence, let your mother describe your father's abuse, but not drag your aunt into the equation to say it all over again.'

'That wasn't the right call?'

Vail sank back in her seat.

'It wasn't enough.' The judge seemed deflated. 'Your aunt would have brought a different perspective from the police officer, and real authority from having seen the horrible dynamic between Marianne and your father play out over years. She could have given examples she'd seen, from small put-downs to nastier instances of humiliation and control. I didn't think it through carefully enough.' She swallowed. 'No. That's not right. I put my own fear of being shown up and embarrassed before your mother's best interests. It was unprofessional and unforgivable.'

Around them, the bustle of the covered market suddenly made

itself heard once again. A woman was choosing ribbons, apparently for her daughter's school play, at a haberdashery stall just along the way. Cherry's eyes skimmed the reels, the colours of the ribbons ranging from purple through deep azure to palest baby blue, tangerine to apricot, crimson to scarlet to sugar pink and so on down the rows. At the end of the aisle, away from the clothing section and beyond the fresh produce, she glimpsed a butcher cleaving apart a rack of ribs and heard a thud as his chopper hit wood.

What was there to say? She could think of nothing. Leaning her head back slightly she gazed upwards at the intricate Victorian roof-lights. She closed her eyes and saw her mother's hair brightly glowing, its deep red and gold strands splitting a ray of sunlight.

'I think what I've told you has been a shock,' Vail said. She sounded stilted. 'Of course it would be. I wondered whether to tell you at all. But it seemed you were searching to build up a picture of your mother's life before...' She stopped.

'Before she and my brother were killed,' said Cherry.

'Yes.' Vail looked straight at Cherry. 'I went to the trial. I sat through every day. I felt I owed her that. And your brother.'

'What... what was it like?' Cherry asked. She could feel the compressed emotion mounting inside her.

Vail was nonplussed. 'Well, each day's evidence was worse than the one before, as we heard more of what had happened in your house.'

'Did anything change for *you* as a result of being there?' Cherry's question came out softly. The control required was immense.

'I... I suppose I felt I should see the effects of having failed to do my job as well as I could have,' said Vail uncertainly. Her head sank. 'I have never been more sorry. Or more ashamed.'

'You think that by sitting through that trial you have any understanding of what my mother went through?'

Vail flinched.

'You will never, *ever* grasp in the way I do how a woman's life can be stripped from her, second by second,' said Cherry, her mouth so dry it was hard to articulate the words. 'Or how it feels to watch your mother lose all dignity. Any shred of power to save her kids. She knew that it wasn't just her who would die, but us too.'

Vail stared at Cherry, silent.

'You work in this world of courts and law where responsibility gets dished out, but only if a woman can prove it. But you know they often can't, or not enough to keep themselves safe. And all of you – judges, lawyers, social workers,' Cherry spat out the words, 'you head home. Because for you, it's just a job. Even when you fail us and people die, you've done your job.'

Cherry stopped. Her mouth was ashes, her heart thudded and she felt both flushed and fuelled by the fury pounding through her.

She leaned back, observed the judge sitting in front of her.

'Don't think you will *ever* begin to know what my family went through. As for being 'sorry...' Cherry forced the words out 'have you done anything – *anything* – since then to make things better for women like my mum? Kids like my brother? Or the ones who survive? People like me?'

Chapter Eighteen

The Hotel du Vin was stylish, glamorous and very Eliza, Cherry thought wryly to herself as she looked around the courtyard for somewhere to lock her bike.

The message that arrived on her phone as she had begun to cycle home from her meeting with Vail had not been a complete surprise; she realised that she'd been awaiting the barrister's reaction to her suggested google search on her family. All the same she felt slightly unnerved at the prospect of being asked questions about the news articles Eliza would undoubtedly have read. Especially right now, in the wake of a meeting which had seen her march blindly out of the café, away from the judge's stuttering attempts to calm the situation.

She had not been able to bear a single word of explanation or soothing from Vail, and had, she realised, fled the scene in a way that would have appeared childish and panicked. Another thing to beat herself up about.

The sound of heels tapping behind her made Cherry look up from fiddling with her lock.

'Strong liquor needed, I think,' declared Eliza, grinning as she took in Cherry's cycling gear, helmet hair and downcast expression. She herself was wearing a knee-length flared dress in petrol blue with black suede ankle boots. Lips precisely stained in cranberry and chunky glitter earrings finished a look which Cherry interpreted would come across to clients as, 'I'm extremely competent, somewhat scary and not as conventional as other lawyers, so trust me, because actually I'm more like you than they are.'

'Hi,' Cherry said, slightly awkwardly. 'Thanks for suggesting we meet up.' She glanced towards the hotel. 'I wasn't kitted up for this. I've not had time to get home to change.'

Eliza rolled her eyes. 'Don't worry,' she declared. 'They'll be delighted to see us. Because I'm taking us for cocktails and *lots* of them. And because Christ knows I need a stiff drink after your suggested bedtime reading the other night.' She winked at Cherry and strode into the hotel, through reception and straight to the bar.

Trailing sweatily behind, Cherry suddenly and unexpectedly felt lighter somehow for being in Eliza's ambit. She watched with amusement as the barrister glided smoothly onto a bar stool and leaned towards the bartender.

'Brandy Alexander for me.' A delightful smile that reached right to her eyes. 'And for her.' The bartender, cool, rugged and younger, smiled uninhibitedly back. Eliza didn't even need to try, thought Cherry ruefully. Some people just had it.

'Well, that was quite the shitty childhood you had.' Eliza's perfectly made-up eyes were focused completely on Cherry now. She'd noticed this before – Eliza's ability to envelop someone in her attention and concern. As a client, it would be hugely reassuring. As a friend – was this them becoming proper friends, now, Cherry wondered, rather than just two people who got on? It was like being held firmly, so you wouldn't – couldn't – fall.

'I don't tell many people, but you'd seen me in that state... I didn't know how to explain,' she started. 'I don't do it, you know,' she glanced at her leg, 'the cutting, because I'm a mess. I mean, I mostly don't do it any more at all. Just sometimes, it creeps up. And I don't want to resist it.'

She took a breath, and sighed it out, sadness suddenly hitting her. 'It started in my teens. Years after my mum and brother were killed.'

'Sounds like you've mostly sorted it then,' said Eliza. 'Except when you're stressed. So. Now you're stressed. Why's that then?'

The laugh that came out of Cherry then was thin and ragged.

'Nice big drink, now,' said Eliza, pushing Cherry's straw towards her mouth. To the barman, she raised her hand. 'Another two of these, sweetheart. Fast as you like.' Turning back to Cherry, she declared, 'So. I'll do the starter for ten. The arsehole with the psychiatric-patient wife.' She raised one sculpted eyebrow. 'Am I right? Yes? Boring. We've discussed him and I've told you the solution. So. Next.'

Now Cherry really did laugh. The slug of alcohol she'd taken – there was only a thin puddle left in the bottom of the glass – had started to hit the spot.

'Fine. Number two. My dad's been in touch. From prison. Yes, he's still there. He's never admitted to killing my brother. So... no parole for him, though he's way past his recommended tariff.'

'He wants to see you, and... let me guess...' mused Eliza. 'He wants to explain everything so you understand.'

'I don't know,' said Cherry quietly. 'He's not said. But anyway, the third thing is, I've hurt my aunt, who brought me up. She doesn't want me to see him. So she's angry.'

'You mean she's worried he'll hurt you,' Eliza clarified.

'Yes, okay. Smartypants.'

Eliza cocked her head and Cherry laughed again. The second round of cocktails arrived. It was easy talking to Eliza. She was unshockable.

'Then – I've lost count – there's the woman I told you about. Kathie. The court case. She's a bit spikey. And brittle.' Cherry confessed. 'Understandably, if she's been through what she says.' Her mouth twisted wryly. 'I do, actually, find Ed easier to warm to, though I've seen him behave, well, it's hard to say definitely, but quite unpleasantly towards her. And I think there's something unsettling about how composed he is. Anyway,' Cherry concluded, 'I reckon Kathie is going to piss off that judge, and by comparison Ed is going to come across as much more together, reasonable and rational.'

Cherry stopped. An image of a younger Judith Vail flashed across her mind, telling her aunt Margaret she wasn't needed to give evidence. And suddenly, shockingly, the sensation of her own face pressed against her mother's hair, the feeling of her cheek against her mother's neck, assailed her.

Eliza put her hand on Cherry's shoulder.

'Okay?'

Cherry shook her head, tried to clear her mind.

'You're going to tell me I'm too involved in this story,' she said. 'And that it's too much like my own.'

Eliza looked at her carefully. 'The problem is, you need to give some weight to what you've been through. What I read about your mum and brother, that was *harrowing*. And I'm used to the worst people can do to each other.'

She reached over to Cherry and hugged her hard, her dark, gleaming hair contrasted against Cherry's auburn locks. 'Christ almighty, *think* about what happened to you. Did you never think that covering this sort of subject was madness for someone like you? Of course you're stressed to hell.'

Cherry's voice was low and muffled. 'I just came across Kathie. And I felt compelled. So, so curious. This kind of story is what drives me. I want to know, *everything*. And I want to tell people. And you know, it's not too much, it really isn't, until, like now, it suddenly is.'

Eliza pushed Cherry's cocktail towards her. 'Come on. Get that down you.' The barrister took an enthusiastic slug of her own, then looked directly at Cherry. 'You think she isn't going to be able to prove the risk. And you think you're going to be a witness to a judicial decision that isn't just unfair to her but is actually dangerous.'

Cherry lifted her drink and tipped it at the barrister. 'You got it.'

Eliza sat back in her seat and thrummed her nails on the bar.

'You don't have to be likeable to be a victim of domestic abuse,' she said. 'I've had clients who are defensive, or aggressive, or they zone out, or they close down, or yes, they seemingly overreact. Those are normal reactions when you've lived in peril for months or even years. But they are not reactions that 'look nice'. And it's a narrow margin, what looks nice in a family court.'

'So what does someone like Kathie do?' Cherry asked.

'They get a lawyer.'

'She can't afford it.'

'Who can?' said Eliza with a faint shrug. 'But that judge, I'm afraid – and I wouldn't say this about most of them – there's something a little bit, well, odd going on there. And so your woman can't do this without one. So, if you'd allow me, and in memory of your mum and your brother, I'll represent her for free if that's what she wants. No...' she stopped Cherry's protest. 'It's not because I believe her – I've never met her, I don't have a clue. It's because anyone who truly believes their partner is a danger to their kids needs proper representation in court.'

Chapter Nineteen

C herry had received her father's reply by return of post.

Dearest Cherry
Thank you. I didn't expect you to say yes, even though I hoped very
much that you would.
It's too late to organise a visit for this week, but your name is on the
list for next Thursday.
I will be so happy to see you.
Ralph Lester – your father

After reading her father's note, Cherry had called Garth. Remonstrating with herself, she had tried to resist the pull – then dialled his number anyway. He had listened with the attention and concern that Cherry knew was what she wanted more than anything from this man who would not be hers.

She had not had to ask – he had offered to drive. And now here they were, a week later, at just gone eight in the morning, in Garth's car, heading towards the Peak District. She already knew it was a mistake.

Cherry's hopes of being comforted by Garth's presence were not realised. There was too much to say and nothing to say. 'How are the girls,' was on Cherry's lips, but any answer would be too painful. As the miles scudded past in nervy silence, she knew that this was, properly, the end.

By contrast with the bleakness of her mood, the meandering route through Derbyshire was a heady shot of early summer. Stone-drawn fields were scattered with lambs, strong and insistent as they butted their mothers. Fields of high buttercups glowed yellow against the tough green grass. There was a fresh, hopeful kick to the air.

Set into a dip in the middle of a moor, HMP Longstone was a stark modern complex, its razor wire a vicious scribble against the sky. Cherry gazed upwards, but its gorgeous azure could not lift her. Instead she felt a dragging sense of dread, given an edge by a sharp, shamed thrill that shot through her every time she imagined seeing her father's face.

Until receiving his letter, she hadn't allowed herself to think deeply about her father for years. As she stared out of the car window, however, she was transported back to her aunt and uncle's farmhouse in the weeks and months after the night of her birthday.

'That night,' as she called it to herself, before skirting over the details. For the first time in many years, she inhabited again the hot, racked body of a small girl sobbing for her mother and brother, and sobbing too, she knew now, for her father.

There was so much that little girl's brain could not make sense of that Cherry remembered feeling it would explode.

She remembered conjuring until it was almost true the sensation of being on her mother's lap at bedtime, encased in warm arms and with a storybook held in front of them as she read aloud. She would re-live how she often edged into her father's workshop after school, and him telling her how to work the tool he was using at the time, his hand curled over hers, pushing it forward on a chisel, twisting it on a screwdriver. His brilliant helper, he would say smiling.

In those first weeks and months at Waun Olau, she would lie curled tight in that picture, feeling Bill's tiny hand clutch hers, her own hand in her father's – and for a few exquisitely sweet and hard-won moments she would be home, and safe. Sometimes Cherry had been able to hold onto her willed creation for long enough to fall asleep. But there was never any respite – each morning's waking would be a sickly plunge into the fresh realisation of all she had lost.

Somehow, she had known that she could not allow herself to indulge in longing. Steely as only a child can be who knows that their job is to survive, Cherry had clamped off her dreaming so tight that when, in adolescence, images and memories periodically punctuated a life that had become mostly happy, she was able to banish them almost without acknowledging they had existed at all.

Right now, though, she was struggling.

There were so many doors in a prison. It felt like potholing, reaching ever deeper into a closed world where the outside became less and less possible to conceive. So much metal and concrete. Every surface hard. The shivering clang of iron as a door shut was exactly as it sounded in films. There really were that many keys.

Did anyone else come to see him, she wondered. She'd heard of women who struck up relationships with men convicted of murder. Had he been written to, followed on prison transfers around the country, visited in anonymous, airless rooms across plastic-topped tables?

A prison officer showed Cherry into a smallish room with a high barred window. She looked around carefully. Institutional lino on the floor. Plain white walls, newly painted, with a wide green strip up to waist height. Two emergency buttons on opposite sides of the room, one of them positioned next to yet another metal door. Two chairs facing each other across a table.

The chairs' physical placement rocked her. They were close, just a table between them. Their orange moulded plastic glared out.

She could not, she immediately realised, sit across this table from her father. She could not let him be so near. But the encounter would take more than a few minutes, and emotionally... she would need to be seated.

Thinking fast, Cherry moved one chair and placed it against the wall facing into the room. The other she left at the table, and sat down.

He walked in.

She had tried to prepare herself, but nothing could.

An instant shock of familiarity. Her memory of her father, now in real life blurred by age.

Yet his height and shape were the same, his walk the same.

And his hands, his hands. His hands, so capable, so strong, the hands that once held her, that threw her wildly into the air and caught her, the hands that wiped her face and dressed her and dried her own hands with a towel.

The hands that had stroked her cheek and then sliced it open and the hands that had killed her mother.

They were the same hands she remembered and the same hands she had wanted, holding her, in the days, the months, the years that came after.

He walked towards the table and stopped short.

She assessed the distance between. Four metres. Enough.

'Cherry.'

His voice a sound that was part of her. A voice that steadied her. Not a shock, and yet vastly shocking.

It would be a greater shock for him, she realised, to see her so changed.

She shifted in her seat.

'I put your chair over there.'

Unbalanced slightly in his forward movement, he halted and looked behind him. For the first time, Cherry raised her eyes.

He saw the chair, noted its distance, nodded.

Cherry watched him turn and seat himself. Not a small man. Not a tall man. But he moved easily, and looked toned for a man in his fifties. He was not entirely relaxed, she thought, but more at ease than she felt.

He looked back at her, eyes crinkling in the way she remembered that implied a smile. His face had so many more creases now. Despite how fit he looked, his skin had a poor colour, she noticed.

She let him begin.

'Cherry.' Such a long pause. 'My gorgeous girl.'

She froze. He saw it.

'I'm amazed you came. And glad.' His voice was gruff. He paused, his eyes intent upon her.

Cherry stared. Again, she had no words.

Her father looked directly back at her. 'What made you decide to come?'

Straight in there.

Cherry had let him start because she'd hoped, she realised now, to see him at a loss, discomfited in addressing her, unable to find words. She'd hoped to skewer him with her poise.

'I will *not* call you Daddy.'

Horror swept through her. Defensive. Before, in her own mind, she had framed this as an interview. She had worked out her tactics, her questions, her route through, her line across the perilous crag of all that was unsaid and unlived between them.

But an interview could not be about her own feelings. Those were an irrelevance. And now she had betrayed herself. Cherry's stomach clenched as her mind cast about for where to go next.

He was sitting forward now, concerned.

'You can call me whatever you like.' He studied her. 'You look like you need a cup of tea.'

Mute, Cherry gave a tiny nod.

He looked over at the guard, his face creased with concern. 'Biscuits too? Could we manage that?'

The guard nodded again.

Could he have whatever he wanted, Cherry wondered. She clenched her fists hard and forced herself to refocus. Keep to the facts. Say the bare minimum.

'I came because I've got questions.'

'You want to know what happened. Of course.'

There it was again, a punch to the stomach. Cherry flattened herself against her chair, nowhere to go.

'I'll help if I can. Of course I will. You're my girl.'

Her skin crawled with a mixture of disgust – and pleasure. How could he call her that? Her hand crept upwards to her face but didn't reach the scars before she pulled it away.

She saw him note the movement and felt his gaze alight on her cheek.

Her face flamed. How could she, in front of him, feel shame at the disfigurement he had inflicted that night?

Was the shame because she hadn't resisted as he cut her? That she hadn't run sooner? That she hadn't begged him to stop? That everything she and her mother and Bill had been to him hadn't been enough, not nearly enough, to prevent the destruction he'd wreaked?

'I am not *your girl*,' she managed. Scarcely able to contain her fury and angrier still that he had seen it, Cherry closed her eyes.

It had taken barely a minute to reach this place, the place she had wanted above all else to avoid. 'I am not your *anything*.'

The obvious and unspoken truth was heard plainly by them both. No rejection by her, no reorganisation of her love, no new allegiance to a new family who loved and cared for her, could change the fact of their relationship.

Or that she had come to him when he asked her to.

Very slowly, Ralph stood, picked up his chair and brought it forward, keeping the table between them. He sat.

Alert as a starving child in the presence of food that had been placed just out of reach, she tracked him.

Her father leaned forward. 'I follow you.' He smiled. 'Around the world.'

That smile.

'I've seen what you do. The places you go. I read everything you write.'

She watched him rest his hands on the table. The movement brought him closer. She calculated each millimetre, recomputing each time he moved how much nearer she could stand to have his body to hers.

'Ask me anything,' he said.

Cherry heard his words in an echo that kept repeating. He followed her work. He cared where she was. He read what she wrote.

Was he proud of her?

'You're incredible, Cherry.' His voice broke with emotion. 'More than everything I dreamed you'd be.'

This encounter she'd so long resisted and so long craved, the moment you meet your father after so many years, should be a joyful thing, a flinging of arms around and tight hugs and laughter and fizzing relief and never letting go, she thought.

The urge to forgive was a deep temptation. She wanted to make the pain go away and only he could do that. Her heart ached to be open – but it could never be.

The dissonance between what she craved and what could not be transfixed Cherry in her seat.

He waited.

He waited for her to come.

The guard's rubber-soled foot scuffed the floor, a muffled squeak, as he set the tray on the table.

Cherry did not take her eyes from her father.

The familiarity of his physical presence was still shocking, as was the sense of ease it engendered in her. How much to tell him? In all her imaginings of this meeting, she had been clear. Only questions. Nothing of herself, of the nights of broken sleep, the half-conscious dreams, the unarticulated screams inside her head on waking. But now the comfort of talking to her father, her own father, the person who had made her, was flooding in. Her defences were not strong enough to withstand it. She would have to bend a little, allow herself to reach for a small part of that comfort, or abandon this meeting entirely.

'I don't sleep,' she said. 'I used to, but now I struggle.' She looked at him, and saw compassion.

She evaluated it, noted it, moved on.

'Since you wrote to me, I see everything that happened that night. Over and over again. I'm in the room and so are you. I can't make it stop.'

Cherry's mind raced. What to tell him? Marianne was hers. And Bill's. She could not permit him any degree of intimacy with their mother whose life he had ended. She would not name her.

'I see what you did. Each time you hurt her. I saw it. I still see it. I hear her.'

He hadn't looked away. He was listening.

She took a breath. 'I want to know what happened after I managed to...' Cherry fumbled. She couldn't say the word 'escape'.

Why not, she wondered. She *had* escaped. She'd climbed out onto the garage roof with Bill and over the edge and then she'd dropped him.

She could still feel the thud of the ground on her back. The breath knocked out of her, then crawling and stumbling and running running running. Her legs heavy so she had to drag them and her lungs burning.

She thought of Bill, his felt-tipped smeared hand clamped to his face as he sucked his thumb. How he'd been annoying and funny and how he'd thought she was the best. She'd always been able to make his upset better.

There was always, Cherry suddenly recalled, a moment in an interview when you had to ask the question that would be heard as impertinent or even rude. There were ways to soften it; you empathised, you were self-deprecating, you apologised in advance for your temerity. Sometimes you flirted your way towards asking the outrageous. There could be none of that here.

'I want to know why you killed my mother.' She choked on the last two words. 'I want to know precisely,' – the word hissed out of her – 'precisely why you did *this* to me.' As she touched her scars, she closed her eyes, reminded herself to keep it simple. Just ask the question.

'And I want to know whether you would have killed me too. If I hadn't got out. If I hadn't run.'

Cherry's hands wrapped around her mug of tea. Heat from its smooth surface scorched her palms. A bead of sweat in her armpit broke free. She felt it roll down her side and into the waistband of her jeans.

He watched her drink, made sure she had gathered herself. The tightness Cherry had felt wind tighter inside her all day had reached a sticking point; she could go no further when he started to speak.

'I wanted to tell you a long time ago what only me and your mother could know about that night.'

In that instant the stench of her mother's fear hit Cherry. She was sweating hard, she realised now. Her armpits, her back, her legs were sticky and hot and cold.

The guard was watching them intently, she noticed from the corner of her eye. A voyeur? A protector?

'I tried to see you,' he said. 'Every year, I asked if you could visit.'

Cherry's mind whirled. How could you ask to see your child when you'd killed her mother?

An image developed. She was arriving at the prison in her old cardigan with gauze taped to her cheek, her eyes black with grief, to see the man who just a few hours or days or months or years before – however long, it was no time at all – had sliced open her face. He was only behind that door. But there were so many doors. Not far now. Just behind the next one. Her daddy had asked to see her. If only she could get to him. How many times had he asked for her? Why hadn't they let her go to him? Why hadn't he tried again and not stopped until they said yes?

It would be her aunt and uncle.

Their decision to say no.

Their fault.

'I'm guessing your aunt Margaret didn't tell you I asked for you.'

Barely, Cherry inclined her head.

He nodded. 'Fair enough.' His voice was pragmatic. 'What were you actually told? About that night, about the trial, about what happened after?'

A shudder ran through her. Reflexively, he reached out his hand across the table to take hers. To comfort his daughter. Cherry flinched.

He withdrew his hand, the moment now clanging and awkward.

She shook her head, hard.

He sat back and studied her. 'I understand. Write it out if you like. I'll read whatever you tell me.'

He reached out and pushed her mug closer. 'It would be a place where we could make a start. Like I said. I'm happy to tell you whatever you want to know. You could come back.'

Cherry's mind split with the intense pleasure of his offer set against the last shreds of rational thought she was able to cling to.

No. Just no. He'd given her nothing of what she wanted. Nothing of what she needed. And now... now he was bargaining? Her memories for his knowledge.

She stared at him, outraged. 'You've not answered any of my questions. I came here for me. Not for you.' Her eyes narrowed. 'You *promised*.'

She watched as her father sank his head into his hands. Seconds that stretched towards the ticking end of their time together. She would not speak till he did.

Finally he raised his head, his grey skin wet with tears.

'What you want to know is complicated.'

He met her eyes, his expression one she remembered as an echo deep inside. Understanding. Kindness. Engulfing love. The look you give your daughter when you want to stop her getting hurt.

'It's going to be hard, Cherry. So much harder than it's been so far.'

Without an instant to think, Cherry's hands grasped his. The shock of their touch catapulted her words.

'I want you to tell me what happened every minute of that night. All of it. You *owe* me that.'

He squeezed her hands, turned them over carefully in his, brought her right hand up to touch his cheek then got up. His shoes were soft on the floor. The visit was over.

'Write it out. What *you* remember. And Cherry, know this. You will always be my daughter. And I will always – always – love you.'

Chapter Twenty

The kids had woken just after six. Brandon needed food. Lola needed milk. But Kathie had to get dressed.

'Chocolate stars on the table. Drink your milk up,' she called. 'I'll be there in a minute. Get your colouring out?'

In an attempt to exert some control over her anxiety as she tried to sleep the night before, Kathie had gone through various options of what to wear for court. One minute she knew it didn't matter, the next she was convinced that it did. The feeling of uncertainty about her choices annoyed her. She had not always flitted from one decision to another in this way.

Maybe it was the exhausted fug of having small children, Kathie thought blankly as she buttoned up a light blue blouse and pulled on black trousers. Lola whimpered. She had about another minute.

What came next? Shoes? Was that what came next?

Kathie stared at the wardrobe with her shoes stacked in the bottom. As Lola's cries rose, her focus scattered. Any shoes. The nearest ones. She pushed her feet into black brogues and picked up her daughter.

Then she heard Brandon call. 'Mummy, the dooooooooor!'

Kathie emerged from her bedroom to see her son at the bottom of the stairs, tugging at the front door. She hadn't heard anyone knock. But now she did. Four raps that rang out in a familiar pattern. Her stomach twisted.

'Leave it,' she whispered.

Brandon, all shiny hair and boot button eyes, the sweetest boy there ever was, looked up at her from the bottom step. She lurched downstairs on legs that suddenly felt wobbly.

'Mummy. It's the door,' Brandon insisted.

She'd reached the bottom.

'Go to the kitchen.'

Brandon drew away, still clutching the door handle.

'But someone wants to come in. They want to come in right now.'

'I mean it. Go back to your breakfast.'

'I mean it. Go back to your breakfast,' Brandon aped her, amusement and crossness mingling on his five-year-old face.

Kathie leant down, grabbed her son by his arm and half dragged him along the hallway into the kitchen. 'Stay here,' she hissed. 'Do your colouring. Do you understand me? And don't move.'

Slowly she moved back along the hallway, Brandon's shocked eyes following her. She should ignore the knocking, she knew, but the raps were insistent.

The figure on the other side of the ruby and blue stained glass came closer. The knock rang out again, sharper this time. Against her shoulder, Lola reared up, startled.

He would stand there, knocking, waiting, till she opened the door. He shouldn't be here, but he was.

She opened the door. The early morning light seared her eyes.

'Hello my love.' Ed stood by the front step, relaxed. 'Are you all right?'

Kathie stared.

'I mean about later,' he said. 'How are you feeling about later?'

Affable, Kathie thought. That was how people saw him. That was how she'd seen him. Laid back. No need to prove anything.

No words came.

'I thought I'd check in.' He smiled diffidently. She'd loved that smile, once. 'We don't need to do this, you know. There's no need for it.' He leaned in. Kathie steeled herself not to flinch.

'Court, lawyers isn't what we do. It isn't us.'

Kathie saw him focus on her clothes.

'Ah. You've dressed for it already then.' His glance swept across her outfit, taking her from top to bottom. Then to her bewilderment, he crouched down.

Disoriented, Kathie saw the top of her husband's head, now at waist level. His hair, tousled and springy, that she had loved to ruffle. That he had loved her to hold.

'Your shoes. Kathie.' He looked up, reproachful. 'You can't carry Lola around like that. What if you trip?'

Kathie gripped her daughter as she looked down. He was touching her shoes. What in god's name was he doing? Oh. No. He was tying her shoelaces, which she had left undone as she'd come downstairs.

Then he was stroking her leg, his fingers sweeping upwards from her bare ankle, along her calf.

No.

She kicked his hand away, but not hard. Pathetic. More of a flick.

'Get off me.' Her voice came so faintly she could hardly hear herself. Like trying to scream in a dream, when you were so frightened your voice wouldn't make the sound. She held Lola with one arm, the doorframe with the other. 'You can't be here.'

He took his time, his smile wider.

'But I will be here, to pick them up, in the future, won't I?' He held her gaze. 'It's a given, Kathie. That's been my legal advice. I expect it's been yours too. So you might as well agree it, rather than us fighting. You can't keep me away from where my children live. It's not practical, and it's not fair.' He raised his eyebrows. 'Give me Lola while you tie up your other shoe.' He held out his arms.

Kathie looked straight ahead at the houses in the opposite terrace. A blackbird perched on the roofline. She could not think of a single word to say. She felt her feet against the ground, made sure of her footing. Pressing her daughter close into her shoulder, she stepped backwards.

He made no move toward her.

She shut the door.

Down the hallway, to the back of the house, to the kitchen, Kathie walked as if pushing through water. Brandon was munching on a slice of jam-smeared bread.

'I got it for my own,' he said accusingly.

He had purple ink on his mouth and all over his hand that was now transferring to the bread. Colouring-in sheets were spread across the table with felt-tips scattered across them.

Kathie could feel panic burgeoning. She had to get out of the kitchen, away from the children. She had to sit down.

'Mummy has to go for... something,' she said faintly.

As her breath started to judder from her in gasps, she knew she was only seconds from collapse. She placed Lola in her playpen and found herself almost undone from the effort of standing back up.

Palms pressed against the wall of the hallway, she managed to stumble towards the stairs. She had to call someone. But she couldn't breathe. She dragged in air, again, and then again. She had to get help. Her mind cast about. Who would pick up the phone so early?

She dreaded telling anyone.

The journalist. Cherry Magraw.

She would listen. She wouldn't judge.

•••••

Cherry sat on the edge of her bed, unsettled. Kathie's distress on the phone had been extreme, and quite different from the anger evident in their previous conversations. She'd been frightened to the point of barely being able to get her words out.

'It's Kathie,' she'd mouthed at Garth. She still could not believe that she had let him stay. The long drive back to Bristol the day before had felt entirely different to the bleakness of their northward journey to the prison: Garth had become the succour she had sought, wrapped her in words of understanding and then distracted her from the immediacy of her distress with anecdotes about his drivers and the demands of his long-haul customers. She had given no thought to resisting when he'd pulled up at her door and turned to look at her, the ghost of a smile on his lips acknowledging what they had both known for at least the past hour: that he was going to come in.

At Cherry's suggestion of calling the police, Kathie had retreated fast. Making more trouble felt like too much of a risk, Cherry suspected.

'I have to get the kids ready,' she'd said. 'Not much time now.'

Would Cherry definitely be at court today, she'd wanted to know. Cherry had reassured her, but wondered how the hearing would go given Kathie's distraught state. Would she hold up? How would she come across?

Cherry sighed and collapsed back into bed, hooking her leg over Garth's lower body. The bubble of their night together had been well and truly broken by Kathie's phone call.

Gently, Garth disengaged, then sat up. He didn't need to say it. He had to go.

Cherry felt the vibration through her body as he banged the front door shut.

With deliberate effort, before sadness could creep in, she made the decision not to think about what this all meant. Then she stretched, extending every limb to a point of tension, and shook the upset of Kathie's phone call out of her body. She had to get moving.

Would Kathie be the 'perfect victim' today, Cherry wondered as she shrugged herself into her cycling jacket, clattered downstairs and prepared to navigate Bristol's snarl of early morning traffic on her bike.

• • • • •

Kathie stared at the floor. In her frame of view was the fringed edge of the rug and a headless Lego minifigure under the sofa. The effort required to get to her feet felt beyond her. But the thin wail of noise was getting louder. As it became a shriek she turned her head. Lola.

The jagged edges of her daughter's cry tore through her. Her heart thudding painfully, Kathie leapt up. How long had she left them? Half way down the hallway, her blood pressure racing unsuccessfully to catch up, Kathie's vision faded and she stumbled, hands thrust out to the wall, saving her fall.

Unconcerned at the noise, Brandon was colouring. His mouth was even more deeply stained with felt-tip.

She moved towards the baby, by now a small shrieking fury, legs pumping against the towel.

'Need to change you now darling.' Kathie scooped Lola into her arms and upstairs. Not much time now before they needed to go. She had to focus. Clean Lola. Change Lola. Fresh clothes, gently now, pull the arms through.

Don't think about what comes next.

Holding Lola close, Kathie walked to the bathroom mirror. She looked pale, that was all. Nobody would be able to tell what had happened that morning. They would see her pushing Lola down the street in her buggy, her hand clasped over Brandon's on the handle to keep his small body within inches of her side. Always on the inside of the pavement, never on the road side. She'd greet the other parents in the playground; she'd never ever say that her husband had turned up unexpectedly that morning and tried to tie her shoelaces and that this had frightened her so much she had collapsed.

In the mirror, Lola's face was reflected back at her; perfect skin, perfect eyes, perfectly rounded cheeks. Tiny fingers delicately spidered over Kathie's face. Toddler rage had transformed into peachy calm.

'Go down now shall we? Ready for out?' Kathie smiled at her daughter. 'Going on a bear hunt? Go to catch a big one?'

Lola's smile split her face. 'I not scared!'

Hand in hand, Kathie and Lola walked downstairs, their steps matching the rhythm of the words. They turned towards the kitchen.

'Bradon, Bradon,' Lola bellowed. 'I not scared!'

As they entered the kitchen, Kathie stumbled to a halt. She saw the side of Ed's head, bent towards their son.

The shock froze her. Then fear hit.

Ed glanced up and smiled, just a quick smile. Then he leaned back towards Brandon. In his hand, Kathie noticed a felt-tip pen, a blue one.

Kathie did not move.

'Dragons aren't blue, Daddy. And cats and dragons don't live together so that's just silly.'

'Maybe they'd make friends if they got the chance to meet each other?' she heard Ed say.

She felt air on her hand. Lola. She watched her daughter run to her father. And now, Kathie realised, he's talking to me. She squinted to lipread the words her brain was not able to compute.

She moved towards the kettle. He'll want a drink, she thought.

She picked her way carefully across the floor.

He's in the house. He's in my house.

Safe. Safe. That's what I have to do. Keep this safe. Keep us safe.

'Sweetheart. You need to keep that back door locked,' said Ed. 'It's not safe left open.'

Kathie nodded, her head going up and down, up and down.

She was stupid. So very stupid. Just like he said.

Her tongue was swollen huge in her mouth. Kathie found she could not utter a word as she waited for the kettle to boil.

Ed drew a cat with the blue felt tip next to Brandon's stick dragon.

Cherry had said to call the police but Kathie's phone was on the kitchen table. She couldn't get to it.

She had to make the coffee but knew she mustn't turn her back when Ed was near the children.

Maybe, she thought, I can pick up the phone when I give him the coffee.

Oh. She had made tea.

Stupid, stupid.

Don't remark on it, she thought, her heart fluttering. Don't say anything. Just start again. But he'd seen.

'Tea, love? Have I ever, since you've known me, drunk tea?'

* * * * *

He's next to me. Refilling the kettle. I start to move away because

I can't be this near to him but he's got my wrist and he's pulling me closer. Check the kids. Can they see? Thank god Brandon has picked up my phone. He's not looking.

Has he really put my hand on the kettle? I can't move. I can't speak.

'You won't keep them from me.' He says it pleasantly.

The kettle's getting hotter.

He says, 'They are my children.'

Second by second. His hand on my hand.

'They're mine. They'll always be mine. No matter what you do.'

It sounds like a conversation except I'm not talking. My hand my hand.

'This life you've taken away from me is my life.'

I turn my head and clamp my lips.

Hotter.

'*My* life.'

Louder in my ear. Searing heat on my hand is all I can feel.

'This house. The kids. You.'

I have to scream. My scream comes out and he lets go.

'Shhh now.' His head bends to my hand.

He licks it.

'Better?' He looks at me, considering. 'You'll never really get away, Kathie. Because of the kids. The kids are our link. Always.'

• • • • •

Kathie held her hand under the cold tap until it ached. As her skin numbed, she watched Brandon who was sitting in the corner playing with a red spaceship, hatch opening, hatch closing.

He'd startled at the sound of her scream, then got up from the table and wandered away. Spacemen were put to bed, then roused again by small fingers digging them out of their plastic capsule.

Kathie scrutinised her palm. The cold water had saved it. Her skin hadn't blistered. He hadn't held it to the hot metal for quite long enough. No. He wouldn't be so stupid.

He'd broken in, breached the non-molestation order that decreed he must not come within half a mile of the house. Burned her, but not badly enough to cause obvious damage to the skin. Threatened and terrified her, but what had he said, really, if she was to report his words? Just his hurt that she'd left him.

The day loomed at her suddenly. It was ten to eight. She was meeting her lawyer in just over an hour. And Cherry.

She pinned her attention tightly to each of the routine tasks required to marshal and equip her children for the day and get them through the door.

Brandon and Lola were good as gold as she buttoned their coats with her left hand and bundled them out of the house.

· · · · ·

A bus pulled out in front of her bike. Swearing, Cherry banged her fist against the side. For once the driver looked penitent. Fine to be sorry when I'm dead, thought Cherry furiously as she pumped her legs to get past him at the lights.

Her pink fluorescent jacket flashing gaudily as she cycled towards the city centre, Cherry diverted onto side roads to avoid the treacherous overpass where a heavy goods vehicle had once nearly ground her to a pulp against the railings.

She had arranged to meet Kathie at nine o'clock in front of Eliza Wynne's chambers, a two-minute walk from the court building. Ten minutes early and ravenous, she locked her bike beside a glass-fronted café on Victoria Street and stepped inside.

Sweatily uncomfortable as she waited to be served, Cherry glanced around. Glimpsing Kathie in the corner of the café, she raised her hand in greeting.

Wrapped in a dark grey coat, Kathie was sitting with an uneaten croissant in front of her. She did not see Cherry's wave. Observing more closely, Cherry saw that Kathie's hands were held slackly in her lap, her eyes were half closed, and her body was slumped in what looked like expectation of defeat.

Cherry left the queue and pushed her way through the tables to

Kathie's corner spot. She barely looked up.

Like you might approach a small child, Cherry crouched down.

'Hey. Kathie.' The sound elicited a brief flicker of a glance and then Kathie's shoulders crumpled inwards, her ability to hold herself upright seemingly spent.

Careful not to make her movements too sudden, Cherry leaned towards her. 'I'm going to help you sit up.' Wondering if she'd heard, she reached over Kathie's shoulders, hooked a hand under her armpit and pulled, holding the slumped figure close, her other arm circling Kathie's shoulders. With another judder, Kathie's bowed head lifted, her eyes still closed against the world.

What had it taken to put her in such a state of collapse, Cherry wondered. She had sounded distressed on the phone earlier, but had rallied, or so it had seemed. How would she hold up in court if her ex arriving on the doorstep prompted this degree of collapse?

Very slightly, Cherry shook her. 'Look at me,' she instructed.

Kathie's eyes opened, barely.

'Do what I say,' said Cherry very quietly. 'Clench your fist.'

Kathie seemed not to register.

Cherry brought her face closer. 'I mean it. Make a fist. Like mine.' She held up her own right hand, and tried to take Kathie's in hers to raise it up.

Kathie flinched and pulled away.

'Humour me.'

Kathie reluctantly clenched her left fist.

'Good,' said Cherry. 'Now lift up your arm.' Cherry raised her right forearm. 'Look at mine. Higher.'

Kathie's body unfurled as she raised her left arm to barely shoulder level. She looked uncertainly at Cherry.

'Now count. Out loud, with me.'

Slowly, as Cherry began to count, she held her fist higher in the universally recognised symbol of protest. On the count of four, Kathie joined her, her voice a whisper.

With each number, Cherry's voice became louder. She'd seen desperate, angry people in a fog of tear gas and assaulted by water cannon raise their fists in protest; she'd seen refugee children in Calais do it as police dragged them off lorries; in her unhappiest moments, she'd done it herself, where no one could see, against the world. She thought she'd been taught the action by her mother although she could not remember when: a remnant of her childhood. Of her life before.

Cherry had discovered that it was impossible to hold this position and remain utterly in despair. It forced you upright. It opened your shoulders and made you bigger. It required you to breathe deeply. It gave you intent, and even, somehow, courage.

The counting, each number getting louder, was Cherry's own invention. On each count, Cherry's fist, and now Kathie's, drove forward in a rhythmic beat. They were oblivious to the sidelong glances being darted at them by other customers.

At the end of her second count of ten, Cherry lowered her arm and gripped Kathie in a hug. 'Don't tell me now. Tell Eliza. Hold it together till we get there.'

Kathie rubbed at her face with the sleeve of her coat.

'Now?' she asked, her low voice once again barely audible amid the clatter of the café.

Cherry nodded. She picked up Kathie's bag and ushered her towards the door. Kathie picked her way tentatively through the spaces between the tables until, almost cowering at the exit, she pulled at Cherry's arm.

'He came back,' Kathie said hoarsely. 'After I rang you, he came back.'

* * * * *

'Now is the moment to tell me. I mean minute by minute from when you woke up. I need to know exactly what we're facing.'

Kathie and Cherry sat across from Eliza Wynne in a small modern conference room in the barrister's chambers on Three Queens' Lane. A box of tissues lay on the table next to a jug of water and four small glasses. Eliza was as usual, elegantly dressed but had subverted the formality of her fitted charcoal suit with red leather boots that zipped up the back.

After accepting Kathie as a client, Eliza had initially been resistant to Cherry attending conferences. Their conversations were legally privileged, she'd pointed out. Kathie had to feel free to tell her anything, even information that was counter to her own interests.

But Kathie had insisted. She wanted Cherry with her for all parts of the process.

Eliza had set her terms. Her responsibility was to her client but also to the court. It was up to Kathie if she wanted her story in the press, but it was up to Cherry to stay within the law or take the consequences.

'Contempt of court can mean an unlimited fine and even jail, you do know that?'

Cherry sighed. She kept being told by assorted lawyers and judges that she'd be banged up and bankrupted if she transgressed. She nodded. 'I am duly warned,' she said.

And, the barrister added sternly, she didn't want to be quoted in any article.

'He got in. He was waiting. In the kitchen, doing colouring with Brandon.'

Cherry's eyebrows jumped. She hadn't known this from Kathie's phone call earlier. The injunction prevented Ed from even approaching the house. Actually entering it was an extreme transgression.

'He told me that no matter what the judge says today or at any other hearing, we're his. We can never get away.' Kathie's sentence ended in a strangled gulp.

'So we will be telling the court that he has broken the injunction to stay away, correct? And that he physically entered your home?'

Kathie nodded.

'And that he threatened you?' Eliza asked.

Kathie swallowed. Cherry saw her press her right hand with her left and wince. 'Well, it felt like that. The way he said it.' She shrugged hopelessly.

Eliza was making rapid notes. 'If we're to persuade a judge that he's such a threat to the children that he can't be trusted to see them alone, every bit of evidence helps. The fact that he's broken the order not to enter the property is vital but unless he agrees that it happened, the judge has to decide which of you he believes. Did a neighbour see him coming in or leaving? Did you call the police?'

'I was in shock,' Kathie murmured. 'I didn't think.'

Cherry's stomach tightened. Should she mention the phone call? She couldn't. She'd been warned. She absolutely couldn't get involved. It took her away from being independent, made her part of the story – she had done this too often and had been criticised for it by editors who told her she was skirting close to a line she could not cross. So she pressed her lips together. But saying nothing felt wrong. Really wrong.

'Doesn't telling my lawyer count?' Kathie stared down at her tea. 'He can be such a good dad.'

Eliza looked at her neutrally.

'He can,' Kathie insisted. 'And I do want him to see them. Just not on their own.'

Eliza gathered her papers together in a neat pile, set her pen on top and fixed Kathie with a direct but sympathetic gaze.

'Yes. And now we need to talk about how it'll be in court.'

Kathie closed her eyes. Cherry could see the pulse jump in her neck.

'This judge – well, you know she's tough. She'll want evidence to back up what you say he's done.'

Kathie glanced down at her right hand, which Cherry noticed she was cradling in her left.

'It's good you've got the photographs,' Eliza was saying. 'They're not conclusive, but they're indicative of harm.'

'What do you mean, not conclusive?' Kathie's voice was incredulous.

'They don't show what led up to the injuries. Or who inflicted them.' Eliza looked at her client sympathetically. 'I know. What are you meant to do... video your own assaults? But even to get to 'probably', the standard of proof family courts use, usually takes a collection of evidence that points inexorably in a certain direction. Not just a photograph. Not just your word that he hurt you.'

Kathie looked into the distance and folded her hands away.

'Right,' she said. 'My word isn't enough. I understand.'

There was a pause. Kathie seemed to withdraw further into herself. Cherry watched her stillness deepen and her eyes sweep closed, as if she was already exhausted.

'If anyone is unpleasant to you, I will intervene,' Eliza continued, more briskly now. 'You need to listen carefully to the questions, and never get into an argument. Even if you think a question is ridiculous or provocative, try to answer politely.'

As if on autopilot, Kathie nodded.

Oh no, you can't disengage now, thought Cherry.

Kathie chewed her lip, her mouth compressing into a line.

'Will the judge believe me?'

Eliza tapped her fingers lightly on her notepad. 'The judge makes decisions about what kind of person you are from the way you answer questions. Even if you think your answer makes you look bad, always be honest. Judges give people a lot of credit for being honest. Even when – particularly when, actually – the answer goes against you.'

Now Eliza glanced at the clock. It was twenty to ten.

'Right,' she said. 'Time to go.'

Chapter Twenty-One

The short walk to court seemed to revive Kathie somewhat. Cherry had watched Eliza steer her client along the street, and when Cherry's phone rang as they reached the plaza in front of the court, the barrister gave Cherry a brisk nod as she hung back to take the call.

'Check the lists to see which courtroom we're in,' Eliza said over her shoulder as she and Kathie entered the court. 'See you in there.'

The name 'Patrick Daunt' flashed up on her screen. Editors calling always made her nervous.

'Patrick.' She widened her smile, hoping it would warm up her tone. 'I'm on a job. In fact I'm on *the* job.'

A laugh rolled down the line. 'No time for small talk then I see.'

'We're just going into court for the fact-finding. I think it's about to get messy.'

She could almost see Patrick's ears prick up. Messy meant good copy.

'Except remember,' she hurriedly warned, 'I still don't have permission to report.'

'Mmm.' Patrick's tone was careful. 'I've been having a talk with our legal department. They want you to ring them to discuss. Conference call. I'll be on it too.'

Silently, Cherry groaned.

'The lawyers need to know what the ex-partner's told you. It's about balance and getting the full picture. Cherry, they're not just worried about contempt. They're worried about libel. The piece has to be fair as well as accurate.'

'All rise,' said the clerk. Yet another youngster who looked as if he had barely graduated, Cherry thought. Were there any experienced court staff left?

The door to the left of the judge's scarlet chair opened. Balancing an open laptop on top of a bundle of papers, Fosse entered.

Seating herself, she surveyed the room from her vantage point several feet above the rows of desks. The large chair was set directly beneath the gilded figures of the lion and the unicorn fighting on the royal coat of arms. Tearing each other to shreds, Cherry thought; an entirely appropriate image for what so often took place in a family court.

Eliza and Kathie sat to Cherry's right; Kathie in the row behind her lawyer. Unobtrusively, Rachida sat at her side.

On the same long wooden benches that stretched across the courtroom, at the far left hand side was Ed, sitting behind his own newly instructed counsel. Cherry recalled James Hallett, an impressively rotund barrister, from a case she'd sat in on several months ago. He'd not been all that keen on her being in court, and had huffed and puffed an objection which, she'd pointed out – she hoped without making obvious the irritation she had felt – was not based on any of the lawful grounds for asking that a journalist be ejected from a courtroom.

Hallett had grudgingly conceded the point and plonked himself back down. Later in the case, she'd observed how the barrister's unctuous manner hid a viciously forensic streak in cross-examination.

Cherry saw Fosse clock her presence with a pursing of her lips. She inclined her head, then busied herself setting up a new document on her laptop as the judge tapped her pen sharply on the desk.

'Mr Sams, Mrs Sams, good morning,' said the judge. 'Both represented today, I see – Mr Hallett, Ms Wynne. Good. That should, dare I say, speed things up.'

Fosse's gaze now alighted on Cherry. 'I note that we have present a member of press,' she said lightly. 'Again.'

Cherry sat up straighter, locking eyes with the judge. What was she going to say this time?

'We are indeed fortunate to have a free press in this country,' – Fosse's voice, though tiny, carried through the courtroom – 'and I am pleased to see that one of its members has chosen my court once again for her attentions.' Her smile was without warmth.

Cherry saw Kathie half turn to glance at her.

'Ms Wynne, given that I understand from the papers before me that your client has engaged in interviews with this journalist, I must suppose that she is in full agreement with her presence here. But I should warn Mrs Sams once again that the prospect of media reporting of this case will make not a scrap of difference to my conduct of it or to any of the decisions I take.'

Cherry saw Eliza's eyebrows shoot up as she stood. 'Of course, Your Honour,' she said.

The judge smiled thinly.

'Mr Sams, I must take account of any relevant reasons advanced against the media being present in a family case. Do you have anything to say?'

Hallett hauled himself to his feet. 'No Your Honour.' He took a breath and glanced at Ed. 'In fact my client told me that he, ah, welcomes, as it happens, the interest that Ms Magraw is taking in this case. He believes that more understanding of how fathers are dealt with by family courts can only be for the public good.' With that, Hallett thumped back into his seat.

Above them all, Fosse flexed and then tightened her fingers.

'Very well. It seems, Ms Magraw, that everyone is delighted you are present. Shall we get on?'

As Kathie made her way to the witness box, deliberately taking a longer route to avoid walking past Ed, Cherry was able to see her face clearly for the first time since they'd entered the court. She looked both determined and frightened. Her hands gripped the barrier tightly as the clerk swore her in.

Kathie had initially listed eight instances of abusive behaviour on what was known as a Scott Schedule. Fosse had ruled that she would hear evidence on four of them. It was only in regard to one allegation, the bite to her underarm, that Kathie had any evidence to corroborate her account: her call to the police and her own photographs.

Precariously balancing his iPad on his palm, Hallett opened in a reassuringly conversational tone.

'Mrs Sams, I have read your statement. You have described an overall atmosphere in your relationship which you felt to be intimidating.'

Kathie nodded.

'I'm sorry Mrs Sams, for the recording you will need to speak up.'

Kathie jumped. 'Oh. Sorry. That is, yes.'

'And you say that over the years you have become scared of your husband, and you have also mentioned a number of instances where you say he acted abusively towards you?'

'Yes.' Kathie's voice was clear but thin. She had averted her head from Ed so that she would not be able to see him, even in her peripheral vision.

'Perhaps we could focus on the first allegation to start with,' said Hallett. 'The day your son Brandon had a hospital appointment. You say in your statement your husband deliberately did not inform you of a change of clinic?'

Kathie gripped the barrier. 'Yes. I'd missed an appointment. Ed had organised a new date. But he didn't tell me when the letter came that we had to go to a different place. I didn't even know there was a letter. He just told me the date and time. So I took Brandon to Frenchay when it should have been St George's. We had to drive from one to the other then wait till the doctor could see us. It took the whole morning.'

Cherry switched her attention to the judge, whose face, she saw, was carefully composed into listening mode.

'Having to drive to another hospital and then waiting around all morning meant I completely missed an important work call.' A note of indignation crept in. 'Brandon was climbing the walls by the end. Ed said it was my fault for not checking and that I'd been stupid – well, he swore at me – for messing things up. But he'd *never* told me about the appointment being somewhere else.'

There was a sharp exhalation of breath from Ed, who folded his arms and closed his eyes.

'Mrs Sams, what are you saying this incident means?' Rolling back on his heels, Hallett looked at her, his head cocked.

'That he'd deliberately not told me the right information.' Kathie looked at Ed for the first time, her face bitter. 'He does this. He creates a situation so I seem to make mistakes. Then he blames me for it.' Her voice came out low and hard. 'I know it sounds like a small thing, but when it's happening over and over again...' She stood up straighter, her voice rising. 'It's just one example but there's only space for eight on the form. I couldn't put them all. And now,' she looked accusingly at the judge, 'I'm only allowed to try to prove four of them.'

The courtroom fell silent.

Fosse sighed wearily. 'Mrs Sams, if you wanted to challenge my ruling on the number of counts of domestic abuse you wished to prove, you should have done so at the last case management hearing, not today.'

'How could I know I could do that?' Kathie expostulated. 'I didn't have a lawyer, I was doing it on my own.'

Cherry saw Eliza start to rise to her feet. Fosse waved her down. 'Ms Wynne, thank you. I shall attempt to explain my rationale to your client, and we shall then see if we can continue, or if we must adjourn.' Reluctantly, Eliza sat.

'Mrs Sams, it is my duty to run this court both fairly, proportionately and efficiently. I selected four allegations from your list, and I chose them to run the spectrum from the minor to the serious. I do not need to hear every allegation someone makes in order to assess the level of abuse, which – if proved – you have been subjected to.'

'But I didn't know it would be like this!' Kathie protested. 'I thought I could explain how all the other things he's done are part of it. How he makes me feel too scared to even try to go against him.'

Cherry glanced at Ed, who had averted his face as if he could not bear to watch. Half closing her eyes, Fosse sighed again.

'Well, Mrs Sams, I assure you, these four instances before us will be enough for me to make up my mind,' she said crisply. 'We will press on.'

Hallett's next words were uttered with extreme politeness. 'Mrs Sams, my client says you are exaggerating and misrepresenting what happened. And he says that you do this a lot.'

To Cherry's surprise, Fosse intervened.

'Not quite, Mr Hallett. I think the point Mrs Sams is attempting to make is that your client deliberately withheld information from her, and then castigated her harshly for the resulting debacle.'

'Well, Your Honour, no,' said Hallett, flushing at the interjection. 'That is not true. As I will now attempt to show.' He glanced down at his iPad, a chunky finger scrolling down the screen. 'Mrs Sams, how good would you say your memory has been since you gave birth to your second child? For instance, have there been any other times that you have missed medical appointments?'

Kathie's forehead crinkled with a frown. 'Er. Yes. Of course I've missed the odd appointment over the years. Once it was because Ed took us all off at the last minute for a few days away without telling me. I only found out once we were headed for the motorway.'

Cherry could see how this might sound like the unedifying playing out of banal grievances that build up in all struggling relationships. Worse, it was coming across as trivial and unfair.

Hallett looked up from his screen. 'So you miss not just one, but two consecutive vaccination appointments for your baby, then arrive in the afternoon for a morning appointment for her twelve month check-up, and finally, confuse the date of a return-to-work interview with your employer, which meant my client had to leave work abruptly in the middle of the day to enable you to attend?'

'You have got to be kidding me?' Kathie's tone was scoffing.

'No Mrs Sams, I'm asking you whether or not these missed appointments occurred.'

Kathie rolled her eyes in weary despair. 'Yes. I was struggling with two young children, pretty much on my own.' She looked at Fosse pleadingly. 'I was *tired*.'

Hallett smiled. 'Mrs Sams, please don't worry. The pressures of motherhood are indeed intense. But do you not think you might, in exactly the same way, and for the same reasons, have got yourself confused about this particular clinic appointment you are now blaming your husband for not telling you had changed location?'

Kathie lifted her eyes to the ceiling and very slightly shrugged.

'No. It happened like I said.'

The judge nodded, her eyes beadily fixed on Kathie. 'I see. Well, Mr Hallett, let's move on.'

Hallett flicked his finger across his large iPad then doubled tapped halfway down.

'Mrs Sams, in the next item, you say, 'He undermines my authority with the children, failing to back me up on discipline and going against agreements we've come to, for example, about the consequences of not eating their dinner. He will, for instance, give them a pudding in front of me, when we have agreed that this shouldn't happen. He makes me out to be the 'bad guy'. This happens repeatedly. It makes me feel helpless and as if there's no respect between us.''

Hallett looked up at Kathie. 'How often would you say this type of event happens, Mrs Sams?'

'A few times a week?' Kathie sighed impatiently. 'It's hard to say.'

'I see. But would you accept that there are bound to be differences in parenting styles, and uncomfortable though it is, parents have to work through them?'

Cherry saw Kathie stiffen at the patronising tone.

'It's not a 'difference in style',' she said cuttingly. 'Reading it out doesn't show how it all builds up. He does intend to put me down. It happens too often, and you can't see the expression on his face when he does it. You can't see how he sometimes shows me he could hurt me. Or shows me how he could hurt the children if I don't do as he says.' She stopped, taking a deep gulp of air.

Fosse cut in. 'Mrs Sams, we are moving into more serious territory here. You are not alleging your husband assaults you as part of this particular aspect of your complaint?'

Kathie exclaimed in frustration. 'No! It's not like... that. It's *how* he does things... he's telling me in lots of ways that he could. And just writing down different examples in this...' she took a raw breath, 'dry court statement just won't work.' Kathie's cheeks were hectic and her voice had risen to a high note.

The judge, Cherry noted, had leaned forward, her eyes intent on Kathie through the violet frames of her spectacles.

'Mrs Sams, do take a moment.'

Kathie nodded, crossing her arms tightly in front of her, unconsciously trying to create an extra barrier between herself and the court.

'Would you like some water?' Fosse asked.

Kathie nodded. The judge indicated to the clerk who scurried over to the witness stand with a white plastic cup, water slopping over the top. Kathie sipped, her hand shaking.

'Now,' Fosse resumed. 'I'm sorry, but time is limited. Is everyone content to carry on? Mrs Sams?'

Kathie shrugged, a jerky movement. Glancing at Eliza, who looked grave, Cherry wondered what any lawyer could do as they watched their client unravel in front of them.

Fosse was speaking. 'We are going to have to dig deeper into these matters, however painful it is,' she said. 'Because, Mrs Sams, you are making more serious allegations from this point in your statement. Mr Hallett?'

The barrister, who had sat down, now rose again. 'Yes Your Honour.' His finger flicked again down the screen of his iPad.

'Mrs Sams, I would like to move on to the third instance you cite in your statement. But perhaps instead of me reading it out, you could instead explain what you say happened?'

'Oh. Yes. That.' Kathie closed her eyes. 'It's hard to know where to start. I'd come home from an evening out. I could tell before I even got in the house that Ed wasn't pleased I was later than I'd said. I couldn't find my keys so I knocked but he didn't answer. I knocked and knocked. I was wondering where he was. At that point I had to walk round the back. I found him on the sofa with Lola. He must have heard me knocking. But he blanked me. Didn't speak to me, didn't even acknowledge I'd come in.'

She paused, casting her mind back. 'He just put Lola on the floor and walked out.'

There was a pause. Cherry could see Kathie trying to think how to explain what happened next.

'I picked her up, gave her a cuddle for a few minutes, then started taking her upstairs. I didn't know where he'd gone but I was dreading an argument. It was even worse because of the silent treatment. Anyway. He was waiting for me on the landing where the staircase turns. He wouldn't let me past. I tried to laugh it off, but he stood there, just not moving.'

Kathie abruptly stopped. In the silence until she could speak again, she began to tremble and tears spilled down her cheeks. 'He handed me a sleeping bag... and a note. It told me to...'

Cherry saw Kathie stop again and gulp for air.

'He'd actually written a message telling me to sleep downstairs. I couldn't believe it. He held out his hands for Lola. I tried to talk to him but he wouldn't say a word. Of course I was going to put my daughter to bed. I was so angry. I tried to carry on up but he held out his hands against the banister and the wall and I stumbled. I was holding Lola and he tried to grab her from me. Then he shoved me against the wall and pushed his arms towards me and was wrestling me for Lola. And you can't let a baby be handled like that, so I just let her go. I let her go.'

Kathie swallowed a sob. 'I tried to follow him but he pushed a finger into my chest and said, 'Don't you dare come up'.' Cherry saw her shudder.

'That was the only thing he said to me. Then he kicked the sleeping bag down the stairs and went up taking Lola with him.'

Throughout all this Fosse had appeared to Cherry to be perusing the courtroom ceiling. At the sound of Kathie's sobs, she looked down, observing the witness for a few seconds.

'Mrs Sams, I know this is difficult.'

Kathie nodded, scrubbing at her face with a tissue, hiccupping as she tried to suppress her emotion.

The judge bent her head over the ring binder in front of her, her expression in shadow as her fingertips tap tap tapped their way down the paperwork. She looked up.

'It is of course difficult to know what to think about matters such as these which take place in the private domain of a family home.' She sighed. 'You say one thing. Inevitably your husband will have a different recollection, or indeed, interpretation, of the events in question. It is my job to assess the evidence you both give as to whether they took place. However...' Fosse surveyed Kathie's dishevelled state with, Cherry perceived, a small moue of distaste flickering across her lips, '... I will now rise. We will return in twenty minutes.'

And with that, the judge alighted neatly from her scarlet judicial chair and disappeared through the door at the back of the court.

Out in the lobby, Rachida put her arm round Kathie's heaving shoulders, as Eliza handed her a cup of vending machine tea.

Acutely aware that her physical positioning had to reflect her neutral position as a journalist, Cherry seated herself apart from the huddle. Ed could not be given any impression that she was on Kathie's side. Though right now, he wasn't anywhere in sight.

Observing Kathie from her vantage point by the usher's desk, as she visibly expostulated to her lawyer, Cherry suddenly realised that her interviewee was not simply upset, she was incensed – and stinging with the shame of not having been believed. In failing to make any headway with the judge, Kathie realised that Fosse assessed her as having magnified and skewed her descriptions of what the judge viewed as trivial incidents, in a malicious attempt to discredit her husband.

It was exactly how Eliza had said these disputes could play out.

★ ★ ★ ★ ★

The police photographs of Kathie's arm did indeed look serious, Hallett observed, as he resumed his cross-examination.

'However, my client has an entirely different account of how the mark' – the barrister repeatedly chose not to call it an injury, Cherry noted, though Kathie's skin had clearly been broken – 'came about.'

Kathie looked steadily at him. 'Is there a question?'

Ouch, Cherry thought. Kathie had a bit more spark about her

– she'd clearly rallied in the break – but that kind of direct challenge did not come across well.

Hallett bridled. 'Indeed there is, Mrs Sams,' he said. 'You do not deny in your statement that you and Mr Sams have often engaged in what is colloquially known as 'rough sex'?'

Kathie stood absolutely still. 'No.' She shook her head. 'I mean yes. We have done that.'

Hallett rolled back on his heels. 'And you enjoyed it?'

'Yes.' She cleared her throat. 'Sometimes.'

'Sometimes?' Hallett paused. 'Can you be more precise?'

'When I wanted it. I didn't always.'

Hallett looked up sharply. 'To be clear, by saying 'not always' you are not alleging that my client has ever raped you, I think?'

Kathie now looked confused.

'No. I've not said that.'

'So shall we, ah, try to avoid from now on any implication that he has had sex with you without consent. Unless you intend to amend your statement? At what would be a very late stage in these proceedings?'

'No.' Kathie shook her head again as if to clear it. 'I mean yes, I'm not saying he raped me.'

Clever, Cherry thought. Ed's barrister had manoeuvred Kathie into a positive declaration that there had never been any non-consensual sex.

Hallett's chubby forefinger was scrolling down his iPad screen. 'So we are now left with your account of how you received this mark, which is at odds with my client's. He says you enjoyed and engaged in sexual activity which sometimes included biting and rough handling, and that this mark came about as a result of sex on, he says, the staircase. You say by contrast that he assaulted you.'

Kathie, by now, Cherry could tell, was unsure there was any firm ground beneath her feet.

'I appreciate you have a police report on what you say was an assault,' Hallett smoothly went on, 'but given that my client says – and you accept – that your intimate life together included this sort of rough, ahhhh, play, shall we say, and that you did not allege – and are not alleging – that he has ever raped you, then I think, perhaps, you will have to accept that there is stronger evidence for my client's account of how this incident happened, than there is for yours?'

Before the start of the hearing, Eliza had informed Hallett and the judge that Ed had broken the terms of the non-molestation order earlier that morning. Kathie wanted this added to her schedule of allegations, Eliza had said firmly. Submissions as to whether it could be allowed as a late allegation would be considered during the hearing, Fosse had ruled.

Now, Hallett finally addressed the issue.

'Mrs Sams, my client denies coming anywhere near the family home this morning, let alone into it,' he declared in ringing tones.

This was risky, thought Cherry, astonished. Ed must have lied to his barrister. She had not imagined he would make an outright denial.

'You have a great deal to gain if this court finds that my client breached the order,' Hallett continued, his voice beginning to boom. 'And if he really did turn up, and you really were frightened, then I'm perplexed, Mrs Sams, as to why you didn't knock on a neighbour's door. Or ring the police. We say it did not happen.'

Kathie looked blankly back at him. 'I was all over the place,' she said, sounding puzzled at her own reaction. 'I couldn't think straight.'

'But surely anyone's first instinct if they think they are in danger is to call for help?' said Hallett, the sound of his voice now filling the courtroom with assumed indignation on behalf of his client. 'You ring the police, you ring your parents, you ring a friend...'

Kathie looked at him, mute, uncomprehending. 'I had to get ready...' she said helplessly, cradling her right hand with her left. 'The kids... there was a lot to do.'

Cherry stood up.

'She rang me.'

During the few seconds it had taken from hearing that Ed had denied breaking the order till getting to her feet, a feeling of doom had engulfed Cherry at the prospect of this moment. Now it was upon her, she felt sick.

Startled, Hallett looked round, searching out where the words had come from. 'Er... oh, Ms... Magraw?'

Ahead of her Eliza Wynne and Rachida turned and were staring. Kathie's barrister looked floored, and the refuge worker was frowning in bewilderment. Ahead and to her right, Ed's head had jerked in reaction to Cherry's words.

The judge looked up sharply; her eyes now flicked between Cherry at the back of the courtroom and Kathie on the witness stand.

'Yes. God. Oh yes. I did call you!' Kathie's voice flooded with relief. 'I'd forgotten. How could I have forgotten!'

Cherry looked at Fosse.

The judge's expression was ominous. 'I believe this is the first any of us have heard about this... phone call?' Her tone was dangerously polite.

Cherry flushed but looked straight back. 'I didn't know it would come up.' She took a breath. 'When it did I felt I should say something.'

Eliza was on her feet, speaking fast. 'Your Honour, my client was distraught when we met earlier today. She didn't mention this to me. May I take instructions?'

Christ, Cherry thought. What had she done? By marching headfirst into the workings of a court of law, she had likely ruined any chance of Ed ever speaking to her again. And he would now undoubtedly oppose her application to report the case. This wasn't her fight, and in trying to simply tell the truth, she had royally screwed up.

Ten minutes later the court reconvened.

'We wish to call Ms Magraw to give evidence.' Eliza's silhouette was upright and, Cherry thought, approaching defiant.

Narrowing her eyes, Fosse tilted backwards in her chair, her voice incredulous. 'Ms Wynne. Am I to understand you are suggesting the court hears from a journalist who is deeply embroiled in reporting this case, who has conducted interviews with Mrs Sams, and who intends to write a story in the national media?'

'Your Honour,' said Eliza, drawing herself up even straighter. 'The paramount concern of this court must be whether my client or Mr

Hallett's is telling the truth about what happened this morning. I am far less concerned with Ms Magraw's professional endeavours than I am with representing my client and making sure that every piece of relevant evidence is placed before you.'

Eliza, thought Cherry, was about to demonstrate the value of having a professional advocate on your side.

'You have pointed out that at present, we have only each party's word as to what happened this morning. Therefore,' Eliza enunciated the next phrase in a tone which stayed only just inside the bounds of politeness, 'I would respectfully suggest there is a strong case to admit first-hand evidence that my client hopes will go some way to corroborate her version of events. If you find, based on what Ms Magraw says, that it is more likely than not that Mr Sams came to the house, this would be a serious breach of a court order, and material to our case.'

Eliza stopped talking but stayed standing. Despite her assured demeanour, Cherry noticed her hands shake when she lifted them momentarily from the table to take a sip of water.

Hallett, Cherry could see, was conferring intensely with Ed. The risk now, Cherry knew, was that Hallett would object, and Fosse would not allow her evidence.

'Ms Wynne, Mr Hallett – we will speak in my chambers.' Looking furious, the judge snapped her laptop shut and almost bounced off her chair before turning to Cherry.

'And you,' she fixed her eyes on Cherry, 'will not say a single word to either of the parties in the interim.'

Fosse stamped out of the room, her shoulders stiff with outrage. As the judge exited, Cherry saw Hallett speak in an angry undertone to Eliza. He jabbed a forefinger on the table to underscore each point. 'Quite outrageous.' Hallett's voice snapped out, his colour high as he uttered his final words before bumping along the row to get out, half pushing Ed as he squeezed his way to the end. Eliza forbore to answer, simply inclining her head. Practising her de-escalation skills, Cherry thought. But she wondered if Eliza was in fact on unstable ground.

As she moved past Cherry on her way to meet the judge, a wisp of a smile touched the barrister's lips. 'If you enter the fray, you have to commit,' Eliza said quietly. 'This next bit won't be pretty, but it's what I'm here for. To put my client's case the best I can.'

Fifteen minutes later, Cherry was sworn in.

Being on the witness stand felt extraordinarily exposing, Cherry instantly realised.

Eliza stood up. 'Please tell us what happened this morning,' she asked simply.

It took just a few minutes for Cherry to give her account.

Then Hallett got to his feet.

'How do we know this happened? That you are not simply protecting someone whose version of this relationship breakdown provides you with sensational material for a news article?'

Cherry froze in disbelief. 'Are you suggesting I made this up?'

'I'm asking, plainly, if you are telling the truth.' There it was. The challenge to her integrity.

'I am, yes.'

'But there is no other proof?'

Cherry's hackles had now risen to levels she had rarely experienced.

'Proof? Isn't what I say on oath regarded as evidence? I can give you my phone. You can see every call received.'

'But not what was said in those calls,' Hallett shot back. 'Was anyone else there to hear this phone call?'

Cherry's eyes widened.

'I'm not sure what you mean?' she said, a spurt of anxiety shooting through her.

'It was early this morning. I think I've been perfectly plain. Do you live with anyone. Did someone else hear the call? Or was it just you in your flat?'

Cherry paused. Hoping her dismay was not apparent, she turned to the judge.

'Your Honour, I'm not sure why the person I was with this morning matters. I've described what happened.'

Fosse tapped her finger sharply on the desk. 'Ms Magraw. As you are unfortunately involved with the people in this case in your professional work as a journalist, your evidence only holds so much value. It may be helpful to have your account of this phone call, and the conversation on your side of it, corroborated by someone else. Someone independent.'

Cornered, Cherry felt her cheeks start to burn. On her pale skin, the flush of colour was unmistakable, and she sensed Fosse scrutinising her with fresh interest. The judge's nostrils flared. Fosse had grasped that there was a problem. And Cherry saw her begin to understand what it might be.

'Please answer, Ms Magraw. Mr Hallett has asked to know who this person was. He is entitled to an answer.'

Fosse was actually enjoying herself, Cherry realised. The judge had, shark like, smelled a ribbon of blood in the water.

She would play it straight. She would not be shamed by this.

'A man called Garth Morgan was with me.'

Hallett rocked on his feet, gazing down at his papers.

'So, to confirm, Mr Morgan heard this phone call?'

'Yes. At least, he heard what I said.' Cherry kept her chin up and her voice steady.

Hallett pressed on. 'Might we know your relationship to Garth Morgan, Ms Magraw?' He paused. 'A flatmate? Your boyfriend?'

'He had stayed the night.'

Faced with the spareness of this response, Hallett paused, taking stock of the situation before pressing on. A slight smirk now curled at his lips.

'With you?'

Cherry nodded.

'We need you to speak your answer, Ms Magraw. For the court recording.'

'Yes,' Cherry said, her head tilting in disdain. 'With me.'

'Thank you,' said Hallett. 'We may now need Mr Morgan to confirm that he heard you take this call.'

Cherry was silent.

Fosse pinned her with a look. 'Ms Magraw, if counsel requests it, Mr Garth Morgan will be required to present himself at this court. I am being asked to find that Mr Sams has breached a non-molestation order, which in itself is a serious matter but in this case it has even more significance because Mrs Sams is arguing that such a breach shows he would continue to disregard her safety, and more particularly the safety of their children. Indeed she argues that he is positively a danger to them.'

Fosse tilted her head. A beam of sunshine filtered through the high window, washing the court with brilliant light.

'What is being sought is a draconian order that Mr Sams never again sees his children on his own. So I am afraid that whatever may – or may not – be Mr Morgan's relationship to you,' – ah, there was the thrust – 'and any possible difficulty in explaining why he was at your home early this morning, if Mr Morgan is called, he must come.'

Chapter Twenty-Two

Immediately Cherry stepped down from the witness stand, Fosse had adjourned the hearing for lunch. Cherry left the courtroom at a clip, and now, awash with adrenaline, stood in the plaza in front of the court building, trying to gather her thoughts.

As she considered the urgent phone call she now had to make to her editor, Cherry noticed that all her limbs were trembling. Watching as Kathie was undermined and shamed on the stand had been bad enough. But Cherry now understood, in a way she never had before, that you could not appreciate the impact of an aggressive cross-examination until you had yourself been subjected to an experienced lawyer politely but forensically slurring your motives and questioning your integrity.

Cherry sank down beside the concrete plinths at the furthest end of the plaza from the court building. With shaky fingers, she scrolled to Patrick's number.

'Cherry.' Friendly, warm. 'Twice in one day...' There was a faint enquiry in his voice.

Cherry had no idea how this conversation was going to go.

'It's tricky.'

Her editor's tone sharpened. 'Okay. Shoot.'

'I was called as a witness in the hearing today. To give evidence. For Kathie.' Down the line, she felt the quality of his attention tighten.

'Riiiight.' There was concern in his voice. 'How come?'

Briefly yet thoroughly Cherry ran through the events of the morning. Her account skittered briefly over Garth's presence in her bed at the time of the call, but she knew she had to explain that the man she was sleeping with might be called to give evidence.

A silence stretched on the line while Patrick absorbed the implications. Cherry pulled her coat tight around her as a stiff breeze swept across the plaza. How could she report fairly and impartially if she was testifying on behalf of one of the parties, she knew he was thinking. She'd been wondering the same. Was she compromised? He was going to pull the commission, wasn't he – and she couldn't blame him. All that work. All that time. Gone.

'Interesting.' Patrick's tone was thoughtful rather than dismayed. 'It's unusual. But perhaps not fatal.'

Cherry breathed again.

'But I have a question. If he's called, your boyfriend will back you up, won't he?'

Cherry closed her eyes. 'It's... difficult.' She felt tears stinging her eyes as her throat closed. 'Patrick, I'm sorry, this is a really awful situation.' She made a sound between a gasp and a laugh. 'He's not some random hook-up I'll never be able to find again, if that's what you're thinking.'

'Random hook-ups are, of course, fine, except when you have to tell them the pay-back for a night of passion is a court summons.' Patrick's voice was amused.

'A hook-up might have been preferable.' Cherry took a breath. 'He's married. Kids. It's messy. And it's over, well, I think it's over. A trip to court will just about finish it off nicely.'

Patrick laughed. 'Doesn't sound ideal. But... well, maybe... I don't want to presume, but if it's over – or at least over-ish – it sounds like this is his problem, not yours.'

Cherry fished out a tissue and tried to blow her nose quietly. 'Yes.' She took a breath, steadied herself. 'I'm just not looking forward to telling him.'

Patrick paused and Cherry heard him decide. 'Bringing this back to your investigation... we can work with it but the only option we have now is to be transparent. You'll need to write about what happened in court this morning, so that the readers understand what's gone on.'

If the judge gives me permission, thought Cherry. A distinctly unlikely prospect at this particular moment.

'Got it,' she said. 'And thank you.' For not pulling the commission, she thought. For not pulling your support. For not binning weeks of work. She didn't need to say it. They both understood.

'But Cherry, remember, we have no room for manoeuvre now – this makes it even more vital to get a full account from the ex. If he's saying he's not abusive, we give him every opportunity to put his case. We listen to him on exactly the same basis that we listen to her.'

As she emerged from the lift after grabbing, but barely tasting, a bacon roll for lunch, the fourth-floor lobby was buzzing with activity. But there was no sign of Kathie, Eliza or Rachida. Cherry glanced at her phone. It wasn't yet 2pm – could the hearing have already started? She walked swiftly to the usher's desk to check.

Leaning against the desk, Hallett was sharing a joke with head usher Fergus. Throwing his head back in a guffaw, he suddenly caught Cherry's eye, and brought his roar of laughter to an abrupt halt. 'Anyway, good to chat,' he said rapidly. 'I'll get on.' Barely acknowledging Cherry, he turned his attention to the papers in his hand, flicking through them busily as he marched off.

'Ms Magraw. The head usher's eyebrows quirked upwards. 'Interesting case? You going to write about it?'

'Who knows Fergus, who knows,' Cherry smiled wryly. 'It's always a battle.'

'Her Honour Judge Fosse, eh?' he said, quietly.

Cherry rolled her eyes. 'Hmm. Not sure she's all that keen on me being in court.'

At this, Fergus reached under the desk. 'Something for you, Miss. I mean, Ms.'

Matter-of-factly, he pushed an envelope towards her. Cherry reached for it and felt something hard and circular inside. Her fingers ran across it questioningly. A CD?

Fergus was already turning away. 'Look smart.' He nodded over to the courtroom, into which Hallett and Ed were disappearing.

'Hearing's about to start.'

What had he given her? No point asking. Fergus was now dealing with a cross-looking woman haranguing him over the state of the broken lifts. Cherry tucked the envelope and its contents into her rucksack, walked to the courtroom and pushed open the swing door.

'Court rise.' Cherry had scarcely got her laptop open when Fosse's entrance was announced by the clerk.

The judge inclined her head. Perched in the resplendent red leather chair, she scrutinised the parties.

'Next, we will hear evidence from Mr Sams. So, Mr Hallett, over to you.'

On the stand, Ed looked remarkably relaxed for a man who had just heard two people give evidence he had broken an injunction.

Hallett heaved himself to his feet.

'Mr Sams, we have two diametrically opposed accounts of what happened this morning at your family home. I will ask this very simply. Did you go there?'

Straight in, Cherry thought. Still, Hallett hardly had a choice.

Without a moment's hesitation, Ed answered. 'No, I didn't.'

Hallett assumed a troubled expression.

'But Mr Sams, two people say you did.'

Ed turned to the judge. 'Your Honour, I don't want to impugn Ms Magraw. It's perfectly possible that Kathie did call her in distress for some reason, and told her...' He tailed off. 'Look, I don't want to say any more. It doesn't help.' He sighed. 'But there's no evidence that I went to the house this morning, and that's because I didn't.'

Fosse looked down at him, her eyes narrowed. 'Be careful, Mr Sams. Your wife's account of this morning's events counts as evidence.'

'Yes, of course Your Honour.' Ed's voice hardened, ever so slightly. 'But no more, I hope, than mine.' Ed paused. Cherry watched him thinking, weighing up what to say next. 'She's understandably fraught. This whole situation is destabilising. For everyone, including our kids.'

Clever, thought Cherry. He was presenting a concerned persona, not wanting to land Kathie in hot water, but implying just enough to plant a seed of doubt about her emotional stability. She found his level of calmness remarkable, given the stressful courtroom context – he had seemed just as reasonable each time she'd met him.

'Mr Sams.' Hallett's voice nudged him back on point. 'Let's rewind a little.'

Ed nodded in brief apology. 'Of course.'

'Please tell the court where you were at the time your wife says you accosted her at the front door and later broke into the family home.'

'In the flat where I'm staying for the moment.' He shrugged, grimacing helplessly. 'And no, before you ask. It was early. And I didn't have anyone with me.'

This is an impossible game of 'he said, she said', Cherry typed into her laptop. Who is more believable? Who is a reliable witness? What does it take to be a credible victim in the eyes of the law? How does any of this back-and-forth get to the truth of what happened?

Five minutes later, Hallett had finished. Now it was Eliza's turn. Would this shake Ed up in the same way that Hallett's cross-examination had undone Kathie?

Eliza, her dark hair swept back and shiny even in the dull light of the court, cocked her head and smiled at Ed. 'Do you ever make things up? Things that aren't true?'

He looked back at her, a small frown crinkling his forehead. 'I do not,' he said.

'Because that would be a wrong thing to do,' Eliza continued.

'Yes.'

'And you and Mrs Sams bring your children up not to tell lies?'

'Yes. Well, Lola is very young, but obviously, yes.'

Ed sounded baffled, not understanding where this was going. Nor, Cherry thought, did she.

'So your wife thinks it's a bad thing to tell lies too?'

Ed's body tensed ever so slightly. 'Yes, I would say so.'

'You've known her to be a generally truthful person, during your relationship, when you were together.' Eliza was stating a fact.

'Yes.' There was a hint, but no more, of reluctance.

Between The Lies

Interesting, Cherry thought. Ed had realised that if he'd said no, he'd be challenged to prove it. Not just that, he'd sound churlish. And he wanted to look gracious, understanding, even caring, about his former partner – at the same time as dragging Kathie's credibility through the mud.

'And yet what you're now saying is, she's a liar?'

'What I actually said was that she might be fraught. Not sure of herself.' Ed wavered, trying to work out what to do. It was the first time Cherry had seen him appear uncertain.

'Fraught is one thing. But saying something happened when it didn't is quite another.' Eliza paused. 'It would be a lie, wouldn't it, Mr Sams?'

Ed raised his chin. 'Yes.'

'So I'm sorry to repeat myself, but that means either you are lying or your wife is. Who was it Mr Sams?'

Ed turned his head away as if in distaste. 'I don't lie.'

Eliza leaned forward, the fingers of each hand splaying on the desk.

'So you're saying, on oath, that my client is lying. But you have absolutely no proof of that. You say she's a truthful person. And she has a witness, an accredited member of the press, who took a call from her, in distress, immediately after you knocked at the door to her house in direct contravention of a court order telling you to go nowhere near it.'

196

Chapter Twenty-Three

Just as Cherry reached the front of the queue for the bar, Eliza bundled through the door.

'Soooo,' the barrister drawled, once she'd navigated through the crowded room. 'This is where us lawyers come to drown our clients' sorrows. So I'll have a double vodka tonic please.' She hefted her capacious shoulder bag onto a nearby table.

As Cherry set down their drinks, Eliza undid her hair from its French pleat, shook it out and clinked her glass against Cherry's. 'What did you think about today?' Her elegant eyebrows arched as she took in Cherry's eye roll. 'Well, I told you things often aren't pretty.'

Cherry thought back to the moment in the courtroom, half an hour ago when Fosse had given her judgment. From the back of the room, she had been able to survey the scene, her eyes flicking between Kathie, Ed, their lawyers and the judge as she touch-typed into her laptop every word Fosse uttered.

'In my assessment, this is a high conflict relationship, not an abusive one,' the judge had begun. 'I make no final decision today on the alleged breach of the non-molestation order this morning. Should Mrs Sams choose to pursue it, I will require evidence from Mr Garth Morgan on the matter of the phone call that was made to the journalist Ms Cherry Magraw, but my provisional view is that were I to find Mr Sams had arrived at the family home this morning, while I would regard such a breach as extremely ill-advised, given it is a single breach, and Mrs Sams did not feel in such danger that she called the police, or even went round to a neighbour's house in any sort of distress, I would most likely put it down to a misjudgement caused by strain of today's hearing.

'Such a breach would be wrong if it had taken place. Court orders must be respected. But given the rest of my findings, I would not regard it as material to my decision-making in respect of the child arrangements orders that I anticipate I will be asked to rule on in the coming weeks.'

As her fingers flew across her keyboard to note the ruling, Cherry glanced briefly up at the court. Eliza was typing rapidly into her own laptop so she couldn't see the barrister's expression, but behind her, Kathie was now leaning against Rachida, whose arm was round her shoulders. Hallett too was typing as fast as his fingers allowed, and Ed... Ed was sitting straight in his seat, his head tilted slightly to one side, his eyes closed.

The tension in the courtroom felt thick, the emotions emanating from both parties swirling around almost palpably, despite the silence into which Fosse uttered her judgment.

'As to Mrs Sams' other allegations, on the evidence before me, I find none of them made out,' said the judge.

As Kathie gasped, Rachida tightened her arm around her.

'The most serious, the bite, which is, I agree, documented and was the subject of a police caution, I cannot say was not caused as part of consensual... shall we say, playful, verging on rough, sex which Mrs Sams agrees she has previously taken part in willingly. Mr Sams may have gone too far on this occasion, he may have made a misjudgement, but I cannot find, given this couple's acknowledged history, that this was an incident of domestic abuse. I'm afraid that I also cannot exclude the possibility that Mrs Sams has made this allegation maliciously, attempting to leverage the revulsion that any decent person must always feel when one individual assaults another, to sway my view of Mr Sams, when in fact what evidence we have of how the bite came about points the other way.'

Suddenly, Cherry heard Kathie's voice cut across Fosse's words.

'You're wrong,' she hissed, standing up, visibly shaking. Everyone's eyes swivelled towards her.

Eliza, turning around, looked horrified and made shushing motions. Ed, Cherry noticed, winced and turned his head away.

'Completely wrong!' Kathie's voice rang out. 'You are putting my children in danger. And me! Do you hear?'

In the pause that ensued, Fosse placed her notes very precisely on the desk.

'Mrs Sams.' In the shocked silence of the courtroom, the judge's tiny voice was crystal clear. 'Please sit down. The time for you to speak is over – you have given your evidence.'

Kathie did not move a muscle. Rachida spoke to her entreatingly as Eliza turned round in her seat, making calming motions with her hands.

'We have to listen now,' Cherry heard the barrister say in an undertone. 'We'll talk later. I promise.'

Somehow, Rachida managed to half usher, half drag Kathie back down into her seat.

'Sometimes,' Fosse continued, 'I fear, there is a tendency to re-interpret events after they have happened, after coming into contact with a domestic abuse support organisation that, quite naturally given its remit, tends to view events through the lens of intimate partner violence being an evil prevalent throughout society.'

Cherry saw Rachida stiffen in outrage.

'But the ramifications of finding that domestic abuse has occurred are so serious that this court requires evidence beyond mere assertion, beyond a *feeling* of being threatened.

'Taking the other two incidents now: if indeed either of them did happen, I am afraid to say that they are the kind of thing that is heard all too often by this court when a couple's relationship comes under strain, and particularly when there are issues relating to contact with children. There may be real and distressing unpleasantness when a couple breaks up, but it is all too easy to re-interpret such unpleasantness as something more sinister.

'I do not deny, and nor would I ever wish to, that domestic abuse and coercively controlling behaviour, which we are all learning more about, is destructive and frightening and must not be tolerated. But it is also important for the court to be aware that exaggeration can easily occur, and quite naturally and understandably so, in the heat and anger of a failing relationship.

'I would characterise this relationship as containing episodes of disrespect, heightened disagreement and tension, but that is not domestic abuse. Even on this mother's own account, these incidents were not threatening, they were not controlling, and even had I found them to have been instances of domestic abuse, they were not of the highest. They would not influence this court's view as to whether this father was a safe person around his children.'

Chapter Twenty-Four

As she turned the key into the lock of her front door, Cherry felt her body slump in relief that the day was over. The long day in court had felt toxic. Hallett was unpleasant, but Fosse's antagonism, covered over with a chilly veil of politeness, and her evident enjoyment in having pinpointed Cherry's vulnerability prompted feelings in her, not just of indignation but of rage. But unless Kathie chose to pursue proving her allegation that Ed had turned up that morning – which the judge had said she would disregard in any case – it now seemed that Garth would not be required in court.

Walking into her kitchen and putting the kettle on, Cherry shook her head as she recalled Kathie's devastated reaction to Fosse's final words: 'I see no reason now, given my findings, for Mr Sams' time with his children to be restricted any longer,' the judge had said.

'In the interim period before the final hearing where I will decide on the ultimate contact arrangements, I order that Mr Sams may have Brandon and Lola to stay every other weekend from, let us say, nursery and school pickup time on Friday to 6pm on Saturday, and the same pickup times one day in the week, to be arranged outside this court between the parties and their lawyers. That time will be unsupervised, and it will begin starting this weekend. Do you have anything to say, Ms Wynne?'

Kathie had cried out in protest as Eliza stood up.

'Your Honour, there is the matter of returning the children after contact. Notwithstanding your finding on her complaint that Mr Sams breached the injunction only this morning, my client is genuinely anxious about him coming to the house, and of course there is still an injunction in place preventing it. My client would prefer a handover location that is neutral and in public...'

'Oh yes...' Fosse's voice had a definite edge. 'The injunction. Well. I think Mrs Sams will simply have to overcome her reluctance, because given my findings, or rather, the lack of findings, it is unreasonable to prevent Mr Sams from approaching the family home.'

'No, Ms Wynne,' Fosse snapped, as Eliza rose to object.

'It is not, in my opinion, desirable for very small children to be carted back and forth to McDonalds car parks or petrol station forecourts for collection, like parcels, especially close to their bedtime. It is disruptive. If Mr Sams will give the court an undertaking not to make any attempt to *enter* the marital home in which Mrs Sams and the children are living,' – Fosse looked over at Hallett and Ed, who gave a brief nod – 'I now discharge the non-molestation order and its conditions, and for the benefit of the children, order that Mr Sams hands over the children to their mother at their own front door.'

Cherry knew she needed to make immediate notes on her impressions of the court day. Turning on her laptop she saw it was almost out of juice. As she rifled in her bag for the charger, her fingers touched an envelope.

God, yes, Fergus. What *had* he given her?

Cherry shook out a CD and looked at it curiously, then slid it into the disk drive of her laptop. As she waited for the disk to whirr itself open, Cherry clicked on a new email that had arrived from Ben Temple.

Dear Cherry, she read.

Of course I remember reporting on the deaths of your mother and brother. I was a young journalist then, and your father's trial was the most serious case I had covered at that point in my career.

I note that you are also a journalist now; I have seen your byline many times. Because I moved away from Bristol, and now live in Dale, not all that far from your aunt and uncle, I've occasionally heard about your family through local networks.

You're welcome to give me a call, or if you're in the area, drop by the

sailing club in Dale which is where I'm based. If you can give me a day or so's notice I can make sure I'm available. I will also dig out my notebooks, which I've kept from that time.
All the best
Ben Temple

Thinking ahead about existing work commitments, she typed a rapid reply.

Dear Ben
Thanks so much for getting back to me. How about a week today? Around lunchtime? I can meet you at the sailing club.
Very best
Cherry

As she sent the email, a .wav file appeared in the middle of her screen. So the CD contained an audio recording. The file name was a jumble of capitals and numbers that would be indecipherable to anyone who didn't mooch around the family courts for a living. Cherry could glean that BS17P00312 was a private family law case, as denoted by the letter P.

What on earth was Fergus playing at? It was a serious contempt for the court audio to be given to anyone, let alone a journalist. If it was found out, he would be marched out of the court building, instantly sacked for gross misconduct. Without a second thought, she pressed 'play'.

It was the start of a hearing. Lawyers' voices chuntered on in the background before the judge came in. How long would she have to listen to the recording, Cherry wondered, before grasping what was really going on? She was about to bin the envelope which had held the CD when she realised that on it had been scribbled *Start 06'57"*. A time stamp, Cherry realised. Fergus was nothing if not efficient. Scrolling forwards, she heard a precise and tiny female voice.

'I know this has been referred up to me but I'm afraid I've had no time to read these papers.'

It was Fosse.

The shock of hearing the judge's voice once again, this time inside her flat, made Cherry's skin crawl.

'I suppose you're going to say I need to adjourn for an hour to read through everything, but that is disproportionate, frankly, for this sort of case.'

A female lawyer's voice was heard next. Startled, Cherry realised it was Eliza. 'Your Honour, as you see there's a considerable bundle including both parties' statements, witness statements, and police disclosure, and I do think you'll need, well, yes, approaching an hour...'

Fosse's voice cut across. 'No I won't. We'll get straight on. This isn't a children case. It's a case where grown adults are squabbling. They are usually a complete waste of court time so let's just sort it out quickly so our overstretched system can get on with looking after children who are really at risk. I'm not even sure why it's come in front of me.'

Eliza tried again. 'Your Honour, this case has been sent up by the magistrates because there is a particularly serious allegation which they felt would be better heard...'

'Yes, well, it's refreshing to hear that magistrates feel they aren't competent to make a decision, given the mess I'm typically presented with when a case has first been in front of *that* bench.' Fosse's tone was so snide that Cherry's eyebrows jumped.

She knew that many lawyers felt disquiet about the way magistrates – lay people, not qualified lawyers, let alone experienced ones – presided over cases, but she had never before heard a judge speak of them with such outright contempt.

There was the sound of flicking pages as Fosse went through the file.

'A child's faeces smeared by the applicant father onto the respondent mother's face. Well, that's novel, at least.'

Suddenly a loud tapping noise came over the audio. Cherry jumped, then remembered Fosse's tic of tapping her pen on the desktop.

'Yes, Your Honour,' said Eliza. 'In fact there are six allegations made by my client...'

'I'm not hearing six. I'll hear the most serious one.'

Eliza was audibly restraining herself at this point, Cherry thought.

'Your Honour, two of the allegations are linked. Those two at least will need to be heard.'

'If they're linked, Ms Wynne, just bundle them up together,' said the judge. 'Let us at least try to be efficient.'

In the pause that came next, Cherry could hear a snuffling sound that she couldn't quite make out.

Fosse carried on. 'I suppose this whole exercise is in aid of the mother trying to restrict the father's contact with the children?'

The snuffling, Cherry now realised, was actually the sound of sobbing caught on the court's overhead microphones, which hung down over the rows of desks at which the lawyers and their clients sat.

Eliza was now clearly having to bite back anger. 'One child, Your Honour, as is set out in the papers. Her name is Tally. She is eleven, and currently unable to attend school due to an anxiety disorder. To answer your question, yes, if findings of domestic abuse are made then I imagine my client may wish to pursue such a course.'

'Look,' Fosse's voice was snappish. 'Whatever happens there's going to be contact.'

Cherry caught her breath. Could a family judge have actually said that?

'Your Honour, I must point out that practice direction 12J requires you to consider how contact with a perpetrator of domestic abuse will impact on the child *and* the victim, and take that into...'

'Ms Wynne, I warn you, do not get ahead of yourself.' Fosse's voice had turned icy. 'There have been no findings yet. And there may never be any. So no more talk of 'perpetrators' please. Now.' Two sharp taps of the pen split the air of Cherry's kitchen. 'Anything else before we get on?'

There was a pause, while, Cherry supposed, Eliza gathered herself.

'Your Honour, yes. My client requested screens in court for today's hearing. They aren't yet in place, so we just need to...'

'Screens? Really?' An impatient sigh. 'Is this going to be one of those ludicrously transparent efforts to make me look more sympathetically on your client? I do hope not. It never works with me, you know.'

'No, Your Honour. It is not that.' Eliza was now biting her words out. 'My client is anxious to...'

Fosse interrupted. 'Because it has been known.'

Eliza did not back down. 'She is *understandably* anxious not to have to give evidence on sensitive matters while being watched by her alleged abuser. She wants to be able to properly engage with the court...'

'Complainants do try to take advantage,' Fosse snapped. 'I've been on this bench for a long time. And it goes on. No, Ms Wynne, there is no use looking at me like that, I can assure you it does.'

Eliza paused, and then spoke calmly but insistently. 'I draw Your Honour's attention to the fact that it has previously been agreed and ordered that screens should be up. That order is in your bundle.' Her tone was studiously neutral, 'At tab B62. I can take you to it.'

'Ordered by the magistrates I suppose? They always seem very keen on screens.' The veneer of amusement was paper thin.

'Ordered by the judge who very briefly case-managed this case before it came to you, Your Honour.'

A single sharp rap rang out. 'Oh very well. But the screens are not very convenient for this courtroom. It will take time for the ushers to sort it all out.'

'I am grateful, Your Honour,' said Eliza evenly. 'I have already spoken to the ushers. They have been most obliging. I believe the screens are on their way.'

Then Cherry heard a rustling sound, and a new voice. A woman was speaking through sobs, her voice low, her anger mixed with hopelessness.

'What... on earth? What sort of farce is this? You...' – the sobs rose, but the voice carried on, pushing through – '*you* can't hear my case. What sort of a judge are you? You've already decided against me.'

Cherry felt herself reeling. With a judge in such a mood, how on earth would the hearing go at the point when the woman got on the stand and was asked in detail about some of the most painful events of her life? And... given the legal ban on publishing any of the extraordinary interchange she had just heard, what on earth was she going to do with such explosive material?

Cherry drained her tea fast, oblivious to its heat. In any other scenario where such damning information was leaked by a whistleblower on the inside, it would be seen as journalistic gold – and she would have no compunction about publishing. Because it was a private family court hearing, however, every word spoken was protected by statute, and the only person who could give her permission to make it public was the judge.

Her Honour Judge Ruth Fosse.

Clearly, she couldn't go and ask her.

Cherry flung herself to her feet, groaning in frustration. The situation was ridiculous. Nobody could talk about what happened in the family court or they were in contempt. Journalists couldn't investigate the veracity of what parents told them by cross-checking against the paperwork or courtroom transcripts, or they too were in contempt. That meant nobody could tell the public when judges behaved abominably, or even unlawfully – and the only way to shine a light on any of it was to make expensive applications, case by case, for permission to publish.

That in itself could put people at risk. Even if Cherry was to request that another judge decide on her application to report the dialogue she'd just heard, awkward questions would be asked as to how she got hold of the audio. Then she would have to refuse to tell the court, because she could never incriminate a source. It was not a fun prospect.

Best case scenario, even if she was given permission to publish and Fosse was publicly embarrassed, she wouldn't be sacked. Judges never were, no matter if what they did was grossly and objectively unfair, or even unlawful. It was a job for life.

Before Cherry could cogitate further, her phone rang. Maggie. Briefly, Cherry squeezed her eyes shut, then pressed the button to accept the call. She was on the back foot – she should have called her aunt back. Guilt now mixed with trepidation. Was she going to face her with what she'd discovered in the newspaper archives?

'Hello lovely.' Margaret's voice was too bright. Cherry could hear the effort in it. 'Steff told me you went. To the prison. Sorry... I... well, I'm just ringing to see how it went with... well, to see how you are.'

'Oh Mags.' Cherry shook her head. She loved her aunt, but having discovered that Margaret had not allowed her sister to come back to the farmhouse after Ralph had been given access to the family home, she felt anger rippling close to the surface. It was why she hadn't phoned back immediately. Plus, Cherry thought, her relationship with her only remaining parent was entirely up to her. She was entitled to visit her father.

'Look,' she said, guardedly. 'I know you're worried sick. But I'm still trying to get my head round all of this. I'm... I'm finding so much out.'

There was a long pause at the end of the line.

'Right.' Margaret fell silent. Cherry realised her aunt was having to exert immense control. After a few seconds, Margaret asked, 'Is there anything you want to tell me about what happened? What he said to you?' Her voice fell away. 'It can't have been easy.'

Her aunt might be concerned about how she'd coped, Cherry thought. But it was clear Margaret also desperately wanted to know what her father had told her, how he'd come across after two decades in prison. But why?

'It's difficult, Mags,' Cherry said. 'Because I want to understand more about what happened. And he can tell me. And...' it came out in an accusatory burst she couldn't hold back, 'you haven't told me everything about that time have you?'

Her aunt stuttered, but no words came down the line.

Cherry took a breath. Okay. She was going to do this.

'I went to the archives in Bristol library. I read the old newspaper reports. You did an interview. You told that reporter you wouldn't let us come back to Waun Olau after mum went to court. When you knew the judge wouldn't stop him coming to our house...' Cherry was suddenly gulping for breath.

'You *knew* he was dangerous and you didn't...' She heaved a breath in and then pushed the words out, feeling a gush of tears on her cheeks. 'You didn't *make* us come back to where we'd be safe.'

Chapter Twenty-Five

Cherry had been staggered to get a message from Ed suggesting that they meet again, this time at the university.

After the way their last meeting had panned out, she was relieved that this interview would be on a more formal footing. No more pubs. No more climbing walls. She shook her head at the memory of being persuaded - tricked? - into that 'deal'. What had she been thinking?

Locking her bike to the futuristic IT building's sleek cycle-racks, she texted Ed to let him know she had arrived and pushed through gleaming glass doors into an airy atrium. There was no reception desk and barely a soul to be seen. The space was dotted with furniture that was all angles and edges. Cherry had barely confirmed her suspicions as to the designed-in unfriendliness of the seating when she saw Ed descending the open staircase. He waved. She nodded back. Friendly but business-like was to be today's setting for the interview.

Ed had a lofty corner office with plate glass windows at right angles giving a vast view over the concrete campus. He ran his hand through his hair as he considered Cherry, who was setting up her audio recorder and notebook at the meeting table.

'It's good of you to come. Here I mean.'

Cherry looked up. 'Well, after what happened in court...' she tailed off.

Ed turned to her. 'I just don't want you to think I would do that, break an injunction, turn up at the house...'

Cherry shook her head. 'I don't know what happened that morning.' She rubbed her eyes. 'It was very awkward, the whole court thing, I'm well aware. I'm just grateful you're still willing to talk to me.'

Ed took a deep breath in and sighed. 'What choice do I have, if I want people to have a proper sense of just how horrendous it all is?' He paused. 'Look, let's focus on today.' He glanced at her audio recorder. 'You're taping this?'

'Just as notes,' Cherry replied quickly. 'Not for anyone else to hear.'

'Right. Right.' Ed walked over to the desk and sat down, then instantly stood up again to make sure the door was shut.

He really wasn't at ease, Cherry realised. That was a first. Having faced cross-examination by Eliza Wynne, surely he couldn't feel anxious at the prospect of being asked questions by a journalist? And the fact-finding judgment had gone his way – he was in a far stronger position now than he had been to date, certainly since the non-molestation order had been put in place a few months ago.

'You're still happy to go ahead?'

Ed drifted across his office and stood fiddling with the coffee machine that was set on a side table. 'Yes. Yes. I suppose – well, court was very exposing about some quite private stuff. I think – well, I want to know how much of that will go in your article?'

'You mean the, um, more intimate allegations?'

'The rough sex stuff? Well, yes, I guess. That. But more what she says about how I am with the kids. Which I am absolutely not.'

'It was all evidence, set out in court. So yes, some of it at least will be in the article, if I'm allowed to report it,' Cherry said. 'It has to be, or nobody will understand why you and Kathie are in court. But remember, you – the whole family – will be anonymous.'

Ed set two mugs of coffee down on his desk. 'Can we be? Realistically?'

'Yes,' Cherry said determinedly. 'If the court gives me permission to publish. I promise.'

Ed looked doubtful.

'It's not just about using pseudonyms, remember,' Cherry reiterated. 'I can change the kids' ages. I can give you and Kathie different jobs. I would never specify where you live. These are the kinds of changes we make all the time so that a story can be told.'

It was up to him now. Cherry sat back in her chair and waited.

Then Ed nodded quickly, twice, and sat himself down opposite her. 'Okay. That seems fine. Let's do it.'

'Great.' Now Cherry looked directly at Ed. 'After that last hearing... how are you?'

To her surprise, given the result had gone in his favour, Ed immediately looked uncomfortable. 'Not great.' He raised his eyebrows at Cherry's questioning expression. 'Well, you saw it. Watching Kathie get treated like that.'

'You got the decision you wanted, though,' Cherry observed neutrally. 'The judge didn't believe her.'

Ed's laugh barked out. 'No. But you're forgetting... she's my children's mother. I saw her give birth. She was extraordinary.' He stopped, his lips pressed together. 'We're linked forever because of that. And who actually wants to end up in a courtroom trying to make the person you loved look like a liar?' Ed rubbed his eyes, the pressure of his hands reddening his skin. 'Sitting there as my lawyer tore into her was fucking grim. I *never* want to see that again. It's not me. It wasn't us. It's a terrible place for a relationship to end up.'

What had Ed imagined would happen when he issued an application to force more contact with his kids, Cherry wondered. That his wife who hated and feared him, would just... roll over and agree?

'So was the court hearing – the process – not what you expected?' she asked carefully.

'It was horrific. Actually, I'd say it was abusive.'

Cherry pursed her lips. She hadn't expected this.

Ed continued. 'What my barrister put her through, I could hardly believe it... and what her lawyer said to me, that vile, passive-aggressive way they put their points, the imputation that we were both there in bad faith, the outright charge that I was a liar, and that she was a liar...' He shook his head again despairingly. 'Kathie and I are just ordinary people. Ordinary parents. With standard flaws and failings. And the *shittiness* of those lawyers' approach to trying to find out what had happened between us just staggered me.' He drained his coffee in a single gulp. 'I just sat there trying to remove myself mentally but inside I felt... rage at what this system puts people through. What it was putting Kathie through.'

Cherry had to challenge him. 'But some might say you'd set off this whole process. What did you think would happen?'

Steadily, Ed looked back at her. 'Two things I'd say to that. First, you don't have much idea before you embark on it, what the reality of a legal fight will be like. But...' he laughed hollowly, 'what option, really, did I have? I didn't treat her in the way she's saying, and I have to prove it, or I lose my kids.' His gaze turned steely. 'And second, I will *not* lose my children. It is impossible for me to contemplate, literally impossible, that I would never be trusted to care for them... watch them as they fall asleep, have them run in and jump on me in the morning... I will *not* have that taken away from me. Not by Kathie. Not by anyone. And certainly not on the basis of a lie.'

Ah. So he *was* now saying Kathie had lied. Cherry saw that he'd caught himself and was looking slightly abashed.

She moved in.

'This is the tricky part, isn't it?' she said conversationally. 'And it's the bit I'm interested in, which is the bit the court doesn't seem to do much thinking about. If Kathie's making it all up, about you hurting and frightening her, and being a risk to Brandon and Lola, why is she doing that?'

She watched as Ed chewed over her question. She waited, refusing to fill in the gap.

Eventually, Ed sighed. 'It's hard to speculate, isn't it?' he said. 'What I think happened, well, I may perceive it very differently to how she saw it. Sometimes I've wondered if the power difference between men and women – I mean the physical difference – means that an action is experienced entirely differently by me than it is by her.'

Cherry nodded. Women were aware of potential danger in a way that men just weren't. Had never needed to be.

Ed's mouth twisted. 'I know it sounds like I'm making excuses. Like with the... well, with the sex stuff.' He looked down at the table, speaking slowly. 'God, this is grim. But I'll have to try, I suppose. When you're playing with control, with power, because it's obvious you both get off on it, then consent, over the years, might get blurred. You might think you have it by default, you might think you know what someone likes. But you might be wrong. Or you might be right sometimes, and wrong other times. So it's not always obvious. And then... your partner might not want to tell you you've got it wrong, to save you embarrassment. Or... they might not always know what they want to try out and what they don't. That giving up of control, well, it might mean allowing yourself to see if something you don't think you'll enjoy – or don't enjoy immediately – ends up being something you actually find you like.'

He squeezed his eyes closed. 'These boundaries are subtle. If you don't have really good communication then things can go wrong, quite fast, without anyone meaning it to.'

One of the risks of interviewing anyone, Cherry knew from long experience, was that of being drawn into their worldview. Because even the wickedest person on the planet felt they were right and justified in what they had done. Ed wasn't the wickedest person on the planet, nor possibly even a bad one. And the human condition, Cherry also knew, was infinitely varied. What Ed had just said made perfect sense. People drew different lines in different places. A shout by a man in the middle of a row could be, to him, just a shout, but as a woman with her own particular childhood history, Cherry would always hear in a man's raised voice the possibility of her own annihilation.

'But you don't deny that domestic abuse happens? That rape can happen inside a relationship?'

Ed looked appalled. 'Of course I don't.'

'What about those photographs? The bruising Kathie reported. She said you bit her.'

Ed shook his head decidedly. 'I am *not* violent. And I have never raped Kathie. The idea is revolting.' He choked on the words, then dropped his head into his hands and rubbed his temples. Muffled, Cherry just about heard him say, 'It makes me feel sick.'

She paused. How far should she push? 'Do you think she made it up, how she got that bruising?'

When Ed took his hands from his face, his eyelids were red and his skin flushed.

'Like I just tried to explain, I think she and I have very different perceptions of what happened. More so towards the end. Maybe she exaggerated some stuff because she was so upset. Maybe it wasn't an exaggeration to her.' He looked intently at Cherry. 'But the judge seemed to grasp that there are complexities in relationships. And they shouldn't be redefined afterwards to make things seem worse than they were.'

They were poised now, Cherry realised, at a critical point, because if domestic abuse had not fractured Ed and Kathie's relationship, what had?

'If she's redefined events, re-interpreted things that happened between you, whether in bed or not – why?' Cherry asked. 'Why has this become such a poisonous break up?'

The silence stretched. At first, it was a gap into which Cherry could almost hear Ed's thoughts clashing against each other in confusion. Finally, he met her eyes with a faint smile and a barely-there shake of the head, as if in wonderment.

'On that count, I have absolutely zero idea,' he said lightly. 'No clue. Not a fucking scooby.'

It was entirely unsatisfactory as an answer, Cherry mused as she cycled home. She'd pressed him for more insight into the deterioration of his marriage, but Ed had been unable or unwilling to dive any deeper. He'd seemed bewildered at what he clearly felt was Kathie's unreasonable, verging on unhinged, refusal to contemplate him spending time alone with Brandon and Lola. And his outrage at the idea that he was a threat, let alone actually abusive, was obviously heartfelt.

He was having the kids that weekend, and was clearly looking forward to it. 'Here, on my own... we can be free,' he'd said. 'It's the only way I can describe it. I can just be their dad, without any suspicion and no need to have anyone...' he'd almost spat out the word, '*supervising* us.'

As she raised an eyebrow, Ed had fixed Cherry with an intense gaze. 'Do you have any idea just how offensive it is to have a judge – the state – tell you that you can't be trusted with your own children? For their mother to tell a court you are a threat? The feelings it brings up... I've never been so angry. Or so humiliated.'

Shamed in front of a court. Then as friends and colleagues gradually came to know the situation, they were further embarrassed. The bitterness of that sting would not dissipate anytime soon, she understood. But Ed's lack of – what was it, willingness, or ability? – to either suggest or analyse possible reasons for Kathie's compulsion to escape their relationship was troubling. He knew she was unhappy, at least to some degree, but had been unable to articulate any reasons as to how that unhappiness had begun, and then grown. She'd got the distinct impression that for Ed, while there had undoubtedly been unpleasant moments in his marriage to Kathie, being her husband had not been intolerable at all.

Chapter Twenty-Six

Cherry had, to her own surprise, taken Eric up on his offer to accompany her to meet Ben Temple, the former Bristol Post reporter, when he'd phoned her the night before to ask if she'd like to meet again.

'Maybe for a better coffee... or something more exciting?' he'd ventured. 'No archive news articles involved?'

She had barely seen another living soul in the days after interviewing Ed. Bashing out copy for well-paying but ultimately unfulfilling copywriting jobs was acceptable in small doses – and right now, they were the only thing keeping her finances afloat – but she couldn't tolerate her own four walls any more, and the prospect of spending some time with a human being who didn't prompt feelings of fury and guilt (Margaret), aching hopelessness (Garth) or trepidation (any thought of re-contacting her father) was suddenly overwhelmingly attractive.

But no, she couldn't go out for a drink or anything else tomorrow evening she'd said, as she was heading to Pembrokeshire.

Were any drinks to be had in Wales, Eric had asked. Because if so, he'd be happy to buy her one there. Cherry had stumbled over her answer. Go on a day trip to west Wales with this man she barely knew, but who seemed to like her... she felt unmoored, not knowing the right answer, or what Eric's intentions were. Then she'd lambasted herself; could he not just want to get to know her better? Was it really so odd for someone to be spontaneous? Also... it had felt simple and just... easy to be in Eric's company the other day. Simple and easy was what she wanted. What she needed.

And so now, here she was, pulling up in front of Bristol Parkway in

a silver Audi saloon she'd hired which was a vision of corporate con-
formity. And there he was, looking ready for a tramp across a wet and
windy hillside.

Surprised at how her mood lifted as she saw him, Cherry slid the
passenger window down and waved.

'Blimey. Should I have smartened up?' Eric glanced doubtfully at
the car, and then at his worn jeans and rain jacket.

'We got lucky,' she said with a grin. 'I asked for the cheapest, but
this was all they had left.'

She had on a chunky red polo neck, grey leggings and black
Converse boots for their trip to the coast, and as a result looked like a
teenager who had sneaked her parents' car without their knowledge.

Chatting to Eric was uncomplicated and fun, Cherry realised, because he did not appear unduly tortured by his own issues or family
traumas; in fact, she found it hard to dig out much about his background at all. She decided to find out more about his academic passion. 'So. Lichens v homicides,' challenged Cherry. 'Convince me.'

'Complex photosynthesising symbiotic organisms made up of
fungi and algae that cover up to ten percent of the earth's surface,' Eric
told her, grinning. 'Intriguing, no?'

Cherry's forehead wrinkled. 'Mmm. Tell me the most exciting
thing about them.'

'Ah. Well. Sometimes fungi and algae decide to split up and go their
separate ways, but sometimes they get tired of being single and team
up with other fungi or algae and become lichens again?' Eric offered.

Cherry squinted at him. 'Thrilling to you, I'm guessing.'

'Well, you're breathing oxygen created by lichens right now so
they're keeping you alive. Which means at least they're useful.'

'And pretty,' Cherry observed.

'Oh, don't get me started on the different varieties,' Eric laughed
darkly. 'Lichenologists can get poetic when it comes to the different
forms and colours. There are a lot of ways of describing yellow and
green. But better to see them.' He paused. 'I can take you to my study
site one day if you like.'

Cherry hooted out loud. 'What a line!' She glanced across at him.

'Sorry. Just... hot date!'

Suddenly they were both snorting.

'I've never taken anyone to my study site before,' Eric protested through gasps.

'Lucky, lucky me.'

Collecting herself, Cherry steered the car onto the M4. As they drove, she had to drag it out of him that once a week, he volunteered at a Bristol project that helped people off the streets.

'That's... really quite worthy,' she teased.

Eric didn't answer.

Shit. She'd hit a bum note. 'Obviously I'm being shallow and flippant.'

'It's just what speaks to me,' he said lightly. 'Some people have more house than they need. Some people don't even have a roof. And without a home you struggle to make much of a life.'

The tide was out as they crossed the Severn Bridge, mudflats visible beneath the shallow wash of water. As they drove past the Newport turnoff, she barely thought of Garth. By the time they'd reached Cardiff they'd diverted to a surprisingly tricksy numberplate game that Eric suggested which involved replacing one of the three registration letters with another to create an acronym. The twist was, you had to know what the acronym stood for. Cherry discovered she was rather good at it, and the bantering competitiveness that the game engendered got them as far as Carmarthen, at which point the reason for her meeting with the former journalist began to resurface.

It was too extreme to characterise her feeling as one of impending doom, Cherry told herself sternly. But Eric noticed her drop in energy.

'Something up?' he asked.

Cherry didn't answer for a while. What could she say? Eventually, she replied. 'Let's have some music.'

Push it all away again, if only for another hour.

The sailing school owned by Ben Temple was operating at full stretch, despite it being early July and school holidays not yet having started. A dozen dinghies with red and yellow sails were dotted across the bay, dashing between buoys as a gusty wind scuffed the sea.

Temple, a compact, muscled man who, Cherry assessed, might just have hit his fifties, was tying up a small rib on the pontoon in front of the Griffin Inn. As she and Eric approached along the gravelly foreshore, Temple jumped out of the boat and walked up the pontoon, the assurance of a man with a physically active life apparent in his step. As he reached the end, his sunburned face broke into a smile.

'So. Good god. Cherry Magraw, from twenty years ago.' She saw him clock the scars on her cheek; that slight narrowing of his eyes and tiny flick downwards and away. 'This doesn't often happen. It is...' Temple paused, unsure how to frame his next word, given the circumstances, then simply nodded. 'Well... it's good to see you.'

She knew how infrequently journalists kept in touch with the people whose stories they'd covered: there were too many tragedies to keep count of. For reporters, she reflected, it was always going to be on to the next. There was a pragmatism in that, she acknowledged as she observed the man in front of her, but often, she also knew from experience, a lingering question. What happened to those people? How did they pick up the pieces? Were their lives forever blighted, or did they, somehow, survive or even, at least in some sense... thrive?

Temple enclosed her hand in his roughened fingers, and then shook Eric's.

'I'm a friend,' she heard Eric say. 'I'm afraid I invited myself along on this trip on the pretext of buying Cherry a drink.'

Temple nodded. 'Right. Well, Dale has drinks. Café or pub? They're both over there.'

Cherry glanced at the Griffin Inn's modern extension with its outdoor seating area on the roof. The day was gusty but bright, and the wind was warm.

'Pub,' she said, decidedly.

Eric brought out the drinks. Cherry didn't bother with chitchat.

'It's strange to meet someone who covered my mother's murder and my father's trial. You know more than me about what happened.'

Temple laughed, slightly too loud. A release of tension, perhaps?

'More about some things, maybe,' he acknowledged. 'But there's a lot I could never find out.'

Cherry's eyes narrowed. 'I know there would have been loads you'd never have been able to publish. That's what I want to know about.'

'Right. Right. Of course.' Temple considered his glass more carefully than beer usually warranted. 'Well, you know I interviewed your aunt. There's not much more to tell you about that, though it was when I first met you. Or rather, saw you.' He looked up at Cherry.

'That was after the inquest. I came to the farm. Your aunt Margaret invited me. Mind, your uncle wasn't keen. Not at all. You weren't speaking then. Your aunt wouldn't let me talk to you. Which was quite right, of course,' he added hurriedly. 'But, I, well, I did use the fact I'd seen you for colour in my copy.' Beneath the weather-beaten tan, he reddened. 'My editor cut that out. Tore strips off me. Said you were entitled to your privacy, and she'd allow no bereaved child to be used to titillate readers into buying a paper. Decent woman, that editor. And yes,' he said, replying to Cherry's frown, 'I was young. Didn't have kids. It was my first big murder. I didn't get it. But I learnt.' He was struggling to look at her, Cherry realised.

'What else didn't you manage to get published?' she asked.

The silence lengthened. Cherry glanced at Eric, whose expression was calm, his focus entirely on the conversation. He pursed his lips, nodded at her – yes, she was right to press.

'I want to know,' Cherry insisted. 'It's why we've come.'

Reluctantly, Temple scrubbed at his forehead with callused fingers, then seemed to mentally brace himself.

'Well. The thing is... I went to see your father in prison. First while he was on remand, and later after he was convicted.' Temple looked at her worriedly.

As she heard the words, Cherry began to feel lightheaded. A journalist had sought out her father's version of the events of that night.

Temple continued, a smear of shame evident. 'It's not that unusual. I interviewed lots of people charged with crimes.'

Cherry inclined her head. Beneath the anger that was starting to build, she also felt a surging curiosity – the curiosity that any journalist would feel. The same desire for information that Temple had felt. *What* had her father told him, just months, maybe even only weeks, after that terrible night?

'There's a public interest in understanding crime, why something happened, the circumstances. Whether there are other, unknown victims. Whether there's remorse.' Temple huffed out a breath in a release of tension, the worst part of the conversation, he sensed, now over.

'Of course, that's rarely how the person who's in prison sees it. They meet us for all sorts of reasons, usually aimed at trying to justify what they've done. Abusers are the worst. They always have a reason. That's why they're so dangerous.'

Now he looked directly at Cherry, his face troubled. 'But I should make something clear. I didn't ask your father for an interview. He got in touch with me.'

Cherry looked over towards the bay, taking in the white tips of the waves. Her eyes registered the dinghies. Deliberately, to calm herself, she counted eleven. She searched and searched to find the twelfth. When she couldn't, her attention wandered southwards to the point where the peninsula curved round, her thoughts scattering as she tried to make better sense of what she'd just heard.

Her father had invited Ben Temple to the prison. Of course he had. Manipulative bastard. He'd just killed her mother and there he was inviting journalists to his prison cell to put out his excuses as to why. At the very same time, she now knew, as he was writing to Margaret trying to get her to bring Cherry to see him.

And now he was still calling the tune, making her work for any scrap of knowledge. Still in her head. Still controlling her life. Still her father. Her only parent. The one person who had known that little girl. Who still promised her he cared.

'Cherry.' Eric's voice cut in. 'Cherry.'

She turned her attention back to the table.

'I'm fine,' she said, her voice clipped. 'Just thinking. So, what did he say?'

Now Temple had managed the first step towards disclosure, he became garrulous in the telling.

'I went twice, as it turned out. The first time was before the trial. My first time in a prison, too – the clang of those metal doors stays with you. He was way more relaxed than I'd expected. Of course I asked him why he'd done it. He said it was complicated.' Temple's laugh was cynical. 'I've heard that one since from other men who've done similar. And I've heard them say how sorry they are, but they won't take the blame. Not really.'

Temple's gaze was faraway, over the sea. 'We didn't know at that point that he wasn't going to enter a plea to the charge of killing Bill. And obviously, we couldn't publish anything till the trial was over. But I got writing straightaway.'

Cherry could feel Eric watching her carefully. She gave him a quick smile, knowing she had to focus on Temple's words, else she might, she felt, simply levitate from the scene and out over the bay, her mind fracturing away from the pain, tumbling and dispersing in the wind.

'It always felt like he was holding out on me, in that first interview,' said Temple, musing on the memory. 'So when I got a note from his solicitor just as the jury went out, I... well, I felt excited. He'd chosen me. I was... probably flattered.'

Eric winced.

Temple acknowledged his distaste. 'Yeah, well. We're stupid when we're young.'

But what *didn't* you write, Cherry wanted to scream. What didn't you put in your story, and why didn't you publish that interview?

'I didn't believe what he told me, you need to know that,' Temple rushed on. 'Of course, by then, our readers were desperate to know why he hadn't pleaded one way or another to your brother's murder. And remember, he never gave evidence. The jury never got to hear from him how Bill died. And so he couldn't be cross-examined on his story.'

Eric spoke now, because he could see that Cherry was too tense to utter a word.

'I suppose the obvious question you'd ask is, 'Why didn't you plead one way or the other to your son's murder?' Eric suggested. 'Did you ask him that?'

Temple guffawed, the noise hitting Cherry like an assault. 'Of course I did! And this is what I mean when I say I didn't believe him. He told me, quite matter of factly, that someone else was involved.'

Cherry froze.

'So why didn't he plead 'not guilty' then?' Eric asked, not sensing Cherry's distress.

Temple shrugged. 'Well, I pressed him on it, because it made no sense. But he clammed up. He wouldn't say another word.'

At this, Cherry abruptly stood up. 'I expect you all speculated in the office, though, didn't you,' she said fiercely. 'I suppose you know where Bill was found, on the path next to the house, beneath where I climbed down to escape. Trying to get us both out.'

Temple's voice was firm. 'It was clear from experts at the trial that your father was responsible for both their deaths, whatever happened afterwards.' He looked at the young woman in front of him, his eyes gentle. 'Your father was no different from any killer who wants to get off. After the trial he was just trying to shape the story, trying to use the press to colour how the family court and prison authorities viewed him. And that's because he wanted to see you. It was obvious he wanted that more than anything.'

Temple took a breath. 'Your aunt told me he kept asking for you to be taken to the prison. That's why we didn't publish his interviews in the end. We weren't going to let him use our newspaper to campaign to see the daughter whose life he'd destroyed.'

Chapter Twenty-Seven

Leaving Dale without driving the forty-five minutes north that would have taken them to the Waun Olau farmhouse felt like a betrayal. Cherry had never been back to this farthest western edge of Wales without the purpose of her trip being to head home. So her instantly negative reaction to Eric's suggestion that she might want to drop in to see her aunt and uncle told her in a way she'd tried to ignore that she was determined to avoid questions from Margaret about her visit to the prison.

The hired Audi was a smoother ride than she'd driven in years, probably ever, she thought wryly as she nosed the car through the winding lanes bounded by hedgerows so high that they gave only brief glimpses of the glittering blue-green sea. Eric, she saw, was gazing out the window as they left Dale, looking south towards the Milford Haven oil depot, once a busy refinery. It had, for Cherry, always been a major landmark of the Pembrokeshire coast.

'You only properly see the old refinery towers from this side of the peninsula,' she remarked. 'On the northern side, you'd barely know it was there.'

'Bet the northern side's more expensive, then,' Eric grinned. 'No industrial nastiness spoiling the view.'

'It's employment,' Cherry countered. 'Skilled jobs. There's not much else round here that is, other than tourism and farming.' She thought of Margaret's determined efforts to build her flower business in the face of frequent high winds, coastal storms and delivery costs, Tom's lifetime of effort to make a living out of potatoes, and, as she moved through her teens, the realisation of the almost total lack of opportunity for herself and Steffan to build a career here in this place they both loved. She felt a nagging ache of sadness. Life would have been so much simpler if she'd stayed in west Wales, she knew. But despite everything she loved about it – the sea's exhilarating chill embrace, watching kestrels hovering over a steep cliff drop, the tangled, barely used footpaths that led from village to village, her bone-deep familiarity with the jagged edges of this land – it had not held her.

But the afternoon was too lovely to dash back immediately to Bristol, Cherry suddenly decided. 'Got any 4G on your phone?' she asked Eric, slowing down.

He fumbled for his phone. 'Er, yep. At the moment.'

'Search tide tables,' she instructed, pulling over at a minor crossroads. 'Look up Musselwick, and check for low tide.'

'Low tide is at 17.47... that's in...' Eric checked his, 'about ninety minutes.'

'Almost perfect,' said Cherry, smiling. 'No point coming all this way and not going for a swim.'

Eric looked at her quizzically 'Sure... but, did you bring your kit?'

'Who needs kit – assuming you're wearing pants of some variety?'

Eric nodded, his expression amused. 'I can't remember quite what variety, but yes, I can almost guarantee that I put some on this morning.'

As she headed for the village of Marloes rather than turning right for Haverfordwest and towards the M4, Cherry's spirits lifted. The Marloes peninsula, a jagged finger of land that demarcated the southern edge of St Bride's Bay, had been a favourite haunt of hers in her teens: as she'd got older and more confident on his boat, Tom and Cherry had motored far out into the bay to fish for mackerel and bass here, exploring the rock arches, sea stacks and smaller coves that were inaccessible by land.

Cherry was driving fast. Eric looked at her inquiringly. 'Are we on a deadline?'

'Yep, we are. The beach at Musselwick only exists for about ninety minutes either side of low tide.' Less than a minute out of Marloes, Cherry parked the Audi tight into the hedge so that she had to scramble across the passenger seat to get out. She pointed at a foot-path fingerpost pointing north. 'Prepare for the most perfect beach you'll ever see. And one of the most private.'

Bright yellow gorse mixed with the mauve of heather as Cherry and Eric picked their way along the rocky and undulating coast path. After a few minutes, she pointed at a blackened sweep of cliff face reaching down to the sea. 'In a second you'll see the sands. But I almost love the black cliffs more.' As the pair scrambled down the rough steps cut into the rock, glimpsing the sea in front of them, Cherry felt something approaching carefree for the first time in what seemed like months.

She could do this. She could research the trial. She could interview Ben Temple again, make him scour his notebooks for the minutiae of what had been said in court, confront her aunt, and, soon, face her father again with what she knew. This investigation was about piecing together her own story; this was her skill, and she could put it to use to make sense of her life and the events that had shaped it.

Suddenly, a man clad in black neoprene shorts and a zipped, black webbed top rounded an outcrop of rock, moving fast. His dreadlocks glistened with seawater, and as Cherry registered him stepping lightly up the steps towards them, she saw he had a harpoon in one hand and a heavy-duty knife strapped to his thigh. She stopped abruptly causing Eric to stumble behind her. She could feel her heart pounding. The gleamingly black-clad man bounded upwards and made to squeeze past them. Cherry found she could hardly breathe.

Cherry stepped sharply away and averted her eyes from the knife, squinting away from the scene and into the sun, pressing her back to the cliff.

'Good fishing?' Eric asked with a smile, unaware of his companion's reaction.

'Not bad,' said the just-emerged Poseidon laconically. 'Too many in fact. Want a couple?' As the man turned, the ominous effect of his black outfit and weaponry was comically offset by a bulging orange plastic Sainsbury's bag held in his other hand. He held open the bag. Just a local guy coming back from fishing.

'Er, we're not really set up for carrying or cooking them,' Eric said, glancing at Cherry, who was looking pale. 'Sorry mate, good of you.'

Cherry leaned against the warm black shale stone, determinedly ignoring the swiftly departing back of the fisherman as he ran up the steps. She knew that the strength and intent of the man's physicality had prompted the start of her reaction. His muscled shoulders and the aggressive military feel of his clothing had been the embodiment of an impending threat. The final trigger though, she knew, had been the knife. It's heft, in its sheath against his thigh. The imagined edge of it.

'Something up?' Eric was puzzled. 'Did you know him?'

Cherry shook her head. She felt the relief of propping her body against warm rock. 'Just need a minute.'

Eric looked at her carefully, then sat himself down on the path too, near but not next to her. There was a long pause.

'I sometimes get... freaked out,' she said eventually. 'Well. Actually, more often recently.' She paused, then said quietly, 'Did you see on his leg? The knife?'

Eric nodded. 'Yep. Serious blade on that.'

'Right.' A shaky intake of breath. Cherry's hand crept up to the thin, double ridge of scars on her cheek. Tears prickled. She turned to Eric, still holding her cheek.

'You never asked what happened.'

A gull chattered overhead. Eric replied, calmly, 'Well, no. But I've wondered.'

'It wasn't reported. I expect they didn't want to make me give evidence at the trial. I wasn't talking, you see, afterwards. Not for months. I don't remember when I started to speak again. But...' Cherry now had to struggle to get the words out, as her voice had gone sticky and she felt tears begin to prickle her face – a surprise, as this was not the first time she had explained how she had come by her scars, and she had always said it very matter-of-factly in the past. 'It was him who cut me.'

Her throat closed up. Why was she telling Eric this? Why now? But she couldn't stop, even though she could only get the words out slowly and every one felt painful.

'My mum was on the floor. I knew it was bad. I was on a chair. He braced my head against his side, then brought the knife up. I remember him looking at me as he cut me. It wasn't to hurt me. It was to hurt my mum.' She shook her head, incredulous at the memory. And with that, Cherry sobbed so hard her whole body convulsed, and a wail emerged that seemed to scour the cliffs around them.

Eric was silent. He didn't touch her. He didn't reach for her.

Eventually, Cherry raised her head from her knees where she'd buried it. The breeze dried her cheeks, and the perfect, empty beach, its yellow sand stretching towards a sea turned sparkling gold, offered the only available promise of release. Unsteadily, she stood, picked her way across the rocks, and, far from Eric and facing west, stripped to her underwear and walked into the water.

Swimming hard, Cherry only spotted the gleaming round head when she finally stopped to tread water and looked back to shore. The dog-like muzzle of the Atlantic grey seal had broken the surface less than ten metres away, and now two dark eyes observed her intently. So close that she could see water beading its whiskers, Cherry stared back, barely moving her arms and legs. Looking up at the rocks where she'd left Eric, she saw from his wave that he'd seen the seal too.

The seal blew water from its nostrils. Its whiskers quivered. Cherry stayed as still as she could. A thrill of delight flooded her body exactly as, minutes earlier, her fear had felled her. There was no shred of apprehension at being so close to a creature that was bigger, heavier and in every way more at home in the sea than she was. The seconds – probably no more than a minute – during which the seal stayed beside her, felt healing. It was a gift of time in which she did not have to strive to forget, sick at memories she could not push away. For a few short moments, Cherry felt she could just, simply, be.

Cherry was shivering by the time she got out and it had taken her a good half hour to warm up, so Eric took the wheel as they drove eastwards. He hadn't joined her in the sea. When she'd asked why not, he'd simply said, 'It was your time.' She had seen him clock the scars on her thighs as she'd walked back up the beach, but whereas those had always been infinitely harder for her to show in public than the scars on her face, she discovered she felt no embarrassment in front of him. The latest cut a livid line between the others. He didn't look appalled, she noted.

'Is that healed enough to get wet?' he asked.

Cherry glanced down, her fingers automatically reaching for the injury. 'Yeah. Just about.' She dressed fast, facing the sea.

Scrolling through her phone to deal with work emails as they sped along, they had just driven the winding route through Haverfordwest, Pembrokeshire's county town, when her concentration was interrupted by the sound of a WhatsApp message.

Kathie.

'Oh god.' Being constantly on call felt wearing at the best of times, but today had been emotionally sapping, and she didn't feel she had much left to give.

'Work,' she told Eric briefly, as she opened the message.

'Ed's just dropped them home,' she read. 'Lola has a lump on the back of her head, bruises on her arms. He says she fell off a swing. FFS. He's shaken her. Fuck him. They're never going back.'

A series of five photographs pinged in. Cherry enlarged the pictures. Distinguishing a lump on the back of Lola's head was too hard through her hair, though Cherry thought she could just about see a raised area. But while the marks on Lola's right arm were barely visible on the quickly snapped photo, those on the upper section of her left arm were obvious. Her outer and inner arm showed what looked like four finger marks and a corresponding thumb, in the places you'd expect if a child had been grasped hard by an adult's hand.

Closing her eyes, Cherry leaned back against her seat, her mind whirring.

'What's up?' Eric asked.

'The mother in my court investigation. She says her ex has hurt their daughter. And quite badly. She's sent pics.'

Another WhatsApp arrived. 'Brandon keeps saying, 'It was an accident',' she read.

Because he's a five-year-old boy and his loyalties to his mum and dad are split right down the middle, thought Cherry. Kathie was pan-icking. She'd doubtless spent the last 24 hours while the kids were with Ed worrying herself into a frenzy. At the same time, she understood Kathie's concern. Picking a toddler up from a fall in a playground however it happened didn't typically result in the kind of bruises she'd seen on that photograph.

Another WhatsApp pinged in, then more, each message a short, staccato burst of rage.

'I'll be making a statement to the police.'

'He CANNOT carry on like this.'

'It's everything I warned about!'

Cherry thought for a moment before typing a response.

'Email Eliza, let her know. Send her the pictures.'

'Will do.' Kathie's message was clipped. Then another message arrived.

'He's not having them on his own again. Ever.'

As the sign for Newport flashed overhead, Cherry found to her surprise that there was no accompanying jolt of pain, just a small shard of sadness. It was gone 10 o'clock when Eric pulled up in front of Cherry's flat. There was no suggestion by either of them that he should come in. As they'd left the Severn Bridge behind, she'd scrab-bled in her wallet and found the card for Clive's Taxis. Eric lived on the other side of the city: she knew it was a cop-out not to drop him home first but she was done in. Clive was waiting when they arrived.

'Not for me this time,' she said, indicating Eric.

Clive nodded. 'Of course.' He looked at Cherry. 'It's good to see you looking so well, my friend.'

Cherry smiled. 'Thank you, Clive.' Turning to Eric, whose qui-etness on the journey she understood had been deliberate, she said, 'Thanks for coming. And especially for... well... not asking too much.'

'I have questions.' Eric looked at his feet, then directly at her. 'It's not that I don't want to know. It's that... I don't know you well enough to wade in, and I don't want to... well,' he laughed quietly. 'Just saying this is already putting pressure on. And I reckon if you need anything, you need a break from what other people want.'

Tears prickled her eyes. Unexpectedly, Eric took her hand and touched it briefly to his cheek.

Formally, he said, 'I'm honoured you asked me to come.' He nodded in place of goodbye then crossed the road to Clive's taxi and dropped into the passenger seat.

Clive gave Cherry a brief wave of acknowledgement, and the taxi drove off.

Chapter Twenty-Eight

As Cherry pushed open the door to her apartment, her phone rang. She groaned. Too late, surely. Nobody called for a chat at this hour. Stuffing her keys in her mouth so she could fish her phone from her pocket, she was surprised to see the name flashing on the screen. Eliza.

Shit. That meant Kathie. Oh god. Could she bear to hear more, right now?

The barrister's soft Valleys accent did not sound so mellow tonight. 'Sorry to be calling at this hour but Kathie's asked me to let you know; the children are going into emergency foster care.'

Startled into alertness, Cherry's keys dropped to the floor as she fumbled for the light switch.

'Sorry, just getting myself through the front door. What on earth?'

The sigh that came down the line was full of mingled frustration and fury.

'You know the kids came back from contact and Lola had bruises, right?' Cherry could hear the clink of wine bottle on glass as Eliza spoke. 'Well. Soon as Ed left, and I assume once she'd called you, she took them straight to A&E. She's still there, and frankly, it's all going to shit.' Cherry heard another slug of wine going down.

'The hospital are taking it seriously; they're investigating the lump on Lola's head after scanning her, as they say it's in a place that's unlikely to have resulted from a fall from a swing, *and* they're concerned about the finger-marks. So social services got called.'

'Wow.' Cherry sat down in a heap on the sofa. 'What does that mean?'

'Well, Ed has *obviously* said it wasn't him, but he's had them on his own for the last 24 hours. So we've now got unexplained injuries to a child. And Kathie says it wasn't her, but she's been alone with them too.'

Cherry blew out a breath. 'Right.' She sat down heavily at the kitchen table. 'And the upshot is... ?'

'They've just been taken into a side room and told by a social worker that they had to sign their consent for the kids to go into 'voluntary' – and I put that word in inverted commas – foster care.' The anger in Eliza's voice was now rolling into Cherry's ear with a ferocity she'd not heard the barrister speak with before.

'Hang on.' Cherry scrabbled for her notebook and pen. 'If the social worker felt the children weren't safe with either Kathie or Ed, what's wrong with doing that?'

'Because it's coercion. It's not free consent. She told them they *had* to sign it or they'd be in court first thing tomorrow and the council would apply for an interim care order. So they did it. They signed. And I am,' Eliza declared, 'so fucked off. Social workers play this game all the time. It's a nasty trick. Legally, you cannot be asked to sign a voluntary agreement under threat. There's tons of case law showing it breaches human rights. But oh no, let's crack on anyway, because who gives a toss about the *actual* law. And so... of course, because parents are terrified when they hear the word 'court', they sign.' She sighed noisily. Cherry heard more wine sloshing into Eliza's glass at the other end of the phone line. 'Why do we fucking bother legislating? Child protection stuff should obviously just be left to a duty social worker making up their own mind, on the fly, out of hours.'

Cherry was taking rapid notes.

'Oh, this whole mess will get unpicked in the end, but not before everyone is totally traumatised,' Eliza went on. 'That social worker thinks she's protecting children but in fact she's shitting all over everyone's rights to a fair process. And she either doesn't know or doesn't care. Kathie was so distraught she didn't think to call me before she signed the paperwork, when I could have made a difference. I'm going to make *mincemeat* of that local authority.'

Finally, Eliza managed a hollow laugh through her rage. 'Sorry. Just... it's unacceptable. Everyone knows it's unacceptable. But somehow, it just keeps on happening.'

In bed, Cherry stared through darkness at the ceiling. Kathie was now in an even worse situation than she had been before. And so, frankly, was Ed. Both were being investigated as potential perpetrators of unexplained injuries to their daughter. As Ed's mother was away on holiday and Kathie had no family locally who could step in, Brandon was being despatched, at that moment, to an emergency foster placement. When Lola was discharged – and who knew when that would be – she would almost certainly follow. Eliza said Kathie had been virtually hysterical as she had told her all this. God knows how Ed had reacted, but Kathie's phone was now out of juice and so she was stuck at the hospital, incommunicado, with the ex-husband she hated and feared.

It was all, in truth, brilliant material for her story. Another potential injustice to write about. How would Kathie cope with her children now removed from her care by the state, rather than by her soon-to-be ex-husband? Would she fight? Or mentally collapse? How would Ed react? If Kathie hadn't taken the children to the hospital tonight, none of this would have ever crossed social services desk, at least if Lola's bump on the head had got better on its own. Ed would blame Kathie for the fact that their children were now in foster care, and just as surely, she would blame him. The toxic spiral of their unravelling relationship would become even more embittered; what the next court hearing might look like, Cherry could barely contemplate.

But she did know that Kathie would now use every weapon she had to fight Ed getting time on his own with the children. And she would see the forthcoming social services investigation into how Lola's injuries had been caused as the perfect opportunity to amass every scrap of ammunition she could against him.

Chapter Twenty-Nine

Stepping through the wood panelled door, Fosse seated herself beneath the fighting lion and unicorn, and swept the cramped courtroom with a cold gaze.

'Well. I am sorry to say that matters are not *at all* where I had hoped they would be this morning,' were her first words.

A reprimand, wondered Cherry, as she began typing into her laptop. Hardly a way to settle two distressed parents. The windowless room felt airless, and with Kathie, Ed and their lawyers seated so much closer together than in previous courtrooms they'd been in, the tension was palpable.

'I have brought this hearing forward at the request of both parties,' the judge intoned. 'I can see that the events of two weeks ago have caused considerable anxiety to both Mr and Mrs Sams, and I decided that the case did, indeed, require some urgent judicial oversight so we could attempt to work out how to move things forward in Lola and Brandon's best interests.'

She tapped her pen twice on the wooden desk and nodded briskly at Eliza. 'Ms Wynne?'

Eliza stood. 'Your Honour. As you'll see in your bundle, the local authority's safeguarding investigation is now complete. It has been impossible to determine to the satisfaction of the hospital how Lola came by her head injury, which thankfully is healing. Meanwhile, the consultant paediatrician is willing, though I emphasise only *just*, to accept that the bruising to her arms could have been caused by Mr Sams picking her up roughly from a fall in a panic.'

Eliza briefly glanced back at Kathie, who was sitting bolt upright, her cheeks flushed, in what Cherry could only characterise as a blaze of self-righteous fury.

'The current situation is that the children are *still* in foster care under Section 20 as we learned this morning that children's services appear to be still considering whether to apply for a care or supervision order.'

Fosse fixed Eliza with narrowed eyes, clearly displeased. 'Still considering? Surely it is obvious what will happen now, which is that the children will be going straight home.'

'Indeed Your Honour. We had hoped a representative would be here today to clarify the council's position, which has not been communicated to us, but despite several calls and emails over the last few days we have been unable to discover their intentions,' said Eliza, pointedly. 'In view of that, the parents' joint position,' Eliza nodded at her opposing counsel, sitting with Ed behind him, 'is that these proceedings remain a private law case, albeit complicated by the fact that the children are currently in 'voluntary' foster care. A situation arrived at *under duress* – against the spirit and letter of Section 20 of the Children Act – and which both parties are keen to bring to a rapid conclusion. Ideally,' said Eliza, in clipped tones, 'today.'

There was a creak at the back of the courtroom as the door opened. Into the room scurried a small, pale man in a rumpled suit holding an open laptop in front of him.

'Your Honour, my profuse apologies, I'm for the local authority,' he said as he virtually ran to the front of the court. 'Christopher Groble.' He pushed his way into the row at the front of the room, causing Hallett to have to shuffle along.

Kathie and Ed looked both bewildered and alarmed. It was the first time, Cherry realised, that she had seen Ed knocked off guard.

As best she could, Fosse drew herself up, looking thunderous.

'Mr Groble. What am I to make of this? Your lateness is extraordinary. Do I understand that the local authority has sent you to intervene in this case when there has been *zero* communication with the parties despite their best efforts to contact the social work department?'

Groble seemed barely to register the judge's displeasure.

'Yes, I am as I say extremely sorry, and having only been briefed this morning. I do apologise as I say on behalf of my client, Bristol City Council,' he rattled out, 'which has very serious concerns about this case and begs the court's indulgence but the department is as you know terribly overstretched. It now wishes me to make representations on its behalf of these children and...'

'Mr Groble. Stop speaking.' Fosse's voice cut sharply across the lawyer's waffling. 'Your rudeness to this court and the parties is unconscionable. You have my leave to remain *only* because this court's overriding duty is to these children's welfare. However, because you arrived late you missed the parties stating that the voluntary foster care agreement was arrived at through means of coercion. If so it is a most dismaying matter. So, before anything else, what have you to say about that?'

Groble threw his eyes to the ceiling. 'The council strenuously – *strenuously* – denies that there was any coercion,' he said at a canter. 'But Your Honour I am afraid, leaving that aside for one moment, I am very much afraid that I am here on an even more serious matter. It appears that Lola was readmitted last night after reporting pain, and an x-ray reviewed by her consultant this morning shows she has a fracture to her arm that was not apparent at the initial scan. As such the local authority wishes now to apply for a full care order.'

The quiet of the small courtroom was shattered.

Over the next few seconds, Cherry watched as Kathie sprang from her seat, crying out in distress. To her right, she saw Ed also leap to his feet, his astonishment plain as he could be heard saying, 'What the hell is going on? What does that mean?'

Both advocates had hurriedly turned to utter a few quick words to their clients before Hallett – Eliza was still engaged trying to calm Kathie down – faced back towards the judge. The barrister's fruity voice filled the low-ceilinged room with outrage.

'This is simply not acceptable,' he said furiously. 'I have never been involved in a case where the local authority told parents in such an insensitive way about an injury to their child.'

The sound of Kathie's sobbing engulfed the room, making it hard to hear Fosse's voice as she tried to regain order.

'Mr Hallett, you are quite right,' Fosse said. 'It is outrageous. Mr and Mrs Sams, please be assured, I will get to the bottom of this.'

She turned to the local authority lawyer. 'I am astounded, Mr Groble. This must never happen again. Even if the diagnosis was made only this morning, their child was admitted to hospital last night. The parents should have been informed. An email or phone call to the advocates would have been all it took to accomplish the task with a degree of respect for the fact that they, and let us remember, *not* the council, currently hold full parental responsibility for these children.'

Groble nodded rapidly. 'Yes indeed, Your Honour. Nevertheless,' he unfolded his hands helplessly, 'we are where we are. And the council has concerns.'

Fosse glared through her glasses. Her voice was steely. 'I want the social worker for these children in front of me – within the hour. I do not take kindly to my court being made into a theatre for a local authority to parade its power, and that is precisely what you have done.'

As everyone trooped out, Cherry glanced around. She urgently needed to hear the conversations that Kathie and Ed would now be having with their lawyers, but could realistically only listen to one of them, and only then if she was allowed in.

Kathie would be more accessible afterwards, she decided. Ed was disappearing into a side room with Hallett, so she half ran, half skipped, over to him. No time for niceties.

'Ed.'

He turned. His face, which had been shielded from her in court, was reddened and wet with tears.

'What do you want?' He indicated towards Hallett, whose back was disappearing through the door. 'I have to go.'

'Can I... can I come and listen?'

'Oh.' He closed his eyes for a second. 'Everything's gone to shit anyway, so yeah, why not?'

Hallett looked startled as Cherry walked into the small side room with his client.

'Mr Sams, I advise against this. Strenuously. Please remember,' Hallett looked at Cherry with distaste, 'Ms Magraw is also in contact with Mrs Sams.'

'I'm well aware.' Ed sat down and folded his arms. 'However I've realised, late in the day, I'll admit, that having a journalist here provides protection in the midst of what I see as a shocking abuse of process.' He looked across at Cherry. 'I want you here. And... can we speak later? I need to ask you something.'

Cherry nodded. 'Sure.' She wanted in on this conference with Ed's barrister, and she could maybe interview Ed after the hearing to get his reaction to whatever unfolded next.

'Thanks.' Ed seemed relieved. 'That's settled then. She stays.'

'Very well,' said Hallett in a clipped voice. 'But some ground rules. Nothing said in here is to be published without Mr Sam's consent. And certainly not shared with anyone else involved in the case. Most particularly Mrs Sams. Understood?'

Cherry nodded. 'Got it.'

Hallett turned to his client.

'Can they really take the kids into care? Forcibly?' was Ed's first question. His voice shook slightly.

His lawyer sighed. 'It smacks of an inexperienced social worker. So that's where we'll start. A care order at this point is disproportionate and unnecessary.'

Hallett had been intensely disagreeable to her personally, but Cherry could see the reassurance his knowledge and experience brought to Ed.

'But we wanted them out of foster care,' said Ed with a hint of desperation. 'That's why we're here today.'

Twiddling his pen in chunky fingers, Hallett looked serious. 'That is now more complicated. You have every right to remove Brandon and Lola without notice from foster care, as they are only there with your consent. In theory.'

'What do you mean, in theory?'

Hallett heaved a sigh, sat back in his seat and folded his arms across his massive chest. 'The judge is on your side, at the moment. I suspect she is not inclined to agree to the council's demand for a care order at this hearing. But putting matters plainly, if you or Mrs Sams leave this court and pick your children up, I anticipate the council will make an application for an emergency removal order. At that point, the judge may take a different view.'

Ed's face bleached of colour.

'And then... the council would *share* parental responsibility with you. And from then on, we are in a whole different ball game.'

Hallett leaned forward. 'It would be far better – strategically, I mean – for us to urge the continuation of the voluntary agreement. We can say that you have been cooperative, and as such there is no *need* for a care order. We then wait a few weeks for social workers to do their investigation, and then, assuming they've found nothing more, we ask the judge whether in all conscience, having the children in voluntary foster care is a reasonable infringement of everyone's right to family life.'

Ed's voice was shocked. 'They could be in foster care for another few weeks?'

Hallett hesitated. 'Well. These investigations take time.'

'I don't have a choice, do I?' Ed's voice rose. 'Kathie and me, as parents, we don't have any options.'

'I'm sorry,' Hallett sighed. 'At this point, there are no good ones.' The barrister heaved himself to his feet. 'Mr Sams, the judge is perfectly aware this case has not been conducted correctly by the council. That is helpful, to us, I mean. What we need to do now is keep you, and, ah, of course Mrs Sams, on the front foot. It sticks in the craw, I appreciate. But it's my best advice, and I would be most surprised if Ms Wynne were not saying exactly the same thing to your wife.'

It was three in the afternoon by the time the social worker assigned to the case arrived at court. A determined young woman in her late twenties with bouncy blonde hair, wearing bright pink lipstick, Veronica Voysey's smile as she entered court looked somewhat plastered on. The social worker was suppressing her irritation at being hauled away from other pressing tasks, Cherry assessed. It soon became clear that she was not at all in awe of Fosse and held her own opinions and judgement in considerable esteem.

'It was an emergency,' she said. 'I explained that the options were voluntary foster care for Brandon, with Lola following on discharge, or we would be left with no choice but to apply to the court for the children to be placed under a care order.'

Fosse narrowed her eyes. 'That might well be characterised as coercion, Ms Voysey. Indeed, the parents say it was.'

'I have of course read many of the judgments relating to improper use of Section 20, Your Honour,' Veronica Voysey said self-assuredly. 'But I did not make any threat. I know this will feel terrible for Mr and Mrs Sams,' she directed a smile towards them, 'but under the circumstances at the hospital that night, we could not allow Brandon to return home with either parent.'

Fosse nodded curtly, but was not letting the social worker off the hook.

'I understand from Mr and Mrs Sams' lawyers that the local authority did not offer to pay for them to take independent legal advice. You'll be aware that this failing is noted in several of those judgments you've read.'

Veronica Voysey opened her eyes wide. 'Your Honour, mother and father both told me, I have to say in rather... emotional terms, but of *course* they were upset... that they had their *own* lawyers who were already instructed in the private law dispute. I... I, well, assumed they would be taking advice from them.' She blinked rapidly and looked up at the judge, contrition written across her face. 'I'm very sorry if I was wrong to do so.' A full wattage smile was now directed at Fosse. 'But facing facts, the outcome would have been the same with or without legal advice: we cannot leave children at risk so, realistically, it was going to be a voluntary agreement or an emergency care order. In my experience, a voluntary agreement is the route parents tend to prefer.'

Chapter Thirty

Cherry nodded goodbye as she left the courtroom to the sound of Eliza entreating Kathie to take a more neutral attitude in the upcoming meetings with social services.

'The judge will view hostility between you and Ed as bad for the children,' the barrister urged.

Kathie was tense with distress, and, Cherry realised, fear.

As she took the stairs to the ground floor, through the glass barriers she saw Ed and his barrister huddled together on a bench, Ed expostulating and Hallett making ineffectual calming motions with his large hands.

Ed looked angrier than she'd seen him to date, his face flushed and his body stiff with fury.

'You need to at least *look* as if you're trying to work together in the children's best interests,' she heard Hallett say.

Should she speak to Ed now, ask him for his reactions to the day's events? It was later than she'd thought and she needed to get home. Eric was coming over. A date? Maybe, sort of. She didn't know. But she wanted to shower and change, and she was going to hit Bristol's rush hour, which on a bike was never fun. She walked quickly out of the building, not saying goodbye to Ed, feeling a little bit guilty, but not enough to turn back. He'd wanted a word. But she could contact him tomorrow.

As she pushed open her front door, Cherry's stomach flipped. A reply from her father. She recognised his writing instantly, though the envelope was half hidden beneath junk mail. She groaned, realising how foolish she had been to include a return address on her letter. Her father had now entered her home. She had given him that access.

Cherry felt lightheaded. She'd eaten almost nothing during the day. Eric was meant to be dropping by before they headed out for a drink, a prospect she had anticipated all day with a mixture of excitement and trepidation, disloyalty to Garth and also deliberate abandon – why shouldn't she see other men if he was never going to commit? And now, when she needed a few moments to gather herself for whatever the evening might hold, a letter from her father.

She headed up to her flat and made for the refuge of the sofa, digging herself deeply into the cushions and then stretching every limb till it ached. As her toes pointed, her right calf cramped. The muscle knotted so tight it took agonising seconds to release it. An echo of the pain remained.

The letter lay on the coffee table, not malevolent, not aggressive, not wheedling, not anything, she told herself. Just a letter. Up to her when to read it. Whether to read it.

Ridiculous to pretend she might not read it.

Cherry sighed, eased herself up and made to scoop up her post. As she wandered across the living room and glanced out of the window, the extraordinary sight of Ed's head viewed from above halted her step. Cherry shook her head and looked again, hardly believing her eyes.

From this angle, she could see his dark hair set off against the cornflower blue sweater he'd worn over a shirt in court. Staggered, she watched as his fingers reached for her doorbell.

How could Ed be here?

How could he even know where she lived?

The sound of the buzzer hit Cherry like a shock.

He must have followed her bike route from the court building. Nothing else made sense.

Cherry stood stock still. What did he want? But she also had to work out whether to answer the door. And what she would be indicating if she didn't.

The doorbell rang again.

'Ed,' she said, coolly, into the intercom.

She heard him take a breath, stumble.

'Er, yes. Hi.'

'You're outside my flat?'

'Cherry.' His voice sounded hoarse. 'I'm sorry. I shouldn't be here... But I needed to speak to you, and I missed catching you after the hearing.'

She leaned against the wall, the plaster smooth on her cheek.

'Ed, I'm so sorry about what happened today. And I'm sorry I didn't stay behind – it ran late and I needed to get off.' She took a breath. 'But what are you doing here?'

'I know. Jesus. What was I thinking?' Cherry thought she heard a catch in his throat.

Why hadn't he just called or messaged, she wanted to ask. But. The trust she tried to build with every interviewee was a fragile thing. You had to offer them trust in return. Otherwise... otherwise they backed off, knowing full well that the deal they thought they'd signed up for had been undermined.

People wanted to feel Cherry had confidence in them. They wanted to feel that she thought they were, if not right about everything, then at least good people. Building that trust wasn't a one-way road; it required trust back. And the relationship was always delicate, and all too easy to break.

Ed's voice was tortured. 'Cherry, I raced after you when I saw you get on your bike but I couldn't catch you up. So I came here because there's something I need to say. In person.'

He must have followed her bike all the way home in his car.

'Did you... follow me?'

Ed ignored the question. 'And I've been wondering whether I should ring your bell or whether I'd freak you out if I did.' He tried to laugh. From above, she saw his hands clench and unclench. 'And now I have. Christ I'm stupid. I'm sorry. I'll go.'

What did he need to talk to her about that couldn't wait? She'd been in court all day. He could have told her anything he wanted in the breaks. But it was clear she couldn't extend this discussion over the intercom system with Ed on the doorstep.

Cherry thought fast. If she spoke to him now, it could be a dramatic turn in her article: a man so desperate that he'd follow a reporter home and demand to be heard.

'Hang on a sec,' she said reluctantly, knowing she was going to have to hear him out. 'I'll come down.'

'Ah, right. Thanks. Actually...' She heard what she thought was a sob swallowed into a cough. 'I'm sorry. I just can't do this standing on the street. I promise it won't take long...' Ed tailed off.

Cherry sighed as, too fast, but tired after a long day, she pressed the front door release.

She'd been climbing with Ed, she told herself. She knew people who knew him. This might feel weird but he wasn't a stranger. Her thoughts spun around as she heard his footsteps thud softly upwards.

Ed had tried to gather himself on his way up, and Cherry opened the door to her flat to find him on the landing, smoothing his hair.

Trying to mask her reluctance, she indicated for him to come in.

'Nice place.' He glanced around. 'Just you?'

A wrong note. They both knew it.

Ed pressed his hands into his eyes, rubbed his face. He looked shattered. 'Sorry. Sorry.'

She showed him into the kitchen where the metal-framed chairs felt less social, and she hoped, less comfortable, than the living room.

'I've only got a few minutes.' Scraping a chair over the kitchen floor, she pulled her bag towards her and dug out her notebook and a pen, to show him that this was work. She sat down, pointed him to a chair. 'A friend's on their way over shortly. So.... what is it?'

Ed sat down heavily. The ensuing pause surprised her. He had seemed eager to speak. The silence lengthened. He shook his head, ducked his eyes. He was, she realised, embarrassed.

'Actually,' he hesitated again. 'I don't have something to tell you. I've got something to ask you. Well, beg you, really.'

Cherry's sense of unease spiked.

Ed's voice emerged so quietly she had to lean in.

'I need to know from you what's going on.'

Cherry frowned, perplexed. 'What do you mean, *what's going on?*'

He stared at her, the intensity of his gaze familiar to her from the focus he had brought to their climbing sessions at the wall.

'When we get the kids back, which we absolutely will, Kathie's not going to let me have them, is she? She's not going to let me see them.'

He exhaled. 'Before all this, it was going my way in court. You've seen. She couldn't back up any of what she said.'

Cherry tightened her focus on Ed. An almost imperceptible incline of the head. To show she was listening. Paying attention to him.

'Even if Fosse orders that I get them for overnights on my own, after everything that's happened, *she's* not going to let that happen, is she?'

'How is she not going to?' Cherry asked, baffled. 'If there's an order, she'll have to.'

Ed's mouth twisted. 'She'll find a way. Object. Obstruct. It'll be back to court, over and over again. She thinks I'm a risk and after what's happened now she's convinced of it.' His voice disappeared in a strangled cough as his face crumpled and he wept, hard, into his hands.

Cherry stared for long seconds as Ed struggled for control.

'I'll lose my kids and I can't...' his voice rose, 'I can't stand it.'

Cherry got up, walked to the sink, ran some water into a glass and silently passed it over. Ed swallowed it fast, his throat working hard.

Had he hurt Lola, Cherry wondered again, a question that had constantly been in her mind. If he had, was it intended? Or had he briefly lost control? She needed to ask. It was her job to ask. But she hesitated.

'There'll be no regular weekends, or holidays. Kathie's already told me... she's said I can't count on anything. She'll protect them from me, whatever it takes.'

He was shaking now, his words choppy. 'Whatever it takes. It's a joke. What does that mean?'

Now. She would ask him now. But as the question started to form,

Ed leaned over the table and grasped her left forearm. 'I've got to know what she's told you.'

Cherry pulled back. What was he thinking?

'Ed.' Her voice came out shocked. Indignant.

He tightened his grip. 'You've spent hours with her. What's she going to do?' His cheeks were wet and his words came faster now. 'She's going to find a way to take them away from me. *Isn't she?*'

Cherry tried to rationalise what was happening. Ed was focused entirely on his own anticipated grief for the loss of his children. He was catastrophising. But... he was also hurting her.

'Ed.' She balled her other hand into a fist and rapped her knuckles hard on the table. The sound reverberated through the flat. 'Let go. Now.'

But there was no release of pressure. Instead, Ed leaned in, pressing her arm into the table. Her wrist bone dug against the hard surface. Cherry gasped, feeling sweat spring up on her face. She tried to say, 'Get *off*' but he spoke over her.

'If you know she's going to do a runner you have to – you know this, don't you Cherry – you *have* to tell the court.'

In a second, Cherry's mind flipped. He wasn't listening, she understood that now. She had to make choices. How to manage the next seconds... minutes? Defuse or attack? Normalise this outrage – offer him a chance to walk out with dignity intact? Or fight?

The skin between her wrist and the table felt as if it was splitting. She pressed down on the panic and the pain. She would restore normality. Push away the possibility of danger.

Her voice was sharp. 'Ed, listen up. This is how it is. You are my source. And Kathie is also my source.'

She felt his fingers press deeper into her forearm. She hadn't thought he could hold her arm any harder. Men's physical strength was always a surprise.

She held the pain away from her. The effort was immense. She considered her pen in her right hand. She changed her grip. Now it was no longer held between her fingers and thumb but in her fist.

'Whatever each of you tells me stays in confidence.'

Her arm was on fire.

'Ed, I'm letting you know that I will not – *cannot* – tell the court or you – anything Kathie says to me.' Cherry leant in, looked directly into Ed's eyes. They were swimming with tears.

'You need...' she took a breath to manage the pain, 'you need to understand I'm not part of this.'

He would loosen his grip. Blood would rush back and the burning would stop.

Ed shook his head as if in sorrow.

Pain blazed through her. What could she say to get through to him?

'Ed. I'm not your friend. I'm not Kathie's friend. I'm here to tell both of your stories. That's my job. It's what I do.'

His fingers, like iron, dug into her flesh. The pain was roaring. Cherry felt fear shoot through her in a sick burst. This wasn't ending. She couldn't reason with him. Was he even hearing her? Or had he heard loud and clear?

She decided.

They both gasped as she stabbed her pen into the bright blue wool of his sweater, pushing into the flesh where his shoulder met his chest.

A beat. Ed's eyes, incredulous, met hers. As his lips curled into a grimace, Cherry pressed deeper. It felt good. Then she pulled her fist down. Hard. Fast. She felt resistance, then give.

'Get... off... me,' she ground out.

They both heard the pen break.

Then he took his hand from her arm.

* * * * *

He had left quietly. Strangely, she'd half waited for him to say a goodbye which never came. Then she had counted his footsteps down the stairs, not moving from the kitchen table.

Cherry felt giddy. She had freed herself. Taken control. *Made him go away.* She hugged herself and laughed out loud. Glee surged through her. She threw herself on the sofa, glorying in the strength she suddenly felt.

Seconds later, elation shifted to a sense of dread.

She had stabbed him. She had done it on purpose.

What would Ed do with that?

In this whole mess of allegation and counter allegation in the family court, the only person who could now be shown to have been violent was Cherry, the reporter who was meant to be objective, independent, standing outside of the case.

Turning her head, she saw a drop of blood that had landed on the leg of a chair next to the one Ed had been sitting on. The blood had rolled down the smooth iron surface, brightest red where it was streaked thin, darkest where the liquid had slowed to a full stop.

There were other drips, she saw now as she turned her head to gaze around her. They must have sprayed when he had pulled out the pen with a grunt, the first sound she'd heard since embedding it in his shoulder.

As his hand had released her arm, Cherry had felt her own blood surge back through her veins, flooding her capillaries. At the same moment, she watched crimson bloom through the wool of Ed's sweater.

He'd got up in a clatter and begun pulling kitchen drawers out.

'Tea towel. Anything.' His voice was rough. 'I need to stop this bleeding.'

Head down, she stumbled to a drawer, handed him a folded cloth.

'What the fuck,' he muttered, leaning against the sink. 'Antiseptic? First aid kit?'

She nodded. Reaching under the sink, she pulled out her kit, handed it to him. Then, she retreated.

She had to stay small. Stay out of his way. Reduce herself. Disappear.

'You're going to have to help.' Ed stripped off his jumper and pressed the wadded tea towel back over the wound. He nodded at a roll of adhesive tape. 'I can't cut it and hold this.'

Silently Cherry tore off a strip and held it out.

'I can't,' he said. 'You do it.'

Cherry had to lean towards his bare chest to tape the dressing on. She could smell his sweat now, and also her own.

She watched as Ed found a roll of clingfilm in a drawer, picked up the broken end of the pen from the table and wrapped a sheet of the thin plastic carefully around it. The creases in the plastic turned red. He'd glanced at the collection of coats hung on the wall, taken a sweatshirt of Steff's, and pulled it over his head.

'Done here, I think,' he'd said.

Then he left.

* * * * *

Her heart was beating too fast, she could feel it. Her jaw clattered but it was impossible to clamp her teeth together and breathe at the same time, she found.

Glancing down, Cherry saw a thick, livid stripe now ran across her left forearm. The deep ache left by the pressure of Ed's full weight leaning down onto the bones in her wrist wasn't slackening.

Her chest was rising and falling faster and faster.

Cherry suddenly felt herself struggle to breathe. Her diaphragm heaved, her lungs gasped, she tried to suck in air but the muscles around her chest had clamped and she couldn't push against them. She couldn't expand her ribs. Couldn't suck air down into her belly.

She couldn't breathe.

She couldn't breathe.

If she couldn't breathe she was going to die.

Her body allowed her only tiny shallow gasps as her eyes widened and that was how Eric found her when he walked upstairs because he'd found the front door open.

'You're having a panic attack.'

He was behind her on the floor, holding her against him as she heaved for breath. 'Cherry, listen to me. This is a panic attack. You're *not* dying.'

Her words hurtled out. 'Feels... like it.' Her lungs heaved for air.

'Hold my hand.' Eric found her right hand. She grabbed it, feeling an almost imperceptible easing in the pressure around her chest.

'It'll ease off soon,' Eric said, his voice coming from behind her ear. 'I promise.'

She half-laughed through her gasps. 'How... d'you know?' She dragged in another breath.

'My dad used to get them.' Eric shifted her so that she was sitting more upright. 'Once you believe you're not going to die, it helps. Well, it helped my dad.' She heard him grin.

The tiny extra amount of oxygen that Cherry had managed to suck in thanks to the slight easing of her diaphragm meant her lungs weren't screaming quite as desperately as before.

She breathed in again, and felt her ribs expand a centimetre more. Another step towards not dying.

Eric leaned round to look at her. 'Bit better?'

Cherry nodded weakly, the relief overwhelming. 'Getting there.'

Chapter Thirty-One

Cherry opened her eyes. Her phone said 10.23am. She'd not slept so late since she could remember. And there was a mug of coffee on the floor next to her bed. It was the smell, she realised, that had woken her.

Eric. He'd stayed over. Good god, after what he'd seen.

She heard a noise in the kitchen and lifted her head to look across to the living room, where a crumpled blanket lay on the velvet sofa. Its cushions were squashed flat where he'd slept.

Eric appeared at her open bedroom door. He was barefoot and his hair was stuck up on one side, she noticed. He held a plate of toast.

'Breakfast?'

'Er, yeah.' Cherry shuffled herself upright. Self-consciously, she took the plate. 'Thanks.'

Eric sat on the floor. 'It's like Mother Hubbard, your kitchen. Bag of rice. End of cheese. That was it. I went out to get bread. Don't you eat?' He looked at her and grinned. 'How are you feeling after stabbing a man then almost suffocating to death?'

Christ. Cherry exhaled, shaking her head. Thank god Eric was here. Though there was nothing jokey about what had happened the evening before, just being with someone who could make light of it was a relief from the sickening lurch of memory which had hit her a second after waking.

'I guess I'd better enjoy my last meal as a free woman.' Would Ed report her? Why the hell wouldn't he? She'd *stabbed* him. He'd have needed medical attention. What would he have said to the doctors at the hospital?

'He'll probably lay low.' Eric crunched his toast. 'He knows he shouldn't have turned up here and threatened you. And anyway, look at your arm.'

Cherry glanced down. Her left forearm was now streaked puce and purple. It looked far worse than it had a few hours ago.

'It's nothing to what I did to him.' The sensation of pulling down hard on the pen, thrust deep into Ed's chest... she'd meant to hurt him. She'd enjoyed it.

'We should probably take pictures,' Eric was saying as Cherry's attention refocused on the present. 'I've already made a dated note of what I found when I got here last night.' He waggled his phone. 'In case you decide to go to the police.'

'What are you, a journalist?' Cherry tried to joke. It came out as a sob. She could never go to the police. Ed might have held her down, but she'd stabbed him. She knew how it would look.

Eric smiled. 'Researchers are highly trained in record-keeping, I'll have you know.'

As he snapped a few pictures of her arm with his phone, Cherry's thoughts swirled. She couldn't stay in the flat. Ed could come back any time he wanted. She also knew that as soon as she opened her emails, there would be at least one message from Kathie asking what she thought about yesterday. Telling her how frantic she felt. Wanting, wanting, wanting something from her. And on the kitchen table still, her father's letter, unopened. She squeezed her eyes shut. Her flat, which she had made her sanctuary, was no longer safe.

Cherry struggled to disentangle herself from the duvet. 'I've got to get going.' She tried to work out how much to say. 'I mean – I need to get out. I can't stay here.'

'You're actually doing a runner?' Eric's smile faded as he saw her stricken expression. 'Sorry. Just trying to lighten the mood.'

Cherry shook her head, trying to lift the corners of her mouth, but finding the effort too hard. She didn't want to say she was scared. But the way Eric was now looking at her, she didn't need to.

Eric watched her pack.

'So,' he said, his tone practical, yet quizzical. 'Where are you running to? Shall we plan an escape route? Will we need a couple of decoy destinations? Suggestions: an anonymous business hotel signed in as Ms Smith; an abandoned Scout hut deep in the Forest of Dean; or,' he hesitated, raising an eyebrow, 'my place.'

Cherry laughed out loud. 'You've got to be kidding.' Then she saw his face. 'Oh. You're serious.'

'Just a suggestion.' He reddened slightly. 'At least there'd be food.'

'Nothing wrong with cheese on rice for breakfast,' Cherry said tartly, shovelling in her adoption file, notebook and laptop.

At the last minute, her eyes fell on the letter from her father. She hesitated, then pushed it into the top of her rucksack before clipping it shut.

She swung round to face him. 'Eric, that's... well that's bloody lovely of you. But I have to get out of Bristol.'

Carrying her rucksack, Eric made for a pistachio green Fiat Cinquecento that was parked a few doors down, clicked open the boot and dropped it in.

Cherry peered in at the retro-styled leather interior. 'My bag isn't smart enough for your car.'

Eric laughed out loud at her evident surprise. 'No, PhD students can't afford a car like this. But I couldn't say no to my gran when she bought it for me just before she died.'

'Right,' said Cherry, wrinkling her forehead. 'Anyway, I didn't expect a taxi service to the station after blowing out last night's drinks. And inflicting... well, all that.' She raised her shoulders in apology.

Eric looked astonished. 'I'm not dropping you at the station. I'm taking you wherever you want to go.'

Cherry tilted her head. 'Don't you have a PhD to go to?'

'That's the beauty of academia.' Eric slid into the driving seat. 'It can be endlessly postponed. And lichens are gloriously static, so they aren't going anywhere.'

Cherry stayed standing on the pavement. 'It's a six-hour round trip to my aunt and uncle's place. And,' she took a shaky breath, 'I don't need looking after.'

Eric paused. His gaze swept over her face, which Cherry guessed must look drawn at best, wrecked at worst. 'No, you don't. But mightn't it be a relief, just for today?'

Yes, Cherry thought. Yes, it would be a relief not to have to deal with the logistics of getting herself back to west Wales, and worst of all, being out in the open, in full public view. Ed could already have gone to a police station, and a vision of police officers manhandling her off a train in handcuffs suddenly flashed through her mind.

'Cherry.' Eric's voice cut into her thoughts. 'It's just a lift. I'm not suggesting selling my granny. Not that I could, or would, obviously. Not after she handed me the keys to this beauty.' He pressed a button. 'Which has a roof that comes down, because she adored convertibles.' He smiled, a little wistfully. 'She made me take her out in it. She loved hurtling around on little country roads. Christ only knows what she'd have done in the driving seat.'

As Eric clicked the roof into its open position, Cherry found herself grinning back at him, gave up, and got in. She closed her eyes, wriggled in her seat – it really was very comfortable – and sighed. 'Alright. I guess we're not quite Thelma and Louise, but if you want to transport a violent fugitive from justice, we might as well get going.'

They'd crossed the Severn Bridge before Cherry's anxiety levels spiked again. She felt her mind slipping.

Children lost in a crowd of refugees, exhausted and crying for their parents. Interviewing a woman whose nine-year-old daughter had slipped from her arms into the sea, who she would never see again. A premature baby, tiny, who had expired quietly in front of her, an hour after being born onto bare ground in a Greek island refugee camp. Almost weightless in his mother's arms, he had barely existed, and then didn't. His mother's blank eyes as she turned her face away.

Cherry felt her heart bang inside her chest. Her hands balled into fists and she dug her nails into her palms, trying to focus on that sensation rather than the throb reverberating through her body. Now she was seeing a boy. But not a boy in a refugee camp.

A boy in a bed. A small boy, heavy with sleep. She put her hands

under his armpits and dragged him off the mattress. He landed with
a thud. She dragged in a breath, then another, getting herself ready to
heave him up.

'You've gone a bit pale and your breathing sounds fast again.'

She opened her eyes to see Eric looking over at her, concern creasing his forehead.

Shit. Shit shit shit. Had she lost it so badly that she couldn't hold herself together on a simple car journey?

'Take it easy.' Eric's eyes flicked between Cherry and the motorway. 'Breathe in for three, out for five. And again.'

She tried to follow him. Breathe in. Hold. Breathe out.

'Any better?' he asked.

'Mmm.' Cherry couldn't trust herself to speak. Tiny tremors shook her. Her arm throbbed. As her breathing calmed, she found tears rolling down her cheeks.

'Right.' Eric sounded definite. 'You're in no state for a long drive.'

'I can't go back!' Cherry heard her voice emerge in a shriek that was whipped away in the wind.

'That's not what we're doing.'

Cherry saw Eric register a slip-road signed as coming up in half a mile. 'I'm taking you to my parents. It's about forty-five minutes from here. Better than two and a half hours to St Davids. And anyway,' his mouth quirked, 'I'm not hanging out at some grim 1980s service station while you get yourself together.'

Wriggling his phone out of his jeans pocket, he passed it to Cherry. 'Job for you. Send a text. Number's under 'mum'.'

He was trying to distract her, Cherry realised. There was no protest left in her, just a deep desire to be able to slough off the strain of the last twelve hours. Pulling smoothly off the M4, Eric turned right, heading north.

'Put, 'coming home, with you by noon, bringing a friend'.' He hesitated, or was he just checking the traffic, Cherry wondered, watching him concentrate at the roundabout. 'Can you get a room made up?' A thought struck him. 'You veggie?' Cherry shook her head.

'That's done then. Press send.'

'No love or kisses?'

He looked at her, eyebrow raised. 'My mother knows I love her.'

As they followed the route of the river Usk, the landscape rapidly transformed from the decaying post-industrial suburbs of Newport towards the rolling Monmouthshire hills. As they passed into Herefordshire, Cherry dozed. She only opened her eyes when Eric gave her a nudge.

'We're here.' As he spoke, he turned the wheel sharply to the right, taking the car between two stone gateposts. A narrow track curved gently through grounds that were fringed with trees in full, green leaf. Blearily, Cherry observed that up ahead, the track became a driveway, at the end of which she could just about make out a roof structure still mostly hidden by the tree canopy.

As more of the building came into view, Cherry realised it was a large manor house built in a warm red brick, the likes of which she had occasionally seen lushly photographed in society magazines or used as film sets.

Glowing in sunshine, she soon saw the house was built around three sides of a courtyard. Purple lavender bushes bordering the edges scented the air.

Eric came to a halt before a flight of shallow steps leading up to an open front door. 'Home,' he said quietly.

'Shit.' Well, someone had to live in the assorted country estates that littered the English landscape, Cherry thought. You just didn't usually meet them working in the city library. You didn't usually meet them full stop.

Eric's expression was unreadable. 'Don't hold it against me.'

'So... your mum and dad...? Am I meeting, erm, aristocracy? Because as far as I'm concerned, all this,' Cherry swept her arm out to encompass what appeared to be a country estate 'should be social housing.'

Eric laughed.

'I'm not kidding.'

Eric grimaced. 'Don't worry. I agree.' He stepped out of the car and lifted her bag from the boot.

Cherry stayed seated. With a sigh, Eric sat on the steps and gave her a quizzical look. 'To answer you: mum and dad are Violet and Hugh. Aristocracy, minor, but yes. For which, obviously, apologies. But, you know, very much remnants of. And as for Vive la République and off with our heads, I'm with you.' He dragged his hand through his hair. 'But until the barricades go up, I reckoned you needed a bolthole and a bit of looking after. And my mum and dad, for all the undeserved privilege, do that brilliantly. They've sort of made it their job.'

He indicated the door.

'So... want to come in? This is actually a hotel, of sorts. Which I reckon makes it an excellent option for fugitives fleeing a possible charge of GBH.' Sardonically, he smiled. 'Alternatively there's an Ibis down the road. Up to you.' Then he leapt up and bounded inside. The sound of him calling echoed back to her on the driveway.

Cherry sat back in her seat. She suddenly remembered that Eric volunteered at a homeless project. Goody two shoes, she'd teased him. But... if this would one day be his... his life wasn't as uncomplicated as she'd imagined.

Right now, she realised, he was asking her to accept an offer of help. Trying to give her something. Safety. And his diffidence told her it had cost Eric something to bring her here – his anonymity for starters. She would never again not know that he came from this background.

She had to face the fact that showing her his family home was also an invitation. To know him better. And despite everything that had happened since last night, that felt good.

She swung open her door and on legs that felt like cotton wool, followed Eric up the steps.

The doorway opened into a high-ceilinged, stone-flagged hall that was bigger than Cherry's entire flat. Somehow, it managed to be both grand in scale and welcoming in atmosphere. No oil paintings of grim-faced ancestors gazed down from the walls. Instead, a radiating warmth was created by a scarlet, cerise and azure Persian rug that stretched across two thirds of the floor. Light flooded in from the enormous window on the opposite wall, and candlelight flickered from several oil burners inside the fireplace. Cherry picked out scents she thought might be rosemary, lavender and eucalyptus. The oils seemed to prick her brain into greater wakefulness.

Eric had entirely disappeared, though Cherry could still faintly hear him calling. As her eyes swept the room, they suddenly alighted on a Great Dane so hulkingly vast that Cherry could hardly believe a dog could grow to such a size.

Startled at the scale of the animal, she stood stock still, but it had seen her. The monster padded over, each gigantic paw thudding softly. As it reached her, it lifted its head mournfully, jowls quivering, and pushed its muzzle into her chest.

At this, Cherry wrapped her arms around its neck and found herself sinking to the floor, the Great Dane collapsing with her into a heap on the jewel-coloured carpet.

'I see you've met Lump.' It was a woman's voice, clear and cheerful. Cherry's head snapped up to see Eric and a woman in her early fifties standing on the galleried staircase looking down.

'I would say mind the slobber, but too late,' said the woman. 'Welcome.' She made her way down the stairs as Cherry struggled to her feet.

'Violet Wilder.' She extended her hand. 'And you must be Cherry. In search of sanctuary, my son tells me.'

Her face changed when she saw the livid bruising on her guest's wrist as Cherry staggered slightly and, in trying to regain her balance, held her arm stiffly away from her body.

'That looks painful,' said Violet, frowning. 'Right. Kitchen. Let's get it seen to.'

Cherry could only stumble a reply. Eric's mother was unlike any of her friends' parents she had met before. Wearing a short kilt set off by bottle-green tights, her tobacco-brown hair effortlessly tousled, Violet Wilder strode towards the back of the hallway and glanced round.

'Come on,' she said briskly. 'No, don't worry, no need to tell me now. You both look like you need something stronger than tea and biscuits. Eric knows but I'll show you where we hide the booze. Given how much some of our guests get through, it's best they don't know where to find the supplies.'

Half an hour and two slugs of cognac later, Cherry gingerly unpacked her rucksack in the pale pink bedroom she'd been shown into. Laptop. Chargers. Notebook. Her usual kit emerged, and with it, her father's letter. Cherry grimaced. She would have to read it. But not yet.

Her left arm was tender beneath the dressing that Eric's mother had wrapped, gently but firmly before fixing it with three neat safety pins. Her skin felt swollen and tight. The bandaging offered welcome support, but the pain was actually becoming worse as the swelling took hold.

Cherry felt an urge that couldn't be resisted to log into her laptop. Thankful that she could still use her right hand, she sat in the armchair by a window looking out over a flourishing kitchen garden, and searched through the Bristol news websites.

No reports of a stabbing. Nothing about police searching for the assailant. It didn't mean Ed hadn't reported her, and it didn't mean the police weren't searching. But if they were, they had not released it to the media, and there wasn't a picture of her circulating newsrooms across the south west, or, god help her, the national news-desks. Yet.

Cherry tried to assess her situation. Ed had followed her home. Would that be seen as stalking? He'd threatened her. But she had no proof of that. He'd assaulted her. She could show what he'd done, but would that be given any weight by comparison with the injuries she'd caused him? Cherry's mind whirred. Where had he gone when he'd left? Any hospital he turned up at for treatment would ask him what had happened. Would he say?

With a sick lurch, Cherry suddenly understood the situation she was in. Ed could tell, or not tell. He held the power. He would always have the hospital records of the injury and his treatment. A constant threat. And it was serious, what she'd done. She'd stabbed him. Torn through flesh and muscle. That was grievous bodily harm. You could go to jail for a long time.

Panicked, she started unwrapping the bandage. What he'd done to her needed to be documented. All of it. Not just the swelling that Eric had photographed earlier but the bruising that was now turning her skin violent shades of purple, blue and red. Bandage trailed from her arm as she grabbed for her phone.

At that moment, she heard a knock. A muffled voice called, 'It's me.'

Eric's head appeared. His eyes widened as he saw her pull the final edge of the bandage off. 'Oh – everything okay?'

Cherry held out her phone. Might as well get him to help now he was here. 'I need to show it looking worse.'

'Right,' he said slowly. 'Because...?'

'Because he's not reported me yet, and if he does, I'll need to give a halfway credible explanation for why I drove a pen into his chest,' Cherry snapped.

Silently, Eric took her phone.

Feeling ashamed of her sharpness, Cherry held out her arm in the light from the window.

'Put your other arm alongside, to compare,' said Eric quietly. He took several more photographs from different angles, then picked up the bandage.

'Let's get this back on. Then bed.'

Cherry looked at the plumped pillows on the enormous bed behind her. She ached for its softness. Closing her eyes, she held out her arm. Less expertly than his mother, Eric bandaged it.

'Nobody knows you're here,' he said. 'He certainly doesn't. You're safe.'

For now, she thought. But nobody could hide away forever. With that thought, and before even hearing Eric closing the door as he went out, she slept.

Chapter Thirty-Two

As her eyes opened into the light of early morning, the half-folded envelope, her father's letter, was the first thing Cherry saw.

She lay still, staring at it. There were words inside the envelope that could hurt her. Or maybe words she could wrap around herself, a thick, soft scarf of explanation. Could there be comfort there? A story she'd never known... lives and relationships she didn't fully understand... places she'd never been and so couldn't grasp.

She closed her eyes. Not yet.

As she sank back into a half-dreamed world, she saw her mother's burnished copper hair glinting, being pulled in by her father for a kiss. Marianne tried to balance the cake against the momentum of his pull. A cake in the shape of a nine. Intricate, delicate icing decorations, swirling and looping across its perfect sugar surface.

'Your mum made that.' His words in her ears. Proud.

But Cherry wasn't looking at him. Her mother's face hovered above the cake, smiling. Candles burning.

She slid her arm round her mother's waist. Hair brushed her shoulder as her mother bent to press her cheek against Cherry's head.

'My gorgeous girl.'

A look into each other's eyes, shining.

The most beautiful cake Cherry had ever seen.

My gorgeous girl.

Who'd said that?

Cherry wrenched herself back to wakefulness. She had to open the letter. Face its contents. Holding her swollen arm carefully, she reached down from the bed and picked up the envelope. Taking out the single page of cheap prison foolscap, she lay back on the pillows and unfolded it.

My gorgeous girl, her father had written. *Thank you for what you were able to tell me. I want to tell you something in return. You are not* – he had underlined the word 'not' – *responsible for your brother's death. Keep hold of that while you read on.*

Cherry put the letter down, then picked it up again between her fingertips as if it was fragile. She read the line again.

You are not responsible for your brother's death.

· · · · ·

Closing her eyes, she telescoped back in time.

Bed.

My blue flowered duvet, carpet squidgy. I want to sink into the carpet and then dive deep into my nice cold sheets.

'Daddy, I need to brush my teeth. Then I need to go to bed.'

His hands holding a flannel, dripping. He never wrings it out properly. Mum hates that soggy never dries germs she says.

'Right love. Bedtime. Yes.'

My cheek. Don't touch it with that. I duck.

'No,' he says. 'This is for mum. Don't worry, we'll sort you out in the morning.'

I can hear her breathing downstairs. A choking cough. Then quiet.

I'm not listening.

Mum said run. Get out and run.

I've been planning. One, get into bed. Two, wait for him to go down. Three, open the window and a wriggle over. Four, hold on and slowly, slowly arms full stretch. Then drop. Not far to the garage roof. Like jumping off a table. Then the garden. That's further, like jumping off a ceiling.

Energy so bursting I nearly can't hold it in. It's pushing me out-wards like when you stand on a roundabout and have to hold to stay on as your dad pushes you faster.

Last two steps and I've got to my room.

'Bedtime you.' He's pushed the door open. 'Hop in.'

Bill's door closed.

'He's all right,' he says. 'He's settled down.'

Why is Bill's door closed? It's never closed. It's white and closed in my face like I've never seen it. At night it's always open.

Mum said run.

But Bill?

Two doors between me and him.

Not into bed. If I lie down I'll be sick.

Bill.

Just check.

I step out of my room. Those choking noises again.

Reach through air, through dark, fingers stretch for Bill's door and handle down. The air he's breathing warm as I stare through the room to find him.

Light from the landing. He's got one hand flung up. My chest thumping. I'm both silent and loud.

My legs moving but hardly. So heavy. How am I going to run with my legs like lumps?

Such a heavy boy. Wake up.

Bill. Get up.

Up!

• • • • •

You know I didn't plead either guilty or not guilty when I was charged with killing Bill. I now realise you think his death was your fault. I didn't think of that at the time – stupid of me. So I'll say again – I didn't kill him. But you didn't either.
Rather than me telling you, I think you should find out how Bill died from the post-mortem.
Let me know if you want to visit again once you've done that, and I will do my best to explain.
I love you, Cherry.

There was a knock at the bedroom door.

Dressed in a much-washed white t-shirt and worn shorts, Eric popped his head round.

'Us being aristocracy and all we've got access to the river. I thought we could go swimming. Plus I've got hot chocolate.' He brandished a flask and a plastic box. 'And ham rolls, and hard-boiled eggs.'

Indicating the letter, Cherry brushed her hand across her face. 'I've just read my dad's letter. It's been a bit of a start to the day.'

Eric's grin widened. 'What's new, Cherry Magraw?'

Cherry marshalled herself. Swung her legs over the mattress and stretched. 'Hard-boiled eggs and private swimming it is.'

Their route took them across a meadow sprinkled with buttercups. Swallows criss-crossed the field at knee level and the air smelled of honey.

Eric had brought towels and a red swimming costume borrowed from his mother. He held it out but Cherry shook her head.

'That's not how you go wild swimming.'

She started to strip, knowing but not caring – well, almost not caring – that he would again see the scars on her legs. She was suddenly desperate to feel the shock of dunking her body into the water. She wanted no barrier. Nothing between her and the river as it rushed downstream.

Now he smiled, looking directly at her, taking all of her in. 'It's icy in there.'

'It'll be fine.' She strode to the riverbank, and lowered herself in. Her feet sank into the gritty mud of the bottom. She didn't wait. Leaning forward, she pushed herself head and front first into the river, her whole body instantly immersed.

Gasping as she felt her heartbeat rise and her breath come quicker, she turned and saw Eric on the bank through the droplets glistening on her eyelashes.

'So,' he laughed. 'It's fine then?'

'It's... definitely fine,' she gasped. The silken cold wrapped itself around her, her skin numbing fast. 'Get in.'

Cherry trod water as she watched Eric lift his t-shirt over his head, drop it on the bank, then remove his shoes.

'I'm looking,' she called.

Eric looked up. 'I know,' he said. There was no trace of bashfulness or embarrassment. 'That is the point of this, isn't it?'

Seeing a new body after being so accustomed to a different one was always a surprise, Cherry thought. Each body inhabited space differently. Every plane and contour was an alteration from the expected. Skin tone, musculature, the way hair was distributed – all different. Slighter than Garth, Eric was also leaner, his edges were more tightly drawn. Eric was, she remembered, easily ten years younger than Garth, and a few years younger than herself.

She closed her eyes and lay back, the water inhabiting every crevice. The sensation was of chilly comfort, but one she would not be able to tolerate for long without moving to raise her body temperature. She held out for a few more seconds, then heard a splash and a gasp. Eric shook out his hair, river water flying in the sunlight.

'I'm not scared of your scars.'

'You say that now.' What was this, Cherry wondered. Was it too soon? She pushed the thought away. Why shouldn't she?

Face on to each other, their arms wheeling gently in the water to keep them afloat, Eric moved closer. 'I like what you look like, and I hope,' he raised his eyebrows 'to find out more. But I'm not fancying underwater sex in what feels like the Arctic. However, I *am* going to race you to the bridge.' He flipped over, kicked hard and began a fast front crawl downstream.

Cherry made a good effort but her swollen arm meant she stood no chance of catching up.

'Unfair!' she shouted as she finally reached the bridge. 'My arm!'

'Excuses?'

Cherry sliced a curtain of water toward him. 'I'm fast when I've not been assaulted in my own home.' As she said the words, her face fell.

Registering the change of mood, Eric moved through the water towards her. Their faces almost touching, arms and legs swirling gently through the water, he leant in.

'I'm not going to kiss you here for the first time, either.' He raised his hand to her right cheek, but did not, as so many had, stroke her scars before telling her they didn't matter. Then he nodded towards the riverbank. 'You know... it's much warmer inside.'

Chapter Thirty-Three

The experience of being thoroughly looked after by Violet and Hugh at the manor house had been welcome, but five days had been enough.

Taking reluctant leave of Lump, who she had smuggled into her room every night, where the Great Dane had taken up delighted residence on her bed, Cherry had begged a lift to Hereford station and taken the train back to Bristol, only gulping slightly when making the required change at Newport.

While Cherry was out of town, the child protection investigation had concluded far more rapidly than anyone had expected. A renowned orthopaedic consultant had been visiting the hospital and had reviewed Lola's x-rays, concluding that there was in fact no fracture. Kathie's frantic questions as to how two experts could make opposing diagnoses had been met by bland reassurances that sometimes in young children, bone injuries were not always clear cut. The consultant's evidence had been accepted by Bristol Children's Services. Veronica Voysey had closed her file on the children.

Back home for a week now and there had been no contact from the police. But tomorrow, she would have to face Ed; Eliza had told her by email that everyone was trooping back to court.

The expectation was that Fosse would now confirm that Brandon and Lola could return home, and hand down her decision as to whether Ed would be allowed to see them unsupervised.

Her phone buzzed.

'Cherry. Hi. Got a minute?' To Cherry's immense surprise, Kathie sounded entirely calm.

'Of course.' Cherry wondered what was coming. 'How are you feeling about tomorrow?'

A brief laugh came down the line. 'Yes, well, that's what I'm calling about.'

Cherry paused. 'You're still happy for me to come?' She was dreading the prospect of seeing Ed, but could give no indication of that to Kathie.

'Look Cherry. I'm telling you this because I trust you. And because I think you do, actually, get what Ed is like.'

Kathie articulated her next words very precisely. 'We are not sticking around to be abused for the rest of our lives by that monster.'

Cherry's mind whirred. 'Not sticking around?'

She heard a snort down the line. 'Christ, Cherry, that fucking judge hasn't taken anything I've said seriously.'

Cherry pursed her lips. Kathie was not wrong in her assessment. And after hearing the recording leaked by Fergus, she knew for a fact that it wasn't just Kathie who Fosse could take against.

Kathie was still talking. 'We've had the evidence in from the medical experts. The lump on her head is actually a cyst, god knows why they couldn't have told us sooner. And the paediatrician has now said that the bruise pattern isn't concerning after interviewing Ed about how he picked her up. I don't agree, but hey, what do I know? Anyway, the local authority has agreed the kids can come home. So tomorrow, that judge is going to put Brandon and Lola in a situation where they're at risk, every time Ed sees them. Even if he doesn't do anything at all, he knows the threat of it petrifies me. And he'll enjoy that.' Kathie took a breath. 'I won't allow it. I can't.' Her voice became even more emphatic. 'First it's him abusing me, then it's the court – I'm not taking it anymore.'

Cherry swallowed. Her sudden suspicions about what Kathie was planning to do worried her.

'I'm still not quite sure what you're telling me,' she said, as a vision suddenly flashed across her mind. Kathie and the kids driving fast down a motorway, holing up in an anonymous caravan park... or even taking a ferry to Europe, or Ireland... living on the run. She knew some women had fled the country, just like this. And she knew the punitive view of their actions taken by the family courts. Judges were ferocious in their condemnation when these women were, almost inevitably, dragged back to the UK.

'I'm sorry,' said Kathie abruptly. 'I'd better not say any more. I don't want to make life difficult for you. But I did want to tell you that... well... if I'm not at court tomorrow, don't be surprised.' She rang off, leaving Cherry staring blankly at her phone.

Was Kathie planning to go on the run? Cherry had to think.

If Kathie absconded with the kids, what status would her disappearing with them have, right at this moment? There was no court order in place. Was it legal? Why wouldn't it be, as Kathie was their mother...?

But Ed would not have given permission, and there was a live court case in train, with contact in dispute... and also... oh god. What was Cherry's responsibility in this emerging shitshow? Should she tell anyone what she suspected might happen?

She gave herself a shake. What was she thinking? Kathie was a source. That meant she was protected. That was the journalist's code.

Source or no source however, she at least had to tell her commissioning editor. And so, with some trepidation, she rang Patrick Daunt. Cherry chewed her lip. If Kathie did run, it was a story she desperately wanted to tell.

'Right, you're on speakerphone.' Patrick's voice travelled through her earphones. 'I'm with Julia Kemble, our head of legal. You know each other, right?'

'Yep. Hi Julia.' Cherry closed her eyes. Julia always scoured her work with a meticulous eye and had overseen all her court reporting.

Briskly, Julia's voice came down the line. 'Cherry. What's up?'

There was no point dressing this up. 'There's a story I'm reporting on in the family court. I think the mother might abscond with the children.'

'Riiiiight.' There was a pause. 'And you're on this story for us?'

Patrick's voice cut in. 'Yes, she's commissioned.'

Another pause, which to Cherry's mind, lasted an uncomfortably long time.

When Julia came back on, her voice was as usual, calm and practical.

'How do you know she's planning anything?'

'I don't,' Cherry said uncertainly. 'The way she put it was, 'I won't let the judge do it to us. I'm going to protect them whatever it takes. We're not sticking around to be abused by that monster'.'

The lawyer's voice sharpened. 'That's ambiguous, certainly. She could be talking about running away. But she could also be contemplating something even more serious.' She left a meaningful pause. 'Parents have, albeit rarely, killed their children when they feel pushed into a corner.'

Cherry's mind raced. Had Kathie ever hinted at that? She didn't think so.

Patrick's tone was even. 'That would be extremely unusual, wouldn't you say? Especially as it's a woman. I've almost exclusively read of men killing their children when it's this kind of custody battle.'

'You're not wrong,' Julia replied. 'But it's my job to set out the risks.'

'Cherry, what's your sense of what she meant?' Patrick asked.

Cherry shifted, thinking back to the phone call with Kathie. How to be accurate and fair about how she presented this?

'She's furious, indignant, and scared. Also determined. I think she was probably telling me, as much as she could, that she intends to find somewhere to hide with the children. While trying not to put me in a difficult position. Though of course,' Cherry laughed hollowly, 'she has. Hence this conversation.'

'So what's your question to me?'

'Well, she's a source and she's told me something in confidence. So I can't tell the court, or the authorities. So, what should I do?'

'What should you do?' Julia's voice was studiedly calm. 'In circumstances where you believe a source is going to break the law? And where children could be harmed?'

To Cherry's relief, Patrick cut in. 'Julia, people tell journalists they're going to break the law all the time. We report on them breaking the law when we cover riots and we don't tell the police or supply them with our footage or interview notes. As a matter of principle. Ever. Why is this different?'

Julia's voice was suddenly exasperated. 'Think about it. Because it's children.' She sighed. 'I can't tell you what to do. There's no law to say you have to report that someone has told you they *might* do something unlawful. Or dangerous. But you have to think carefully. If you say nothing, and the kids get hurt – can you live with that?'

The line fell silent as Cherry and Patrick took in the import of her words. Then Julia spoke again. 'Patrick. Cherry is freelance, so ultimately she makes her own decisions, but you have something else to think about – the criticism we as an organisation might be faced with.'

'Yes.' Patrick's voice was grave.

'In my view that risk is small, but as children are involved, it could not be more serious.' Again, she paused. 'It's a risk I would advise against.'

Cherry mouth went dry.

'And this isn't the kind of story that we'd go to the wall for,' Patrick said, glumly. 'No.' He sighed. The pause thickened.

'Cherry, I'm sorry,' Patrick said. 'You're committed to this story and obviously you know it inside out, but I have to balance other considerations.'

'And put frankly, a story about a woman's fear that her husband will hurt her kids won't get you anything *like* the same industry kudos as exposing international money-launderers, will it?' Cherry's voice was ice. 'Or celebrities who go off the rails. Or politicians who tart up their homes on taxpayers' money.'

'Woah, Cherry, hang on...'

'No, Patrick.' Cherry bit out the words. 'I tell you what. Let's leave it till Kathie or her kids are hurt or killed by her ex – there are quite a few who get murdered every year after all. *Then* you can run a comment piece going, *Isn't it appalling that abusive men sometimes kill their children?'*

'That's not fair,' Patrick protested. 'I'm trying to...'

But rage had overwhelmed Cherry. '*Much* better not to take on any corporate risk than for the paper to really, properly unpick how complicated victims are failed in the family courts by judges who think it's more important that a petrified child sees their abusive parent every weekend than have a childhood free of fear.'

In the shocked silence that followed this outburst, Cherry felt her body shake with the pounding of her heart. Patrick didn't know about her mother or her brother. Tears stung her eyes.

Julia's voice, ultra-calm, came through her headphones. 'Cherry, we hear you. But please can you think about this: I gather there are no particularly serious findings of domestic abuse against Ed. A court has heard evidence and Ed hasn't been found to be violent or otherwise abusive.' She paused to let this sink in. 'The family justice system is a binary one. Officially, now, Ed is not a domestic abuser. That gives us very little wriggle room, in case we need it, later on.'

'But the process I watched in court was ludicrous!' Cherry expostulated. 'I was leaked court audio from a completely different case where the judge's attitude was shocking. I know this sounds like I'm taking sides, but Fosse's attitude... she was against Kathie from the start.'

'But Cherry, how do we actually *know* any domestic abuse happened, as a matter of fact?' Patrick's voice came on the line. He sounded professional, cool; he was holding at bay his reaction to the emotion of her outburst. 'What, objectively, do we have, to say that Ed is a controlling, coercive, dangerous man who would hurt Kathie, or his kids?'

And now here she was, Cherry thought, in the exact place she didn't want to be, the place she'd tried to avoid – bang in the middle of a story she was meant to be telling from the perspective of a dispassionate observer.

She had to tell Patrick now, or beat a retreat – it was the only chance she had to save the commission.

'I know he's dangerous, because of what he did to me.'

'I'm sorry?' Patrick sounded bewildered. 'What he did to you?'

Cherry squeezed her eyes closed. Why hadn't she told him at the time? Shit. Really, just, *shit*.

'After the last hearing, Ed followed me home. He persuaded me to let him in. He wanted me to tell the judge stuff Kathie had told me when I interviewed her. When I told him I wouldn't – couldn't – he... hurt me.'

'*What?*' The shock in Patrick's voice rang down the line. 'Hurt you how?'

'My arm.' She stopped. How to explain the hell of those endless moments – or the fear of what might come next? 'He ground my forearm into my kitchen table. The pain... it was... I begged him to get off. But he wouldn't let go.'

'Why the hell haven't you told me this before today?' She could hear Patrick's concern. 'Cherry, my god, you should have said. I would have taken you off the story immediately.' A pause. 'I suppose that's why you didn't tell me.'

Cherry swallowed. 'No. Well, not really.'

'What do you mean, not really?' His sigh was impatience mixed with worry. 'Are you okay now? Your wrist? Did you get it checked out?'

'No. Patrick, listen to me. I had to get him off me,' she said in a low voice. 'The pain... it was horrendous.' She closed her eyes. She wouldn't go back there, to that place, where she had been captive, a blaze of agony, no hope of release. 'I... I stabbed him. To make him let go.'

'You stabbed him?' Patrick's voice was deadly calm.

'Yes. I had to. To make him stop.'

Patrick pulled the commission.

'I have to be blunt, Cherry. You broke his skin,' Julia had said. 'You did it intentionally, so it could be charged as grievous bodily harm. That is serious. And it could still happen. Ed could hold it over your head forever, and certainly, when the story comes out... think about it.'

Bleakly, Cherry listened to the lawyer's dispassionate assessment of the situation. Patrick had terminated the call shortly after, with a quick, 'I need to think. I'll be in touch.'

Half an hour later, she'd received an email formally withdrawing the commission. She would be paid half the agreed fee, plus any expenses she'd incurred. He was sorry that this was the outcome, and wished her well.

As she absorbed the blandness of this message, Cherry felt her stomach roil. It was the worst possible outcome. She had destroyed her relationship with her editor. Ed could still report her to the police at any point. Fosse had as good as said she would never allow her to publish any details of what had gone on in court. And now she was holding all the risk of suspecting Kathie was about to abscond with her children.

She was on her own.

Chapter Thirty-Four

It was with a sense of trepidation that Cherry arrived at the Bristol Family Justice Centre the following afternoon. Quite apart from whether Kathie would turn up or not, this would be her first encounter with Ed since his unannounced visit to her flat and all the horror that had ensued.

She had pedalled hard across the city in an effort to dispel the sick feeling she'd woken with. It hadn't worked, and now she felt jittery as she veered off Redcliff Street and made for the bike racks in front of the building.

The hearing was listed for 3.30pm – the fag end of the court day. It was obvious Fosse wanted this case off her desk. A dull grey sky bore down on the city, the air heavy and hot. Cherry wiped a film of moisture off her face. This heatwave needed to break; lifting her helmet off hair damp with sweat, she saw a darker edge to the clouds over to the east. Maybe today would be the day. Swapping cycling shoes for trainers, then unbending herself from tying the laces, Cherry's eyeline swept upwards and across the back of Kathie's head disappearing through the glass doors to the court.

So. She had decided to attend the hearing. Cherry felt sharp relief. Kathie at court meant the kids were still with their foster carers. Nothing irrevocable or potentially illegal had been done that Cherry could have foreseen and prevented.

Having made it through the security barriers and ignoring the broken lifts, Cherry headed to the usher's desk on the first floor. Phone clamped to his ear, Fergus spotted her and stabbed his forefinger upwards.

'Scuse me,' he spoke into the phone, then covered the mouthpiece with his hand. 'Fourth floor. Think they're all up there. Court 7. Final hearing?'

Cherry nodded. 'Think so.'

Fergus nodded. 'She looked white as a sheet. He was sweating so bad he looked ill. Not the usual Mr Cool.'

A jolt of adrenaline hit Cherry in the stomach. 'He's up there already?'

'Yep, good and early.' Fergus held up his finger, finished his phone call with a quick, 'Yes ma'am, I'll get that sent up,' then looked at Cherry directly. 'I see all sorts in here,' he said, his usually avuncular voice now sharper edged. 'I sit in those courtrooms, I watch them give evidence. I see them outside court too, which the judges don't. Nobody notices ushers – we're just the staff.' His eyes twinkled at Cherry over an uncharacteristically thin smile. 'But we notice everything. I used to be in the military.' He lowered his voice, leant in. 'Special Forces. But it's not all guns and glory. You go on a recce, you learn how to look properly. And you keep looking when people think they're not on show.' The head usher's mouth tightened. 'I know what sort of man he is. My dad was just like him. Didn't like to be crossed.'

He beckoned Cherry closer. 'Fosse... she might be a woman, but she's the same.' He dropped his voice. 'Well, you've heard her. Bullies people. Pays lip service to the law. And gets away with it.'

Cherry slipped into court only after watching Ed and Hallett disappear through the swing doors, followed by Christopher Groble for Bristol City Council, and finally, Eliza and Kathie, their heads close together; from a few words that floated across the lobby, Eliza appeared to be urging her client to agree a way forward and Kathie was resisting.

From her usual poor viewpoint at the back, Cherry watched as Groble formally withdrew the council's application for a care order to be made.

'Despite the, ahhh, distress we know separation from Brandon and Lola must have caused Mr and Mrs Sams, we hope the court will agree that this has been unusually speedily resolved and we must all be most grateful for that,' Groble oiled, clasping his hands together.

'What about the distress to my children!' Cherry heard Kathie hiss to Eliza.

Fosse heard it too and looked up sharply.

'Mrs Sams, we know that child protection measures can be upsetting,' she said, her tone short. 'But the welfare of your children is this court's paramount concern. You and Mr Sams both had contact sessions facilitated by the local authority. Given all the circumstances, the council could not have acted other than it did. And nor could I.'

Kathie shot to her feet, knocking her papers off the desk. Eliza looked around in alarm, making urgent hand motions to her client to sit back down. But Kathie, Cherry saw, could no longer help herself. 'My children's emotional wellbeing has now been damaged precisely *by* this process,' she said forcefully, 'and it's *me*, not you or social workers who will have to work for years to try to deal with the trauma they've been caused by this local authority and *this court!*' She remained on her feet, panting slightly and staring furiously at the judge.

A sharp tap echoed through the courtroom as Fosse brought her pen down hard on her desk. She stared straight ahead, ignoring Kathie's words entirely. After a few painful seconds, Kathie sat. What else could she do, Cherry thought. But the humiliation was intense, and intended. Kathie's cheeks and neck had flushed a mottled red.

Cherry observed Ed turn to watch his wife. It was a measured look. There was no compassion in it. Then, deliberately, he turned his head the other way.

'Now Ms Wynne, Mr Hallett, I think we are getting to, I very much hope, the end... and the *resolution* of this case,' said Fosse. 'And I must give my judgment.' The judge picked up a piece of paper and nudged her glasses up the bridge of her nose.

'No facts of domestic abuse or other behaviour by either party against the other were found that were so serious that I would have any doubts about either of them spending time with their children. Until the youngest child, Lola, reaches the age of five, I order that they live with their mother, and spend every other weekend, from Friday after school or nursery, until Sunday at 6pm, with their father. They will also spend half of each holiday with Mr Sams. As is standard, there is to be one weekday overnight per fortnight with their father.

'I hope and expect that the parties,' Fosse looked over at Kathie, whose averted gaze was determinedly set on the wall of the court-room, 'will be able to be flexible with regards to which night this is, given Mr Sams' professional responsibilities which mean that he must at times travel abroad for academic conferences.'

Ed's shoulders had relaxed, Cherry saw, and Hallett was looking over at him with a reassuring nod.

'However,' continued the judge, 'I make it clear to Mr Sams that this contact cannot be 'rolled up' if his job takes him away. That would be disruptive to the children. It is ordered on a 'use it or lose it' basis. That is my judgment.'

Ed nodded, his face suddenly unlined, his whole body looser.

Cherry heard a sound from Kathie's side of the courtroom, and turned to see her tapping Eliza's shoulder and urgently speaking in the lawyer's ear.

Eliza stood up slowly. 'Your Honour, my client asks one question. You did not specify whether this contact with their father will be su-pervised or unsupervised.'

The judge's expression became fixed. 'I thought I had made myself plain, but I do apologise if I was not specific enough for your client.' Her eyes flicked to Kathie.

'Mrs Sams has failed to prove that Mr Sams poses any risk of harm, let alone any serious risk. The contact will therefore naturally be unsupervised.'

Fosse stood up, gave a curt nod, her gleaming bob swinging, and disappeared through the door in the wooden panelling.

Chapter Thirty-Five

The heatwave had finally broken as lightning split the sky and thunderclaps shook Bristol. Racing along the Portway under the Clifton Suspension Bridge as the rain sluiced down, the wheels of Kathie's car flushed jets of water up from the road. The Portway was becoming a waterslide, the torrents unable to drain fast enough into the river below. Cherry felt the car plane and then skid. She had to steady herself as Kathie wrenched back control of the wheel.

'You need to calm down.' Cherry could hear the tension in her voice. There was no acknowledgement. Cherry wondered if Kathie was seeing the road. Alarmed now, she rapped on the dashboard. 'Kathie. Slow down. We'll get there.'

As Kathie turned towards her Cherry was shocked to see her paleness.

'Fuck slowing down.' Spittle flew with the force of her words. Her knuckles tightened on the steering wheel. A sheet of water from under their wheels engulfed a cyclist who skidded sideways, then shook his fist, mouthing silent curses.

Her anxiety heightening now as she realised Kathie was beyond taking care, Cherry braced herself against the dashboard. They lurched right off the main road and Cherry watched newly built executive homes flash past as Kathie drove, barely slowing, through the estate. The car juddered as the brakes failed to gain traction on the road surface and slewed to a messy halt after jumping the curb at the end of the cul-de-sac.

'Jesus.' Cherry expelled a breath. She had to get a grip on the situation. Twisting to face Kathie, who had already unbelted herself and was reaching for the door release, she put her hand gently on the other woman's arm.

'Take a minute.'

'I might not have a minute. I need to get them out of there. And before they're in bed.'

Baffled, Cherry stared at her. 'You called before we left to let the foster carers know you're picking them up?'

'Christ no.' Kathie was defiant. 'I don't have to explain myself. Not to them. Not to anyone. They're my children. They're only there by 'consent'. If you can call it that.'

Cherry took a breath. How to calm Kathie so she had time to think through the likely result of snatching her children back without warning the council? 'You're right. Absolutely. But the kids might be a bit... alarmed if we turn up suddenly and they weren't expecting to see you?'

'I'm their mum, of course they won't be alarmed,' Kathie scoffed.

'Kathie...' Cherry felt desperate. 'Ed could use this against you. He could say you're putting your needs to see the kids before their welfare. And there's a court order that he can see them. He could say you're obstructing him doing that.'

Kathie banged the steering wheel so hard the car shook. 'If I'd told the foster carers in advance they might let him know. He still has,' she spat it out, 'parental responsibility. Which is a big, fat joke.' Kathie's face suddenly loomed towards Cherry. 'After everything, do you still not get it? He's going to use that court order to hurt us. He can't see them. I won't take the risk. I can't take any risks at all.'

Kathie dashed through the now sheeting rain and banged her fist on the front door of the only detached house in the road. Her mind spinning with what Kathie intended to do once she had the kids back, Cherry watched with a sense of deep misgiving as the door opened.

* * * * *

They had exited the court building two hours earlier. It was gone five o'clock. Standing outside the tall glass doors, Eliza stepped forward. 'It's not the result we hoped for. I'm so sorry.'

Kathie shook her head. 'What can any of us do against these bastards.'

'It wasn't the judge we'd have hoped for either, I grant you that,' Eliza said dryly. Hoiking her bag over her shoulder and indicating the direction of her chambers, she said, 'I need to draft the order. Any preference as to which week night the children go to their father? A Wednesday is often what parents agree – though I'll have to consult with Mr Hallett as to your husband's wishes too.'

'Christ. Wednesday. Why not?' Kathie closed her eyes.

'The key thing from now on is to try to communicate,' said Eliza. 'It's difficult, I know, when you don't agree with the court's decision.'

'When I don't agree with a judge who has put my children in danger,' Kathie cut in. 'And who now expects me to cooperate with the man who abused me. Difficult. Yes. I'd say it is.'

Kathie had walked away at a clip. With a worried look at Eliza, Cherry said a rapid goodbye. 'I'll go after her.'

Eliza nodded, her mouth a thin line. 'Crap result for her. I'm sorry.'

Cherry gave the barrister a brief hug. 'What more could you have done?'

She caught up with Kathie just as she reached the bridge and steered her into a bar overlooking the river. Kathie seemed surprisingly unfazed, Cherry thought, as she ordered two glasses of chilled white wine. She had expected frustration, fury even. Not the heightened energy she observed emanating from Kathie, who Cherry soon realised, was increasingly giddily determined to retrieve Brandon and Lola from their foster carers that same evening.

'Is that a good idea?' Cherry ventured. 'Fosse suggested that you and Ed would go together, tomorrow.'

'Fuck that.' As Kathie spoke the words, her phone pinged. Digging into her bag, she read the message, laughed and passed the phone to Cherry.

'See? He's already controlling what's going to happen.'

The message was from Ed. 'Thanks for your draft order. My

barrister has amended. As I've not seen B and L for the last ten days, we suggest I collect from foster care tomorrow at nine. Drop off with you after lunch. Trust this suits as the children have had longer without seeing me.'

Wordlessly, Cherry passed the phone back. Kathie's face was set. 'Right. That does it. I'm getting them now.'

• • • • •

Rain blurred the neat, blonde woman who arrived on the doorstep of the townhouse, holding a toddler in her arms. There was no doubting her alarm after hearing Kathie's first words.

Lola's head was on the woman's shoulder, her thumb in her mouth, eyelids closed. She was clearly asleep, and as Kathie reached for her the woman stepped back, her expression confused, her free hand making calming motions. From the car, Cherry could see the woman flattening herself against the wall as Kathie, with not a moment's hesitation, marched inside.

The front door was left open as the woman too turned and disappeared into the bright interior of the house.

Cherry dug herself deeper into her seat. This was not going to go well. Kathie might have the legal right to turn up and take her children back whenever she wanted, but the minute she left, with or without the kids, those foster carers were going to ring social services. God knows how Veronica Voysey would construe Kathie's unannounced collection of the children, but Cherry had a good idea: she could almost recite the words that would be written in the social worker's report.

'Notwithstanding Mrs Sams' right to collect the children without notice from foster care, it is questionable whether she was thinking of their best interests in arriving at bedtime, having given no indication to their foster carers of her intention to remove them. The disruption they suffered was entirely avoidable. Given her failure to think about their welfare on this occasion, we now have concerns that she will in future prioritise her own emotional needs over that of the children's...'

Cherry groaned.

As she refocused on the doorway, a small figure appeared just inside, at the bottom of the stairs.

Toothbrush in hand, Brandon stood gazing out of the front door. His head turned back inside, and a joyful shriek of 'Mummy!' reached all the way to Cherry as the little boy scampered back down the hallway towards his mother.

After that it was quick. Clutching a now bawling Lola tight to her shoulder, Kathie bundled a beaming Brandon down the path towards the car. The blonde woman hurried after them clutching a bag into which she was stuffing two coats, a teddy bear and a sippy cup, which dropped and rolled down the pavement.

Cherry got out of the car and bent to pick it up. The woman, who she could now see was flushed with upset, grabbed for the beaker, dug into the bag for wipes and scrubbed at the lid. Then she thrust the bag at Cherry.

'That's her cup with milk in it. There's nappies. Wipes. Two changes of clothes for each of them. A couple of snacks and water for Brandon. That was all I could manage. In the time.'

Her indignation, anger and worry were evident as she saw Kathie strapping Lola, still crying, into the car.

'I have absolutely no idea what's happening,' she said helplessly. Cherry could see a man, presumably the woman's partner, just inside the doorway, holding his phone to his ear. Calling social services already, then.

'I know she has the right to pick them up, but it should never be done like this.'

She glared at Cherry, her mouth twisting. 'The state she's in, you should be driving, not her. Don't you think?'

⁙ ⁙ ⁙ ⁙ ⁙

Kathie hadn't needed convincing to let Cherry take the wheel. Instead, she had rolled the passenger backrest down and turned almost completely around so she could stroke her daughter's head with one hand while holding Brandon's chubby fist with the other.

Lola settled almost immediately, her eyelids closing with a soft flutter as she sucked on her thumb. Brandon's eyes were fixed on his mother.

'We're not going home,' Kathie said.

Cherry sighed. 'I think I'd guessed that.' She turned right onto the Portway. It took less than five minutes to reach the farthest outskirts of the city. At this point, Cherry realised, a more concrete decision than 'not going home' was required.

She pulled into a lay-by and kept the engine turning over.

'Okay. Where?'

Kathie pressed Brandon's hand to her cheek, sighed, then heaved herself round to face forward. 'We can't be anywhere he might think to find us.' She stared at Cherry. 'You do get that? He's going to come after us. Nothing will stop him now. He thinks he's got the right. And thanks to the court, he does.'

Cherry could see that she had tipped into a zone beyond the distress that had assailed her earlier in the day to a state of resolve that could not be gainsaid.

Deep in her bag, Kathie's phone buzzed. Both women started. Kathie dug for the phone, and opened a message.

'I know you have them. I know where you are. I'm on my way.'

Kathie gasped. Her finger tapped on the attachment.

A picture message showed a thick blue line crawling across a map of Bristol. It showed Kathie leaving her house; parking near the court; driving to the foster carer's house. Ed had tracked her movements.

Kathie began to shake so hard that Cherry grabbed for the phone. As she stared at it, the blue line suddenly extended itself to stop on the western side of Bristol. At the spot where they'd parked.

'My god.' Cherry stared at the screen. 'It's an app. He knows exactly where you are. All the time.'

In the half light, Cherry could see Kathie collapse into the foetal position on the reclined seat. Cherry grabbed her shoulders, pulled her upright.

'Listen, there might be a tracker on the car too. Or in your hand-bag. Or your coat. And I have no idea where to look. What I do know is that we have to lose the phone, dump this car, your belongings, everything you've packed. And then we have to disappear as fast as we possibly can.'

Wildly, Kathie looked at her. 'I can't lose the phone. It has my life on it. Everyone I know. Pictures of the kids from when they were tiny.'

'We turn it off then,' said Cherry. 'And it doesn't go back on. At all. Got it?' She pressed the off button, watched the screen die.

Kathie looked frantically at the two sleeping children in the back of the car. 'We can't just get out here.'

Cherry was already letting off the handbrake and pulling back into the stream of traffic, her foot hard down on the accelerator. 'No, we can't. Not with the kids. But we're going to make a dash for it over the bridge and I'm hoping someone will meet us.'

She handed Kathie her own phone, feeling an uncomfortable mix-ture of reluctance and resignation. 'Find a number for someone called Garth. Call it. Put him on speakerphone.'

Garth picked up almost immediately.

'Cherry.'

He sounded surprised but not guarded: Cherry judged that he hadn't yet gone home.

'Hi.' She saw the bridge ahead and picked up speed. 'I need your help. So listen up.'

She heard Garth take a breath. 'Righto.'

'I need a vehicle. A van. Or a truck. I don't really care. And I'm nearly at the bridge, so I need you to meet me in twenty minutes.'

'Going to tell me anymore?'

'Can't. Sorry. It's complicated.'

She heard the pause.

'Garth, I need this. It's urgent. I wouldn't ask otherwise.'

She could sense Garth's characteristic caution down the phone line and knew what was coming.

'It's that woman, Kathie, isn't it?' He gave a sigh. 'Christ, Cherry, can't you just stay away? I told you she was trouble.' His voice rang out clearly from the speakerphone.

Kathie was startled. She leaned into the phone.

'Hi Garth. This is Kathie.'

Silence filled the car. Then, unexpectedly, catching each other's eye, both women spluttered with laughter, the sound warming the damp interior of the car, relaxing the tension that Cherry realised had crept into every part of her.

Kathie recovered first. 'You know, Garth, you are so right, I *am* trouble,' she said into the receiver. 'The kind of trouble that comes with wanting to protect my kids. And I am fierce, *fierce* trouble to anyone who'd try to hurt them. So they're in my car right now because we're fleeing my maniac ex who's put a tracker on my phone, and quite possibly on the car too. And I'd appreciate your help. But if you'd prefer not, let me know and we'll, I don't know, hijack a train or hike our way to somewhere he can't find us.'

They had reached the Severn Bridge, high winds buffeting the car so it swayed perilously across the lanes.

Without saying anything to Kathie, Cherry glanced in the rear-view mirror, as she had been doing ever since she'd realised about the tracker app on Kathie's phone. If he'd been tailing them all day, he'd likely be behind them now, and there was nothing to be done – if he had a tracker on the car as well as her phone they probably only had ten minutes start on him.

Garth's voice interrupted her thoughts.

'Is what you're doing illegal?'

Cherry's mind flickered. Kathie was within her rights to take her children out of the foster home at any time. There was, however, no shred of doubt in Cherry's mind that social services would have been alerted the second they'd driven away.

Cherry also knew Kathie intended to defy the court order which said Ed should see the kids. But until Ed's contact time with the children was next due, strictly speaking nobody was doing anything wrong. Ill-advised, certainly. But not, at this point, against the law.

'No,' she said shortly. 'But I don't want us on CCTV, so you can't meet us at any of the services. How about we meet you at the quarry a couple of miles up from junction 24?'

'Right,' said Garth resignedly. 'I guess me and the van will be seeing you shortly.'

He was waiting when they pulled into the quarry entrance at the wheel of a small truck which, Cherry noticed, was not branded with the company logo.

'Sensible,' she said, as he jumped out of the cab.

'Stripped down for refurb,' Garth replied. 'Not that I don't want to be associated with this, but... well, evading court orders isn't my core business, is it?'

Gently, he carried Brandon in his car seat, strapping him in behind the driver's bench.

'You've done that before,' said Kathie.

Garth glanced at Cherry. 'Well, yes,' he said briefly. 'Anyway. I gather we don't have much time.'

He indicated the open door. 'Shall we?'

As the truck rattled along the narrow road back towards the M4, Cherry's mood lifted. They'd eluded Ed. If he did have a tracker on Kathie's car, he might come across the car but he couldn't have any idea where they were now, what direction they'd travel in or where they'd end up.

Garth braked as he approached a crossroads. Headlights swung up to meet them, and a grey Volkswagen loomed out of the rain, barely slowing for the driver to scan for traffic.

Kathie gasped. 'It's him.'

'Down!' Cherry hissed, pulling hard on Kathie's arm. The two women crouched below the dashboard.

'What the hell...?' Garth had already pulled smoothly across the intersection and was gazing down at the two women, bunched up in the footwell.

'That was Ed,' said Cherry, unfolding herself awkwardly. 'Which means I was right that he had a tracker on the car too.' She laughed a little wildly.

She could feel Kathie shudder next to her. Cherry leaned forward to turn the heating up and felt a comforting surge of hot air against her legs.

'All right?' she asked Kathie.

Her only reply was a silent, huddled nod. Leaning round to where the children were sleeping, Cherry found a dusty rug and wrapped it round her.

'Look, we're going in the opposite direction,' she said. 'He can't possibly follow us now. And we're going somewhere he doesn't know about. He'll never find us.' She pushed away the thought of what would be happening now at the council, whether the police would be on alert, searching for two disappeared children.

Garth's voice interrupted her thoughts.

'We're about to join the motorway. East or west?'

Cherry smiled. 'West. We're going home.'

By the time they reached Port Talbot, the steelworks were barely visible but for tiny flames flickering at the top of narrow chimneys. Cherry's eyes took in the yellow and red lights dotted around the sprawling plant. In the last half hour Kathie had fallen heavily asleep. Garth had stared determinedly ahead, but now, as they drew towards Swansea, she could feel the silence swell with questions.

She stared at Garth's hands on the steering wheel. She'd asked for – no, pretty much demanded – his help, and he'd given it, but she didn't yet know the cost.

'Thank you,' she said.

The silence lengthened. He didn't take his eyes off the road. She tried again.

'Her ex, he's violent. I have proof.' A beat. 'Garth, I have never felt so frightened as when I realised he was tracking us.' She scrubbed at her face with both hands, trying to find a way to explain the flight im-pulse that had been impossible to deny. 'Look, I'm sorry for calling you. I didn't have many options.' But she'd called Garth automatical-ly, she realised. Not Eric. What did that say?

Finally he glanced back at her. Cherry shrank at the look on his face.

'When you called...' She heard the emotion in his voice and relief swept through her, the sensation akin to the adrenalin hit of earlier, but this time, warming, relaxing. A place of safety, if only for an hour or two.

Then he sighed. 'It was the girls' school play tonight.'

Cherry's mind understood immediately, but her body took a moment to register. Oh god. What could she say. There was nothing. Nothing.

'It had just finished. I left the hall in a rush.'

The motorway lighting washed his face with amber. Cherry could see his jaw, held tightly against the emotions pulling him in opposite directions.

'I have absolutely no idea what I'm going to say to any of them when I get back.'

What do you do when you can't tell the truth and a lie won't cut it either?

Awkwardly, she leaned over and rested her head against his shoulder. It wasn't comfortable. She straightened herself. As they reached Haverfordwest, she rang the farmhouse number. She needed her family's help, and she needed no questions to be asked.

Chapter Thirty-Six

The children had settled immediately on arriving at Waun Olau. It was now three days since they'd turned up late at night to be tucked under blankets on the living room sofas, and they seemed entirely at home on the farm.

Cherry had observed how Kathie, too, appeared to relax, chatting happily to her aunt and uncle as she washed up after mealtimes and helped cut for the flower orders in the polytunnels.

Cherry, however, felt only a constant, dragging sense of dread. Her anxiety levels spiked at every news bulletin on the kitchen radio as she listened for an alert on 'mother on the run after abducting two children' blaring over the airwaves.

It hadn't come yet, but it could, and Cherry thought, it almost certainly would. What action had Bristol Children's Services taken after realising Kathie had abruptly removed Brandon and Lola from foster care? Had they gone back to court to compel the police to search for the children, and remove them by force from Kathie? Had Ed?

She didn't know, and she couldn't contact Eliza to find out. Numerous missed calls and three increasingly furious voice messages from the barrister had arrived on her phone. She had ignored them all. Of course Eliza had a duty to her client, but Cherry knew her overriding duty was to the court. If the barrister knew where the children were, and she was asked the question, she could not refuse to answer.

And now it was the fourth morning since that chaotic dash and Cherry had woken in a sweat just after five, then tossed and turned in a damp haze of unease until she heard her aunt go out into the farmyard a couple of hours later.

Would this be the day a judge allowed the media to publish the names and photographs of Kathie and the children in a bid to locate them? Would police officers turn up at the farm? Softly, Cherry groaned. What could she have done differently? There had been no stopping Kathie that night. Ed had shown his true colours in even more frightening form, and the children had needed a place of safety. But the current status quo could not continue, Cherry knew. The cogs of family justice and child protection would be turning right now. An order would be made. The police informed. And then... then the situation for Kathie would become very much worse.

Somehow, a way had to be found to wrest back the initiative. But how? She needed to talk to someone who would listen. Someone with no stake in the outcome. And someone who wouldn't judge.

'Brandon, put that down – right now!'

As Cherry descended to the farmhouse kitchen, she heard Kathie's voice, then Brandon's, half indignant, half wheedling. 'It's just a game, Mummy!'

Kathie glanced up when Cherry entered. 'Sorry for the noise. I've just come down. Lola's been grizzling for ages and finally dropped off. I was going to make a coffee, but now I'm having to clear up after all this.' She rolled her eyes, sweeping her arm around the room.

Brandon was clutching a rolling pin and a roasting tin. He had built an entire townscape that stretched across the kitchen floor. He'd used chairs, stools, cereal boxes, tin cans, saucepans, bags of pasta, crockery, condiments and bits and bobs that he'd found on the now almost-bare Welsh dresser. Roads had been created with trails of Rice Krispies in between 'buildings', and in the middle of it all, the cat was lapping vigorously from the emptied fruit bowl that was full to the brim with milk.

'The cat likes my lake!' Brandon said, looking up at Cherry with long-lashed, beseeching eyes. 'Look!'

A wail from upstairs cut through the air. 'Oh for god's sake!' Kathie exclaimed. 'Brandon, this is *naughty*! Put everything back while I go and get your sister – no!' she snapped as the little boy's face crumpled.

'We can't turn this place into a tip for everyone else. Tidy up!'

'Not a tip! I've made where we live!' Brandon pointed. 'Our house.' His finger traced its way along a Rice Krispie road. 'My school. The Co-op. The playground. I made a seesaw!' A wooden spatula was balanced on an egg cup.

The crying from upstairs was getting louder. Kathie squeezed her eyes closed. 'Brandon, please just do as I say while I...'

'No! I won't! Brandon's fists clenched and his body went stiff. 'I made it! I made it!'

'Jesus, Brandon...'

Cherry stepped in. 'Kathie, it's fine. Go and get Lola. Why don't I take him out for a drive?' She glanced at Brandon. 'In the Land Rover? Shall we go and get some nice breakfast? Bacon butty? Go and see the boats?'

* * * * *

Brandon had chattered happily to Cherry as the Land Rover rattled along the lanes towards Dale. By the time they reached the village on the other side of the peninsula, she knew about his teacher, his best friend, his worst friend and the fact that he didn't think much of the food at the foster carers. 'Too much broccoli. Too much carrots.'

They sat at the outside tables at the seafront café. While Brandon wolfed down a bacon sandwich washed down with hot chocolate, Cherry scanned the beach for Ben Temple who she hoped would be out and about getting the dinghies ready. There was no sign of him though, so she got out her phone and messaged. 'In Dale. I'm buying breakfast.'

Ten minutes later, the former journalist turned sailor walked briskly along the seafront, hopped over the wall, and sat himself down at the picnic table.

'Morning. I'm off shortly to pick up some clients for a day's fishing. So, who's this?'

'I'm Brandon. This is my hot chocolate.' Brandon looked up at him, his face serious. 'It's nice. You should get one.'

'It looks nice. But I've had my morning coffee, so maybe next time.' Temple turned to Cherry. 'This is a surprise. What's up?'

Cherry glanced at Brandon. 'Hey, do you want to watch YouTube on my phone?' The little boy nodded vigorously. Cherry handed it over. 'You stay right here. Me and Ben are just going to be over there, right?'

As Cherry perched herself on the wall in front of the café, Temple looked back at Brandon and asked, 'This feels like... trouble?'

As Cherry explained her investigation, how the family court case had ended, Ed's tracking of his wife and her decision to help Kathie escape to the farmhouse three nights before, his face creased with worry.

'God almighty, Cherry. This is serious.' He paused for a moment to consider, then shook his head. 'You're out of options. You can't hide them forever. You'll have to go to the police.'

Cherry rubbed her eyes. 'That's what I think. But Kathie won't agree to it. She's frightened. And... she's right to be.'

Temple looked at her intently. 'He's tracked her car and that's bad. He's broken a non-molestation order to come to her house, you believe but you don't *know* it happened. Yes, he's come to your flat and threatened you, hurt you – but the court made no findings that he's abusive. What evidence do you have that he's dangerous, rather than nasty and paranoid?'

A pause opened up, then stretched away from Cherry as her mind scrambled and she became increasingly bereft of words. How do you explain menace to someone who hasn't felt it, she wondered. How do you make them grasp that you can be at risk of your life and know it at your core, when they have never and will never know the self-unraveling horror of incipient annihilation at someone else's hands? She got up, walked over to Brandon and took her phone. 'Back in a minute, sweetie.'

Scrolling through her photos, she found the pictures of her wrist, taken over the two weeks from when Ed had turned up at her flat.

'I tried to explain what it was like. This is what he did,' she said, holding out the screen to Temple. 'This is what he's capable of.'

As Ben Temple flicked through the photographs she glimpsed the puce and purple bruising of her injury. His expression became fixed.

'Do you see now? This is what he did to me. And I'm nothing to him. I was a means to an end. He wasn't in a rage. He chose to do it, deliberately. And he didn't stop. I thought he was going to grind my bones through my skin. If I hadn't stabbed him I think he would have broken my arm.'

'Would you show me?' Temple's voice was quiet.

Cherry held out her arm. The bruising was by now a faint yellow smear travelling from her wrist up towards her elbow. 'It still aches.'

He looked at it for a moment, then up at her face, where her scars were unusually livid in the bright morning light. Gently, he took her left hand in both of his.

'I've not told you this, but all those years ago, when I came to interview your aunt, and I saw you at the farm, I could see how you'd been... hurt.' He indicated her cheek. 'I put that your face had been slashed in my copy. I was horrified. Aghast. How dare he mark you like that. I wanted people to be angry, even more angry, with your father. So I wrote about your scars.' He paused, glancing out at the sea where wind ruffled the surface of wavelets that lapped the stony beach. 'From the outside, you try to imagine the inside of that fear, but you never can, not really. I was trying to bring readers into the reality that night as you'd experienced it. As you had to keep living with it.' He swallowed. 'Thank you for showing me those terrible pictures,' he said. 'I see now. And I'm sorry.'

Cherry's phone rang, breaking the moment.

'Oh god. It's Kathie's barrister.' Cherry breathed out hard. 'Again. What the hell are we going to do?'

Temple stood. 'I've got to head to the boat to pick up my fishing guys. But this is what I think. Unless you're planning an escape to South America, Kathie and you will have to make a full report to the police about what's happened and re-open the criminal case. Yes...' he stopped Cherry's protest. 'Everything. The assault on you, and yes, the stabbing. The tracking device on her phone and car. Kathie may just have to accept that Brandon may need to give evidence about the breach of the non-molestation order. She needs every bit of ammunition she can get to support a criminal prosecution. Once you've talked it through, I'm going to call the superintendent in charge of Swansea police station. She sails from here and I know her. I can try to prepare the ground. The best you can hope for is a soft landing.'

Chapter Thirty-Seven

By the time Cherry and Brandon got back to Waun Olau after going for a swim in the sea at Little Haven, it was late morning. Cherry went out to the polytunnels to help her aunt with the flower orders. Wandering back to the farmhouse an hour later for lunch with Kathie and Lola, she picked up her phone from the hallway and heard it buzz. Two missed calls from Ben Temple and now a WhatsApp voice message. Surprised, she pressed 'play'.

Temple's voice blared out, loud and stressed.

'Cherry? I'm calling from the boat heading to Porthclais, sorry if I break up. I've just had Ed turn up here at the sailing school, raising hell about his Kathie and the kids. He thinks they're with you. He's been asking everyone in Dale if they've seen you, and it's not like a woman with red hair and scars is a common sight round here, so I'm worried someone will know who you are and direct him to St Davids.'

Cherry's eyes widened, as Kathie grabbed for her daughter in shock. The message went on.

'Obviously I didn't tell him you were over here earlier with the boy. But he was angry, Cherry. He tried to hide it but he wasn't pleasant. Pretty much threatened me, the people in the watersports shop and the girls in the café. Let me know how things are? And call the police.'

The message had been left fifteen minutes ago. Kathie had heard every word. As Cherry turned, she saw her leaning against a stone wall for support. Cherry grasped her arm.

'Let's get you into the house.' As she half propelled, half dragged Kathie inside the farmhouse and dropped her into a chair in the kitchen, Lola started to cry.

Cherry's mind raced. How on earth had Ed ended up in Dale? It sounded like he'd virtually accosted Temple – how could he have any inkling she and Brandon had been there that morning? But even as her mind formulated the question, Cherry's heart sank. She knew. Fiercely, she turned to Kathie.

'Where's your phone?' she demanded.

'What?'

'Your phone. Where is it?'

Moving like an automaton, Kathie felt in her bag that was slung over the chair she was sitting in.

'Oh,' she said blankly. 'It's not here.'

'No,' said Cherry furiously. 'It's not. Brandon must have it. And he's turned it on.'

Cherry ran through the farmhouse. 'Brandon!' she shouted. 'Brandon!' Not in the sitting room. Not in the farm office. Not in the downstairs loo. Not in the utility room. Cherry raced upstairs. All their precautions. The personal risk she'd taken. And Kathie had left her bloody phone in her handbag, just waiting to be found by a small boy who loved playing games on it when he was bored.

Clattering downstairs, she stood on the stone flags of the hallway, wondering if there was anywhere else to look before combing the outbuildings. At that point, a small squeak emanated from the old wooden settle.

Goddammit. Cherry moved towards the tall seat that sat against the wall next to an overcrowded coat rack. Two sets of toes could be seen poking out from beneath the piled coats.

Another chuckle from deep inside. Cherry dived in, pulling Brandon out. His grin disappeared as he saw her face, and he whipped his right hand behind his back.

Cherry tried to keep her voice calm.

'Brandon, give me the phone.'

He shook his head. Tried to resurrect the smile. 'No phone!'

Cherry knew she didn't have time to cajole and persuade. Clamping the child against her, she reached around and wrestled the phone from his grasp. Brandon let out a wail. 'That's my daddy on the phone!'

Cherry froze. Was Brandon actually speaking to Ed? But there was no call in progress. Thank god. Ed wasn't on the line.

'What do you mean?' she demanded.

Brandon's limpid, five-year-old eyes gazed up at her. 'I listen to my daddy on mummy's phone,' he said. 'I miss him.' His voice wobbled. 'I put him in voice memos. When he comes to visit us at home. When he's talking to me. When he's talking to mummy. I brought him with us this morning and...' his voice was tinged with sadness, 'I played him when you took your phone back.'

Cherry took a breath to steady herself.

She crouched down, knowing every second counted, knowing that an enraged Ed was undoubtedly right now hurtling along country roads straight to their door.

'Brandon.' She held out the phone. 'Show me voice memos.'

The boy smiled up at her. 'I know how to do all the phone things!' His grin widened. Chubby fingers pressed on the screen and suddenly, Cherry could hear Ed talking to his son.

'That's a great dragon, so detailed,' she heard him say. 'I like the yellow scales. Can I draw some blue ones on its tail?'

'Daddy helped with my picture,' said Brandon. 'My dragon wasn't blue but I let him colour in some scales anyway. Then he wanted to draw a cat. But a cat wouldn't be next to a dragon. Then mummy came in.'

Knowing what was about to unfold but hardly believing she was going to hear the reality of the exchange that Kathie had recounted to her, Cherry reached out her hand for the phone.

Losing interest, Brandon relinquished it and wandered off to the kitchen.

'Sweetheart. You need to keep that back door locked.' Ed's voice could be heard in perfect quality. 'It's not safe left open and it's easy to forget to lock up when you're in a rush to get out.' There was a long pause.

So he had been to Kathie's house. And he *had* come in through the back door, just as Kathie had said in court.

Cherry could hear Ed murmuring to Brandon about the drawing. Then she heard him say, 'Tea, love? Have I ever, since you've known me, drunk tea?' His tone was light, but not entirely pleasant.

Cherry heard the sound of water running, a kettle being clicked on, the low growl of boiling starting, and, barely audible, a gasp from Kathie. Then Ed again. 'You won't keep them from me. They're mine.'

A pause in which the sound of the kettle became louder. Then, a more forceful tone from Ed. 'They're mine. They'll always be mine. No matter what you do.' The sound of Kathie breathing hard. Then whimpering. 'This life you've taken away from me is my life. *My life.*' His voice lower now, but harder. 'This house. The kids. You.'

A pause. Then a shriek. Cherry jumped.

She turned down the volume, frightened the children would hear. But Brandon had heard it already, surely? Good god, she thought, what happened there?

A pause, then Ed saying, 'Shhh now,' and then the sound of Kathie, weeping.

Ed again. 'You'll never really get away Kathie.'

Now his voice is low. Intimate. 'Because of the kids. The kids are our link. Always.'

Cherry stared at the phone for a few seconds, then turned it off. Counting down the minutes since she started looking for Brandon, she estimated that Ed was now five minutes closer. Given the time he'd left Dale, he was likely to be no more than half an hour away, possibly less. She walked swiftly back into the kitchen.

Kathie was exactly where she'd left her, Brandon playing with a train at her feet, Lola on her lap. 'Cherry, I'm sorry, I'm so sorry.'

Cherry shook her head. 'No time for that. Ed knows where we are. I'd say he's about thirty minutes away. Might be less. Get yourself and the kids in the car. We've got to get you out of here. And, Kathie, it's gone too far now. We've got to tell the police. That's where I'm taking you.'

Grabbing her rucksack as she dashed out the door, Cherry ran the hundred yards to where Steff and her aunt were working in the walled garden. Yes, Kathie and the kids had to leave, and right this minute, but she also had to warn her family that a furious man was about to arrive at the farm and would raise hell when he realised his wife and children had, once again, fled the scene.

She had to make it clear to Maggie and Steff – Ed could be given no information, no confirmation, no indication at all of where they had gone. Or... and Cherry's mind raced... maybe they could misdirect him?

Whatever, she had to get Kathie and the kids to Haverfordwest police station, play them that voice memo of Ed threatening Kathie. Her mind ran on... she'd have to drive there via the smaller roads, not the main route out. Or, should she go north via Fishguard instead, but that would take longer...

Cherry had just reached the polytunnels when she heard the engine of Maggie's van start up. Snapping her head round, she saw Kathie in the driving seat, slewing the vehicle across the yard, tyres squealing as she hauled the steering wheel to the right and disappeared onto the road.

As Steff and Maggie, now running, reached her, Cherry shouted after the van in utter frustration.

'What's she doing?' Maggie asked, breathless, her voice high with alarm.

'She's escaping from her ex, because he knows they're all here. No,' she stopped Steff's question. 'It doesn't matter how. The only thing that matters is he's coming to the farm, he's angry, he's dangerous, and he's probably very close.'

Kathie flung the van along the narrow road. She hadn't turned left towards St Davids and freedom via one of the routes to the east; she might pass Ed on the single-track road. In slowing to pass, he'd have seen them. So she had to go in the other direction. West.

Then what?

She couldn't think. Her mind blurred with panic. She just had to get away.

Brandon, in the passenger footwell where she'd shoved him with Lola, was grasping hard onto his screaming sister. The screams seared themselves into Kathie's brain, driving her on.

The judge hadn't believed her, the family court hadn't protected her, the police didn't care, so she had to get away, as far as possible, as fast as she could. Out, away, gone. It was her only thought, her only choice, the only way to keep her children safe. She could never see Ed again, she knew, or the panic she felt at even the prospect would consume her so totally she would... but she couldn't go there.

Her foot pressed hard on the accelerator and the van leapt forward, roaring down the lane, its engine competing with Lola's shrieks and Brandon begging her to stop.

A mile and a half further on, as they neared the coastal path, Kathie ran out of road.

Pulling the children roughly from the van, Kathie hoisted her daughter onto her shoulders and held out her hand to her son. The clasp of Brandon's chubby fingers around hers bolstered her resolve.

Perched high, with a view of the sea, Lola stopped crying in that abrupt, disconcerting way that two-year-olds can decide to do. She pushed her thumb into her mouth and grasped her mother's forehead with her other hand.

'Come on,' Kathie said, her voice low but determined. 'We're all going for a little explore.'

'Remember, when Ed gets here, stall him,' Cherry instructed her aunt as Steff started up the farm's Land Rover. 'And Maggie... he's desperate. You need to be careful.'

They found the abandoned van after taking the westbound road faster than Cherry could ever remember. Jumping out, Steff scanned the fields. 'Nope. Can't see them.'

Cherry groaned. There was no way of telling which way they had gone. And she knew that for Kathie, trying to run as fast and far as she could from a man who terrified her, with two small children in tow, on this crumbling coastal path, the hazards were clear.

Cherry closed her eyes. Kathie wasn't thinking, so she had to think for her. A woman with two young children dashing along a rough path that would take them down steep sections of rocky ground onto stony slivers of beach, and then make them climb hard up again to the cliff top... they would soon become exhausted. They wouldn't get far. They'd have to stop.

But Kathie would refuse to come back, Cherry knew. She would not agree to return along the coast path knowing that she might well come face-to-face with Ed. And Cherry didn't blame her. What she'd heard on the voice recording had chilled her. And the memory of Ed's unrelenting grasp on her arm, the agony of him pressing her wrist into the table, and her frightened submission to his commands after she'd stabbed him meant she understood as no one else could how dangerous he could be when crossed. She pressed her eyes shut at the memory, feeling her breathing go shallow. No. She couldn't let herself panic. She had to be practical.

If she couldn't get Kathie and the kids to safety by land, the only other option was to take them off by sea. The RNLI lifeboat station was close by. But that would likely mean delay – at least twenty minutes while the crew mustered, possibly more. The police would take even longer. And she knew that Ben Temple was already in his powerboat, on the water heading to the nearby Porthclais harbour, and by now not far away.

She unzipped her pocket to reach for her phone. Looking up 'recent calls', she pressed his number.

'Ben.' Cherry pressed her lips together. 'Where are you?'

'Just heading into Porthclais.' Ben Temple's voice was instantly worried. 'All okay over there?'

'We might have an emergency on the cliffs. Can you get your boat round to St Davids Head?'

The signal went out for a few seconds but she heard him splutter and the end of a sentence. '... should get the lifeboat guys.'

Damn the signal up here, always fading in and out. 'There's no time,' she half-shouted down the phone. 'It's Kathie and the kids. They're on the cliffs and I need your help.'

Now she heard him loud and clear. 'Cherry, it's just me on the boat.'

She clenched her fists. 'Their father... Ed... he's on his way here. He's chasing them down. We can't wait.' She took a breath. 'You know he's dangerous. Ben. He's dangerous like my dad was. I need you to come.'

'Cherry.' She ended the call to see her cousin pushing a hank of climbing rope he'd taken from the back of the Land Rover into a rucksack. Steff handed her another bag so stuffed with rope it was bursting out of the top. 'Harness in there too,' he said matter-of-factly. 'We've got no idea which way they've gone and they'll probably be fine, but we need to be prepared.'

Cherry nodded, her breathing slowing in response to his calmness. Thank god for Steff, always focused on a solution. 'You head north,' she said. 'I'll go south. I've got my phone. Keep in touch.'

The cousins jogged together along the footpath to the cliffs. Ramsey Island to the west gleamed emerald in the late afternoon sun. Where the path forked Steff peeled off to the north and Cherry turned south, shifting the rucksack on her back to adjust the weight of the rope. Calculating in her head, she realised they would have left the farm around seven or eight minutes ago. Where was Ed now?

She'd assumed he would race up the road from Dale. It would take, what, forty minutes tops, to reach St Davids. Another five to the farmhouse... She increased her pace. If she turned her head, she could still just about see Steffan, who was loping northbound along the coast path, heading away from her. She pressed on, slowing to clamber down a steep section of path towards a narrow storm beach.

Two minutes later her phone rang.

'I've found them. It's not good.' Steff's voice was tense. 'They've ended up in a gully. Kathie's holding Lola, but it's mainly scree and they've slipped too far down for me to reach. Brandon's even lower, held up by a gorse bush. I'm going down once I've found somewhere to anchor a rope.'

By the time Steff stopped talking, Cherry had already turned to climb back up, knowing she had to keep her pace measured, try not to break into a run that she would not be able to sustain. Terror turned her breathing ragged, so when she reached the top, she forced herself to stop and take ten deep breaths, exhaling hard each time. Only then did she allow herself to jog slowly across rough ground towards what she hoped would be a rescue rather than a disaster.

At least five more minutes had passed. Which meant Ed was five minutes closer.

The sound of Lola's wails reached Cherry thirty seconds before she came upon the scene at the gully.

Steff had been right – the red sandy ground was steep and flaking, with the rock face starting about twenty metres down from scrubby tufts of grass and gorse. Where soil turned to bare rock, the uneven slope turned close to vertical until it reached the sea.

To her dismay, Brandon was further down than she'd imagined from Steff's brief message, past the point where ground met rock. The little boy looked up at her, his body rigid, his entire weight supported on a knobbly ledge created by the roots of a gorse bush.

Kathie and Lola were a couple of metres further up but in fact, Cherry assessed, they were less secure than Brandon: Kathie had wrapped one arm round a tree root and was holding Lola tight to her chest with the other. She was talking soothingly to both children, though Cherry could hear the fear in her voice.

If it had just been Kathie, Cherry thought, they could have passed down a looped rope that she could have secured under her arms; with both of them pulling, a fit adult could have scrambled up the slope. But Kathie couldn't do that with a toddler in her arms. Even if an ascent was possible, they couldn't risk meeting Ed up here on the clifftop, or on the road. And they had to work fast, because if Brandon panicked, if he moved even slightly, he would fall.

Steff had just finished tying off two ropes around the thick, gnarled trunk of a hawthorn tree. He pulled hard to test they were secure.

'What do you reckon?' he said under his breath, as Cherry upended her own rucksack to unload her hank of rope onto the grass. 'I'll go down on my rope, fix Lola to my harness and put Kathie on the second rope. You come down on the third and secure Brandon?' He handed her a sling he'd fashioned and a heavy-duty carabiner.

'But then what?' asked Cherry, thinking rapidly. Gravity and the crumbling terrain was against them. 'We can't climb them up. We're going to have to abseil them down.'

'What?' Steff stared at her. 'There's nothing but sea if we go down.' He peered over the edge. 'I mean, there's a ledge at the bottom, but the tide's not fully in yet. It'll be under water soon. How is down a good option?'

Cherry looked straight at him. 'They've slipped too far. And, remember, Ed is nearly here. If he finds us... do we want to meet him on this clifftop as we try to grapple them up to the top?'

Lola's wails turned to screams that cut the air.

'Look, Ben Temple is motoring round to where we are,' said Cherry rapidly. 'I've sent him a location pin. He won't be long. I say we go down, take them off on his boat, then go straight to the police.'

Steffan reached Kathie and Lola first. Using a sling he'd tied to his harness, he lengthened his abseil device, then gently took Lola from her mother. Placing the toddler on his lap, he attached her through the closed loop of the sling. Lola's weight was now taken by a carabiner, and Steffan knew he could control their descent, holding the child close but hanging free of his body, which would give him room to manoeuvre on the way down.

Lola secured, he had to trust Kathie to abseil down under her own steam. He looked over – what state was she in? Kathie's teeth were now chattering, but she managed a small smile; relief that her daughter was now safe, he thought.

'Abseiled before?' he asked her.

'No,' Kathie whispered. 'Brandon has. At the wall. But not me.'

'It's nothing like as dramatic as it looks,' said Steff. 'You just lean out and step by step, walk backwards. Keep your feet flat on the rock. The rope holds your weight. You control how fast by feeding the rope out. I'll show you how to brake.' He smiled at her, reassuringly, he hoped. 'Small steps. I'll be right next to you.'

Lola had quietened. She was now looking floppy and worn out, Cherry thought, as she moved smoothly past them on the third rope. She hoped to god Kathie could stay calm enough to listen to Steff guiding her down.

Peering up briefly, Cherry glimpsed Steff snapping three carabiners together before feeding rope through. He was fashioning an ad-hoc abseil device for Kathie.

Cherry nodded to herself. Steff had this. He would get them down.

Brandon's eyes did not leave Cherry as she descended. As she neared him, the little boy reached out his arms imploringly, causing the gorse bush to shake.

'Don't move, sweetheart,' Cherry said, trying to mask her fear that he might, so very easily, plunge downwards. She pushed away the thought of his body hitting the water.

'Stay still, like a statue. I'm nearly with you. Nearly, nearly... I'm here!'

The gorse bush, she saw immediately, was no longer securely attached to the rock face. Some of its roots had been torn out by the impact of Brandon's fall. Those which remained were straining under his weight.

'Your mum says you've done abseiling at the climbing wall?' she said, smiling at him.

Fractionally, Brandon nodded. 'With daddy.'

'That's great. It's a brilliant skill.' As she spoke, Cherry fed one of her slings between his legs, then threaded another through each of its ends, joining both closed loops high on his chest with a carabiner. Using a third sling, she fixed Brandon's makeshift harness to her own, knowing she had to wait until the others were down to shift him across to a free rope. Even if he fell now, he was attached to her.

'You can show me how good you are at it.'

Cherry glanced upwards to see Steff leaning away from the rock, his feet planted firmly. She watched him encourage Kathie to do the same. Slowly, they started to step backwards, Kathie shakily at first, her eyes clamped to Lola until Steff told her firmly to focus on her rope.

As she reached Cherry, Kathie stopped. 'I'm so sorry,' she whispered. 'For all this.'

Cherry could only shake her head. 'Just get yourself down,' was all she could bring herself to say. 'There's a boat coming.'

As Cherry watched them descend, she could feel the panic she had suppressed rising. Every minute counted. It was beyond question that Ed would have reached the farm by now. And where the hell was Ben Temple with his boat? Without that boat, they were finished; she knew they couldn't make it up the cliff, but they couldn't stand around on the rock ledge below as the tide swept in either. As she tested and re-tested the autobloc she'd fixed to Brandon's abseil device which would break his fall if he slipped, Cherry reached into her pocket to check her phone. A message; one word from Ben Temple: 'Coming.'

Thank god, she thought – but when?

A couple of minutes later, Cherry heard Steff whoop below her; a quick glance downwards showed him standing on the large boulder which formed a ledge some two metres above the sea, holding Lola close. With his free arm, he helped Kathie gain her footing as she reached the horizontal.

Cherry felt a small rush of exultation – they were safe, at least for now.

But she still had to navigate a frightened five-year-old down the same route. And she couldn't do it for him. He would have to save himself.

Cherry looked across at Brandon and grinned. 'That's a very nice position you've got there.'

'Ropes free!'

She looked down to see Steff had unclipped himself and Lola from one rope and Kathie from hers. They were down and safe for now.

Two ropes hung free. Cherry would shift across onto one of them. Although she would keep Brandon connected to her via a sling, she would descend on the rope Steff had just released. The third rope, no longer needed, hung free.

'Lean out.'

Brandon uncurled himself from the gorse bush and into what was clearly a familiar stance. He looked suddenly far less vulnerable. Cherry watched him angle his body away from the cliff, holding his rope, hand down by his hip, locked off.

Brandon looked up at her, his eyes serious. 'Daddy says I'm good at this.'

'Well... excellent.' Cherry shot him a grin. 'Shall we do it then?'

Brandon nodded, looked down, then paused. 'I don't like that noise.'

'Oh, the sea?'

He nodded.

'It's just the waves talking. They're a bit loud aren't they?' said Cherry.

Brandon considered this. 'Yes,' he said. 'Shouty.'

Cherry gave a little tug on his rope. 'Never mind them. Shall we?'

Ed had taught his son well, she thought, as they progressed downwards. Brandon was taking it slowly, but when he stumbled he didn't panic. He just found his feet, planted them flat on the rock face and leant out again, reversing in steady steps.

They had progressed about halfway down and were about ten metres from the ledge when Cherry heard the sound of a motor. Turning her head to the right, she saw Ben Temple's boat appear around the headland from the south. She suppressed a sob. They were safe. Almost.

'Boat coming to get us!' she said to Brandon. 'Keep at it. You're doing great.'

The child nodded, his gaze not leaving the rock face, his small hands working steadily to feed rope through the abseil device as he stepped backwards and down.

They had covered three more metres of the remaining height when

Cherry felt a sharp tug on her rope. Her eyes jerked upwards in alarm.

Ed was standing on the cliff edge, at the top of the scree slope.

He saw her see him, and deliberately, slowly, tugged the rope again. To let her know, Cherry understood in an instant, that now her life and his son's were dependent on the ropes, and he held all the power.

Brandon had seen him too.

'It's Daddy!' His grip faltered. 'Is Daddy coming to get us?'

Transfixed, Cherry watched Ed step over the one free rope, then loop it over his shoulder and around his body. A classic rappel as used by climbers a hundred years ago before safety kit was invented: a method that would allow him to abseil down using only the friction of his body against the rope to control the pace of his descent. Only a highly experienced climber would use this technique – or a desperate one, Cherry thought. Ed was both. Her legs suddenly felt shaky.

Ed's face, when she'd glimpsed it for those few short seconds, had been expressionless but utterly intent. Small stones and clumps of earth fell past them now, dislodged as he worked his way smoothly and fast down the slope towards them.

'Brandon.' Cherry's voice was sharp and clear. 'We have to go down. We keep going. Got it?'

The child was staring upwards at his father. Cherry blinked to clear her eyes of falling debris then tugged on Brandon's rope to jerk him back to the present. 'Now!'

The little boy turned to her, his face starting to crumple. But Cherry shook her head. 'We keep going.'

Brandon began to step backwards, but his head was craning upwards, his steps less certain.

They managed only another two metres before Ed appeared once more, his face looming over the edge of the near-vertical cliff, a dozen metres up.

'Daddy!' There was joy in Brandon's voice.

He hadn't seen that Ed was holding a knife. They were still the height of a house above the ledge when Ed cut Cherry's rope.

Cherry lay on the rock, the breath knocked out of her, pain

blooming through her chest and legs. Brandon was splayed across her torso, screaming. Her fall had been partially broken because Brandon, on his own rope, was attached to her harness, but her weight had torn him downwards, and they had both tumbled hard against the uneven surface to land on Steff, standing on the ledge below.

To the side of her Steff choked and heaved, trying to suck in air from the impact of their fall.

Then Cherry felt more rope fall heavily on top of her. It kept coming, coils of yellow nylon and metal gear that hurt as it landed.

What was happening? Where was it all coming from? She wriggled painfully away to avoid another slither of rope as it landed on the ledge and fell into the sea.

Finally it stopped.

Opening her eyes, Cherry saw Maggie at the top of the cliff, holding something that protruded from her clenched fist. It glinted silver as her aunt turned and disappeared from sight.

Her gaze moved downwards. Ed was no longer secured by a rope.

Brandon was still screaming.

Cherry's eyelids squeezed shut. Opened again. She could only take in the world in narrow slices.

Ed was clutching at the rock face, staring fixedly upwards.

Cherry wriggled out from under the loops of rope that had fallen onto her. Pain rocked her.

Her aunt had cut Ed's rope. There was no way back now. Not for any of them. And not for Ed.

Her eyes closed again.

Now she felt Kathie pulling a shrieking Brandon off her, tearing the ropes away, urgently demanding whether Steff could breathe, if he could sit, if he could stand.

Her eyes opened.

Ed was now looking down at them from far above. His mouth moved. She couldn't hear him.

She turned her head. She saw Ben Temple, his boat now steered in close to the ledge on the rising tide. She watched him throw a rope, ask could she catch it, was she all right?

Somehow, unbelievably, she discovered that she was.

Ben Temple brought his boat close in to the rocky ledge. Steff stumbled, half falling into the boat. Working together, Cherry and Kathie handed the children in. Kathie took them to the stern and sat them on the floor, covering them with her body and a tarpaulin, ostensibly for warmth, but really, Cherry realised, so they could not see their father.

Looking up, Cherry could see that Ed was at full stretch. Since Maggie had cut the ropes from their tree-anchor he was climbing free.

She saw when his left foot began to slide and lose its grip. His fingers, stretching, grasped for a hold in the rock.

She saw his toes regain some purchase, then lose it, then scrabble for an edge, an indentation, something, anything that would hold him. There was nothing. All he could do was press himself in hard against the cliff face.

Her gaze flicked upwards. Her aunt had disappeared. Her eyes moved down the cliff. Dispassionately, she observed Ed, clasped against the rock.

It was not a big move he had to make, just a shift in weight, then a short reach with his arm to a hold that would take him to safety. But the rock face curved away – he couldn't see it. Cherry watched, counting the seconds. Fifteen. Twenty. The boat motor growled as Temple worked to keep the vessel tight into the cliff.

Against the rock, Ed hung pinioned like an insect in a collector's case. His legs, she knew, would soon shake with the effort of pressing against the cliff, with only friction to hold him. His biceps would already be burning. His fingers would be locked into claws, unable to risk any release. Cherry stared up a moment longer, then turned away. Her eyes met Ben Temple's. He looked from her to Ed and back again, an eyebrow raised.

It was not a big move she had to make. A small jerk of her chin, and her gaze set firm to westward. Ben Temple nodded, and swung the wheel. The boat turned out to sea.

Chapter Thirty-Eight

Bill Bill Bill Bill. Put my finger on my lips. He smiles. His finger on his lips now, fat finger, curled on his lip.

Nice and quiet now.

In this darkness I need to find a way out. Quick, but quick isn't quiet, quick will make him ask why Cherry. Come on Bill. But he won't walk. Think.

I see Truckie. Bill loves Truckie. Truckie is red and made of plastic and has a yellow steering wheel and a horn.

'Cherry take you on a night ride.'

He claps. No. Bill Bill Bill Bill shhhhhhh.

Put his legs in their jammies over the top of Truckie. Don't make a sound. Now. My room.

My eyes sting in the landing light. Bill on Truckie. So heavy. Stay on stay on. I bend to push. No creaks or squeaks. There mustn't be any sound at all.

He's pleased.

We're in. Bump to my bed. Now I have Bill in my room I gulp at the air and more and more but my chest can't get enough.

We're not finished yet. I still don't know how. I look up at the window.

'Again.' His face grinning up at me. 'Push Bill.'

Oh Bill oh no shhhhhhh shhhhhhh shhhhhhhh.

'Cherreeeeeeeeee.'

I creep on whisper tiptoes and shut the door so there's a big thick block between us and downstairs and I don't listen to downstairs as the door closes and the last bit of light from the landing disappears.

The heavy wave is closing on me. Mum said run. She held my hand. Then there was air on my skin.

I cuddle Bill. I hold his hand.

Come on Bill. Let's go desploring.

A thought rushes into my head and shoots from my mouth.

There's birthday cake in the garden. I hid it! Let's look for it out the window. Lift Bill ooof onto the sill. He's curled up and looking down.

'Cake,' he says. 'Cake cake.' He's laughing.

We have to go and find it Bill I say. I twist the catch and push the window open.

A graze a heave a reach a stretch of arms and Bill is out and there's no time left. He's heavy he's hard to hold. Grab his wrists he's hanging I'm at full stretch it's not too far. I can't get him any closer.

Thud onto the garage roof. Don't look. Out out me NOW I clamber over and like I thought it's like jumping off a table.

I pick him up and turn my ears off from a noise above us. The roof is gritty on my soles. Hold Bill tight but he's not struggling now thank you Bill for being good.

It's only eight steps. Now the edge.

I'm holding you Bill and I will not let you go.

The noise again. *He's* there.

I'm not listening.

I'm not looking.

We're at the edge. My arms are burning but we're here we'll get away.

We're going now Daddy.

I hold Bill tight around his tummy and feel it squash. I swing my legs over.

Then my arm, my arm is empty.

* * * * *

Ed's body was found by fishermen out checking their lobster pots by the village of Porthgain.

In the meantime, a witness statement given by Maggie at Haverfordwest Police Station described how Ed had cut two of the ropes – the ones which held Cherry and his son – from a height that could easily have killed them both. Steff, it emerged, had suffered a broken arm, fractured ribs and a punctured lung as he threw his own body under theirs in a bid to break their fall.

The recording made by Brandon on his mother's phone, played out by Kathie on speakerphone in front of sober-faced police officers, had demonstrated how her husband had broken the non-molestation order. She could prove he had lied about it in court. They found the tracker Ed had installed on her phone, and on Kathie's abandoned car. And Cherry's witness statement describing Ed's assault together with the photographs Eric had taken of the bruising to her arm were further evidence of the danger he posed.

The police investigation was wound up quickly. A week after Ed's body was found, officers arrived at the farmhouse to tell Kathie their investigation was closed. No further action would be taken. They shook their heads, muttering condolences as they left.

* * * * *

'How are you feeling?' Cherry sat down opposite Kathie at the kitchen table, the sound of the police car disappearing down the lane.

Kathie laughed. The sound was harsh. 'I'm fine.' She laughed again, the sound wilder this time. 'I don't care that he's dead.' Each word enunciated. Relished? Cherry winced.

She had not asked her aunt any questions about her actions on the cliff top. They had simply looked at each other, understanding that they would not speak of it again. Margaret had looked after Kathie and the children with a fierce tenderness since they'd all arrived back at the farmhouse.

'I should care, obviously.' Kathie's voice was in no way repentant. 'He's the children's father. Maybe I will, one day.' She stretched her arms above her head, breathed in deeply, arched her back and smiled. 'But right now, I'm just relieved.'

'Right,' Cherry nodded. What could she say? She was in no position to judge. Her decision to leave had ensured Ed would fall. She'd known there was no one to save him.

'Tea?' asked Kathie, briskly, rising to put the kettle on. She was at home in the farmhouse now, Cherry thought. But Kathie's action reminded her of a question she'd been bothered about for a while.

'Why didn't you tell us about when he burned your hand? You could have said something before court that morning. You didn't.'

Kathie frowned and shook her head. 'I wasn't actually burned, not so it would show.' She grimaced. 'And me feeling terrified didn't show either. You heard how Eliza said the court was only interested in evidence. I didn't have any.' She clattered two mugs down from the dresser. 'Anyway, the photos of the injuries I *did* have weren't believed. So what would have been the point?'

She was right, Cherry thought. It would have been futile to say anything. Fosse might feasibly have thought she was fabricating the assault out of spite, so it could even have gone against her.

'Anyway,' Kathie slopped milk into the tea and stirred a spoonful of sugar so vigorously it spilled. 'That whole hideous farce is over now. And I'm glad I met you that morning at the docks. I'm glad you followed and saw what he was like when no one was looking. And I'm glad you left him on that cliff – oh yes.' Kathie's lips quirked as Cherry's face paled. 'I saw.'

There was a pause.

Cherry's mind raced. She had thought Kathie was busy at the back of the boat comforting the children. Her voice stuck in her throat.

Kathie put a mug of tea in front of her, then calmly sipped her own. 'No need to say anything. He hurt me. He scared me. And he meant to. It's not just that I don't care. I'm actually glad he's dead.'

Chapter Thirty-Nine

The pathologist's house was a rambling former rectory just outside Ross-on-Wye that needed a lick of paint on the window frames and someone to cut back the thicket of a garden.

A diffident figure in a worn V-necked sweater and collarless shirt opened the front door. Dr Ian Benton shook Cherry's hand.

'It's good of you to meet me,' she said, tentatively.

'It's a long time ago. I hope this is useful,' said the man who had carried out the post-mortem on Bill and Marianne, two decades earlier.

Cherry noticed that Benton struggled to meet her eye as he ushered her into a drawing room that was furnished with threadbare upright chairs and a round, journal-strewn table.

'This is the report I did on your brother.' The pathologist opened a buff cardboard file and handed Cherry a few pages of densely typed text. 'And your mother, though you didn't mention wanting to see that one.'

As she took the file Cherry's eyes fell on Benton's hands. Medium sized, unremarkable, capable: these were also the hands that had sliced into her brother's body, handled his organs and listed the damage done.

Benton watched her. Pathologists held a macabre fascination for lay people. He was accustomed to the flicker of unease, even distaste, that crossed relatives' faces when, rarely, it happened that they met him.

He had done many post-mortems on children in the course of his career but in the seconds before he picked up the scalpel, their bodies affected him in ways that no adult corpse ever did. He knew that for some pathologists it was different – they developed strategies for distancing themselves – but Benton had always been acutely aware that a dead child was a world-changing catastrophe for all who had known them; a murdered child laid out on his table was an abomination he had never come to terms with. He didn't know if that made him a better pathologist or a worse one.

'Would you like me to talk you through it?' Benton asked, gently. 'The terminology can be difficult.'

Cherry looked up.

'Er, maybe,' she said. All these people you had to be polite to. 'I want to read it for myself, so I understand all the details.'

Benton nodded. 'Of course.' He tilted his head in the direction of the kitchen. 'I'll leave you to it. Feel free to settle yourself in here.'

Cherry's mind stumbled. She hadn't intended to read it right now, at his house.

'Can't I take it away with me?' She heard her words spill out. 'It's my brother. I want to keep it.'

Half out of the room, Benton turned. 'These things aren't easy reading,' he said mildly. 'I can make you a copy, yes. But I'm also happy to answer any questions. It might not be a bad idea to make a start while I'm on hand.'

Cherry heard him close the doors and the noise of the kettle starting up. She gazed at the paperwork before her. The report's brevity was disconcerting. Just four pieces of paper, Cherry thought. So little to describe a child's death.

She wanted to know exactly how her brother had died. Whether he'd lived beyond the fall. Beyond the frantic scrabble of her hands as he slid from her grasp, the sudden loss of his weight and the looming sight of her father's face above her at the edge of the roof.

The report was dated 8 October 1998. The day after, then. The time stamp given for the start of the post-mortem was 16.10. Bill hadn't been dead a day. And where had she been while her brother's body was being cut open, invaded and explored? At the police station? Having her cheek sutured? Or was she already in the social worker's car being driven to Waun Olau? She started to feel her chest raise shallowly, her breathing race.

No. This wasn't getting her anywhere.

She squeezed her eyes shut. Cause of death. That was what she needed.

A third of the way down the second page she found the heading she was looking for.

'Cause of death' the old-fashioned typewriter print spelled out. 'Linear non-displaced parietal skull fracture. Associated posterior subdural haematoma with evidence of significant cerebral oedema. Some separation of the occipital suture line. Damage to the upper body of the corpus callosum consistent with focal axonal injury. No retinal haemorrhages. No diffuse axonal injury.'

Cherry's eyes skipped along. Two words she did understand. Skull fracture.

Over the page was a line drawing of a child's body with Bill's injuries mapped in cross hatches and shading.

'Fracture of right tibia and abrasions to the back of both legs were observed, all sustained post-mortem,' the report continued. 'Abrasions to right forehead, nose, right cheek, right ear, also sustained post-mortem.'

Cherry's mind skittered.

She turned back two pages to the original cause of death. This time, her mind began to more clearly register each phrase.

'Linear non-displaced parietal skull fracture.' Yes. When she dropped him his head had smashed into the stone flags. But what were the post-mortem injuries?

Cherry looked up to see Benton in the kitchen putting mugs on a tray. She rose from the desk. She'd have to tell him. He'd made a mistake.

'How are you getting on?' Benton's tone was friendly, though seeing Cherry's face, pale and deadly serious, he took a step back.

'There's something wrong,' she said abruptly.

'Oh, er, right.' Benton ushered her towards the kitchen table, pulling out a chair. 'What's that, then?'

'This.' Cherry held out the report to him. 'It says Bill broke his leg, and there were bruises and other injuries. But you wrote they happened after he was dead. That's not right. I was holding him when he fell. He was alive till I dropped him.'

It is hard to tell people, Benton thought, that one has dealt with so many bodies that even a child's corpse is no longer entirely singular and unique. But he had of course re-read his own report in advance of the journalist's visit this morning, and refreshed his memory of the injuries on which he had given detailed evidence at her father's trial.

Carefully, Benton handed Cherry a mug of tea. 'What were you told about how your brother died?'

'I wasn't told,' she managed. 'But I know, because I was getting us out.' Her face was set, tight. This was private, her last moments with her brother. 'I was *with* him,' she repeated, glaring at Benton, frustration and bewilderment combining to make her words emerge with startling ferocity.

He should no longer be surprised, Benton thought. People often don't face up to death as adults, let alone give children accurate information about how those they love most have perished.

But he faced a problem that he was only just beginning to grasp.

'Cherry,' the pathologist said slowly. 'When do you think Bill died?'

Late afternoon sunlight streamed through the kitchen window as Cherry gazed at the pathologist.

'Well, pretty obviously he died when he fell off the roof,' she said coldly. 'When I dropped him.'

Benton glanced down at his report, then lifted his eyes to Cherry's baffled, bitter gaze.

'You are correct in thinking that Bill was found on the flagstones just under the roof of the garage,' he said quietly. 'That is what was recorded and it is as you remember.'

Twenty years ago, he thought, he would have unzipped a small white body bag and gazed at a toddler's face, torso, legs, as they were revealed. He wouldn't necessarily have registered his name, though his assistant would have noted it, handed the paperwork to Benton, who after a taking moment to reset his mind to a place where it was possible to view simply as evidence the body of a child who had died only hours before, would have picked up his scalpel and made the traditional Y shaped cut from each ear to the child's sternum, and then straight down his chest.

'When I examined him, Bill had some injuries consistent with a drop of several metres, but those injuries were definitely sustained after he had died,' Benton continued.

Cherry stared.

'None of those injuries would have killed him.' He paused. 'Your brother died from a blow to his skull, some time before his leg was fractured, or the scrapes and bruising that were sustained in the fall. He was dead before he hit the ground.'

Cherry could not reconcile what the pathologist was saying with what she knew. She'd held Bill, shushed him.

'But I went in to get him,' she whispered. Her mind raced backwards, shuffling her memories over and over. 'He said 'Cherry'. I told him we had to go exploring. I put him on his toy truck. We escaped together.'

There was a pause. Benton tried to work out how much he could say – how much he really knew, and how much it would be responsible, given his lack of expertise, to suggest.

'This isn't my area,' he said carefully, 'but it's well documented that our minds can construct alternative realities when we are placed under extremes of stress.'

The ensuing silence stretched.

'Are you suggesting,' Cherry said coldly, 'that I've made all this up?'

Hoping that the facts would not entirely unravel the young woman sitting before him, Benton tried to think how to explain.

'I'm going to go through what we actually know,' he said finally.

Cherry nodded, a brief inclination only, prepared for another assault on the memories that had made her.

'From what I remember of the trial coverage you were found that morning, huddling in the entrance to your school by a teacher who'd gone in early.'

She nodded again. 'Yes.'

'You were covered in blood and your cheek had been cut. When police went to the house they found your mother's body inside and your brother's body outside by the garage.'

Yes. This she knew to be true.

'Nobody can know exactly what happened in your house that night,' said Benton. 'If you'd tried to escape with your brother and found him unresponsive when you went into his room to get him, it's entirely possible that your mind could have refused to believe he was dead.'

He paused, waiting for her to absorb his words. 'As a child of, what were you – eight? Nine?'

'Nine. Just.'

'So... you might simply not have been able to grasp the reality of what you faced. Your focus on getting Bill out might have been so intense that your mind refused to register that he wasn't breathing, or talking to you, or that his body was floppy and he didn't move.'

'But he *did* talk to me!' Cherry burst out, her voice brittle. 'I had to tell him to shush.'

Benton's forehead creased. 'This is going to be hard to accept,' he said gently, 'but your memories of that night may not be reliable. Or, at least, some of them might be and others might not.'

He thought for a moment. 'You say you got him to your bedroom on a toy car?'

Barely, Cherry nodded. She felt again the heft of her brother as she shoved him onto the seat and pushed him down the landing.

'Do you think you might have put him on the truck because he wouldn't – couldn't – walk?' Benton asked. He was acutely aware he was speaking well outside his specialism. For this young woman's sake, he mustn't get this wrong.

'Some of what you remember may be exactly as things happened that night, and some events might have been so traumatic that your brain couldn't afford to process them at the time. Your psyche – your mind – had to maintain its focus on other priorities, and survival always trumps everything else. Everything.'

The pathologist paused, reaching for a way to help her understand. 'Cherry, your entire being was focused on staying alive,' he said. 'Our minds are extraordinary and they will do everything they can to help us to achieve that. If the only way you were going to leave was with your brother, then your brain, despite having to deal with multiple traumas, will have helped you find a way to do that.'

Cherry, he could see, was far away now. He had to bring her back to reality, which was the only reassurance he could give her.

'If I'm expert in nothing else I'm expert in how people die,' he said.

'I examined every inch of your brother's body, and I can guarantee you that Bill was already dead when he fell.'

Chapter Forty

The alarm went off on Cherry's phone. Five minutes until he rang. As if she hadn't been counting down the seconds. She'd had to force herself to work all afternoon at the kitchen table at Waun Olau, knowing this moment would come. She felt stifled, sitting inside. She needed air with the tang of the sea on it to clear her head.

Cherry made her way across the worn cobbles to the storage barn where she hoped nobody would be working. She had to find a place to take this call alone, with no chance of anyone interrupting. Waiting, she picked at the weeds growing out of the concrete floor, then, finding satisfaction in the tearing of their roots, ripped harder.

What was she going to say? She had invited this conversation with her father – well, she had arranged it, at least. Her skin itched with anticipation.

Her phone rang.

'Hello. Cherry?'

Her father's voice.

Warm. How could it be so warm?

'Yes.' Clipped. She tried to soften her voice. 'Hi, it's me.'

He laughed for a second. 'I thought it was.'

'Mmm.' Cherry sank onto the concrete, crouching. There was a pause. Her father filled it.

'You wrote to say you'd been doing some research. And you wanted to ask me some questions.'

'Yes.' She stopped. Where to start. How much to reveal. 'I went to see the pathologist.' Her throat stuck. 'Who did the post-mortem on Bill. He said...' she closed her eyes, tried not to imagine her brother's body on that slab, 'he said Bill died of a head injury. Not from falling. He was dead before he fell.'

Cherry desperately didn't want to tell her father what she remembered of that night, and yet desperately did. Because how would she ever find out what happened if she didn't say more? He was her father, he'd said he wanted to help her. But she knew too that this was a trade, information as a bartering tool. Information as intimacy. He wanted her to let him in.

'He actually said Bill was dead before I got him out of bed, before I took him onto the roof.' Her chest constricted. 'But I don't know how I got him out of bed, if he was already.... and Bill and I talked to each other that night. That's what I remember. So now it feels like I don't know anything anymore.'

'I'm here.' The voice on the prison phone caressed her. 'Cherry, I'm here.'

'Yes.' She hung onto her father's voice.

'Take a minute.'

Cherry paused to gather herself.

'How's your breathing?' he asked.

A mixture of a sob and a laugh. 'It's been better.'

It was hardly a joke but they both snuffled.

This is the first time I've laughed with my father, thought Cherry, for over two decades.

'I expect it was hard, meeting the pathologist.' Her father's voice turned serious. 'You sound, well... you sound upset. I don't want to say more than you can cope with.'

She pressed herself against the barn wall. 'I'm okay.'

'You're not okay.' The voice at the end of the line was dry. 'But I want to know if you're okay enough to hear more.'

Cherry felt a surge of indignation. That's what this phone call was for. This was her story and she was going to hear it now.

'It's not up to you. It's my life. *My* brother. *My* mother.'

Her father's voice was sadder than she'd ever known a voice could be. 'I'm worried about whether you can stand knowing.'

'Jesus!' Cherry exploded. 'I've already coped with more than I should ever have had to. It's my choice. And I choose to know. I *deserve* to know. So you just tell me. Now.'

The line went so silent that after a few seconds, Cherry thought it had gone dead.

Sharply, she said, 'Hey!' She couldn't say 'dad'. 'Are you there?'

'I am. It's not really the moment to ring off, is it?'

Cherry massaged the top of her thigh. The wound had healed but if she pressed down, the nerves told her that they'd been injured. It comforted her, the soreness that remained.

'Cherry, this is going to be hard for you. It would be better if I told you in person.'

'What?!'

'I'm sorry, I just think...'

'*No.*' The word came out staccato and furious. 'I've done what you asked. Don't you *dare* make me come to the prison again. Stop stringing me along. Just tell me.'

'Haven't you ever wondered why I didn't plead to the charge of murdering Bill?'

Cherry shook her head, incredulous. 'Of course I have.'

'This is why it's so hard, Cherry.' She heard him heave a breath, and... was it a sob?

'I wouldn't plead not guilty, because yes, I had some responsibility for Bill's death. But I wouldn't admit I killed him, because I didn't.'

'Right.' Cherry could not say more. She could barely even breathe.

'That night was chaos.' He stopped, and Cherry heard him catch his breath. 'Bill's death... it involved your mother too. I need you to know what happened. But I had – still have – no idea how to tell you the truth without hurting you even more. It needs to be in person. And we'll need time. So I've had to tell a lie.'

There was a click. The call had ended.

Chapter Forty-One

It had always been Cherry's habit, at the end of a sea swim, to flip onto her back and let the coldness cradle her. She could spread her arms, tip back her head, gaze at the sky and, weightless, simply be. With no exertion needed, her skin numb and her muscles exhausted by the effort, she felt as if she had no physical reality at all. Those moments were pure consciousness with no shape and no edges. No landmarks in the sky. No tethers to the earth.

As she heard her father's words, Cherry found herself transported to that place of no landmarks and no tethers. No reference points she could rely on in her past... because if Bill had been dead when he hit the ground, and her father had not killed him, then who did that leave? Her mother? The smashed, torn heap she had last seen slumped on the living room floor. Who she had last heard urging Cherry, 'Run!'

It seemed incredible.

Impossible.

The door to her bedroom at the farmhouse opened. She saw Eric, carefully holding two coffee mugs in one hand and a bottle of whiskey in the other.

'From Maggie. She thought you might need something hot – with a kick.'

Cherry nodded wordlessly. Eric had absented himself while she took the call from her father. But he had come to find her in the barn, had walked her back over to the farmhouse, had taken her hand to lead her upstairs, placed a blanket over her before heading off to find sustenance.

'He says he didn't...' Cherry's tongue felt thick. How could her father have left her with more questions? How could he imply it was her mother who was responsible, her mother who had only wanted to keep them safe? 'He said my mum was involved. My mum. But I don't see how. And he didn't say.'

She could see Eric, but from a distance, it seemed, though she knew he was sitting right beside her. She saw him turn towards her, his eyes searching her face.

'Cherry.' His voice was sharp. 'Stay with me. You're going to be fine.'

She wasn't. She wasn't going to be fine. Not ever. Nothing was ever going to be fine. Questions whirled across her mind. What possible scenario could end up with her mother causing Bill's death?

What had Benton said? Pathologists saw Bill's type of injuries all the time. Falls from height, deliberate blows, but also sustained in playgrounds and domestic settings...? Children fall against hard surfaces all the time, he'd said. But her mother would never have harmed Bill, and if he'd fallen and hurt himself she would have stayed with him... Eric was gripping her shoulders. She knew he was trying to calm her, but she heard only her father's voice in her head. 'It's complicated.'

'He said he wanted me to know.' Cherry knew she was missing something. 'What? What does he want me to know?'

Putting the mugs and whiskey down, Eric reached round to his back pocket. 'Maggie said this had come for you.' He handed her a letter, his face guarded.

The envelope bore the logo 'The Parole Board' across the front.

Cherry laughed, faint hysteria in her voice and ripped it open. A leaflet fell out. She read the single sheet of letterhead. Her face went blank.

It was too much pain. It had to stop. Somehow she had to take control. Before the thought was fully formed, she plunged her fist into the mug of coffee. The scalding pain felt welcome. Familiar. Almost instantly, Cherry felt her breathing ease.

It took her a moment to register Eric's cry as he pulled the mug away, coffee splashing dark against the wall. In one movement he pulled Cherry off the bed. Dragging her across the hall to the bathroom he pushed her into the shower and turned the cold water on full blast. They sat together on the tiled floor, Eric holding the spray against her hand, the flesh bright red and tender.

She wasn't going to apologise, and Eric didn't remonstrate or ask questions.

After five minutes, he turned off the shower, wrapped her tightly in a bath towel and swaddled her against him.

Cherry's teeth were chattering. 'It says he's confessed to Bill's murder.' She clenched her jaw so hard it ached. 'Not that he bothered to tell me just now.' Her breath shuddered out. 'That means he's eligible for parole. They've written to tell me there's a hearing in three months. The Parole Board wants to know my views.'

Eric looked at her, his expression unreadable. 'We should get out of here. Fancy a swim?'

Without telling Maggie what had happened they left Waun Olau and headed for the cliffs. Cherry led the way, taking a faster route across the fields than the designated footpaths could offer, finding her way between stretches of boggy ground, clumps of gorse and wind-tortured hawthorn.

'He's using you,' said Eric, conversationally, as they neared the rough steps that would take them to the beach.

'I know.' Cherry kept walking.

'He's playing everyone. This is about what he wants. Not what's best for you.'

Cherry didn't reply, conflicting emotions tugging her back and forth. Belonging to someone. Her father's voice. His hands, those hands that had cradled her. That had cut into her. Her father, who wanted her.

The moment she'd stepped off Ben Temple's boat after handing Lola and Brandon to Kathie flitted across her mind. On the road by the Griffin Inn, an ambulance and two police cars had waited, alerted to the crisis by Temple's radio message. By then, Ed would have fallen, Cherry knew. They all knew. She'd watched Kathie walk up the swaying pontoon towards the road, Lola held tight in one arm, Brandon's hand clasped fiercely in the other. Her step was firm, her head unbowed. Vindicated, Cherry thought.

Kathie had made the choices required to protect her children. Her own mother had done her best to protect her and Bill too, she knew it absolutely. Whatever her father told her about Marianne being involved in Bill's death. Whatever had happened that chaotic, terrifying, long-ago night.

This Cherry knew, was what she had to do now. Protect herself and survive. So she had to choose. She did not have to wonder about her father's changing versions of events, interrogate his words, cajole more detail from him, even though that meant she would never know, exactly, how or why Bill died. Inside that knowledge gap, she knew, she could speculate forever; create lurid narratives in her mind.

Instead, she could choose to anchor herself to the knowledge of her mother's love. She could decide now that she knew, for sure, who was responsible for her brother's death. However it had come about. And she did not need to help her father redeem himself, if any kind of redemption was even possible after what he'd done.

Cherry and Eric picked their way across the pebble beach. They stripped fast, then waded faster into the waves. Mid-September and the water was only just warmer than skin-shrinkingly cold.

Cherry allowed her body to immerse, the saltiness of sea water a balm to her burned hand. Eric was ahead of her, swimming hard. This was one of the many storm beaches along the coast that her uncle had sailed into, two decades ago. The seal pupping season had been almost at its end. As a young girl perched silently in the bows, she had watched the tiny cream blobs of fur lying helplessly on stony ground, their heads lifting with hope as their mothers heaved themselves gracelessly out of the water, determinedly pushing their way up the beach to feed their young.

The first pups of this season would already have been born, Cherry thought as she began to swim front crawl, urging herself towards the open sea. Later that month and into October, she would walk these cliffs and gaze downwards from hundreds of feet up, searching out their small, pale bodies below. And she would hope that they grew strong, withstood the autumn storms, made it out to sea, learnt fast, got lucky, and survived the perils that batter every life.

© Camilla Reynolds

Louise Tickle is an award-winning journalist and broadcaster who specialises in reporting on domestic abuse, family courts and child protection. In 2022, her Tortoise Media investigation, Hidden Homicides, was nominated for the Orwell Prize for Exposing Britain's Social Evils. She was previously shortlisted for her work on the BBC One film Behind Closed Doors and her Guardian reporting on domestic abuse.

Louise lives up a winding hill in the Cotswolds, and heads west to the Pembrokeshire coast and its spectacular island wildlife with her partner and two sons whenever she can.

Between the Lies is her first novel.

Acknowledgements

My first and biggest thanks must go to everyone who has trusted me with their experiences of domestic abuse and the family justice system. Something I learned fast as a journalist investigating these issues is that there are precious few happy ever afters. It is hard to fathom the enormity of what you have gone through, or the damage wrought.

The stories that inform the world of this novel are not easy ones, and I am immensely grateful to have had the backing of remarkable editors whose trust allowed me to investigate, explore and learn, in particular at Tortoise Media and The Guardian. My very special thanks to Archie Bland, Patrick Butler, Basia Cummings, James Harding, Clare Horton and Susanna Rustin. This could not have been written without you. Also my enduring gratitude to Alice Woolley who spent fifteen years editing me, and who, article after article, insisted that simple is better and less is more. I will keep trying.

To Brian Woods of True Vision TV and Anna Hall of Candour, I did not know what persistence was until I worked with you, and your determination to tell these stories in a way that captivates and compels has been a wonder to behold and a lesson in commitment and grit. To my superb producer Gemma Newby, with whom I've been immensely lucky to work on some of the most sensitive and distressing stories I've reported on, thank you for your brilliance, friendship and support in the harrowing moments we've shared on this beat.

To the many legal professionals who have helped me understand the world of the family courts and how to navigate my way through, I'm beyond grateful; I would have messed up in spectacular fashion without your guidance. In particular, I'm extremely lucky to have met barrister Lucy Reed (now KC!) not long after I first set foot in the Bristol Family Justice Centre: she has been my friend, my critic and my formidable champion in applications to relax reporting restrictions, fighting to win me the chance to tell stories I believed mattered. It's been an education, a blast, a privilege and a (taxi) ride. To Paul Bowen KC, who generously offered me expert representation in an appeal without us at that stage ever having met, I'm more grateful than I can say for all your support, both then and since – and in particular for clear and firm advice that undoubtedly saved my bacon.

To the splendid women who kept me going when I doubted and flailed in the writing of this novel: Cath, Juliana, Liz, Patricia, Rachel, Rin and Sarah - Doodles forever.

To Sophie Mumford for her unstinting enthusiasm, belief and interest, Juliette Morton for her candid and always on-point editing, Kate Weinberg for staunchly supporting me through the final, painful stages, and Victoria Scott for practical help on how to get published, I'm blown away by how generous you have been. John Wilson, I have adored our WhatsApp conversations, conducted late into the night, about the travails and joys of writing (and I am *very* pleased that you got to keep those NHS pyjamas).

Special thanks to Peter Beaumont, who kindly did not snicker at my attempt to write a cliff rescue scene, and whose climbing expertise and constructive comments on my various rewrites mean that any claim to plausibility this chapter may have is down to him, not me.

To David Chaplin, Helen Lacey and Hannah Shergold at Cinto Press, who instantly understood the world of this novel, believed in it and took a chance, thank you. It's been the best fun working with you.

To Mummy, who read, watched and listened to all my reporting, and who told me it was important and worthwhile, my love always and everywhere.

Finally, to Jim and our gorgeous boys, a bare 'thank you' for your time and support (and the ferrying to swimming lessons and staying out for all those Saturday mornings that meant I could write this) is simply not enough – and I'm sorry it took me quite so many years!

Louise Tickle
October 2023